GOSSAMER

GOSSAMER

Book One: The Gossamer Ravel Trilogy

Anna Bailey

SNARLED YARNS PRESS

SNARLED YARNS PRESS

Berkshire, UK

First published by Snarled Yarns Press in 2025

Author photograph taken by Janette Bailey

ISBN: 9781036911409

For the people and the places I call home:

I carry your stories with me wherever I go.

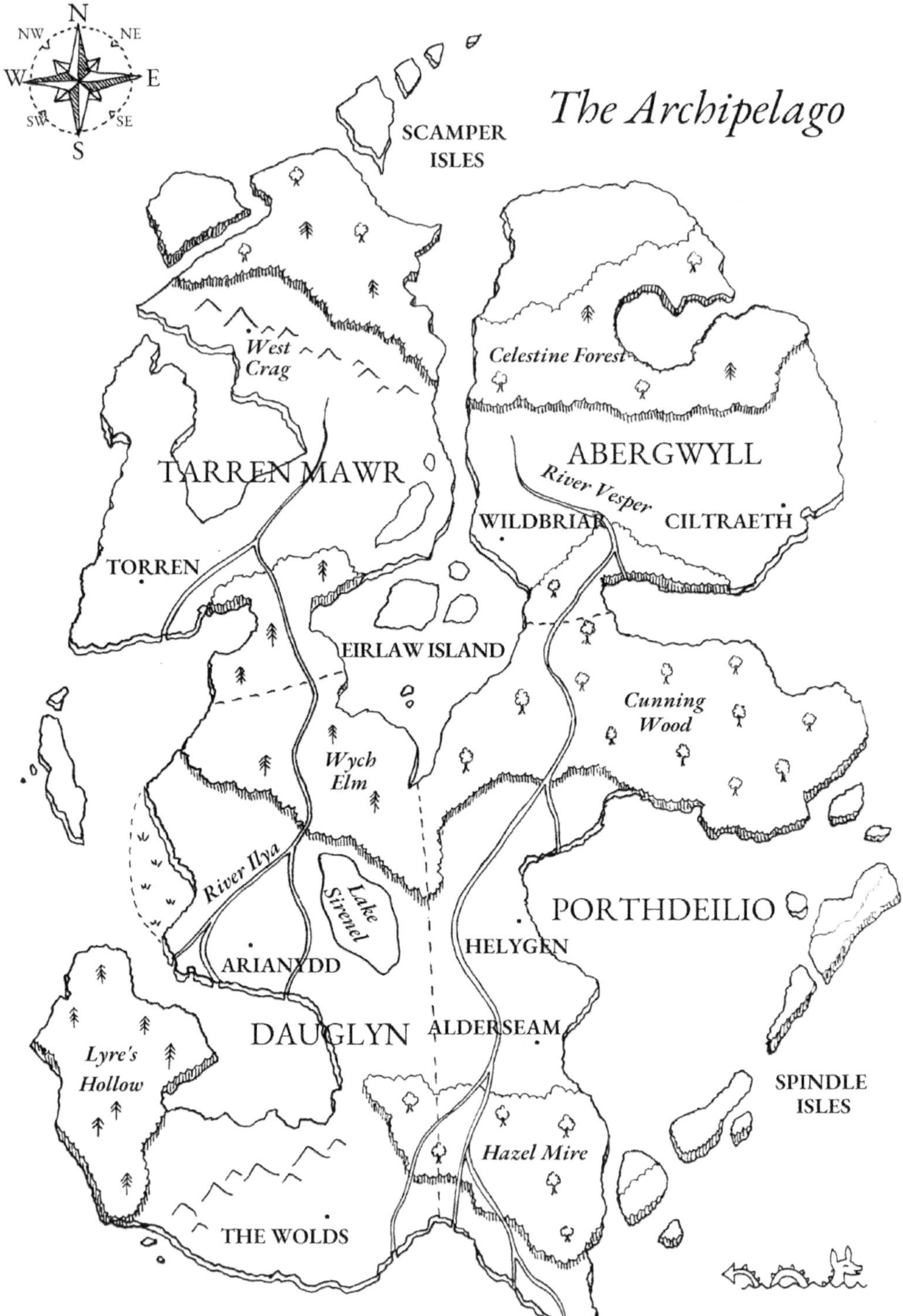
N
NW
NE
W
E
SW
SE
S
The Archipelago
SCAMPER ISLES
West Crag
Celestine Forest
TARREN MAWR
ABERGWYLL
River Vesper
WILDBRIAR
CILTRAETH
TORREN
EIRLAW ISLAND
Cunning Wood
Wych Elm
River Ilya
Lake Sirenel
PORTHDEILIO
HELYGEN
ARIANYDD
DAUGLYN
ALDERSEAM
SPINDLE ISLES
Lyre's Hollow
Hazel Mire
THE WOLDS

The Fallow

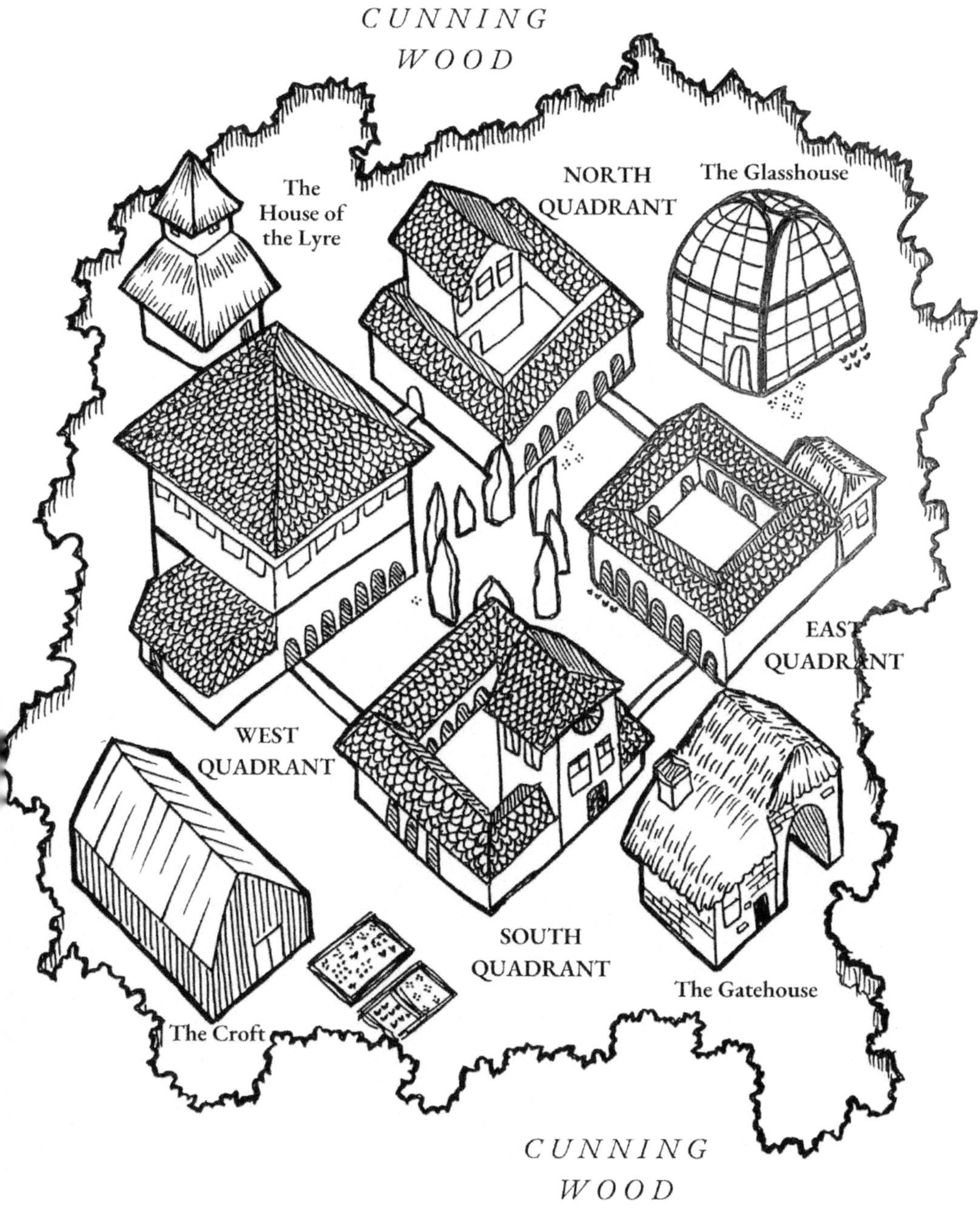
CUNNING WOOD
The House of the Lyre
NORTH QUADRANT
The Glasshouse
EAST QUADRANT
WEST QUADRANT
SOUTH QUADRANT
The Gatehouse
The Croft
CUNNING WOOD

Contents

PART III

PART IV

PART V

PART I

Chapter 1
Eirlaw Island

Magda never did learn why the Skelbrights left without saying goodbye. One day the house across the road from them sat beaming, defiant in its pebbledashed alcove and faded chintz curtains, and the next it was a hollow. *A gulf*, said Enio, proudly, because he had learned the word two days ago in Miss Sachar's geography class. *Shame. We'll have no one to throw snails over the fence at now.*

The house sat empty for precisely two weeks before the plants started to creep. Perhaps they could smell the temptation of that sucked-out, soulless void, or Magda certainly thought they did. Black mountain hawkweed was the first to curl its long green tongue over the cobblestones, trying out the taste. But before it could properly sink its teeth in, a new foot strutted its way down the path and squashed it flat. The foot was slick purple leather with a heel sharp enough to gut a fish. And the day afterwards, the *ar werth* sign had vanished altogether.

So that was that.

Peeking out through the shutters, Magda and Enio never saw the upper half of the woman. *Perhaps she's a morgen, but the halves got swapped around. Fish on the top, woman below.* She's an estate agent, said their mother, sounding tired. And stop staring. Our house would look exactly the same if we hadn't lived in it for three weeks.

That was the thing. No matter which way she looked at it, Magda couldn't help but think something else had happened to the house over the road. Its eyes were misted up, and the velvet moss of the curtains had thickened.

*

It was easy to forget about anything when you were looking at a puffin. And so, by the time they got to Eirlaw Island, Magda had forgotten all about the Skelbrights. She dismissed the smell of salt which lingered in the driveway. She chose to look instead at the sultry orange auk that was now strutting before them.

'Glorious, that is,' said her dad, proudly. 'Such majesty for a tiny being.'

They observed in silence as the bright-beaked bird lifted its head, a silver herring flapping helplessly in its mouth. It was smaller in real life than it looked in pictures, but Gabriel Corrales was entranced. His expression reminded Magda of the time he'd brought home a dozen pistachio tarts from the bakery — except the tarts smelled decidedly better than day-old fish.

'Look, love,' he nudged his wife. 'Isn't it wonderful? I'll have to get another sketch for an acrylic, or maybe something in watercolours ...'

Without warning, the little seabird took off. Magda laughed like someone who had nothing to fear in the world, and the boat listed softly in the silver breeze.

'Your father never changes,' her mother shook her head. 'If only he'd pursued that career in baking instead of becoming a painter. I could've had nice romantic meals on the terrace, glorious sunshine, homemade desserts...' She glanced wearily over to where her husband was now encouraging their son to throw a handful of sprats into the water. 'What did I get instead? A lifetime subscription of weekend trips to the frozen coast.'

Apathetic, the water replied with nothing but a wan verdigris smile. Magda went to join Enio in throwing sprats to the rest of the puffins, who flapped and gawked for each shining morsel as it fell. It seemed like minutes instead of hours before afternoon had turned to early evening, and deeper currents were tugging them back home.

That was the problem about Wildbriar. It was a town as peaceful as it was predictable: and if adventure or thrilling escapade ever came knocking, Magda was certain that it wouldn't be here. Of course, she couldn't know that getting exactly what you wished for was sometimes terrible. Nor could she know what had happened to little Alice Skelbright, whose room now sat vacantly pink and green, a posy of bishop's lace still resting on the dresser.

Magda's mother, on the other hand, had her suspicions. She counted her lucky stars each day that Wildbriar continued to be a backwater town whose name nobody remembered, or even particularly cared about.

*

An especially spiteful bout of rain had thrashed several daisies from the driveway, and Magda was bored to death. Holed up in her room, she'd gotten to the dire point of contemplating homework, when she heard a crackling in the street below.

'Lucía?' called a voice. 'Come and help me with these boxes!'

Across the road stood a young girl with thick, dark hair that curled in tight ringlets down to her waist. She had light brown skin and flashed a brilliant smile at the two other girls who'd appeared behind her, one slightly taller. Envious, Magda glanced in the direction of Enio's room. She wished *she'd* had sisters. Instead she'd gotten one exceptionally irritating older brother who'd somehow inherited the worst of both parents: their dad's mercurial sense of humour, and their mother's talent for spinning yarns without ever actually getting to the point.

'Magdalena!' shouted the devil incarnate, as if he'd overheard. 'Look. Our new neighbours have finally arrived.'

'Don't call me that,' she scowled, but pattered down the corridor to where her brother was crouching.

The pair of them peered through the window like owls in a hayloft, surveying the street below, where an entire family stood surrounded by boxes. Their own parents had already gone out to make introductions. *Come over for a coffee later this week!* her mum was saying. *The kids will be so glad to have some new friends; the last few weeks have been hard on them.* Smiling, the new house's dad nodded *of course*; the mum, whose beautiful hair was even curlier than her daughters', was holding out a slip of paper.

'Bet they're exchanging pigeon roosts,' muttered Enio. 'Not as if they need to. We live two metres away, for scrim's sake.'

Half an hour later, their mother returned clutching a scrawled note in one hand. 'You'll never guess who we just met! Go out and say hi, why don't you? There's a new family just moved in, from over in Dauglyn. They're lovely.'

Dauglyn was the southwestern quarter of the archipelago, though Magda had never been to visit. It was a place on a map that looked faraway and beautiful, and full of things that wouldn't grow in the frozen soil of the northeast.

'Did you get their pigeon number?'

'Yes! It'll be perfect for when I'm out at work.' The Old World had trialled its fair share of correspondence techniques, but it had been far too easy for messages to get lost in transmission — or worse, corrupted. The great thing about pigeons was that they always reached their destination, and they could crap on anybody who tried to intercept a message.

'Told you so,' said Enio. Then, looking hopefully towards their father, 'Hey Dad, can I go to the park with Kasim and Stuart after school tomorrow? It's rugby trials next week, they'll kill me if I don't get on the team.'

'You can go when you've finished your homework,' said Gabriel. 'And after you've said hello to next door! Their eldest daughter's into sports, so you'll have plenty to talk about.'

'And they've got family in Costa Rica,' Aisling smiled. 'You know what that means. More chances to practise your Spanish!'

Magda groaned. Trying to keep on top of her Welsh schoolwork was bad enough, without adding extra classes into the mix. 'Do I have to?'

'Of course you don't have to, love.' Her mother placed an arm gently on Magda's shoulder. 'But I think you should go and say hello anyway. You might even make a new friend — and let's face it, you could do with some more of those.'

'Mum!'

'She's right,' Enio raised an eyebrow. 'We can't all be local legends.'

'Enio Corrales, you are *not* a local legend,' said their father, sternly. 'You're fifteen. Just because some girl gave you her pigeon number last week, it doesn't mean she's the love of your life.'

'Isn't that how you and Mum met?'

Gabriel Corrales suddenly found himself blushing. 'That was an entirely different, and significantly more romantic, encounter.'

They'd all heard the story before: their father had been visiting one of the rainforest reserves for some sketches, and he'd stopped by at the local museum afterwards, where their mum worked. Aisling Nyfer, however, was a woman of many talents. Not only could she talk for hours about the polypody ferns which made the ecosystem so unique, but she could talk a man into travelling three hours from the south of the archipelago to take her out for dinner.

The rest, as they say, was history.

*

It took Magda three goes to summon up the courage to introduce herself. The first time she crossed the street, she worried nobody would hear her knock. The second time, she told herself they would be too busy unpacking to talk. The third time, she feared the worst: they would find her dull as a brush, uninteresting, and reproach her efforts.

It wasn't until she caught sight of the face in the window that she realised someone had already spotted her. Magda could hardly blame them. If a stranger had been loitering outside their front doorstep, she imagined she'd have gotten curious, too.

'Are you okay?' asked the girl who was watching her. 'You look a bit lost.'

'Sorry for, um, lurking. I just came to say hello.' Magda could feel herself blushing. The words already sounded feeble, and anyone with a scrap of common sense would have thought to bring a housewarming gift. 'I'm Magda. We live just over the road from you.'

'Ah. You're the pigeon woman's daughter, right?' The window swung open wider and the girl leaned out. Her voice was bright and lovely. 'She mentioned you might come by.'

Magda blinked in shock. The pigeon woman?! Her reputation was dissolving before her eyes. 'I promise she's not always like that.'

The other girl grinned. 'I'm Muriel. It's nice to meet you.'

Chapter 2

Turning Tides

Back at their old house in Furze, the girls had never stayed out after dusk. Not in summer, when the long shadows were sweet and inviting; not in autumn, when the harvest moon cast its coppery glow; and not even in winter, when the candles were lit for Invernal. The small hours were dangerous in unspoken ways, like an undeveloped photo, and Muriel often wondered what would happen if they waited in the darkroom. Poured the solvent; fumigated the area. Watched to see what would emerge from that eerie blank canvas.

Now she'd never find out, because they were moving north: far, far away from all those terrors. The last thing she photographed was her bedroom. The camera was greedy, keeping all her best moments for itself, and laughing at how precious they became. But something told Muriel they wouldn't be coming back to Furze for a long while. *Snap* and the memories stayed safe. *Click* and they couldn't be betrayed by time.

She got into the car without looking back. If her old town was a wax-sharp postcard, then Wildbriar was a place rendered soft by familiarity, by well-worn lanes and routes only the locals knew. More unsettlingly, it was a place where wild things moved while you blinked. Here, the roots tangled under your feet. Here, the water rippled like a dream.

Too many nasty rumours, said her mother, as their old house receded into the distance. *Furze's all talk and tattle these days. It'll be good to get away from it.*

There was no question of changing their minds. The estate was sold, the journey begun, and every part of their lives up to now was written in past tense. So Muriel spent the first hour of the trip counting flowers. *Daffodils. Thyme. Bird's nest orchid.* One for every carriageway they crossed; one for each new road they navigated.

Rhosynnau. Camri. Briallu.

She could count them like the lines on her mother's forehead, growing wrinkles of worry that nobody else seemed to notice. Only soothing sentences, and a placating voice — *we'll be there soon, cielo* — followed by the smile that Muriel knew was a farce. *Everything will be okay then. Just a few more miles to go.*

When they did get there, things were far from perfect. For starters there was only one other house in the vicinity, leaving the two cottages abandoned like lost sheep on their lonely strip of hillside. More unsavoury, though, was the sad white plastering. If the Silvanas had been hoping for a crisp gingerbread fairytale, what they got was porridge-thick and stodgy.

'We'll do it up,' their father promised. 'Get rid of those ugly curtains and decorate the whole place.'

'And that garden could do with a trim,' said their mother. 'Did the last tenants not think to cut it?'

It rapidly became clear the last tenants had not thought to do a lot of things. The unaired kitchen reeked of salt. A pair of frilly pink socks had been left in the drawers of Muriel's new bedroom. And nobody liked the look of the mirror in the hallway, although it was impossible to put their finger on why.

Being houseproud, the redecorations began immediately. A chiffon curtain here, a shaded lantern there. Some green moiré cushions, and a nice tapestry to cover that wall — wasn't that so much better? It was a task which kept everybody occupied, not to mention the overly-zealous new neighbours who'd come over to introduce themselves.

Secretly, Muriel wondered if they were the same.

Why else come here, live *here*, in the middle of nowhere, when the Brenin's new law had just come into force? As of last month, the Folk knew to remain hidden. She'd seen enough to know what happened to those who broke the rule.

'By the goddess, that's ugly.' A hollow laugh came from the corridor upstairs. Peeking open the door, Muriel found Lucía and Isadora staring at something in a tall jar. 'Hey, small fry. Come and have a look at this!'

Muriel took a step forwards, inspecting the imprisoned creature. 'You caught a frog?'

'Actually, it's a toad,' said Lucía.

'You have to put him back,' she protested. 'He's an indicator species. He's *important*.'

Isa rolled her eyes. 'Unlike you.'

'I'll tell Mum.'

'Don't worry, we'll release him in a minute. It's just so ... slimy. Like a slug.'

They stared at the toad in contented silence for a moment. *Did toads have dreams about swimming through endless ponds?* Muriel wondered. Could they talk to each other? And what would they even say?

'Who's that outside the window?' Isa squinted, her long pigtails falling into her lap. 'Oh. It's that girl from across the road.'

'Maybe she wants to say hi,' Lucía shrugged, adjusting her new glasses. They were diamond-studded and glamorous, like most of the things she owned. 'We could invite her in for some coffee. You know how to use the cafetera, small fry?'

'Of course I do,' Muriel retorted. In truth, she'd only ever seen their mother use it. The bitter smell of roasted beans made her eyes water, but Lucía didn't have to know that. 'I'll be back in a minute.'

First she spooned four tablespoons of grounds into the filter-cloth. One for each person. Then, hooking it over the metal stand, she set the kettle on the stove to boil. By the time she returned to the hallway, her sisters were already at the door.

'Morning,' said the girl outside, her white skin flushed. The moisture in the air had frizzed her wavy brown hair, and Muriel felt a pang of remorse for the darkening thunderclouds in the distance. 'I thought I'd bring you some dragontails. It's what our old neighbours brought over when we first moved here.'

She gestured to a tray of pastries which were piled precariously high on their platter.

'That's very kind of you,' said Muriel. 'Do you want to come in? It looks like it's about to pour out there.'

'Are you sure?'

'As long as you don't mind the mess. We're still unpacking.' They stepped neatly over the piles of boxes which were crowding the hallway. 'These are my sisters, by the way. Isadora and Lucía.'

'Magda, right?' asked Isa, already halfway through a dragontail. 'These are really good. What did you put in the jam?'

'Damson and rosehip. It's a family recipe.'

Muriel took a bite, marvelling at the explosion of fruits and spices that danced on her tongue. 'It's a lot better than Dad's baking. What do you think, Luz?'

'Not bad.' Lucía paused, taking a long sip of her coffee. 'But have you ever tried tamal asado?'

Magda shook her head.

'Well,' said Isadora. 'Don't suppose you're busy this afternoon?'

*

Sidonie and Rafael Silvana returned home from the greengrocer's to find all three of their children miraculously silent.

'Somebody pinch me,' Sidonie nudged her husband. 'I don't think I've ever seen them this quiet before.'

On the kitchen table were the remains of the baking expedition. An empty jug of sour cream, a torn packet of harina de maíz, and half a bag of milk lay stranded on a tray: the only witnesses to sweet treats which had long since been devoured.

Muriel's father shook his head. 'Anyone would think there was a pack of wolves here. Should we go back for extra flour?'

'You already bought some yesterday,' smiled his wife. 'Memory like a sieve. At least there'll be enough to go around tonight.'

'You want to cook, or shall I?'

'We can both cook.' Sidonie smiled, finally allowing herself to relish the space. Their new home — even if the peeling wallpaper hadn't been fixed yet. Here, she dared to hope, their family might be safe from the storm that was brewing in the South. 'Let's make leek and stilton cawl. Your favourite.'

*

At dinnertime, Lucía was keen to relay the events of the afternoon. As the eldest, she had of course taken charge; Isa had been a good helper with the ingredients, although she'd nearly made the disastrous error of adding salt instead of sugar, and Muriel was their chief taste tester.

'It was a perfect batch,' she said proudly. 'Magda and Enio brought us some dragontails, too! Don't worry, we saved you a couple.'

Rafael peered over in amusement at the tray that Lucía was holding. There were only two small pastries left, nestled among a pile of crumbs. 'Enio. Is that Magda's brother?'

'Yeah.' Isa rolled her eyes. 'He's the one who won't shut up about Ivor the Bard and operatic rock. He kept trying to play new phonograms while we were weighing out the ingredients; it was incredibly distracting.'

'Ivor the Bard, eh?' Rafael smiled approvingly. Magda and Enio seemed like nice kids, especially if they could put up with all three of his daughters at once. 'Maybe he's going through an alternative phase. Happens to the best of us.'

'Dad, there's no need to dig out your old records.'

'It wasn't *that* awful,' Lucía argued. 'I thought that some of the harmonies were rather complex. He said he'd see if there were anything else at the shop next week.'

Muriel snorted with laughter. It was unbelievably on brand for Lucía to take the high moral tone, but this was getting ridiculous. 'Haven't got a crush, have you, Luz?'

'As if!' her elder sister glowered. 'I'd rather poke my eyes out than see *him*.'

'Calm down, the pair of you. How about we get some food on the table?' Sidonie reached for the soup-cauldron and offered everyone a ladle. Cawl was best served hot, and its hearty qualities succeeded in settling many an argument where other methods failed. 'Before we eat, we give our thanks. To the Great Weaver and the Great Destroyer; to the spider and the moth goddess.'

'*We give our thanks*,' replied her family.

'For silk and the sacred oak.'

'For silk and the sacred oak.'

There was a moment of silence before Rafael gave a mischievous grin. 'I'm starving. Come on, let's dig in.'

He waited for Sidonie and his daughters to begin first. In his mind, the food at this table could never be beaten: not by elaborate cuisine, not even by the finest cook in the world. Because this was the only table where he got to sit alongside everyone he cherished, all under the same roof.

This table was theirs.

Chapter 3

Pigeon 493

You could always tell the pigeon had been when there was shit all over the doormat.

Cringing, Magda stepped neatly over the pile of droppings outside the front door. 'Enio, could you tell that girl to stop writing so often? This is disgusting!'

Her brother only poked his head out of the window above and grinned. 'You're just jealous you haven't got a secret admirer.'

'If she sends you any more letters, I'm going to kill that wretched bird!'

She didn't mean it, of course. Pigeons were rather lovely creatures, totally unworthy of the bad reputation they'd once been given. With their soft pink cheeks and downy grey backs, they reminded Magda of the sky in early spring: white clouds blossoming, just as the wild campion unfolded their reddish flowers.

Her favourite was Pigeon 493. As her own personal messenger, she'd grown accustomed to watching his little shape grow larger in the distance, until he landed in a clumsy bow at her window ledge.

'Thank you,' she unfolded the little scroll. The last one had been a week ago – one of the girls in town was having a party. Tegwen Price. She'd politely declined; not because she was busy, just because she couldn't stand the girl. 'Here you go,' she'd returned the note to Pigeon 493. 'You should have a name, shouldn't you? I think you'd suit Murdock. No? Or ... Mauricio? Or ... Hergest.'

The pigeon gave a low trill as Magda stroked his back.

'Okay. Hergest it is!'

'What's going on in there, Magda?' called her mother, who was getting ready for work.

'Hergest brought me some post.'

Her mother frowned. 'Hergest?'

'Well. Pigeon 493.'

'They're not supposed to have names, darling. It's meant to be impersonal, to stop strangers from being able to identify them.' She didn't add that it made pigeon deaths less upsetting to deal with. A number could be replaced; a name meant grieving. When Pigeon 493's short lifespan inevitably came to its end, she didn't want her daughter to feel any more wounded than necessary. 'How about we find you a nice blackbird instead? I'm sure they've got plenty at the pet emporium.'

'But I don't want a pet,' Magda protested. 'Hergest is my friend.'

Sighing, Aisling went back to the letter she had been in the middle of writing. She could finish it on the bus; she just hoped it didn't sound embarrassingly formal.

Dear Sidonie and Rafael, read the letter. *Next weekend is Magda's thirteenth birthday, and we're planning a party with some of her friends from school. It's been so good to see her getting along with Muriel, Isadora and Lucía — I was wondering if your family would like to join us? Please let us know if you can make it. All the best, Aisling and Gabriel.*

That was probably too long and rambly. Or maybe she'd repeated the word 'would' too many times. But, considering she had never been good at writing letters, Aisling decided to send the thing before she could change her mind.

In the meantime, there was a birthday party to plan.

*

Saturday hit the Corrales family like a brick. Not only was it blowing a gale outside, but the rain was coming down in thick ribbons over the pebbles.

'Do you think we should cancel it?' whispered Magda, her hands pressed against the window.

'No, love,' said her father. 'We'll just have the party indoors, instead.'

He couldn't bear to see his daughter looking so *sad* in her best dress. It was deepest indigo, the colour of the night, and embroidered with a handful of shimmering beads. On the inside tape, Aisling had embroidered Magda's name in silver thread.

Suddenly, her face lit up. 'Look! Someone's arriving!'

A carriage had pulled up outside the front door. Gabriel recognised the horse; she was a bay mare who belonged to the Davis family in town. 'Hey, Winnie,' he reached out to pat her damp velvet nose. Then he glanced upwards to where three cloaked figures were disembarking from the carriage. 'Harlo, Sienna, good to see you. And who's this little princess!'

Their daughter, a dark-eyed girl named Chalcedony, was dressed in a floating gauze of taffeta. Its colours ran from green to auburn in a way reminiscent of the sunrise; in fact, Magda might even have been jealous if she wasn't so elegantly dressed herself.

'Mum, Chalce is here!' Magda beamed with delight, helping her friend down the steps and into the house. 'I'm so glad you're here. We've got sandwiches, and jelly boats, and potatoes. Oh, and the cake! It's got three layers: blue velvet, chocolate, bara brith ...'

While the pair of them continued to chatter, Gabriel heard the doorbell ring again.

'Come on in, you'll get soaked standing out there!' he called. The carriage door opened and he put out a hand to help whoever was inside. 'Quickly, you'd better not —'

Then he realised who was smiling back.

'Thanks very much, that's awfully kind of you,' said a clipped voice.

Sharla Price and her husband. Who in the Weaver's name had invited *them*? Magda hated their kid. Aisling hated her mother. Gabriel disliked the lot of them by association, and not even because they had no regard for the fine arts. They'd vetoed his proposal for a new gallery at the edge of Cunning Wood, and they refused to acknowledge the value of the museum in town. But above all they were insufferable bastards.

'Did Aisling send a message?' he asked, without thinking. Worse still, had they turned up uninvited? He needed to tell his wife, to warn her, except that was physically impossible. She was busy entertaining the guests in the living room, and the Silvanas were making their way across the road behind them.

'A birthday is a birthday,' smiled the thin-lipped white woman. 'It would be rude of us not to offer our congratulations, no?' Her hand felt like ice in Gabriel's, and he wondered briefly if this was how it felt to invite a vampire into your home. 'Tegwen! Bring the primrose truffles, won't you?'

They stepped past him like a ghost. Gabriel stayed frozen, unable to process what had just happened. *What were the Prices doing here*? he wondered, stupidly. *Why now?*

'Gabriel,' said another voice, much lower this time. 'Are you okay?'

He looked up to find Sidonie Silvana looking at him with a furrowed brow. It brought a smile to his lips: of course the Silvanas were the only ones with enough sense to bring an umbrella. 'Oh, everything's fine,' he forced a cheery tone. 'You'd better come on in.'

*

The party was a riotous success. Magda had a wonderful time with her friends, the party food was cooked to perfection, and not even the weather could dampen the spirits of twelve hyperactive pre-teens.

At least, that was how the children experienced it.

'I don't like that man,' whispered Rafael, after they'd dropped off the girls at the Corrales' house. 'He's been looking at you funny. At us.'

Sidonie turned to see who he meant. Beside one of the vehicles was a malnourished-looking couple wearing too much jewellery and not enough waterproof clothing for the season. 'Let's go home, then. Before he asks any questions.'

But it was too late. Clocking them, the couple had begun to make their way over.

'Hello,' said the scrawny woman, with a thick Porthdeilio accent. 'I don't believe we've met, have we? Sharla Price. Enchanted to meet you.'

'Sidonie,' replied Muriel's mother, with a terse smile. 'I suppose we live too far out of town to have crossed paths before.'

'And there was me thinking you'd just moved in!' remarked Victor Price, with a laugh, but the comment sent a sliver of glass through Rafael's stomach. 'That house has been on the market for too long. Nice to see somebody's taken it at last. Those your girls?' he gestured back to the window, where the back of Isa's head was visible.

'Yes,' said Rafael, stiffly.

'Three daughters,' mused Sharla. 'Richly blessed indeed.'

The Silvanas knew they were lucky. Some couples spent their lives longing for daughters and only got sons who couldn't inherit. But something about the way the pinch-faced woman said *richly blessed* made Sidonie want to wipe the smirk off her face.

'It's getting late,' she said shortly. 'We'd better be off. Pleasure meeting you.'

The other couple nodded, still smiling faintly. 'May the goddess go with you.'

Chapter 4

Five Forests

One of Muriel's favourite things about the archipelago was its abundance of forest. Temperate rainforest, to be specific, and the lush seasonal climate which allowed its vegetation to flourish. It made adventuring easy: all you had to do was walk a hundred metres off the path, and you were stood inside a soft-mossed, fern-fronded haven of greenery.

The summer of the previous year, they'd gone back to visit Costa Rica. Muriel missed the swampy mangrove beaches and the ruffled layers of jungle canopy, dancing so lightly in the breeze. Moreover, she missed the guatusa that always stole their coconut husks from the compost, and the aracaris which forbid anyone from ever harvesting an unripe papaya. The landscape here was slower, more deliberate, than the rapid unfurling of pink pinecone ginger and collapse of rotted palm fronds. A part of her heart would always be lodged in her grandparents' hometown across the sea.

Despite their vast differences, Muriel knew some things drew fine threads between the two countries. A few years before the Rift, the Costa Rican rainforests had been decimated, just as Wales's wildwoods had been bulldozed for new development. It was an outrage. An ecological crisis of the highest order. And since the dawn of the New World, both forests had regrown with a vengeance.

She wanted to be like that; to exist with a vengeance.

'How long are you going to be in there?' Her mum tapped at the door. Muriel and Lucía were weaving Isa's hair into a thick crown braid, but the sheer volume of it meant it was taking longer than anticipated.

'Just a couple more minutes!'

'Hmm. Lunch will get cold if you're not done soon.'

The velocity of the braiding immediately increased. Then another thought struck Muriel. 'Mum, can Magda and Enio come over to play after school?'

'Of course, cariño. Siempre son bienvenidos, ya lo sabes.'

They went back to braiding in silence. After their mother had gone, it was Lucía who broke the glamour. 'Those kids across the road ... do think they're like us?'

A dimple of worry flickered in Isa's cheek. 'Mum said we're not supposed to talk about it.'

'Haven't you wondered, though? Why they're so nice to us?'

'Maybe they're just kind people,' Muriel shrugged. Did everything have to have an ulterior motive? Was it so awful to hope someone actually wanted to be her friend?

'Maybe.'

'You think they're hoping we'll help them back.'

'If what I heard was true, then they've got good reason.' Lucía looked away guiltily. 'Their mum, Aisling Corrales. They say that she's a visionary.'

There was stunned silence.

'Luz, you can't start rumours like that,' whispered Muriel. 'It might not be true. You could put them in danger.'

Isa, however, had frozen. 'Do you think their children know?'

'They're too naïve. Too unafraid. And they haven't spent half their lives living right on the Brenin's doorstep.'

'We were supposed to be safe here,' said Muriel, feeling her stomach lurch.

'Yes,' sighed her eldest sister. 'But that's only as long as no one finds out.'

About the secret that lived under their skin.

About the Tidal Folk.

Because this was the last place they had to run to.

*

As Muriel left the house, she picked up the empty milk saucer quickly. Really, they shouldn't be leaving such things outside for the bwbachod anymore — but who else was going to spare a dish of cream for the poor things, now that all magic was forbidden? She could only thank the goddess that none of their other neighbours were nosy, and set off hastily for school.

When she got there, Mrs Sachar insisted upon grand, elaborate introductions for their newest student. Muriel just about wanted to step out of her own skin, but her embarrassed protests went ignored.

'Now that we've all said hello to the wonderful Miss Silvana, let's get back to geography! It would be remiss of us not to leave time for the Five Forests,' Mrs Sachar's brow was lined with seriousness. She was a short but intimidating woman who kept a carefully-chosen stack of books on her desk. 'Here in the north, we are richly blessed with the Celestine Forest; just south of us lies Cunning Wood. And I'm sure you've covered Wych Elm and Hazel Mire with Miss Drina already.'

The class nodded *yes*. Muriel's gaze stayed fixed at carpet height, where dark brown skin peeked out from between the gold straps on Mrs Sachar's shoes. Rumour had it she ordered every pair direct from Porthdeilio: today's were stylish green leather heels, but Magda had warned her to expect a new fashion every week.

'So here we have it,' Mrs Sachar gestured to the map covering the wall. It was a thick tapestry that had been torn in one corner, leaving a patch of Wildbriar dangling precariously. 'The Five Forests of Wales.'

Cunning Wood. The Celestine. Wych Elm. Hazel Mire. Lyre's Hollow. Five forests so different, and yet the same Sickness ran through all of them.

A skinny white girl named Annest stuck up her hand. 'Mrs Sachar, why aren't we allowed to visit Cunning Wood?'

'Ah,' Mrs Sachar's expression changed altogether. 'Because, my dear, it is poisonous. Setting foot into that forest is a fate which I would not even wish upon my worst enemy.'

'But it looks so pretty,' Annest hung her head. 'Are you sure it's a bad place?'

'Not everything that *looks* pretty is pretty; that's a lesson that will serve you well, my girl. Now let's get back to our mapwork.'

They turned towards the map again. If it hadn't been for the distracting golden thread, Muriel would have said the tapestry looked hastily completed, rushed in certain areas and others skimmed over entirely.

'Now,' Mrs Sachar cast them an analytical gaze. 'Who can tell me why the forests are in danger right now?'

Nobody replied.

'Because of the prophecy.' Muriel glanced around awkwardly, wondering why the other students seemed so oblivious. Didn't everybody know that the prince had vanished? Or were they too scared to speak? 'The forests are sickening, and won't return to health until the Brenin's son comes back.'

'Indeed, Miss Silvana,' nodded Mrs Sachar, gravely. 'What I ask of you all is to be very, very careful. This is a dangerous time for us all. One can never be too quick to fear the Folk.'

A wave of burning shame crept through Muriel. It couldn't be right, to feel like this. Like her family was something fearful. When the class ended she crept out in silence, grateful for the cover of the storm.

Chapter 5

A Vision in Red

The day that everything went wrong, Aisling was on her way home from work as usual. She wondered what Gabriel would have made for dinner, what the kids had gotten up to at school, and all the other mindless mundanities that people took for granted. She detected nothing out of place as she crossed the street; nothing inherently ominous in the weather. Then, on the path outside the driveway, she stopped dead in her tracks.

There was a pigeon nailed to their front door.

Not a wing, not a feather; the whole bird. Blood dripped down its pathetically puffed chest, staining the feathers an ugly shade of scarlet, and its head was drooping sadly. Aisling felt the sudden urge to cry.

It couldn't be Pigeon 493. It had to be someone else's bird — the goddess knew it would destroy Magda to see her beloved pet killed in such an awful way — but why, why would anybody do this?

Trembling, Aisling stepped towards the door.

It wasn't Magda's pigeon.

It was Enio's. She removed the nail from the door with fingers that felt numb, finding a place in the nearby woodlands to bury the little body. But even after she'd washed her hands clean, she couldn't stop them from shaking. There could be no mistaking a message of this kind.

This was a threat.

*

'Dilys stopped writing to me.'

They were sitting at the breakfast table, but Enio was slumped over his hands.

'I think she fancies someone else. There's this boy in our Welsh class, he's always got the right answer. She looks at him like he's some sort of demigod.'

A pang of guilt shot through Aisling. 'Oh, love. It might not be anything to do with him. I'll check in at the pigeon office, see if anything has come up, okay?'

'Okay,' said Enio miserably.

'So that's why he's been playing so much loud music lately,' said Magda, after he'd left. For weeks she had been plagued by Ivor the Bard's latest hit, *Tourmaline*. 'If only he'd develop a sense of discernment. That stuff's hardly poetry.'

'At least it's keeping him occupied,' replied her mother. 'He'll get over her, just you wait.'

'I wish he should hurry up.'

Aisling stifled a laugh. But something uneasy was stirring in her stomach. 'Magda, if anyone talks to you at school ... has any funny questions, or anything like that? You *do not talk to them*. Do you hear me?'

Magda met her eye, confused. 'What do you mean by funny questions?'

'I can't ... I can't really explain it to you right now. One day you'll understand. But for the minute, just steer clear of any conversations about things that feel suspicious.' Stitches, this felt just as deceptive as she'd feared. 'Stick to your normal friends, okay? And avoid that Tegwen Price.'

*

Later that afternoon, Magda gave Hergest the pigeon a letter to take to Muriel. *I'm bored. Want to go explore some of the woods?*

The reply came back almost immediately, carried by an elegant black-and-white pigeon with golden claws.

Sure. Meet in half an hour?

It was raining by the time they got outside.

'Sorry for the short notice,' Magda apologised. 'Enio's sulking because his girlfriend stopped writing to him. And Mum and Dad seem upset, too, though I'm not sure what about.'

'Your brother's got a girlfriend?' Muriel raised a questioning eyebrow.

'Not anymore, he hasn't.'

Dilys Laire was the prettiest girl in the school, with dark brown eyes, warm brown skin, and braids that tumbled down to her waist. Practically every boy in the school had a crush on her, along with some of the girls, but Magda had never deciphered what Dilys saw in her brother.

'She wrote to him for a little while,' she went on, 'but the pigeon stopped coming, so he thinks she got bored.'

Muriel bit back a smile. 'Lucía will be thrilled.'

'Lucía?'

'She keeps asking about your brother,' she smirked. 'And going to the phonogram shop. I think she's hoping he'll walk in and compliment her on taste in music.'

'She'll be sorely disappointed,' Magda raised an eyebrow. 'I wouldn't bother with someone who doesn't know his bryophytes from his lichens, either.'

'Last time she went into town, she bought a copy of *Blodeuedd*.' Muriel made a face. 'You know, the new album by Caspar Arcay?'

'Never heard of it.'

'Wish I could say the same.' The truth was Lucía's listening habits had grown so persistent that Muriel was beginning to nurse a small headache. 'My dad keeps telling her to turn it down.'

'Huh. Maybe she and Enio would get along, after all.' Magda picked idly at a stray gorse bush. It was Enio this, and Enio that, and she was beginning to get fed up with the whole thing. 'I heard there was a new thicket of blackberries near the glen.'

Muriel's eyes lit up. 'No way.'

'Yeah, seems like they've come early this year.'

'Race you there?'

As they sprinted, the oak trees gave way to a hazel thicket. Tall birch and ash boughs crowded over, speckled with tree lungwort and dark orange dog-lichen. Magda gazed upwards into the canopy. It was quieter here, and she let the quietness settle over her shoulders like a scarf.

'No blackberries,' Muriel inspected the briars, disappointed. 'Someone must have beaten us to them.'

It was annoying, not least because blackberry crumble was a great way to cheer up a crowd. Some kind of funk had come over the house, and Magda had slightly hoped that she could have found a solution out here.

She glanced over to the empty bough that Muriel was studying. 'My dad painted a whole glade of blackberry bushes, once. Reds, purples, greens, all dark and inky.'

'He's an artist?'

'Yeah. I reckon his last watercolour went down badly at the auction, though. He's been so stressed lately; that must be why.'

For a moment Muriel didn't speak.

'It's been the same with us,' she said, eventually. 'Both my parents are acting ... prickly.'

'Maybe it's the crap weather.'

'Possibly.' Muriel contemplated, letting go of the thorny branch. The tiniest drop of red blood had scratched her knuckles, and she wiped it away fast. 'I think they're scared, after what happened before.'

'When you were living in Dauglyn?'

'It wasn't easy, back there. There were too many people close to the Brenin.'

'What, like the Prices?' Magda made a face. 'I don't know why they bother. He doesn't even know they exist.'

'That's why we moved, anyway. We needed a fresh start.' Muriel looked away, but couldn't get her sister's words out of her head. *Was* Magda's mum one of the Tidal Folk? Did she have a clue what was going on? It was impossible to ask out loud, which left Muriel to tiptoe around the question. Anything more was too risky. 'Do you know anything about the new law in the South?'

Magda shook her head.

'What about the Folk?'

'Course I know about them,' Magda laughed. 'Everyone does. Not that there are many around here, though.'

That's what you think, thought Muriel.

'What if there were? Would you be ... concerned?'

'Nah,' the freckled girl grinned. 'It would make Wildbriar a lot more interesting, that's for sure. I've been trying to spot a water-leaper for weeks. I bet *they'd* know where to find one. And imagine being able to cast spells, just like that!'

Muriel swallowed hard. 'Magda ... The Brenin's introduced a mandate against them. All Tidal Folk are to be killed.'

The breath caught in Magda's throat. 'What?'

'They're calling it the Scarp Mandate,' Muriel said quickly, regretting the words. 'Don't tell anyone I told you. I just thought you should know, because...' She broke off. How could she explain the kind of fear that Magda didn't even know yet, might not even *need* to know? 'I thought you should be careful. You and your family.'

'Right.' There was an odd tightness to her voice. 'Maybe we should go back, in that case. The woods being full of magic, and all.'

'No, I didn't mean... I just meant where people might overhear. At school, or whatever.'

'Okay.' The ghost of a smile tugged at Magda's lips. 'Want to go pond-dipping?'

The shadow of the previous conversation passed over them like a cloud on an overcast day. By the time they reached the pool, it had winnowed away into sunlight.

'Is this the place?'

'Let's go to the shallow end. Better view over the rocks.'

Neither of them could be sure how long they spent by the water's edge. Freshwater ponds were full of marvellous creatures, as well as elusive ones, and there was a long stretch of quiet before the first catch.

'Look, I got one!' Magda yelped, suddenly waving her line in the air.

Like an angry dragon, the water-leaper was puffing out its cheeks and hissing. Llamhigyn y dŵr were notoriously temperamental. If you didn't catch the little froglike creatures by the tail, they'd flap their boggy green wings and escape.

'Wow,' said Muriel. 'I thought they'd be much bigger than that.'

'Looks like it's only a juvenile.' Luckily for them, it hadn't grown its stinger yet. 'Let's put him back. When he's full grown, he'll be a menace to the fishermen at the coast.'

'I'll have to ask my dad if he's ever caught one,' smiled Muriel. Her father was the manager of an international firm; sometimes he worked with fishing companies around the dock areas. On the other hand, he might crack some awful joke about Muriel's mother being the best catch he'd ever made. 'Do you go into town much?'

'Yeah. My mum's an art historian.' It was a small mercy that she didn't work at the museum right next to Magda and Enio's school, though she'd threatened them with relocating more than once. 'We're saving up to go to the Valleys next spring, there's a textile exhibition she's hoping to see.'

'Really? I bet my mum's heard about it, she'd be so jealous!' Sidonie Silvana's career as a fashion designer meant she frequently brought home richly coloured fabric samples, but Muriel's favourite was the one patterned with deer foals. One poked its nose out into the tall grass; the others gazed up at the spangled starlight. 'Did she say when?'

'I already forgot,' said Magda, sheepish.

They stared back into the pond.

'What are you looking so thoughtful about?' asked Muriel, after a while.

'Right now?' Magda leaned forward to rest her hands on her knees. The pool shimmered green with rackweed, flintlocked in the dying light. 'How to get away with scavenging some of the Sunday roast for Hergest.'

'Magda, pigeons probably shouldn't be eating roast potatoes...'

'I know. But he seems to love them.'

*

Gabriel Corrales knew that something was up from the fact his kids were so quiet at dinner. Had somebody failed a test at school? Had a fight broken out on the playground? Or what in the Weaver's name was all this grim silence about?

'Eat up, Enio.' Aisling shot their son a worried look. 'Come on, what's wrong?'

'It's nothing.'

'Go on, try some,' Gabriel offered the plate of sardines on toasted bread, attempting a smile. 'Nice and crispy!'

'I'm fine, Dad.'

They glanced over to the other side of the table, where Magda wore an equally sullen expression.

'Sweetheart, why aren't you eating? Are you feeling okay?'

Setting her fork down with solemn precision, Magda got up. 'I'm not hungry.'

Gabriel and Aisling exchanged a look. *You or me?*

You, said Gabriel. *You've always been better at this. I'll only make it worse. I'm sorry.*

The apology was a silent excuse. He wished there was some way of traversing those perilous waters, but every time they closed over his head.

'Enio, stay there. I'll be back in a moment.' Aisling tucked in her chair and followed their daughter up the stairs. 'Magda?' She knocked on the bedroom door. 'It's only me. Is there something wrong, love?'

There was a moment before the door creaked open. Hot tears were streaming down Magda's face, her cheeks puffy. 'Mum. What's the Scarp Mandate?'

Aisling felt something cold clasp its fingers around her heart. *No,* it said. *Not this. Not now.* She was supposed to be a good mother. And didn't good mothers protect their children?

'Sit down, love.' She took her daughter's hand, feeling the quick pulse in her fingers. 'Who told you about that?'

'One of my friends,' sniffed Magda.

'Was it Tegwen Price?'

'No.'

'Okay,' Aisling breathed out. 'I think we need to have a chat with you and your brother about this. Can you go and get Enio?'

They sat down uneasily on the bed, like two owls looking up at their mother.

'Some people,' she began, 'are not kind to everyone they meet. Sometimes, it's because of how they look. Sometimes it's the way they dress, or what they believe. And sometimes, it's because of who they are.'

'Then they're mean old stinkers,' Enio muttered. 'What's that got to do with us?'

'I need you both to know that you are the most precious thing in the world to me and your father. There is nothing, *nothing*, that could make us think otherwise,' said Aisling, firmly. 'And because you're special, other people will be jealous. They'll try to trip you up. You mustn't let them.'

'Why not?'

'Because the ruler of this archipelago has just made a very dangerous law.' She took a deep breath, watching her children's anxious faces. 'Remember you're safe here. But if you see or hear anything to do with the Folk, with magic, or the like, you must avoid it. I know it's wrong. And I know it's unfair. But that is the only way to keep you safe right now. Is that understood?'

Two nods.

'Dw i'n caru ti,' she bent down to kiss their heads. 'Now, how about some hot chocolate?'

*

Gabriel came to bed late. Sometimes he sat downstairs and did crosswords about toadstool species or coastal birds in the Eastern Isles, especially when he was stressed from work. But Aisling knew him well enough to know that this was something else.

'How much did you tell them?' he asked quietly, staring at the ceiling.

Aisling rolled over to face him. 'Not a lot. But enough.'

'Did you tell them about us?'

'Not yet.'

'You know we'll have to, one day.'

One day, thought Aisling, as the pair of them fell asleep. They were both so sure they'd have more time for these discussions; more time for everything, everything, when it came to it.

Chapter 6

The Selvedge

After the first rain-glazed weeks of term slid by, curiosity became an art form. Muriel felt as if they were digging, excavating fossils in the clay; marvelling at each bone-white remnant to be found there.

And Magda had a wicked sense of humour. She cracked jokes at school, told stories at lunch, and gave them both stitches from drawing the world's worst portraits.

'Is that supposed to be Enio?'

'Obviously. He's an ugly git, but I've done him a favour with my artistic license.'

The crayons blunted, and the paper yellowed, but their weekends of creative mischief knew no bounds. One afternoon, however, Magda found a new pastime.

'What happened to you?' Muriel stared, horror-struck. From the other girl's mud-grimed appearance, it looked less like she'd been dragged through a hedge backwards, and more like she'd voluntarily crawled through several.

'Went exploring. You'll never guess what I found.'

'Don't tell me you went outside the village.'

'But that's where all the interesting places are,' Magda protested. 'And this time I managed to get inside the library!'

The library in question was an abandoned-looking shack with more rats than functional windows, which naturally meant Magda had fallen in love with the place. She should have looked a state, being covered in dust from exploring. But instead, the autumn sun cast her face in crimson light. A glorious red flare skimmed the tops of the hedgerow, and — for just a moment — everything looked like a picture, burning.

'I can't believe you,' Muriel shook her head. 'You went there again?'

'I found a whole hidden diary in the back shelves! It's brilliant.'

'But you know it's forbidden. If anyone catches you, they'll have your guts for garters.'

'Enio only said that to scare us,' Magda dismissed the warning. 'All that talk of flames and the wrath of the goddess? You can't possibly believe it.'

No one knew where the tales had begun: the ones that said if girls or women entered a house of books by night, they'd burn. As far as Muriel knew, there was no truth in it. And Magda had been in several libraries during the daytime, without any consequence.

But still.

'They say those kinds of fires don't hesitate before they tear the flesh clean off your bones.' Lucía had shivered, when Muriel told her the whole escapade back at home. 'Sometimes they're so quick you can't even scream.'

Isa said nothing. The silence clotted in the coldness of early evening, just as they heard their mother calling them for dinner.

*

Going out to buy fabric, Muriel grumbled, *should have been a simple task*. It was late Sunday morning. Skirting her way through the maze of cobbled streets and old-fashioned looking shops, she caught flashes in every window of the reputation their town had garnered as a market district. Rare goods. Prized goods. Trade on every corner.

This was central Wildbriar. As the hub of the Abergwyll, you never knew quite what you'd find around the corner, but Muriel's favourite place was Milliner's Lane. Home to a dozen haberdasheries, it had beads and buttons and trimmings galore. The most fashionable shops were sold out within hours — and the most fashionable of them all was Tanya Okada's. From the glistening bolts of silk to the soft crimp of the wools, it was as much a tactile as a visual experience. Needed a new dress? There was taffeta that shimmered coolly between your fingers; lawn cloth with its crisp handle. Had an old jacket that needed patching? There was fustian, damask, and all the wondrously coarse weaves in between.

'Good morning,' called a familiar voice, as Muriel opened the door. Tanya Okada was a middle-aged woman who made her customers feel right at home, and every outfit she wore was a stunning advertisement for her craft. Today's crisp linen jumpsuit was embroidered with neat white stitchwork, and her straight dark hair was pinned back into a low bun.

'Hello, Mrs Okada,' said Muriel. 'I was looking for some fabric. Could you help me find it?'

'Of course. Has anything in particular taken your fancy?'

Muriel cast a glance towards the rolls of glittering beaded fabrics, which were lamentably marked *price upon request*. 'Just some slubbed silk, I think. My mum's got a new client who wants some designs for a day dress.'

'That's a pity,' sighed Mrs Okada, scooping up a skein of embroidery floss which had been misplaced by earlier customers. 'We're fresh out of the last roll, and you know we don't stock plastics.'

Of course Muriel knew. Synthetic fabrics were a cheap and ruinous fad which had generated huge amounts of textile waste before the end of the Old World, but there were still the odd few merchants who'd try to make a quick featherfold that way. Mrs Okada, on the other hand, made her distaste quite clear.

'Can I interest you in some seaweed linen instead?' Reaching past a roll of unbleached calico, the tailoress pulled out a bolt of pale green cloth. 'It's a marvellous choice for steady stitching; doesn't snag the way your satins do.'

Muriel cast a wary glance outside. 'I think it's got to be the silk, unfortunately. I'll have a browse and come back tomorrow if I've no luck.'

'No trouble. Take care.'

Muriel grimaced as she closed the door. The truth was that her mum needed the fabric samples tonight. There was a tight deadline by which she'd been asked to create some designs, and it seemed pathetic to let her down on such a simple errand. So she buttoned up her cloak a little higher and set off towards the other side of town, the southernmost market district that ran dangerously close to Cunning Wood. The area, known to locals as the Selvedge, was home to an equally infamous stretch of cloth houses as Milliner's Lane. Unfortunately, it was famous for vastly different reasons.

Once every few years, a human skeleton would be found at the verge of poisoned woodland that ran alongside the Selvedge. Another time it might be a bloodstained handkerchief, or a smashed pocket-watch, or a week-old deer carcass with the eyes rotted out. Muriel was no stranger to tales of terror, yet those haunting snippets sent a certain chill down her spine.

Trying not to dwell on the grisly legend, she hurried towards the nearest fabric shop. Eyes, high; price, low. Somewhere among the rows of cloth would be the perfect bolt of silk. But Muriel's mind kept returning to the rumours whispered at school: the ones that said going into Cunning Wood was sentencing yourself to an excruciatingly painful death. That, she reasoned, was only if you were stupid enough to cross its borders in the first place. As long as you stayed clear of the Forest's edge, it couldn't hurt you.

*

That night the rain cast a layer of gossamer over the town, slicking the roads black. All five of the Silvanas sat together in the living room: Sidonie and Rafael having a heated debate about the necessities of garlic bread, and Isadora peering over her sisters' sewing. While Lucía was hemming an old skirt, Muriel's needle and thread darted in and out of thick spider silk. A pattern like the moon was beginning to form over the damasked surface.

'Where'd you get that fabric?' Isa peered over, envious. 'You'd better not waste it on another pair of socks.'

'Socks are a perfectly respectable garment,' Muriel replied defensively. 'And it's just an offcut from Mum's sewing stash. Nothing special.'

'Come on, she hasn't made anything that sparkly in ages. Did you go to Mrs Okada's?'

Muriel said nothing.

'Or the shop on the corner?'

Another stitch punctured the fabric with vicious precision.

'Wait.' Isadora's eyes narrowed. 'You got it from the Selvedge, didn't you?'

Pausing from her work, Muriel glanced up. 'I might have done.'

There was quiet triumph in her voice. Things that precious didn't usually come cheap at the trade quarters at the edge of town, but she had struck a careful deal. They called it the Selvedge because it was where the town ended and the woods began: just like the raw edge of a fabric, shorn to a halt.

'What did you trade in?'

'I bargained half a featherfold for it,' Muriel admitted, 'and they let me have it.'

'I can't believe this,' Isadora shook her head. 'And to think that you were the one preaching to Magda about being dangerous!'

'At least I'm not risking my neck to sneak into derelict buildings!'

In spite of everything, Muriel spoke with such regal disdain that it was impossible to argue. Isa secretly thought that her sister talked like a queen who might have been.

Chapter 7

Plover

Time flew like white petals in Wildbriar. It was like watching dandelion clocks, drifting until they separated into hours and minutes and seconds: and before the Silvanas knew it, a full year had gone by in their new home. It was the same fateful day that they got a dog.

Perhaps it would be more accurate to say, the dog got them.

'Diosa mía, Rafa, ¿qué coño es eso?' Muriel's mum came storming round to the front of the house, pointing at the very large and very unavoidable fact of a wire-haired grey dog outside their front garden.

'Don't blame me!' Muriel's dad threw his hands up in protest. 'It was here when I got back. *I* didn't do anything.'

Muriel immediately went to pat the grey-eyed monster. 'Mum, can we keep him?'

'I don't like dogs,' sniffed Isa.

'He's so big and hairy,' Lucía added.

But it was too bad. The dog had already decided it was here to stay, and it wanted to make friends with everyone.

'I mean, what do you even *feed* a dog?' asked Sidonie, tying her long crinkly hair back into a ponytail. This beast was going to put more lines on her forehead than she needed, and it looked far too cheerful for its own good. 'We haven't got anything for it to eat.'

It was true. Land-farmed meat was reserved only for the holiest of days, which meant that a large part of their pantry was stocked with vegetables and the occasional fish. As happy as it looked, she didn't think the dog would take much of a liking to beetroot or chayote.

Meanwhile in the kitchen, Rafael was slicing green plantain for patacones. 'You could try him on some boiled rice? He looks hungry.'

'Oh, so it's *he* now?' Sidonie folded her arms. 'Give him the rice, and let's hope he clears off.'

*

Six days later, the dog had still not cleared off.

'He needs a name, Mum,' Muriel pleaded. 'We have to keep him.'

Sidonie and Rafael had quietly agreed that it was futile to argue, although neither of them were exactly pleased about it. 'We can keep him, as long as you take him for regular walks. And he can find his own dinner.'

'He's a good hunter, you don't need to worry about him,' Lucía beamed. Since the dog had foraged and brought home some chestnuts of dubious origin, she'd changed her tune about owning a pet. It was quite miraculous how he seemed to intuit what was missing from their pantry; not even Isa could keep up with the groceries as well as he did.

'How about Diego?'

'Or Vincent?'

The dog was too busy chasing his tail to listen.

'What about Gelert?' piped up Muriel.

The dog broke off from his spinning. With one ear cocked, he sat back at his haunches and Muriel could've sworn he met her eye.

'Where did you hear that name?' frowned her mother. 'It's a horrible story.'

Muriel shrugged. 'Nowhere. Just thought he looked like a ... Never mind.'

In the end, they settled for Plover. He was shiny and grey, just like the national coin. Not only was the silver plover an aesthetically pleasing currency — for each one bore the stamp of a bird's foot — but the hexagonal shape made it impossible for them to roll away if you dropped it.

Meanwhile, Plover the dog had a knack for achieving the impossible. He frequently fitted into spaces where he wasn't supposed to be, pieces of bara planc would mysteriously go missing from the cookstone, and not even the towels were safe from getting chewed up.

But as she watched him sleeping, curled up in a nest of stolen goods, Muriel couldn't help but think Plover was a good omen.

*

Soon the wolfhound began following her to school. Reluctantly, she left him outside the gates and headed inside for the morning's lessons. Today was history: and although Miss Drina was the kindliest of their teachers, her classes were so boring you could fall asleep without trying. Even worse, fresh parchment was set down when Muriel entered the room. It looked like this was going to involve some kind of test.

'Good morning, everyone,' smiled Miss Drina, her wrists shimmering with bracelets. She was a dark-blonde Spanish woman with an affinity for collecting charms: on one bangle was a pigeon, a cat, and a pwca; on the other was a puffin, and a sparrow. 'I hope you've all brought your copy of *Pre-Rift Histories: Collections from the Archives*. Can everyone open to the chapter on the twenty-first century?'

Muriel took out her copy of the hefty textbook. Sat at the desk beside her was a quiet white girl called Ruth Snade; further down the row was Leah Okada, the tailoress's daughter, followed by Annest Jones and Jasper Roy, a boy who Muriel had befriended a few weeks ago. Since learning Jasper lived next door to their favourite coffee shop, Muriel could finally understand why her sister was spending so much time hanging around Brookit Bridge after school. *Are you sure it's just the coffee?* They'd all burst into peals of laughter at Isa's sudden bashfulness.

'Miss Drina?'

'Yes, Leah?'

The girl folded open her notebook, scanning the lines of writing. 'Will we be covering the Convenience Years?'

'Yes,' nodded Miss Drina. 'In fact, let's begin there. During the latter part of that century, large companies found cheaper and cheaper ways to produce goods. The goods got worse, but consumers didn't care enough to look elsewhere... the entire thing was highly profitable. What could have solved the issue was the proverbial basket.'

Muriel leaned forward, making quick notes. Baskets. Since when had baskets gone out of style, anyway?

'Think about it. Let's take a plastic bag: utterly obsolete, of course, but you could screw it up and take it with you easily. Requiring little thought or effort, until the point where you must dispose of it.' Miss Drina took a languid pause, clearly enjoying the theatrics of her debate. 'Now compare this to the humble wicker basket: functional, flexible, lightweight. It might take longer to weave, but it will serve you for years on end. Never underestimate the power of small choices, or the good that they can do.'

Muriel was struggling to copy down the words fast enough. From across the room, Magda shot her a *put-me-out-of-my-misery* sort of look. It was the expression of eternal boredom, but to no avail. Miss Drina was already searching for a new passage.

'Another fundamental breakdown of the Convenience Years was the lack of climate-proof architecture, that is, buildings designed to meet the ecological needs of a particular area ...'

It felt like hours before they finally trailed out into the sunshine. But at least a boring class was the worst that could happen at this school. At Muriel's old school, the breaktimes were unpleasantly long and there was an abundance of bullies.

'I thought we'd never get out of that class,' said Jasper, as they made their way down the path. 'Another minute, and I'd have had to make a break for it. There's a concert tonight. If Miss Drina thinks I'd be late to it, she's got me all wrong.'

Muriel smiled. 'Yeah. What were you listening to the other day, by the way?'

'*You* want to know what I was listening to?'

'Isa's been asking. It's the only way to get her to shut up.'

'Fine,' Jasper gave a broad grin, pulling a phonogram out of his pocket. 'It was the Midnight Pheasant, of course.'

He handed her record to inspect.

'Very original,' Muriel rolled her eyes at the cover art. *The Midnight Pheasant* was a boy band who sang primarily about girls who'd broken their hearts — not that it was surprising, from the way they behaved. 'I thought you'd given up on them ages ago.'

'What's the matter, not a fan?'

'You can't seriously think that 'Starlight Eyes' is profound listening material.'

'Maybe it's not about being lyrically profound, Muriel,' Jasper laughed. 'It's the musicality of it. The intonation! Doesn't that just make you want to sing?'

'I guess.' Muriel handed the phonogram back with a wry smile. 'I'd better get home, anyway. See you tomorrow lunch?'

'You bet. Don't forget it's llymru at the canteen.'

'As if I'd forget!'

Outside the gates, she was surprised to find Plover was still waiting for her. She ruffled his soft grey head. 'Poor old boy, you've gotten all cold and damp. Come on, let's get you back inside. Somewhere nice and warm.'

Chapter 8

Seventeen

Enio couldn't remember the first time he'd heard about the prophecy. It had always simply been there, omnipotent, as a fact of life for them all.

When the royal heir disappears, said the wise-women in town, *the Five Forests of Wales shall be condemned to sicken. They will slowly perish and fall to ruin: only the lost prince's return will restore them to health.*

His parents said it hadn't always been this way: just years ago, the birches grew thick as thieves and fen violets blotted the wetlands. Now they all shrank back. And their only hope, or so Enio had been told, was that the Brenin's son would return to set things right one day.

It drove him crazy.

How was anybody supposed to concentrate when the world around them was in slow decay? Right now he was training to join the Temperate Coastlands Alliance, where he would work in conserving what remained of the Welsh rainforests. By the end of the year he'd leave home for Eirlaw Island, and by the end of *that* year he'd hopefully be earning enough to start cutting a path for himself in the world. But every now and then, he collected rare clippings of hawkweed and meadow saxifrage, fearing they might be the last.

Even that was now the least of his worries. Occasionally he remembered Dilys Laire and wondered what had changed. It brought a smile to his lips — one that disappeared quickly when his family was around. They all acted as if he was still fifteen, laughing and chattering and going about their day as if everything was perfectly fine. Enio wanted to be perfectly fine. He wanted to make them proud.

Next year was Eirlaw Island, and all he had to do was get there.

*

Lucía was waiting outside the door to the phonogram shop, *Bevan & Trove*, when Enio rounded the corner, slightly out of breath.

'Sorry I'm —'

'Late?' she glared at him. 'I'll bet. Twenty minutes I've been here, Corrales. Jamás conocí a un tipo tan necio como eres —'

'Alright,' he raised his hands in defence, trying not to smile. Unlike his dad's Spanish accent, Lucía pronounced her 'c's as a soft 's'; it meant that even her insults sounded softly shimmering. 'How about I buy you a new gram to make it up to you?'

There was a moment's deliberation before Lucía nodded.

'This one,' she pointed to the flower-patterned phonogram in the window. 'It's the new single.'

'Caspar Arcay decided to take a turn for the gothic, huh?'

The band's horse-skull motif was intertwined with withered petals and clouds of ink.

'Looks like it,' she tilted her head to inspect the small script with the name of each track. Phonograms worked through aerotechnology: you unfolded the fan-shaped piece of wood, threw it into the air, and let it swirl there like a wind-chime, as the air blew through it and sounded the notes.

Maybe one day, Lucía dared to hope, she'd have her own phonogram shop. It was the reason she'd first picked up the banjo: making music was all she'd ever really wanted to do, and in her family it went back generations. Her grandmother had been a virtuosic lyre player — not that Lucía could hope to compete. But was it so terrible to want the walk the same path; to leave her voice and tell her story?

She didn't think she could bear it any other way.

'Hey,' Enio nudged her in the shoulder. 'Guess what I just found.'

She peered over, adjusting her glasses. 'Are you going to let me see?'

'Alright, alright.' He reached into the back deck of phonograms with glee. 'Here it is.'

Lucía took one look at the cover, then burst out laughing. 'Sheronne and the Mountaineers? Really?'

'Come off it, you know I've got good taste.'

'Not with women, clearly.'

He laughed, pushing the phonogram back into its slot. 'Your parents still think we're dating?'

'Nah. I think they have their suspicions.'

He smirked. 'I can't believe you used to fancy me.'

'Did not!' she blushed. 'Anyway, fat lot of good it would've done.'

'At least your family's easygoing. They probably wouldn't care if we *were* going out.'

'Enio,' she met his eye. 'It'll be fine, whenever you decide to talk to them.'

Except it might not be. Except he didn't know when, or how to even begin.

'Let's hope so.'

'Trust me,' said Lucía. 'It'll be fine.'

They went back to browsing through phonograms, lifting each one in turn to poke fun at its cover art, at the lyrics, at anything and everything they had to throw. He'd miss this, next year. Being around Lucía felt so easy. It was a rarer feeling than he'd realised.

'Wow,' Lucía stopped, suddenly. 'Look at that sunset.'

A stream of tawny light was pouring through the window. It scattered the shop with shadows and riddled Lucía's deep brown eyes with amber, like a vein of gold in a coal seam.

Enio glanced down at his watch. 'It's getting late,' he realised. 'Give me those. I'd better ring them up at the counter, or I'll be late home for dinner.'

A knowing sparkle twinkled in Lucía's eye. 'No need.'

'What?'

'I already got them.' She held out the bag. 'Happy seventeenth, necio. You thought I'd forget?'

'Aw, thanks Luz,' Enio grinned, his mop of dark hair falling into one eye. 'You're the best.'

'I know,' she laughed, watching him turn away to the long road up the hill. Then she began to make her own way back, the long way, along the coast.

Sometimes she wished he didn't smile at her like that.

Chapter 9

Grimoire Malgarty

By the time they were in their penultimate year of school, Magda had almost forgotten about her mother's warning. The Scarp Mandate seemed nothing but a far-off whisper in the capital, and she was fifteen. She was unstoppable. What could a stupid law mean to her, a mortal, with the world at her feet?

The look on her father's face cut the thought short.

'They're introducing a new programme,' said Gabriel, glancing up from where the pigeon had dropped his weekly paper. 'At all the schools in town. Each pupil is to be tested for symptoms of "the occult".'

'"The occult"?' Aisling gave a sharp laugh. 'I can't believe this. Besides,' she gazed firmly at Magda. 'You've nothing to worry about. It'll be fine, love.'

Meanwhile, there was an alarming tapping sound coming from Magda's bedroom window.

'Hergest, what are you doing?' She pulled up the shutter to let the bird inside. He was holding a scroll of black parchment, and looked decidedly frightened. '*Miss Corrales*,' Magda read. '*Your screening will take place this afternoon. Please arrive punctually.*'

There was a split second where she might have raised it with her parents. Might have complained, or torn up the parchment and forgotten all about it. But then her father was out the door, and she began to pack her bag for school. What did she have to fear?

*

'Frankly, I don't see why this is necessary.' Mrs Sachar folded her arms, tapping the heel of one turquoise boot impatiently. The classroom felt sapped of its usual warmth, like it could sense the foreboding beneath the surface. 'These girls are perfectly ordinary. There's nothing wrong with them, not so much as a hair out of place.'

'It's merely a precaution,' replied a low voice. 'I promise no harm will come to them.'

A silvery kind of woman had stepped across the threshold. Her long hair fell in bright black curls, flecked with streaks of white and grey, and the twinkle in her eyes made all of the girls stare.

'Everyone, this is Grimoire Malgarty. Wildbriar's head physician,' explained Mrs Sachar. Her tone betrayed any notion of reverence that the sentence might have carried. 'She'll be with you for the next hour or so — and then you can go back to your usual tasks for the day. Just a quick test, alright?'

She might as well have been talking to a wall. Everyone was too busy staring at the feline creatures which wound themselves around Grimoire's ankles to pay attention. They couldn't be called *cats*, exactly, but they moved in such a way their colour seemed to shift in the light.

'What are those?' Muriel sounded awestruck.

'Ah, you mean Caravaggio and Maelstrom?' smiled the grey-eyed woman. She reached down to stroke the back of the first one, eliciting a low rumbling purr in response. 'They're grimalkins. Gio can be a bit haughty, but don't mind him. They'll warm up to you in no time.'

The pair of them sidled unctuously around her feet. The first one was golden as a wheatfield in the height of summer, but the second was a stormy grey colour, tinged with blue. He glared at Muriel without a shred of remorse.

'Maelstrom!' scolded Grimoire. 'Stop that. It's rude.'

'I'd best leave you to it,' said Mrs Sachar, awkwardly. 'One hour and no more. Got it?'

The students were separated into pairs and escorted out of the room, each waiting their turn to be summoned. Muriel's stomach felt queasy as molten pewter by the time she and Magda were finally called upon.

'Our last pair already! The time does fly, doesn't it?' said Grimoire. 'I haven't even asked your names yet. Awfully rude of me.'

'I'm Muriel. It's nice to meet ... well, all of you,' she glanced pointedly at the blue-grey grimalkin.

'And I'm Magda.'

'A pleasure to make your acquaintance, ladies.' Grimoire reached into the large leather briefcase at her side. 'Perhaps I should begin by reassuring you that I've been in this line of work for many years, and everything that happens next will remain utterly confidential.'

Muriel wondered what exactly *this line of work* entailed. The woman looked far too mysterious to work an office job; even for a physician it all seemed oddly esoteric.

'I understand that this next part may sound quite strange. But the reason I explain this is because I need you girls to trust me.' Grimoire laid out a scroll of paper and several jars of coloured ink. 'With your consent, I would like to conduct a test of your aptitudes — so that we can understand how best to protect you. Is that okay?'

Slowly, Magda nodded. Her body felt as if it was prickling with tension, but it wasn't fear. 'I thought all of this was to find out if we're among the Folk. That's what you're here for, isn't it?'

Grimoire paused, and a sad smile crossed her lips. 'I suppose it is. But let's take a look, first; there may be nothing to worry about. May I?'

The woman dropped three splotches of blue ink across Magda's outstretched palm.

'Hold your hand over the parchment.'

Magda felt a curious burning sensation — not a painful one, but as if the ink was prickling its way beneath her skin. Finally, the ink began to drip down and onto the paper. It left a series of swirling greenish marks. The tawny-coloured grimalkin had sidled over to inspect them, but Grimoire swatted him away. 'Gio! Keep your grubby paws off that.'

'What does it mean?' asked Magda.

With a serious expression, Grimoire met the girl's eyes. 'You have a strong bloodline. There may have been traces of it in your family, or perhaps not. But you, my dear, are a visionary.'

'What's a visionary?' Magda asked, worried. It sounded bad.

'It's somebody whose dreams are ... uncanny. They often experience visions of the future, or readings of the past, which unnerve those around us,' said Grimoire. 'Don't be fooled, in the Old World there were many who *called* themselves visionaries — but they were nothing but charlatans. Your gift, on the other hand, is true.'

'Well, what am I supposed to do about it?' asked Magda, afraid. 'I've never had weird dreams, or visions, or anything like that. And my mum never said anything about it.'

Grimoire sighed. Of course she hadn't: any mother would want to protect her children at all costs, but she could hardly tell that to the small, bright-eyed girl in front of her. 'Promise me this,' she said at last, 'that you will keep this a secret between you two. If you tell *anybody*, then you will be in danger.'

Magda nodded quickly. As long as she didn't think about it, didn't say the words out loud, then maybe it wouldn't be true.

'Now your turn, Miss Silvana.'

Determined not to show her fear, Muriel stepped up to the grey-eyed physician. The inks and parchment lay waiting.

'Hold still.'

Just before they began, however, Caravaggio gave out a mournful *miaow*. He was getting hungry. When were they going back to the cottage for some food?

'Later.' Grimoire poked him with her foot. 'We have important business right now, okay?'

This time, once the reddish ink had turned to purple swirls as it dripped from her hand, Grimoire looked more bewildered than anything.

'What is it?' asked Muriel, anxiously.

'This ... I haven't seen this in a long time.' Grimoire lowered her voice. 'Miss Silvana, you have veridian heritage. Veridians are powerful sorceresses of the Forest, gifted with a rare and elder magic,' she explained. 'They draw energy from the woodlands and wildernesses. In many parts of Wales, they are considered one of the most powerful of the Folk.'

The slow aftershocks rippled through Muriel like water. Lucía had been clear. Isa had been clear. But she, the youngest daughter, bled with the same magic as her mother.

'Prove it to me,' she said at last. In the face of terror, the only thing worth offering was a challenge. 'I've never felt an inkling of magic in my life. You say you're a physician – but why should we trust you? How can you be so sure about something like this?'

Grimoire raised an eyebrow. 'You disbelieve your fate.'

'I said prove it.'

Reluctantly, the woman reached one hand into her briefcase. Sometimes people got exactly what they asked for, and it was a dreadful thing to witness. 'This is a hummingbird orchid,' she explained, scooping a small flower out of the briefcase. The purplish red flower unfolded in the shape of a tiny bird, and smelled like cinnamon. 'They're quite rare, but you can find them in some parts of the cloud forest. They thrive in the humidity, being epiphytes.'

Muriel stared at the delicate specimen. 'What am I supposed to do with it?'

'Let's see.' Grimoire paused, and raised a foot. Then — before either of the girls could protest — she crushed the flower beneath the heel of her boot. 'I think reviving it would be a good enough test, don't you?'

Muriel stared. This had begun like some kind of bad joke, but now it was getting worse. 'That's not possible,' she said flatly, staring at the miserable, crushed flower.

'Well, it certainly won't be with that attitude. Pick it up,' Grimoire prodded, placing the remains of the orchid into Muriel's cupped hands. 'Now, speak to it, as if you were begging it to live again.'

It felt like a stupid prank, but Muriel clutched it between her fingers and tried to think. *Live*, she thought, urging the flower to hear. *Grow. Flourish.*

Nothing.

She glared accusingly back at Grimoire. 'It didn't work.'

Grimoire cocked her head, and saw what she had missed before. Neither of the girls had even *realised* this kind of destiny might await them. She wouldn't need to worry about them keeping the secret: they would hide from it, run away for as long as it was possible — but in the end, it would always catch up.

'You're right. We've seen enough for today,' she said gently. 'One day, it will be safe for you to speak of these things. But until I see you again, promise me that you will keep this to yourselves.'

Muriel nodded, eager to be shot of the whole hideous conversation. Who was this woman — this *physician* — to tell them what they were?

'Thank you,' said Grimoire, before she opened the door to the hallway. 'Mrs Sachar? We've finished for today. The girls' tests were clear; there are no problems.'

The relief on their teacher's face was visible. 'Oh! That's wonderful news. Not that many women with your gifts of perception,' she added. 'Now, girls, we'd better get you to your morning classes.'

As they were ushered down the corridor, Muriel didn't dare look back at Grimoire Malgarty. It was almost pretty, the way the air had shimmered around her and the grimalkins at her feet. The things that Grimoire had said about *them*, on the other hand, struck fear into Muriel's heart. The test must have been misguided, misjudged, misrepresented; besides, she had failed to bring the orchid back to life. So why did she feel like there was something sinister hanging over them?

*

Sidonie was waiting outside the school gates. She'd been afraid of this day since her daughters had begun school.

Never would she forget the afternoon Isadora had come home crying, after some spiteful girl had left a handful of teeth in her satchel. *Enchantress*, they'd shouted, even though she'd done nothing to deserve it. Even though her test was clear. The worst part was that the teeth didn't belong to any animal Sidonie recognised; if anything, they looked frighteningly human.

'Well?' she whispered, the second they got beyond the grounds. 'Tell me what they said, Murie.'

Muriel looked back at her. Her mum hadn't used that name since she was little. 'They said it's nothing, Mum. That I'm clear.'

A sigh of relief escaped her. 'Oh, darling. That's wonderful news,' she murmured, pressing her daughter into a tight hug. 'I'm so glad.'

Chapter 10

Invernal

The year that Enio left home, a strange void opened in Magda's life. It was inevitable, of course, just as her own eighteenth birthday would be. They'd all helped her brother pack, watched fondly as he waved goodbye from the omnibus, and walked back up the path to the house without a further word. But although the trees were just as green, and the kettle sang its same intolerable limpet-song as always, something had changed. Magda hadn't been expecting the amount of laughter in her life to suddenly halve.

I hate this, she sent across the road by pigeon. *There's no one to help me defend myself against Mum and Dad any more. No one to play cards with. And I have to do* homework *now.*

That's rubbish. It's been weird since Lucía left, too, Muriel replied. Her eldest sister had left to attend a conservatoire in Tarren Mawr, all the way across the Channel. *Obviously I'm happy for her. But it's sort of lonely being the one left behind.*

Yeah. Why'd they have to get all stupid and grown up so soon?

Luckily for Muriel, Plover was determined to fill the gaping void that had been ripped in both girls' lives. Their trips to the bramblings grew more and more frequent, with the wolfish grey hound in the lead and his followers just behind.

'Are we nearly there?' Magda panted for breath.

'Just a little further!'

They were looking for wild fruit to make winterberry pie. Invernal was coming up soon, and there was so much to do. But perhaps the best part about holidays was precisely their ability to keep you busy and take your mind off other, less pleasant things.

Neither of them had broached the topic of Grimoire Malgarty.

At the very least, Invernal was a great excuse to forget all about the visit — even as more reports rolled in of what was happening in the south. *Coven of witches discovered near Furze; hazard safely eliminated*, read one paper. *Caution: lakeful of gwragedd annwn sighted on the west coast of Dauglyn*, shrieked another.

Magda ate her porridge in silence most mornings. She didn't trust herself to answer her parents when they raised the dreadful topic anymore. Pigeon mail became a daily comfort, and Hergest was happy to oblige in carrying her extra papers.

Anything fun happening at yours? Things are boring here.

Worse here, replied Muriel's pigeon, a chirpy bright-backed creature. *I'm stuck in my room while Isa practises the drums. It's the most dreadful sound, you wouldn't believe it.*

I never thought I'd say this, but I sort of miss Enio's bad music.

I miss Lucía's, too. But at least Plover doesn't steal my clothes all the time.

A smile crinkled the corner of Magda's cheeks. She sat back on her bedroom floor, head aching, and stared out the window into the grey rain.

*

At long last, the holiday preparations were ready. It was the Eve of Invernal, and all the townsfolk had descended into the streets to celebrate.

'I can't believe we're finishing school next year,' whispered Annest Jones. She liked being sixteen just fine; seventeen meant scary decisions and things she wasn't ready to consider yet.

'We'll be okay,' Muriel said firmly. 'The goddess blesses our path.'

In the distance, you could just make out the bank of the River Vesper. Although it stayed hidden by day, it was now illuminated with spectacular blooms of light. At Invernal, many citizens made the journey to the river to release fireflies over the water. It was said that the insects would carry wishes for the new year over the land, and those which reached the ocean would come true. It was also a rare occasion where the girls were permitted a nocturnal outing.

'Slow down, Magda,' said Gabriel, from behind them. 'Por la diosa, my back's killing me, I can't have my legs giving in on top of that.'

'But we're almost there,' Magda protested. 'Look! You can already see the lights in the river!'

They were beautiful. Like floating wisps, the fireflies lit up the stretch of water that rushed from the mountains all the way down to the sea. Magda sighed into the breeze. Lately, she had detected an inexplicable sense of fear, one which sat like an all-too-comfortable guest in the pit of her stomach. But tonight she pushed it down: this was no time for sorrow or mourning. Right now, the world was blazing bright.

Right now, she was incandescent.

*

Several days passed before the dull ache returned, the telltale sign of post-Invernal boredom. At first Magda tried to ignore it. Even if Enio wasn't there to keep her company, she had other friends. After all, the town was full of snow: surely someone would be around to go sledding with her? But Muriel was with her family. Chalcedony was with hers, so were the others, and even Ruth Snade made hasty apologies to excuse herself. Suddenly there was no one to forage horse mushrooms with, or bake berry whirls, or go exploring at the edge of the woods. The feeling grew. Soon darkness was falling on another long, sleepy weekend, exactly like the last, and Magda couldn't bear it any longer.

She needed an adventure.

'Magdalena,' her dad remarked as she tried to sneak out, 'just where are you going dressed for the arctic?'

'To the shops down the road! Not all of us have antifreeze for blood.'

'Oh, okay.' A hopeful expression came over Gabriel's face. 'Could you be persuaded to pick up some extra marshmallows while you're there? *Someone* seems to have finished the last of them.'

Magda paused. 'What was it you were saying about trial and hardship the other day?'

'That the greatest hardships make the strongest warriors.'

'Exactly,' she beamed. 'May you become a strong warrior.'

'What do you —'

'Bye, Dad!'

She picked her way across the road, laughing down the hill, and finally along the road out of town. The old ramshackle library stood unobtrusively in the snow. It was a place so ancient it seemed to stand still in time, entirely forgotten about, and chilly white drifts stuck to Magda's calves. She knew exactly how Muriel react if she knew.

That library's a bad idea. You know what they say about those places!

Magda was well aware the library was a bad idea — that was the whole point, wasn't it? If Enio had still been at home, he would've nodded in a flash. But it was just her now, and a small midwinter foray could surely be forgiven. She pushed open the door to the library, coughing at the musty smell of books, neglected in the damp. Why did nobody seem to care about storing these things? There could be all manner of priceless texts inside, and on her last visit she'd barely scratched the surface.

The library watched her while she worked. Its two unboarded windows shone like eyes, sorrowful with sleet that dredged the glass. Meanwhile, in a similar manner to a harvest mouse, Magda shuffled through papers and pored over its stories until it was beginning to get dark, and her stomach was beginning to rumble.

She thought that she'd made it back unscathed. Only once the front door creaked shut did she feel a stern hand on her shoulder.

'And where exactly have you been?'

Magda gave a nonchalant shrug, trying to look innocent. 'At the shops. Ask Dad.'

'That's rather interesting,' replied Aisling, 'because you seem to have left without any groceries.'

Damn it.

'Where were you *really* sneaking off to?'

'I just wanted to go for a walk,' Magda sighed. 'There are lots of interesting old buildings. Houses. Libraries. It could be good for my architectural studies at school, couldn't it?'

'You mean that run-down old library outside town?'

'It's a piece of living history!'

'Magda,' said her mother, as gently as she could, 'places like that are the reason that girls like you go missing.'

'You can't actually believe that old legend, Mum. It's even older than Bampi Owain.'

Aisling fixed her daughter with a steady gaze. 'Magdalena Corrales, folk stories stay alive for a reason. And I've heard stories of too many girls who end up burned to death, or hurt in unspeakable ways, to let you find out whether it's true or not.'

Hanging her head, Magda gave a stormy *hmmph*.

'It's not fair.'

'Remember, love,' her mother patted her shoulder softly. 'Read as much as you like but never trespass after dark. The library by night is not what it might seem.'

Chapter 11

The Bramblings

Plover didn't think much.

He was only a dog, and most of his judgments were to do with food. Namely, the quantity, consistency, and pursuit of it (though beggars couldn't be choosers). But while he'd greatly enjoyed the family feast at Invernal — managing to scrounge a cutlet of roast lamb, and even a few scorched trimmings — a creeping sense of fear brought up the hackles on his back. Even while the family exchanged gifts, wrapped with brown paper and tied with a mistle branch. Even now, he could tell that something was wrong.

And it was lurking in the woods.

Don't go into the bramblings today, he tried to tell his household. He ran threatening circles around the Silvanas' house, as if he could ward off the threat with some kind of talismanic charm. *Stay home. Stay together.*

'Look, Mum! Plover's chasing his tail!' Isadora bent down to give him a pat. 'Good boy, aren't you greybeard?'

Plover growled in frustration. Clearly she was oblivious.

Stay away! Bad things in the forest! he tried to convey, running to the nearest tree and barking with considerable vigour into its canopy.

'Seen a squirrel, have you?' Muriel chuckled. 'I'll be right back. Maybe I'll even find something for you to eat!'

Humans could be so frustrating sometimes. But although his cunning plan had failed, Plover still had one last twist in his tail. He would follow the girl's tracks: that way, if things turned nasty, he could jump in and save the day. At least that was what he told himself.

*

All afternoon, Plover faithfully trailed the youngest Silvana through the bramblings. She paused to find the most quizzical creatures. A missel thrush, a sprig of withered corncockles, and even a curly-tailed shrew. At one point she nearly jeopardised the mission by drawing the attention of an attractive red squirrel, but it vanished before Plover could lose his focus. A short while later they emerged on the other side of the woods. It was a light walk back to the cottage, and the wolfhound breathed a shaggy sigh of relief. He had done his duty.

He had kept his herd safe.

That was when he heard the ruckus that was beginning to unfold down the hill. There were voices somewhere, high-pitched and tangled, along with the sound of rushing water. Plover's ears flattened against his skull as he ran, padding quicker and quicker towards the noise. The very bad thing was still lurking in the woods: just not *this* part of the woods.

Now it was coming for its prize.

*

When Muriel returned from the woods, she had hardly noticed Plover disappear. The dog was like a shadow: if he sometimes slunk off into the dusk, everyone knew he'd be back by suppertime. What she did notice was her father calling out from the kitchen window, looking slightly desperate.

'Cariño, ¿me ayudas con algo? Isa ya se marchó con tu mamá.'

Muriel set down the basket of wild garlic she'd foraged, wiping her hands on her trousers. 'Sure. Where'd they go?'

'Just into town. I imagine they'll be heading back soon.'

Her mother had probably gone to the dye shop, thought Muriel; there was a new tincture she'd been meaning to try on silk. Sometimes the girls helped her grind the cochineal to make a pigment, but the best part was watching their mother paint with it. Thick lines; thin lines, dancing together on the canvas until only a beautiful stencil remained.

'Lucky you're here to lend a hand,' Rafael passed his youngest daughter a brush. 'I was hoping to get it finished before they came back.'

Muriel stared at the wall where her father was kneeling. He'd stencilled a series of swirling lines over the wood, leaves and tendrils and budding flowers. An inkwell full of dark liquid was set on the countertop.

'Is that enchanter's nightshade?' asked Muriel, eyeing the careful lines.

Her father nodded proudly. 'And that's white bryony. Here's fairy-flax,' he pointed to another cupboard, 'and that one's wood anemone.'

'They're all of mum's favourite flowers,' Muriel realised. 'You're painting them for her.'

Brow furrowed in concentration, Rafael lifted his pencil to finish the sketch. 'If I could bring her all the flowers in the meadow, then I would.'

They sat for a while, watching as the wildflowers grew across their walls.

Then Muriel frowned. There was a slow, heavy knock coming from outside. She could hear Plover snuffling somewhere, whining at the window, but the louder sound was coming from the front door.

'Dad, have we got visitors?'

The tapping sounded urgent — but why wouldn't Muriel's mother and sister just use the back gate, which was left unlocked?

'Hmm. I'll get it.' Her father went to the door, setting down the little inkwell he'd been mixing. The padlock, however, wouldn't budge. 'Maldito candado. Why won't it —'

Suddenly the door swung open. All Muriel heard was a shocked gasp, and a crash of broken porcelain. The inkwell shattered on the tiles like a dropped child.

'Dad, what's wrong?'

Outside, the cochineal dye had begun to trickle across the floor like a new river delta. Crimson ink was dripping over the doorstep, and onto the cobbles below.

Then Muriel realised what her father was looking at.

'Don't,' said Rafael, his voice trembling. 'Don't ask me to let you in right now, please. I'm so sorry, but I have to look out for my family.'

The girl outside the door looked haggard. Her feet were bare, splattered with carmine liquid, and Muriel could hardly bring herself to recognise her. It was Magda. The graceful curls of her hair were now matted; her eyes, bloodshot.

'I didn't mean to do it,' Magda took a trembling step forward. Her hands were covered with something red and awful.

'What happened?' urged Muriel, aghast. 'We'll get you inside, we'll get you safe. Right?'

But her father was shaking her head.

'Oh, Magda.' His voice was strained. 'We tried our best to keep you safe.'

*

Magda, please talk to me, Muriel sent via pigeon that night. *Please.*

It was useless. Even after they'd cleaned the redness from the walls — well, from everywhere it had been splattered — Magda had stayed silent. Right now, Muriel couldn't sleep for the thousand thoughts racing in her mind.

Had her best friend been attacked? There were creatures in the woods, and maybe one of them had lashed out in a fit of fury. Or had Magda tried to get into the library outside town, and somehow gotten stuck? There were frightening myths about girls who visited libraries by night, and the image of dark ink swirled grotesquely in her memory. Or maybe, and Muriel truly hoped this was not the case, it had been Magda who had injured someone else. Why else would she be seemingly unharmed? Why else would her dad have stared in that horror-struck way? She didn't dare to let the idea linger.

Whatever it is, it'll be okay, she tried, one last time. *You can tell me, Magda, I promise.*

The moon flickered outside. They were getting close to the longest, coldest night of the year, and not even the stars wanted to be out. Just as Muriel was about to give up, her pigeon came back with a scroll shivering in its claws.

It was Tegwen, read the note. The handwriting was thin and broken. *Tegwen Price.*

Chapter 12

Ether

At dawn, the town clock chimed with its traditional announcement: nine days had passed since Invernal. Nine chimes for each dull, cloud-shriven haze. Thin tapers were set in the windows, veering lopsided like grisly wax smiles, but the village was shivering with unseasonable cold.

Aisling Corrales peered out over the valley road that led down to town. Her daughter had not spoken in hours, and nothing could shake the tremored expression from her face. The talking had been done, she was forced to admit, by everything else.

They'd washed the dark red streaks from her hair. They'd burned the sodden clothes. They'd asked no questions, destroyed the note which Sharla and Victor Price had shoved through their letterbox, and sent back a satchel of gold heavy enough to make a goblin weep. In kinder times, that might have been enough to keep the fear at bay.

But times were merciless, and Aisling squinted as a cloaked white figure became visible in the distance. Someone was galloping up the little road on the hill. An iridescent hood cascaded over her shoulders, draping both grey horse and rider in shimmering gold. It was a mirage almost beautiful enough almost to make her forget the sanctity of the day. At sacred times like this, travelling was frowned upon: the roads were empty of cars and carriages; horses and bikes.

And still the figure rode on.

'Cariad,' she turned to call up the staircase, 'I need help with something.'

But her husband either could not, or did not hear her from the eaves of their snow-covered cottage. The clattering of hooves echoed louder in the distance, thundering up the road. And before Aisling could pull down the shutters at the front, a knock came on the door.

'Hello?'

Aisling froze. It couldn't be the rider from the road. It had been faster than any person should have been able to travel, swifter and more seamless than even the most gifted horseman could manage. The only possible explanation for this was a bad vision. If she stayed here and waited, maybe the premonition would go away.

'Good morning,' a voice sang through the letterbox. 'Would you be so kind as a to spare a moment for a weary traveller?'

She couldn't move.

She couldn't even raise a hand to protest as the door swang open, unaided by any lock or key. A tall white stranger stood behind the glacial breeze, and Aisling felt the blood cooling in her lungs.

It was golden-cloaked rider from the road. The brilliant cloth spilled over her shoulders, as if she'd slaughtered the finest ray of dawn she could find and stepped into its skin.

'A blessed Invernal to you, kind stranger. May I come in?'

'I'm afraid we're unable to offer our hospitality,' Aisling managed, hoping desperately that her family was far away upstairs. 'If I were you, I'd stop by the town hall down the hill. They might be able to help you there.'

'Oh, but I insist,' the woman took a step inside, gloved hands pressed against the doorframe. 'I have heard most wonderful things about your hospitality.'

Aisling paused then, inspecting the woman's face behind the hood. It was like staring down a cat: she didn't trust herself to look away, for fearing the thing might have moved away entirely.

'Who are you?'

'My name is Stefania. I have travelled a long way to get here.'

'Well, I'm afraid we cannot help you.' A step towards the door and Aisling's fingers clenched the handle. 'May the goddess guide your path.'

To her horror, the door didn't budge. Stefania's vicelike grip held it ajar, with fingers that were deceptively strong, the thin white knuckles terse as iron.

'May I make myself clearer,' she strained against the door. 'Your presence is not welcome. If you do not leave, I will have to make a formal complaint to the council.'

One corner of Stefania's lip curled upwards. 'A formal complaint?'

'Of the highest order.'

'Perhaps I should explain this in a different way.' Stefania relaxed her grip on the door, which hung suspended in mid-air. It felt as if the north wind had stripped the house bare of any lies it might tell. 'I represent an institution called the Fallow. It's an extremely prestigious college, one that takes special care of our more ... gifted youths.'

'Gifted youths? I'm sure the local school has quite enough capacity for academic talent.'

The woman's smile burned like ice. 'The Fallow lies just south of Abergwyll, near the Middle Isles. I believe your daughter would be very happy there.'

'Absolutely not. Our children are perfectly content. And as for your intrusion, I think it would be best if you —'

But Stefania raised one hand in a strange gesture, and Aisling's sentence was severed. Her eyes went wide, as if she were choking on her own tongue.

'It wasn't a question,' Stefania cast her a pitying look. 'Now if you would be so kind, I have been sent to collect your daughter. Magdalena.'

She didn't elaborate. In her opinion, there was no point: Wildbriar would soon become nothing but a distant house of memories for these children.

'Where is the girl?'

Instead of replying, Aisling made a lunge for the coffee table and hefted it above her head. She could not afford to miss. But as the antique missile found its target, the wood simply crumpled to splinters. Stefania stood unscathed.

'My, my. What terrible manners,' the woman picked a shard of alder from her shoulder. 'This gown is a precious heirloom, you know.'

So was my coffee table! thought Aisling, furious. Why wouldn't her stupid voice work? And how was she supposed to get this hideous stranger out of her house?

'Ash?' called her husband, hearing the commotion downstairs. 'Ash, are you okay?'

'Your wife won't come to any harm,' said the cool grey voice of a stranger, 'so long as you remain compliant.'

The moment he reached the bottom of the staircase, Gabriel's heart dropped through his stomach.

'You,' he stared, paralysed. 'What do you think you're doing here?'

'Merely my duty.'

There was no time for words.

As Gabriel made a lunge for the pair of them, something caught him in his tracks. He was thrown back by an explosive gust of wind, one that knocked the air from his lungs. It wasn't natural — he knew that much — but it wasn't enough to stop him from trying again. 'This is your last warning,' he staggered to his feet, trying to look menacing. 'Get out of my house.'

'I'm afraid I can't do that, Gabriel Corrales.' Stefania swept back a lock of hair, absent-mindedly. 'Tell me, did your wife take your surname out of true love? Or did she do it to conceal her identity?'

Gabriel burned with anger. It was against tradition for a bride to take her husband's name, but the woman's suggestion cut him to the quick. 'You've got no business here. Take your filthy hearsay and leave us alone.'

'Dad?' came a small voice from behind him. 'What's going on, Dad?'

Unperceived by all of them, Magda had followed the noise downstairs. There was a pale stranger at the door. She didn't like the look of this.

'Go back upstairs, love.' Pain welled in her father's eyes. 'I'll be there in a minute.'

'Mr. Corrales, it is a constitutional offence to shield Tidal Folk from the Brenin's law.' Stefania turned back to where Aisling stood frozen, held by some unseen force. 'Is your wife, or is your wife not, a visionary?'

Tidal Folk.

Visionary.

The words rattled through Magda's head like stones. Surely not. Not after all this time.

'No,' said Gabriel, through gritted teeth. 'She ... I ...'

Like a cat bored from toying with its mouse, Stefania suddenly released whatever spell was holding Magda's mother in place. Aisling gasped for breath, falling into her husband's arms.

'You know, if it weren't for your daughter we would be less lenient,' sighed the stranger. 'Because even among the Folk, there are those who are weaker.'

Gabriel shot her a look of pure contempt.

'Speak about Aisling that way again, and it'll be the last thing you say.'

'Like I said, we never wished for it to come to this.' A thin smile crept across Stefania's lips. 'But if you will not accept these terms willingly, I'm afraid I may have to put this to you a different way.'

There was a crack of thunder so loud it split the air.

Magda stared, horrified, as her father took one step forward and then crumpled to the ground. His legs had folded beneath him and a large, ugly gash now marked his arm. Its edges were black and gaping, like something already dead, but no rush of red blood came.

'Dad!' she screamed. Parents weren't allowed to get hurt; they were the ones who were supposed to stay strong against it all. 'What did you do to him?'

'Magda, get back,' whispered her father. Then, to the stranger. 'You'll pay for this.'

'That's the thing, Mr Corrales. I don't think I will.'

Somewhere far away, Magda could hear her mother screaming, too. Everything seemed to move in slow motion, as if they were underwater, and then unseen hands were pulling at her shoulders. They guided her towards a carriage outside the door, even as she shouted *stop* and *take me back* and *let me go!* Words had never been enough, in this world where little girls grew like moths around a flame.

She didn't remember what happened after everything went dark.

PART II

Interlude

Three Days After

It was a Tuesday morning when Enio Corrales's world decided to tear itself in half. The sunlight outside was fair, the crop of rocks visible from his window, and it would be a glorious afternoon for tidewatching – he just knew it. Eirlaw Island was that perfect distance from home: close enough that you might dream of going back, but far away enough that you could walk without fear of treading on eggshells.

He could hardly believe he'd once hesitated about joining the Alliance. With the work being almost entirely outdoors, new sites to analyse every day, and the darkest night skies for a mile around, it couldn't be much further from perfect. Did he sometimes regret the decision when he returned to headquarters with a bootful of mud? It had its limitations. But they were few, and so very far between.

'Morning,' came a familiar voice from outside the door. If a voice could saunter, that was the word for it: Wilbur sounded like he was perfectly at ease wherever he went. 'You've got post.'

'Let's see it, then.'

Enio smiled as Wilbur opened the door and sat down on the bed beside him, his dark curly hair swept back in a loose ponytail. The sound of the messenger pigeon echoed down the hallway behind them, softer and softer until it disappeared altogether.

'Here,' Wilbur handed over the green envelope. 'Think it's that new phonogram you ordered?'

Enio shrugged, slicing at the paper with a blunt knife. He'd opened a million letters this way. He almost never got it right the first try. The two of them perched silently, struck by brilliant sunshine, as the envelope finally came loose.

'Maybe it's a note from your sister?'

'Hardly,' Enio laughed. 'My parents already know you're coming over for the next Solstice. I doubt they've told Magda yet, or she'd probably explode from excitement.'

'It'll be cool to finally meet her,' grinned Wilbur. Reaching back into the post-satchel which the pigeon had brought, he retrieved a second envelope in different handwriting. 'Hey, look at this! Seems like the Royal Court finally replied to my application.'

'Go on, open it then.'

He unfolded the elaborate scroll casually, sunlight skimming his brown knuckles. '*The Palace extends its greetings from Helygen to Mr. Wilbur Carvallo. We are delighted to offer you a place among the Royal Guard, and will be sending further correspondence over the coming months to confirm arrangements for next year. We will also —*'

But he didn't get any further than that, because Enio had practically crushed the air out of his lungs with a hug. 'That's the best news! I told you they'd accept it, and you didn't believe me but —'

'Hey, I never said I didn't believe you!' Wilbur elbowed him, still laughing. 'Only that it was a bad idea to celebrate prematurely.'

Enio threw him a look. 'Come on. They'd have to be stupid to turn you down.'

'Lots of people are stupid.'

'Yeah.'

'Lucky you're not, at least.' There was that knowing grin again. 'What did your letter say in the end?'

'Oh!' Enio had completely forgotten about the envelope, which was now lying discarded on the floor. 'Let me see. It says ... Oh.'

'What?'

'That's weird,' said Enio. His gaze had fallen to the bottom line, where curiosity always got the better of him. 'It's from my mum.'

'So?'

'It's from ... *just* my mum. Normally it's from all of them, my parents and Magda, but ...'

Then he began to read the rest of the letter. It didn't make any sense at first — there was none of the usual wittering, trivial details about the yarrow in the garden and what new book his father was reading, none of those delightfully unimportant luxuries that surrounded their lives. Then, slowly, the pieces began to constellate. It made a horrible kind of sense.

'What's wrong?'

Enio said nothing for a moment, staring bloodlessly at the piece of paper. 'I have to go home.'

'Shit, but that's — you'll miss training.' There was a question in Wilbur's dark brown eyes now. 'How bad is it?'

How?

How on earth could he describe this?

'Really fucking terrible.'

'Enio...'

But Enio shook his head, fighting the insane urge to laugh. He turned away and wondered if Wilbur would stay. This was the one thing he hadn't learned to doubt yet. But just as he was about to get up, there was a hand on his shoulder.

'I'll be here when you get back,' said Wilbur. 'You know that, right? Send me a message if there's any trouble.'

'Okay,' said Enio, even though it absolutely, completely, wasn't. It was just about the unfairest thing he had ever experienced. *You should have known better*.

'Do you want me to cover your shift tomorrow night?'

'No, I'll have to speak to the head deputy. I think it might take longer than a day or two.' He hardly dared meet Wilbur's eye. This was Wilbur black-coffee-three-sugars, don't-sweat-the-deadline, who-dares-wins Carvallo — and even he looked concerned. 'I'll be back by the Solstice, at the very latest.'

'You promise?'

Somehow, Enio had always assumed that lives came unspun one golden thread at a time. He'd never even imagined that his might come unravelled in one fell swoop, in one single gunshot of a letter.

'I promise.'

Chapter 13

Fallow Ground

The first thing Magda saw when she woke up was a feather-patterned curtain: dark green and golden, like a lost peacock. Hard wood covered the walls. The sky was impossible to locate. And the ground was moving, lurching from side to side, while someone else's shoulder jostled into her ribcage.

'Muriel?'

'You're awake!' Muriel met her gaze, cramped uncomfortably into the seat beside her. A large bundle of fabric lay in her lap, her slender brown fingers clenched tightly around it. 'Thank goodness you're awake. I've been poking you for ages.'

'Where are we... What's going on?' Magda blinked. Her head hurt.

'Don't know. Dagger-eyes over there won't say anything.'

All Magda could see of the woman driving the carriage was her glittering cloak. But it was the same one, she was faintly aware, who had caused something bad to happen — something that she couldn't quite remember yet.

'Dagger-eyes,' she repeated slowly. Those eyes *had* been like daggers, now Muriel mentioned it. Cold and flinty with no edge of sympathy anywhere. 'She came to our house. Did she come to yours, too?'

'Yes. And now we're being kidnapped,' Muriel sounded like she might start spitting venom. 'When I tried that door handle, it was like red-hot iron.' She held up a set of five scalded fingers. 'Useless.'

Magda sucked in a breath. From what she could tell, the carriage was moving faster than it would be safe to jump out of, anyway. Although she didn't get the idea that they were going somewhere safe.

'What's that outside?'

They were travelling through a wooded area, somewhere with tumbling pine trees and moss-shrouded hillocks. Through the window she could just make out dark pink wingtips, skimming the skyline, but slowly catching up.

'Hergest,' she realised. 'It's Hergest.'

The pigeon gave a loud *coo*. Somehow, amid this horrible mess, these small creatures remained. Holding them in place. Quietly punctuating their existence.

'Keep your voice down,' Muriel glanced warily towards the front seat. 'Dagger-eyes doesn't like us to talk too loud.'

'But we need to open the window. He's looking for us!'

'Don't speak of those wretched birds,' snapped the woman in the front seat, silencing both girls with a filthy look. 'They're unclean.'

Magda felt as if she'd been slapped across the face. In Abergwyll, pigeons were sacred. *Paloma* was the same word for pigeon as for dove. In fact, it had been one of her dad's nicknames for her: *his little dove*.

'Oh,' she sucked in a breath. The memories came back to her in flashes: a black gash, a broken coffee table, an icy wind. 'Oh, no.'

'What?' Muriel's brown eyes were round and worried.

'My dad. His arm, I think it was —'

The pale woman turned back to glare at her, silencing the words in her throat. Stefania. *That* was her name. And she looked like bad news.

'Nothing,' Magda swallowed the painful lump in her throat. They were alone in this carriage, wherever it was going. It was dark and claustrophobic. And she couldn't shake the feeling that they were no longer the girls they had been.

'You can't keep us here,' Muriel shot the pale horsewoman an evil look. She was trembling, whether with fear or fury, Magda couldn't tell. 'Let us out!'

'Did I give you permission to speak, Miss Silvana?'

'They'll come looking for us, they will. And then you'll be sorry!'

The wheels creaked ominously.

'You're very welcome to leave,' drawled Stefania, gesturing to the door. 'But should you do so, I believe you'll find a rather swift death among these shrubs.'

'We're going South?' Muriel's eyes darted from tree to tree, realising. 'You told my mum we were going to the Middle Isles. You said we shouldn't be passing through anywhere dangerous.'

'Shouldn't,' Stefania yawned. 'What a lovely word. Luckily for you, the carriage is warded. You won't be harmed, so long as the windows remain *closed.*'

The realisation hit both girls with terrifying force.

They were travelling into Cunning Wood: the deepest and darkest of the Five Forests. So much as a graze from the forest would mean death, for the poisoned woodland took no prisoners. Magda's head was a flood of sticky memories and ugly thoughts. It had all gone so wrong, in such a short space of time.

'Tegwen,' she murmured, remembering that, too. A rushing brook. A pale figure. Golden hair tangled among waterweeds. 'I'm sorry. I'm so sorry.'

As they sunk into numb silence, Stefania began to talk.

The Fallow did not often receive new intakes, she explained. It was a marked privilege to even receive an invitation. And from now on, they would address her as *Ether* Stefania.

All the while, the carriage rolled further and further, through the depths of a jungle so old it had no paths. Polypody ferns sprawled over every inch of bark. Lichens dripped from the canopy like bridal trains. Bromeliads formed caverns where frogs and lizards could swim in the rainwater that collected there. This was the beauty of the primary Forest, but it was filled with enough toxins to kill a man where he stood.

'The Fallow lies at the heart of Cunning Wood,' Ether Stefania smoothed back a strand of chestnut-coloured hair. 'I hope I don't need to explain to you the consequences of trying to run away.'

Hot tears prickling her eyes, Muriel took Magda's hand. This was the kind of thing that happened in bad dreams. Why couldn't they wake up?

*

It felt like hours before the carriage began to slow. Magda watched as the flurry of green floated past the window, darker than before. Home had never seemed so far away.

'Here we are,' said Ether Stefania, casually. 'Get out. I'll show you around.'

They had come to a stop at the edge of a wooded glen. It was set with slate-grey buildings, whose sculpted stonework stood tall as a citadel. Rose windows, spires and lancets sprawled across a lawn which was surreally, almost suspiciously, green.

'Get out?' Muriel narrowed her eyes. 'I thought you said...'

'The grounds are charmed to the parameters of this clearing,' replied Stefania, giving the girl a helpful shove. 'The Fallow will be your new home until you are eighteen. Everyday activities will take place in three Quadrants: classes, meals, prayers, screenings.' The tall woman gestured to four sets of slate-roofed cloisters, each with a courtyard at its centre. 'The North Quadrant houses all students' living quarters.'

It looked like a place where small birds roosted, each dormitory set high into the eaves with a wide-berthed window. Magda could no more imagine living here than living in a dovecote or a pigeon loft.

'What about that other house?' Muriel pointed to a short, grey-bricked cottage on the far side of the glen. 'Who lives there?'

'That's the Gatehouse. You'll take your prayers there once every week.'

As they walked on, they learned other new names like *Observatory* and *Glasshouse*. The vowels flowed like flightless birds above them; however, it was the enormous central lawn which drew the greatest intrigue. Seven standing-stones were arranged in a huge ring around the centre, and Magda wondered if some kind of invisible force field lay within.

'No need to look so scared,' Ether Stefania stepped lightly over the boundary. 'These are the Ceremonial Grounds. In time, you'll come to pay your own respects here.'

'Why?'

Stefania waved a dismissive hand. 'Ask your questions later, after you've met the other Ethers. You can think of us as your guardians if you like.'

If you like. Except the cold smiles and silence already warned against it. Magda and Muriel had unknowingly moved from Wildbriar into a coven of wolves.

'Stefania. I've been looking for you,' said a woman who had just emerged from the cloisters to their left. 'Are these the girls?'

She was dressed from head to toe in a cloak that glittered with precious metal. It was the same cloak that Ether Stefania wore, but it shone with an esoteric glamour which made it impossible to call a *uniform*.

'Girls, this is Ether Lorna.' Stefania ducked her head gracefully. 'She'll take you to your rooms, and lay out a few of the house rules here.'

'Come with me,' the kind-eyed woman led them down a narrow path. Her hair was short, dark, and wavy, and she carried a basket that smelled faintly of cress. 'You look scared stiff. How about a cup of tea before we head over to the North Quadrant?'

Magda and Muriel didn't need to be asked twice. As shell-shocked as they felt to have been dumped here, surely it couldn't get any worse. Shivering like dormice, they sipped mugs of the piping liquid while Ether Lorna talked.

'Right now, I can understand if you're feeling frightened. You might be distrustful, or confused, or just plain angry,' Lorna met them with dark hazel eyes, her brown cheeks dimpled with sorrow. 'You have every right to those feelings.'

'We just want to go home,' replied Muriel. 'Can't you tell us how to get back?'

Lorna set down her cup of tea with a sigh. 'Miss Corrales, Miss Silvana. I'm afraid that this is your home now.'

Fallow girls, they would soon learn, were not normal. This place was one of few where girls with *gifts* would be given safe haven and trained in how to make use of their talents.

For now.

Chapter 14

Low Dawn

It was a crisp, bright day when Rhoswen Merrick first felt the winds of change sweeping the Fallow. At morning prayers, Ether Lorna had been distracted: she'd cast too much Artifice, turning the ceiling to a claggy murk of impenetrable darkness. They'd had to praise the Great Weaver extra loudly to dispel it, and even then a fine layer of soot had stayed resting over the carpets.

Stranger yet, Ether Rhiannon's Triolatry class later that morning had lacked the usual fastidious attention to detail. The tall, proud Ether seemed to trip over her words and even misnamed one of the dates, for which she'd apologised profusely. But finally, at lunchtime, Rhos was certain something was afoot: because Ether Stefania was nowhere to be seen. The woman's presence was like a haunting, and the absence of that ghost was palpable.

It could only mean one thing.

Fresh blood.

'Hey,' Rhos tried to catch Alarice's attention, later that afternoon. 'Did you see how weirdly the Ethers were acting earlier?'

The dark-eyed girl sighed, concentrating hard on a section of diagonal basting. 'It's no different from normal, Rhos. They always get grumpy during winter.'

'But this is different. Ingrid, don't you agree?'

Unfortunately, everyone was too caught up in their Weftwork to pay attention. Fabric and pins spilled across the desks, while Rhos's wild theories lay discarded in the scrap fabric pile. Ingrid's brow was furrowed over a stubborn piece of interfacing. Alarice picked away at a tricky seam, her long braids resting lightly over her shoulders. And Catrin was attacking her basting with the sharp precision of a raptor.

'Those pieces look badly aligned,' Rhos observed helpfully. 'Did you know you're missing a whole notch?'

'Mind your own business, Merrick!'

They were working to create coats for several towns in the north-west, and Rhos was just about fed up. Each class left her feeling exhausted, and the work she produced was never good enough to satisfy Ether Rhiannon's discerning eye. It was probably the heaviness of winter. But sometimes, it felt like some vital piece of her had been stitched into the fabric, along with all the shining thread.

It is not enough to produce fine garments; you must produce the finest garments of all. Ether Rhiannon's words rang in her head as they made their way back to the dormitories after class. A sharp ache had settled between her ribs, and it was growing more acute.

'Rhos, you look constipated,' Ingrid dumped her scarf over the back of a chair, sinking back onto her bed. 'What's wrong?'

'Nothing's wrong,' Rhos avoided her gaze. 'And if anyone *was* constipated, it wouldn't be me.'

'No, it would probably be Catrin. Everything disagrees with her.'

Everything and almost every*one* disagreed with Catrin, although Rhos didn't say that part out loud. Things just hadn't been the same since the last Progressions Council. Now that the Lissa and Shay were gone, Catrin and Alarice had moved up to occupy the top room. What remained was a void in between the dorm that Rhos shared with Ingrid, and the final chamber.

It was a cavern waiting to be filled.

'Was that the pigeon bringing you post earlier?' asked Ingrid, shuffling through a pile of papers at her desk. 'You didn't seem too thrilled. I'm assuming it wasn't some secret admirer.'

'Hardly,' Rhos collapsed into the comfy chair in the corner of their dorm. 'Unfortunately, I think living inside a poisoned forest would be enough to make any handsome prince reconsider his intentions.'

'I mean, you never know.'

'Why don't you take a look if you're that interested?'

It was a collection of newspaper clippings from outside, posted to her by her father. Most of the headlines were bland or pedestrian; others downright depressing.

'Sounds like things are only getting worse out there,' Ingrid folded the paper. 'Are you going to keep them?'

'He'd be upset if I threw them away.'

'Okay. But if anything needs destroying, there's a hex I could try.'

'A hex?' came a third voice. 'Now that sounds interesting.'

They turned towards the doorway, which now swung ajar. It was Alarice.

'Sorry, I didn't mean to interrupt. Are you two busy right now?'

'No, we were just discussing Merrick's fascinating collection of newspaper clippings. Really, it's something to be beheld.'

'Well, I can always leave you to it,' the tall Black girl flicked an amused eye towards the pair of them. 'Unless you could be tempted to a quick game of gwyddbwyll? We're about to set up a board in the cove.'

'You mean a rematch?'

'Naturally.'

Rhos smiled from the sidelines. Both girls had a competitive streak, and for a moment it seemed that the evening might pass away peacefully. They would go to the cove, set up the board, and the challenge was on. That there would be shrieks of laughter; spilt bowls of crisps. At the end of the night, they'd have nothing more than a lost game to fret over.

That fantasy crumpled when they turned the corner onto the landing.

Three figures blotted out the doorway: a dishevelled-looking white girl, a shorter girl with light brown skin, and Ether Lorna, all of them framed by the failing daylight. The first looked like she was about to be sick. The other stared out defiantly from her dark curls, a determined expression on her face, while the corridor gaped its horrible, hanging laugh. It was a small mercy, thought Rhos, they'd been escorted by one of the kinder guardians — not that they had any particular reason to be grateful right now.

'There you are,' Ether Lorna flashed them an apologetic smile. 'I was hoping you'd be able to welcome the new girls to their rooms, and help them settle in?'

Ingrid raised an eyebrow.

'New girls?'

'New girls,' Rhos repeated. She tried to tidy the loose strands that were fraying from her red pigtails, but found they wouldn't cooperate. 'I knew it. This is what's been going on all day, isn't it? You're from Wildbriar, right?'

'You knew we were coming?' asked the freckled girl, weakly. The hall where they'd been left was narrow, with three doors that opened into dormitories, beds stacked in pairs against the walls. '*We* didn't even know we were coming.'

Alarice looked pointedly down. 'I think your school uniform is giving you away.'

A slow blush crept across the new girls' cheeks. They were wearing still cardigans emblazoned with the school crest, matching skirts, and laddered tights.

'Don't worry,' Alarice added. 'We've got spare clothes you can change into.'

'That sounds wise. Miss Corrales and Miss Silvana will be joining you in the North Quadrant, so please make them welcome,' the cloaked Ether bowed her head. 'Given the hour, I'll leave you girls to it.'

They watched as she made her way down the staircase, candles extinguishing behind her. Muriel caught a glimpse of their reflection in the window-pane. She and Magda looked utterly out of place beside the other three girls, who were dressed from head to toe in elegant fabrics. The girl who'd offered them clothes had eyes that were the soft hazel of a secret library, and her dark brown skin shone with the glow of the lanterns. Meanwhile, the stocky white girl wore a lapis-blue pelerine that contrasted her long red hair, and the tallest girl wore a long burgundy top that fanned out over her pale wrists.

'You're lucky it was Lorna who brought you, not Stefania,' said the first girl. 'She's a wolf in, well, wolf's clothing.'

'It doesn't really matter,' Muriel flustered. 'It's not like we can stay here long. Our families will be worried.'

'That's what everyone says when they first arrive.' The girl in burgundy stuck out her hand. 'While you are here, though, maybe we can tolerate each other. I'm Ingrid.'

'Muriel. And this is Magda.'

'Alarice.'

'Rhos.'

'Well, it's very nice to meet you all, but we have to go back home,' Magda interrupted. 'Can you help us?'

'Maybe we should sit down for a minute,' Rhos gestured to a chair. She was wearing a pair of short kid-leather gloves, which by this point felt like a second skin, but she could tell it unnerved the girls from Wildbriar. 'Since you're new, you've got the empty middle dormitory. Me and Ingrid are in the first room to your right, Alarice and Cat are on the other side.'

'Dormitories.' Muriel repeated, deeply uncomfortable. 'You all *live* here.'

'And so do you, now.'

'But... they can't just decide that! That Stefania woman just grabbed us out of nowhere!'

'She's a gorgon,' agreed Alarice. 'But there's no going back now. What is, is.'

'I didn't even get to say goodbye to my brother,' Magda seethed. 'That can't be how this works. It's not fair. It's not *right*.'

Alarice chewed her lip. 'Trust me, this wasn't easy for any of us here. I'm sorry for what you went through. The only thing I can say is, it's over now.'

They all jumped at a sudden *tap* against the window.

'What in the Weaver's name was that?'

'Oh!' Rhos felt her cheeks flush with colour as she went to pull up the shutters. 'It's probably Norbert. I forgot to get him some asphodel berries earlier.'

As the window fluttered open, a hefty-looking beetle fell into Rhos's cupped hands.

'He's a ... giant stag beetle?'

'He's a resplendent goldstone beetle,' Rhos corrected. They fascinated her, as did most animals whose existence was highly improbable. 'Want to see?'

The beetle wriggled its legs grumpily.

'For the Weaver's sake, Rhos,' scolded another voice, just as its owner appeared around the corner. Her white cheeks were framed by a blaze of snow-gold hair, and a set of overcrowded teeth glinted as she spoke. 'Shut up about bugs, or you'll freak them out.'

'Who are you?' asked Muriel.

'I'm Catrin.' Her hair rippled as she turned to face them. 'Welcome to the Fallow.'

*

'So how many girls are there here?' asked Magda, at dinner. Ingrid's eyes hadn't left them, her irises a quivering dark brown. 'Did all of you get taken, too?'

Ingrid grimaced. 'Well, now that you're here, that makes eight of us in the North Quadrant —'

'But the Progression Council was only last week,' finished Alarice, as if this all made perfect sense. 'The two eldest girls left. That's why you've got a whole room to yourselves.'

The flurry of new information floated right over their heads.

After supper was served, Muriel and Magda were handed a dull grey smock to change into. *Your personal effects will be retrieved within a few days*, Ether Lorna told Muriel, when she'd asked for something less lumpy and uncomfortable to wear. *Until then, I'm afraid you'll have to make do with the Fallow's provisions. Cosmetic supplies and haircare services from the capital will be available once a month.*

'So, shall we cut to the chase?' asked the blonde girl, Catrin, from the end of the table. Her rust-brown eyes were the colour of clotted blood, and Magda didn't like the way she was looking at them. 'Everyone's here for a reason. Care to enlighten us?'

There was a mud-thick silence.

'It's no concern of yours,' Muriel raised her chin. 'We're not going to be here long, anyway.'

'Oh, that's what everyone thinks.' There was a curious gleam in the Catrin's eye now. 'Come on, can't you even give us an inkling?'

Muriel thought of two nights ago. She thought of Magda's hands stained scarlet, standing at their doorstep with that haunted look in her eyes. *It was Tegwen Price*, said the messenger-pigeon. What had she done? No matter how awful, it couldn't be the reason why they were taken.

Could it?

'Catrin, leave them be.' Ingrid shot the other girl a look. 'They can't be expected to know the rules right from the outset.'

'Oh, don't tell me,' scoffed Catrin. 'They do realise what happens to the Folk outside of the Fallow, right? Maybe they'd be better off out there if they're so good at holding their tongues. Some of us can't help but be a little less subtle.'

She pronounced the word *subtle* as if she'd meant *insignificant*.

'I don't care what you think about the Tidal Folk,' said Magda, bristling. 'But whatever this place believes in, I promise you they won't get here quick enough to stop me from —'

'That's enough!' shouted Alarice. 'We don't need to be threatening each other. It's hardly necessary, when the entire archipelago's already against us.'

Magda blinked in surprise. She was more relieved than angry that Alarice had cut her off, but the words unsettled her. 'Do you mean to say ... you're all Tidal Folk, too?'

There was a pause while the girls exchanged glances. Silence didn't mean assent, and a *yes* or a *no* couldn't be fabricated from empty air alone.

'They might call us the same,' said Ingrid, carefully, 'but we are not alike. And if I were you, I'd keep my voice down. You're attracting attention.'

Muriel hardly processed the words. Her thoughts were still scattered through the outskirts of Wildbriar, through the fields where they'd played as girls; even through the woods. But it was no good. There could be no going back to a home that had already forsaken them.

'Look,' Magda muttered under her breath. 'Everyone's staring at us.'

From across the room, a table of younger girls had paused to look at them: one held her hand over her mouth, one pointed, and the others turned away as a bubble of laughter frothed into the air. Muriel drew back, feeling the intense injustice of the ugly grey smock covering her shoulders. She wanted to rip the garment into shreds.

'It's always like that when we get new intakes,' said Rhos. 'They're only kids, though. They'll stop gawking before long.'

The remainder of the meal passed in uncomfortable silence, until the view from the window gradually waned to a deep blue hum.

'It'll be lights out soon,' said Ingrid. Her short, dark hair glistened in the moonlight. 'We'd better go.'

Relieved to not have to finish the last scraps of her meal, Muriel pushed back her chair and followed the others up the long staircase. 'How long does it usually take new students to settle here?'

'Oh, a few days.'

'Couple of weeks.'

'Not longer than a fortnight.'

Muriel was astonished that they could all speak so decisively on the matter. She would never do the same. How could she forget her family, everything her life had been before, in a matter of weeks or months — let alone days?

'Is there really no way to escape from this place? I mean, surely there's some way around Cunning Wood. Has anyone ever managed to get out?'

Alarice fixed her with a steely glare. 'There are several girls who've tried. Trust me, you don't want to be one of them.'

Why not? Muriel almost yelled. *Why would we want to stay here?*

But she stopped short. In Alarice's dark brown eyes were stories that Muriel didn't want to know the ending to, and she swallowed the question that was scorching her chest.

'In case you were wondering,' continued Ingrid, as if they were discussing the weather, 'this stays between us. The Ethers aren't to be trusted, and Stefania's the meanest of the lot. Think she's got it out for you now? Wait until you've had a screening. Once a month; quickest way to ruin your morning.'

'What about the others?'

Alarice shrugged. 'Well, you've got Ether Rhiannon for Weftwork. She's not so bad, but she never misses a trick. Don't think you can get away with sloppy work; she'll catch you right out.'

'And Ether Lorna's alright,' said Rhos. 'She teaches Botany.'

'Fat lot of good that is. We only get her classes once in a blue moon,' Ingrid added, wondering how much the new girls wanted to hear. 'I'd tell you things get better, but the best advice is really just to develop a thick skin.'

'Right.' Muriel nodded faintly, grateful for the warning. She wanted to like these girls: and yet there was something that made her wary to give in. Being accepted here would mean that she was *one of them*. She snuck a glance sideways. If Magda wasn't ready to give up yet, then neither was she.

'Have you got any way of contacting outside?' asked Magda. 'A messenger pigeon would do. I just need to write a letter to my parents.'

'They've got pigeons, but outside correspondence is strictly rationed. Only once every four weeks.'

'If you're desperate, you could send a crow,' suggested Rhos. Crows were less reliable messengers, but they got the job done more often than not. 'You can probably call one from the roost in the Middle Isles.'

Muriel's heart jumped. 'Could I send something to my sisters that way?'

'Absolutely. Catrin sends crows back to Tarren Mawr all the time.'

'That's a long way to go.'

'Not long enough,' said Rhos, with a wicked grin. 'You haven't heard about the boyfriend yet, have you?'

'He is *not* my boyfriend. We've been friends since we were kids, for scrim's sake.'

There was a collective eye-roll. Foxe and Catrin had been exchanging letters ever since she'd arrived at the Fallow. As the story went, they'd been neighbours first, enemies briefly, and then firm friends for the last five years. Ingrid warned that any new correspondence would be brandished excitedly at the dinner table.

'Please, it's not like they're anything *scandalous*,' Catrin blushed. 'It's mostly just notes on geology, or what's been happening back in the village.'

'And yet you treat them like the holy grail each time.'

While the others clamoured round, Ingrid said nothing. The letters were sweet, but with affection came lovesick loneliness and false hope. Who wanted anything to do with that?

*

The moment they were alone, Muriel felt the vice around her chest tighten. Everything was wrong with this dormitory. The drawers were in odd places, there was no lamp over the dresser, and the walls were stripped bare. It was the peculiar sensation of cooking in somebody else's kitchen: things that should have been easy to locate eluded her, while the most unnecessary items offered themselves freely.

She could hear Magda scrambling around the other bunk bed, trying to pull the sheets down.

'Mags, are you okay?'

'Not really.' There was a small sigh. 'Are you?'

'I keep thinking about this morning, when Ether Stefania came to our house.'

'What happened?'

'It was so fast,' Muriel shook her head, the blood pooling in her cheeks. She hated this, she really did, but it had been scorching her chest all day. 'My parents tried to stop her, but it was no use. I never saw anyone use the kind of powers that she did.'

'Yeah.' The other girl stopped scrabbling, sitting back and folding her knees in. 'She made it look so easy. Was your family okay?'

'They will be.'

But there were things that Muriel couldn't say out loud, not yet. Isa's beaded necklace, torn and scattered like a string of lost teeth. The noise their grandfather clock had made, shattered across the hallway. Orphaned minutes slipped between the cracks in the floorboards; jagged hours clung to the paintwork.

'I just ... I just feel so *angry*. Who gave her the right? Who was she to sweep in and ruin our lives like that?' She pulled the blanket tighter around her shoulders. The words rang hollow in the dark. 'I don't think it's even sunk in yet, not properly. I keep thinking we'll wake up and be back in Wildbriar, just the way it should have been.'

'Yeah,' Magda's voice sounded tight. 'It doesn't feel real. I'm scared for my family, but especially my dad.'

'They hurt him?'

'I don't really know what they did. It was like everything froze, and suddenly he had this enormous gash on his arm. It looked horrible, except...' She paused. 'Except it didn't look like a normal cut.'

'What do you mean?'

'There was no blood, or pus, or anything. Just emptiness.'

Muriel wrapped her in a hug. 'I'm so sorry, Mags.'

'It's okay.'

It wasn't okay.

Everything hurt, the unspoken fears more than anything.

Chapter 15

Hiraeth

There was a specific word in Welsh for homesickness, a feeling of deep yearning that extended even to places where you'd never been. Muriel lay in the dark blue coverts of the night, thinking its name.

Hiraeth.

It sounded like an exhalation, a final shaky breath. It sounded like yesterday morning. Because right as she'd been dragged out of her house, her mum had thrust a bundle of ornate fabric into her arms.

Here, Sidonie urged her, *I wanted you to have this. Take it, quickly.*

It sank into her arms like a baby animal. Before Muriel could even ask why, there were cold hands on her shoulders, a high-pitched scream, and then everything had turned to shadows.

She folded the blanket open, feeling the patches like squares of field in a valley. She hadn't dared to inspect it sooner. Each square was slightly different from the last; each cut from the same satin-woven cloth. Many animals produced silk — silkworms, spiders, even some types of mussels — but this one was soft and thick as eiderdown. Tricking its way through it all was a dense ridge of embroidery, knotted carefully into tiny figures that looked like a line of people dancing.

Except they weren't people at all. They were letters.

For you, my youngest daughter, read the first dark line. *Today was your fourth birthday. One day I'm sure you will be tall as the trees and strong as an oak tree. You have such beautiful eyes, did you know that?*

Muriel blinked hard, surprised at the tenderness with which one could greet a stranger. How long had her mother been making this blanket? Was there an entry for every year, for every month of her life? She turned the quilt to another side, and another, and another.

The rainstorm last night reminds me of wet season in Puerto Estrellado, read a finely stitched moth-green square. *All the trees used to shake in the wind, and the little geckoes would dance across the ceiling. One day, when you're old enough, we'll go back again. I'll take you to the beaches.*

She turned it again.

This Invernal you lit the firefly-jar for the river. I think you wanted to jump in with it!

And again.

Tranquilo, mi amor. Todo va a estar bien.

Every panel was thick with words, and they enveloped her like a hug. Laying down the blanket, Muriel took a shaky breath. The words should have sung like sweet music. Instead, they reminded her of what she'd lost in the space of mere hours. This was the family she'd had; this was the family they had taken. In a long line of powerful enchantresses, she was only the latest victim.

Rain began to spatter at the window outside. Drowsy and half-asleep already, Muriel read another square of the quilt. It was written in Spanish, one of her mother's three languages, and she scanned the lines for hidden links. It was a game her dad had once taught her: searching for the threads that twined the world together.

Cinio, in Welsh. *Cena*, in Spanish.

Miel, in Spanish. *Mêl*, in Welsh.

Tymestl. Tormenta.

Nos. Noche.

She stared at the folded words until they floated free altogether. As she slept she dreamed of bridges, because there were pathways even between oceans, when you knew where to look for them.

*

Morning broke with all the grace of a smashed glass, and Muriel wished she could curl back under the covers. Unfortunately, a loud bell had rudely awoken them at seven o'clock sharp. It was time for breakfast.

The Ethers hovered like watchdogs just outside the doors to the dining hall, effectively ensuring that nobody could enjoy a meal without feeling like someone was breathing down their neck. There was the dagger-eyed Stefania, the wiry, decidedly more affable Lorna, and a third Ether who Muriel didn't recognise. She was a young Black woman with bright eyes and the most beautiful pair of shoes that Muriel had ever seen. They were midnight sharp and detailed with pearls, seashells, and a golden crescent-moon for a buckle.

By the time breakfast was served, Muriel found she was hungrier than she'd realised. It felt wrong to have an appetite under the circumstances. But the steaming plates smelled so good it was impossible to resist, and she scooped a large helping of cockles onto her plate.

'Ether Lorna?' Muriel asked tentatively, after they'd eaten. Everyone else had already left to get ready, and she was grateful to be alone. Along with a hearty portion of *teisennau cocos*, cockle cakes, anxiety curled tight in her gut. 'I wanted to ask you. Why are we the only new girls here?'

'We maintain a strict quotient of students each season,' Lorna said evenly. 'Try not to feel out of place, you'll fit right in soon enough.'

'It doesn't seem like it.'

'Give it time. The Fallow's aim is to sharpen your talent, you know. To ensure you *use* the gifts you were born with.'

'Right,' Muriel cast her a worried glance. 'Will our families be able to visit us?'

Part of her was still holding onto a dying hope, but Lorna's expression told her it was misplaced.

'For your safety, your families cannot be permitted here. Certain outsiders do not have your best interests at heart,' Lorna sighed. It was the face well-meaning strangers wore when they were about to talk of tragedy, like it was something best held at a distance. 'This is an institution which believes in *opportunity*. By eighteen you must be ready, and the best of you will serve under His Majesty. It is the highest honour to be selected.'

'What about the Scarp Mandate?' asked Muriel, bitterly. The Brenin was the reason why girls like her lived in fear. 'Aren't we a "threat to society"?'

Ether Lorna paused for a moment. There was no way to deny the legislation's existence – but it wasn't the *whole* truth, either. 'I imagine you will have heard many things,' she said carefully. 'Some of them are true, but others are mere distortions. Please trust us when we say you will not be harmed here.'

Muriel didn't reply. The woman's unblinking gaze made it feel as if you were being scrutinised by a large bird of prey, and it wasn't entirely clear how one avoided being eaten.

'Why us?' she asked at last. 'I mean, what's so special about me and Magda?'

And what if we don't want to be selected by the Brenin?

'I'm sorry, Miss Silvana,' Lorna shook her head, 'but I really must get to class now. I have a group of students waiting for me in the orchard.'

Muriel watched her cloaked silhouette recede down the hallway. Maybe Lorna was too afraid to say the reason out loud. But if these girls were monsters – even talented, valuable monsters – then why any of this luxury in the first place? Why teach them at all?

Dismayed, she started to climb the staircase back to the dorm room. Magda would probably be worried by now, and she felt bad for having taken so long, but the room was strangely quiet when she knocked on the door.

'Come in,' said a low voice. 'Quickly.'

As she entered the room, she saw Ingrid was kneeling at the foot of the first bunk bed. The air smelled sour, and the curtains were drawn closed.

'What's wrong?'

'That's what we're trying to find out,' said Rhos, holding a small lantern over the bed. 'She's breathing now, but she wasn't a few minutes ago.'

Muriel pushed closer to the bedside. It was Magda who lay there, her pale skin shining eerily in the gaslights. A ceramic mug lay in splinters on the ground next to the bed, brown liquid seeping into the rug.

'She fell down?'

'We heard the noise, so we came to check on her.'

Horrified, Muriel took hold of one wrist and felt for the pulse. It was slow, reluctant, like mud in a river delta. But it was there, and she was alive.

'Mags, talk to us. What happened?'

Her best friend's face was damp with sweat, her eyes wide.

'I had a nightmare.'

*

If the nightmare was the first bad sign, the second bad sign came later that afternoon. Even after their morning induction ended, there were deliveries to be picked up and formalities to trawl through. A little bundle of their clothes had arrived from Wildbriar, although they smelt of smoke and a dark, pungent foresty smell that was impossible to pinpoint. Muriel changed into one of her old dresses and found herself shivering. It felt like stepping into the skin of a stranger.

'I keep having these dreams,' said Magda, clutching her head. 'This image — I can't get it out of my head. A blonde-haired girl, dressed all in red. She looks like Tegwen Price.'

'Do you think it's got anything to do with ... that day in the woods?' Muriel asked carefully. She still hadn't dared to broach the subject of exactly what happened the night before they were taken, the night that Magda had come home with her hands stained scarlet. She wasn't sure she wanted to know. 'What was it that Grimoire woman said about you having visions?'

The pair of them were sitting in a large common-room kind of area near their dorms. The other girls had called it 'the cove' in passing, which Muriel could only assume was due to its rounded shape and smooth, whorled stone. She disliked the way it made her words echo and echo.

'Of course it's not anything *visionary*,' Magda looked away. 'That old lady can't have known what she was talking about. It's nothing to do with her.'

'You don't think she could have known something we don't?'

'Well, you tell me.'

'What?'

'Is it true what she said about you?'

Muriel stared. 'If I suddenly developed magic, you'd be the first person I told! You can't seriously think I'd be keeping stuff hidden.'

'Yeah. Sorry. It's just...' To her credit, Magda looked ashamed. 'You seem to know more than I do. Everybody seems to know more than I do right now.'

There was a long moment while Muriel considered how she should answer.

'Grimoire Malgarty said that veridian magic ran in my bloodline. My mother had the gift, I know that much. But neither of my sisters inherited it.' A pause. 'So, I suppose I thought, *why should I*?'

She often bargained with the empty air, asking that same question. *Why me? Why any of us?* Why couldn't somebody else take all the suffering for once?

'You never told me that.'

‘I know,’ Muriel shrugged. ‘And when Grimoire said those things about me, I really hope it isn’t true. There’s been no sign of it so far.’

Magda looked like she was concentrating on something that eluded her. ‘Your mother was a veridian. Did people know about her?’

‘Well, that was the issue. When the law changed, we moved because our old town had too much talk. It was too dangerous to stay there any longer.’

And look how that turned out.

‘That must have been awful.’

‘It was better than moving to this place.’

‘Then we’ll think of a way to escape,’ said Magda, with a look of such naïve hopefulness that Muriel could have punched her. ‘We’ll find somewhere new to live, once we’ve got a way out of here.’

‘We can’t,’ she replied sharply. ‘We’re trapped by a poisonous forest on all sides, in case you forgot.’

‘But things change. Who knows what’ll change next?’

‘I don’t want things to change again.’ Muriel’s voice fractured like ice. ‘I miss my sisters. I miss my parents.’ She averted her gaze. ‘I want them back.’

‘That’s not what I ... Sorry. I didn’t mean to upset you.’

‘It’s not your fault.’

The morning grew a shade colder around them.

Chapter 16

The House of the Lyre

Out in the orchard, Ether Lorna's class was hunting for agrimony. Each hill in the distance poked up like threadbare knees: a crop of purplish velvet, broken here and there by the bare skin of the mountain.

'Is this right one?' Catrin lifted a handful of roots, fraying white flowers dripping from the stalk.

'They're supposed to be yellow, not white,' said Rhos. 'Like these.'

'Excellent, Miss Merrick.' Ether Lorna inspected the bundle of flowers that she'd pulled up. Agrimony was an excellent plant for staunching wounds, as an astringent, and for dyeing. 'Can everybody fill up a basket, please? We'll use them for tinctures later this week.'

As they began to pick fistfuls of the yellow-tufted shrubs, Rhos observed the scene around her. Alarice and Catrin were engaged in a heated conversation about Julia Saez's new album, but her own roommate had barely spoken all morning.

She pottered over to where Ingrid was working.

'Hey. Do you need a hand with anything?'

'I'm fine,' came the taut reply. It was always perfectly clear when a conversation was over, and right now there was a distinctly *please-stop-talking-to-me* arch to Ingrid's shoulders.

'Okay. I was just worried in case, you know, something was wrong.' Rhos paused. 'You hardly ate any breakfast.'

'It's not like yesterday was a catalyst for a thriving appetite.'

'I suppose not. But at least we'll have dorm neighbours again,' Rhos attempted an encouraging smile. 'What did you think of the new girls?'

'There's nothing to think yet, since we've barely gotten to know them.' There was an aggressive *rip* as another tuft of agrimony came loose. 'And I'd like to continue in peace and quiet, now.'

'Okay. I think they're nice, anyway.'

'You think everybody's nice.'

'That's not true! If you're so concerned, how about we invite them to a game of Teller at the end of the week?'

There was a dangerous silence.

'You don't trust them, do you?'

'They're outsiders,' said Ingrid, reluctantly. 'They might *seem* fine, but who knows? You saw the way that girl collapsed earlier. We don't know the first thing about the magic they're harbouring!'

'We were outsiders, once,' Rhos cocked her head. 'That never seemed to bother you before.'

'That was different. You were never like them.'

'What, because I'm easy to read? Because I look like I couldn't throw a punch if I tried?'

'That's not what I meant,' Ingrid drew back, flushed with guilt. She and Rhos might have shared a dormitory, but their temperaments couldn't have been more different. 'What I wanted to say was that maybe we should be more careful. Not everyone wears their heart on their sleeve.'

Rhos sniffed. 'I don't think they got much of a choice.'

'And neither did we.' Ingrid turned away, rootling for more shrubs in the dark earth. 'None of us got what we wanted. We only got what they decided we'll have.'

*

After the day's induction was over, Magda and Muriel were relieved to rejoin the others.

'There you are,' said Alarice, striding down the corridor to meet them. 'You're just in time for last class!'

'What did we miss?'

'Botany,' Catrin grimaced, pulling a stray leaf from her hair. 'I'm sure you would've loved carting five barrowfuls of weeds over to the storehouse. Stupid agrimony.'

'Sounds delightful.'

'Better than what's coming next,' Ingrid eyed her watch. 'Come on, or we'll be late for Ardracy.'

Together, they walked to a strange, crooked-looking building above the West Quadrant. Its walls were a drab grey from the outside, but inside they shone with a patchwork of jewel-coloured stone.

Magda's heart choked when she saw who was standing at the back of the room. Ether Stefania, wearing her usual cut-glass smile.

'How nice to see our newest students joining us,' the pale woman beckoned them over. She seemed untouched by reflection of sunlit stones, an ice-white hollow among the coloured light that filled the rest of the room. 'Welcome to the House of the Lyre.'

Muriel looked around doubtfully. 'I thought we'd be having our lessons in the main building?'

'Ardracy is a study of magic, and this will be your classroom. Please take your seats.'

Magda shifted uncomfortably as they sat down. There were only eight of them in the room, and the room's jewel-eyed ceiling burned down like an eagle's glare. It could only be described as an absence of shade.

'Since our new students will be expected to catch up quickly, let's begin with a recap of the magical denominations,' said Stefania, opening a large leather-bound book. There was an identical copy on each of the girl's desks. 'Outside of the Fallow, the Scarp Mandate remains in force: all those who possess magic will be subject to its legislation. Of course, the blanket term *Tidal Folk* encompasses a wide array of capabilities, including elemental magic, elder magic, and spectral arts ...'

As she continued talking, Magda tried to copy down the flurry of notes. The content itself was no walk in the park, but it was the woman's tone that unnerved her. How on earth could she talk about the law so calmly, as if it weren't the thing that had driven a stake through the hearts of friends, families, lovers? Besides that, what could the Fallow possibly gain by sparing them the same fate?

'The select few, such as yourselves, have been given the opportunity to prove your worth to His Majesty. It is a great honour and responsibility to help your people.' Stefania paused, as if allowing the weight of that responsibility to settle over their shoulders. 'Your sessions here will relieve you of the sharpest edges of that magic. The useless variants shall diminish, and the rest shall be honed to their finest degree.'

Magda wondered what exactly qualified as a useless variant. She thought of the bwbach who had visited their old home back, and its cavity of hidden tricks and treats: from folding the linen, to scrubbing the doorstep. Would her parents still leave an offering for it outside? Would they be allowed to keep the sprigs of rosemary in the garden? More worryingly, the bwbach might decide to take matters into its own hands and abandon them altogether. Then their house would be without favour: a sorry fate indeed.

'Now that that's settled, let's return to the syllabus content. Today's topic is lyresses: Folk whose power comes through their voice, be it via melodic incantations or poetic englynion.' Stefania gestured to the third chapter of the book, and they each opened their copy. 'Can anybody tell me the common ailments which may arise from exposure to a lyress's song?'

Smoothing out her parchment, Magda contemplated the tangled-sounding word. Englyns were a traditional lyrical form, although Stefania didn't seem the kind of person who enjoyed poetry.

'Anyone?'

Magda kept her head down. She dreaded the thought of getting picked on, especially when she hadn't the foggiest clue about the question.

'Yes, Miss Gosselin?'

'Common ailments include lethargy, temporary impairment of the senses, and swelling around the wrists and ankles,' said Alarice. Her dark red nails shone as she turned the pages of her notebook, revealing rows after row of neat, curled handwriting. 'Most effects are short-term, but depending on the strength of spell they can take effect over a longer duration.'

'Very good. If a lyress ever came to these grounds, I dare say you'd be the first to sniff them out.'

Magda threw a glance over her shoulder to where Muriel was scribbling down notes. She looked equally overwhelmed, and a little wary. None of it made sense: first their exemption from the Scarp Mandate, and now an education in all matters relating to the Folk. But Ingrid had warned them to develop a thick skin, and she didn't want to be singled out on their first day. So she kept her head down and went back to the book.

'For those of you who've already read the required reading on *cyrch a chwta*,' said Stefania, 'please see the appendix for additional sources. Once you've finished, there will be a short test.'

Magda bent over to read the lines of slanted, curling script. Catrin had taken out a pair of reading glasses, and who could blame her when the text was this crabbed? She could barely make out the first paragraph, let alone the more obscure writings.

Casting a desperate glance about the room, she found everybody was utterly absorbed in their reading — everybody except Ingrid, whose hand was raised.

'Yes, Miss Leyshon?'

'I was meaning to ask about something you mentioned last week,' Ingrid peered down over her notebook, as if the answer was hidden beneath the rows of script. 'You said that every class has its place among the order. But what would happen, if a new order of Folk were to be discovered someday?'

Stefania's cheeks turned pink. 'That's not possible.'

'It must have happened before,' Ingrid went on. 'So it could happen again. What does the Brenin do with a spirit he'd never seen before?'

'This is not the place for insolent questions, Miss Leyshon.'

'I was only curious. I'm sure our newest students would appreciate your answer, too.'

Magda felt her throat tightening. She couldn't understand why Ingrid would drag them into this, even less why the girl had decided to pick a fight with the most intimidating woman in the building.

Stefania took a terse, tight breath. 'It is not the Fallow's place, or right, to question the Royal palace. What the Brenin commands, must be done.'

'Right. Point taken.'

Magda wondered if that would be it. Stefania was a shark, toying with her prey. And the waters hadn't calmed yet.

'Miss Leyshon?'

Ingrid looked up. If she was scared, she didn't show it.

'Please see me after class.'

Nobody dared to raise a question after that, and they worked in silence for the rest of the hour. Every scrape of someone's chair, every slash of a pens ticking against paper, scratched at Magda's brain. It was all the worst parts of school, with the added exception that their teacher was a demon. Right when it seemed like they might be able to escape, there was a tap on her shoulder.

'Excuse me, Miss Corrales.'

'Ether Stefania.' Magda stopped writing. She didn't want to look into those dagger-eyes, grey and opaque. 'Is something the matter?'

'I wondered if we might find a quiet moment to discuss your situation over the coming days. I'm aware that we may have ... gotten off on the wrong footing, over recent days. You and Miss Silvana are quite a special case, as I'm sure you're aware. It was important to ensure that transit was not delayed.'

Transit? Is that a new name for kidnapping?

'I see,' said Magda, still not looking up. There was something unnatural about those horrid eyes: because When Stefania looked into you, it felt like she saw your soul. 'You made that quite clear.'

She picked up her pen again, not trusting herself to say any more.

You're not forgiven. You'll never be forgiven. I'll despise you as long as I live.

'Thank you for understanding. Needless to say, we expect great things from you both.' There was a shuffling of feet as Stefania turned to face Muriel's desk. 'And you, Miss Silvana. We have all heard the most interesting things about you.'

Muriel didn't speak. There was such disdain in her expression that Stefania should have shrivelled like a weed under boiling water. The problem with weeds was that they were easy to stamp down, but infuriatingly difficult to destroy.

'Well, girl? Have you nothing to say?'

'That depends,' Muriel set down her pen, with a calmness that could have been mistaken for composure. 'To you, I have nothing to say.'

'Well, isn't that pretty.' The Ether glanced towards the clock, almost casually. 'Would you look at that? It seems we're out of time for today. Make sure to keep up with your readings, and I'll see you all next week.'

They walked down the corridor in silence. *That was bang out of order,* someone was saying behind them. *Did you see the look on their faces?*

Bloody psychopath, that old bag.

They were almost at the staircase to the dormitories now.

Then Muriel said, 'I'm going to kill her.'

Not loudly, not quietly. As plain and mild as a cup of tea.

Magda considered it. 'I'll join you.'

Chapter 17

Snarled Yarn

By the time Magda woke up, her pillow was already warm from the morning sun. Muriel was sitting cross-legged in the alcove of one window, haloed in the amber rays. A large blanket was spread across her lap. It was the same one Magda had noticed in the carriage on the way to the Fallow, and it was covered in tightly-stitched knots.

'What's that?'

'My mum made it for me,' said Muriel, her gaze fixed on the dark lines of needlework. The enormous quilt covered everything but the hem of her old jeans, which still smelled faintly of smoke. 'She gave it to me that morning, right before they took us away.'

'A blanket?'

'Of sorts. It's more of a diary, really. I didn't even realise she'd been making it.'

'That's amazing. Can I see?'

'If you like.'

Intrigued, Magda scrambled out of bed and went over to sit in the alcove. Sure enough, the densely-packed stitches were not knots, but letters. Words. Entire paragraphs: all worked into the fabric. 'They're so intricate. And she wrote them all just for you?'

'Yeah. It must have taken her years.'

They sat there, marvelling at the vast detail of the blanket. The morning light had draped itself over the room like a set of sheets, while motes of dust made slow voyages across the canvas. Magda wished she had something from home. Her mother's words were mostly scribbled under holiday pictures, pinned up on a little board. And her dad's had been held in a blur of ancient summers, of trips back to Spain when they would visit their grandparents.

'Look. That one's from this time last year.'

Muriel peered over to the square of the quilt where her friend was pointing. *Today while I was practising the harp, I could hear you singing! I think you've got an ear for fine music, or at least you certainly performed a nice rendition of 'Cuando las olas dejen de hablar'. I always did like Siya Sirena.*

The blanket felt soft and weathered between Muriel's fingers. To be honest, she wondered why her mother had never passed her it sooner. Why she'd never even *mentioned* it before. Why now, at the cusp of unprecedented change? What good could a shawl do now that they'd been kidnapped?

Magda sat back, inching towards the window. 'I didn't know you sang.'

'Not often. Only sometimes. I keep wondering if there's some sort of secret message in here,' Muriel sighed. 'But it's just words.'

'She probably didn't want you to feel lonely.'

'I know. There's only so much a blanket can do, though. She's still hundreds of miles away. We're still trapped here.'

'Maybe we should go down for breakfast?' Magda ventured. 'We could go and join the others.'

'And get stared at? No, thanks!'

'It can't be worse than yesterday.' Magda cringed at the memory of the Ardracy class, cooped up in that horrible building. 'Besides. If we don't go, they'll think it's weird.'

'They already think we're weird,' Muriel pointed out. 'That Ingrid girl stares at us like she's just seen a gwiber. What's the point in trying to be friends with someone who's not interested?'

'Then let's show them why they *should* be interested,' said Magda, firmly. 'Because you, Muriel Silvana, are not only the best friend I could ask for, but the brightest flint in the magpie's nest. You ace every class at school, you've got the quickest wit I've seen, and what's more, you're a genuinely decent person. Anyone who doesn't want to be your friend isn't worth the time.'

Muriel hesitated for a moment, the beautiful quilt caught between her fingers. 'Okay. Let's go and socialise.'

When they got downstairs, the dining hall was in various states of disarray. The younger girls' table looked like it had been attacked by locusts, and the North Quadrant's breakfast spread was only marginally better.

'Late to the table,' Rhos arched an eyebrow. 'Keep that up, and there'll be nothing left for you!'

'I know,' said Muriel, wearily. There were still several pieces of toast available, but she scooped some onto her plate before that changed. 'My sisters used to make sure of that.'

To her left, a smile crossed Alarice's lips. 'Let me guess. You were the youngest?'

'How'd you know?'

'I've got a little sister back home,' Alarice nodded. 'Mischief, that's what she was. You lot get away with everything!'

A faint, warm memory blossomed in Muriel's mind. She was twelve, and standing on a rocky beach. Isadora had found a crab and Lucía was chasing her with a strand of slippery seaweed. A purple, lightning-wrought sky and its jewel rain, dancing over the rockpools...

'Did your sisters inherit the same gifts you ended up with?' asked Catrin, carelessly. 'It must be more complicated, with there being three of you.'

The toast suddenly went dry in Muriel's mouth.

'Don't bring my family into this.'

'Alright, no need to look so distraught.' The blonde girl smiled, crumbs stuck between her teeth. 'I was only asking 'cause I'm an only child. No sisters for me to compare notes with.'

'That figures.'

'What time's our first class?' asked Magda, loudly, before anyone else could start an argument. 'I'm starving. Pass me the lemon curd, I can eat while we walk.'

*

The first class of the day was called Weftwork. To Magda's relief, it was Ether Lorna who stood at the front of the hall this time: an ordinary, warmly lit room on the ground floor. If Stefania had blown like an icy draught through the building, then her colleague was the soft chartreuse of spring foliage.

'Good morning, everyone,' Lorna smiled at them. 'Please accept my apologies on behalf of Ether Rhiannon, for today's absence. She's taken leave on urgent business to the Palace, and will be back to take your lessons by the end of the week.'

Alarice frowned. 'What happened?'

'I'm afraid that information is confidential. But you may rest assured it's nothing to trouble yourselves over.'

They settled into their seats behind heavy wooden desks, and Magda was distinctly grateful for a normal-looking room with four walls and a door. A sewing machine sat at the corner of the tables, and at the back stood a glass-fronted closet filled with bolts of fabric. Everything about the House of the Lyre had felt cryptic and disorienting. This place, on the other hand, felt like it existed for a functional purpose.

'Here at the Fallow, a refined understanding of the textile arts will be essential to your training as seamstresses.' Ether Lorna's voice was like seaglass: smooth, but heavy. 'Upon your Progression, should you be chosen as one of the Brenin's select artisans, it will not be enough to produce fine garments. You must produce the *finest garments of all*.'

Magda blinked. 'We're training to be seamstresses?'

'That's correct. I'm sure Ether Rhiannon will give you a much more comprehensive background to this than I can, but a core component of your learning here will centre around the textile arts — with the end goal of becoming a seamstress in the Brenin's service.'

Magda couldn't believe her ears. According to Lorna, each girl would gain the hand-sewing skills, tailoring techniques, and theoretical knowledge to construct any garment from scratch. Being selected, so they said, was the highest honour. The very notion made Magda's skin crawl.

'Is that quite clear?' The Ether looked slightly apologetic. 'If there's anything you wanted to go over, we can, er, revisit this another time.'

'I think that's enough for right now,' Muriel said quickly. 'Thank you.'

Magda gave the tiniest nod. She decided then and there that she'd sooner make waistcoats for stray mice than serve the Palace.

'We'd better get started with our work now.' Ether Lorna went to the back of the room to retrieve several vast baskets of yarn. They were cornucopia-like and shimmering with all manner of slub yarns, fancy yarns, and loop yarns. 'As I'm sure you're all aware, the frosts have been getting harder. Today we'll be weaving winter shawls for the southern districts of Brenarthe. Please take your looms.'

They did as they were told. In contrast to the colourful wool, Lorna's own dress was comparatively plain. At the hem of her long white skirt, however, Magda noticed frills and fronds, fine eyelets and curls like lichen over bark. Her quick fingers discarded the right yarns from the wrong ones with ease, until every girl had been given a skein of ivory floss to work with.

'Let us bless these threads with our gratitude to the Great Weaver: she, who wove these lands from nothing. We thank her for these gifts.'

'We thank her for these gifts.'

'You will begin like so.' Lorna took the heddle loom and set the weaving comb to one side. 'Don't rush, or the yarns will snarl.'

Across the room, Rhos and Ingrid began pulling thick lengths of the silk fibres from the bundles at their feet. Magda hurried to tie her warp yarns. It became easier once you got into the rhythm of it, and the girls soon began to weave on instinct, as if they were spiders themselves. But she and Muriel were still so much slower than the others.

'Mine keeps getting stuck,' Muriel began to undo a section hastily. 'Mags, is yours working?'

'Not exactly.'

A louder, more confident voice interrupted them from the front. 'Is this right?'

Ingrid had somehow already finished the first portion of her shawl, and was holding it up proudly. Magda felt a pang of inadequacy. How on earth could she and Muriel compete with students who'd been practising for months?

'Very good, Miss Leyshon,' nodded Ether Lorna. 'I dare say you'll snag the role of high seamstress if you keep up that quality.' Then she turned to face Magda. 'Miss Corrales, how are things coming along here?'

'Er. Well. I got the first part started, and I thought maybe it would look better if I added some colour — just a bit of silver, to break up all that ivory, and ...'

'I see.' Lorna ran a finger over the rippled surface with a sigh. The girl had woven in an extra strand of silver, and it caught the light like a misplaced constellation. She hated to undo it. But she hated more the idea of what Stefania would do if she discovered they had been incompliant.

'Did I get it wrong?' Magda looked up, anxious. She hated unpicking things. It was all the effort with none of the joy of creation.

'Not entirely. However, I'm afraid you're going to have to redo this.' Ether Lorna placed the woven sample back on her desk. 'The Tidal Folk are not dangerous because of the magic they possess inherently. They are dangerous because of what they do with it. When the Folk disobey, it means they can't be trusted.'

'But it's just a bit of thread.'

'I'm sorry, Miss Corrales.'

Reproachfully, Magda began to undo the work. As much as she would have liked to protest, she was already tired. It would take less energy to undo the extra thread than to waste another hour arguing.

'Remember, girls, the Brenin values you enough to honour you with *contracts* after you leave,' said Ether Lorna, as if that could lighten the mood. 'You'll make us proud, I'm certain of it.'

Magda said nothing. *Maybe*, she thought darkly, *the contracts that awaited each girl were exactly what they promised.* An insidious thing that lurked in wait, then slithered around you and slowly, imperceptibly, began to tighten. One day it would *contract* altogether, choking you where you stood.

'Do you need a hand?' Rhos asked, quietly, after half an hour had passed. 'I've finished mine, if you needed some extra help.'

'I'll be okay. Thanks, though.'

As Magda went on with the shawl, the movements became more and more strenuous. It was only a heddle loom, for goodness' sake. Yet it felt as if some vital filament was being strained out of her soul. No matter: she would show Ether Lorna that she was made of tougher stuff than they'd imagined.

At long last, after the other girls had long since finished, it was done. Magda handed over the shawl right as the beginnings of drizzle began to tap at the windows.

'Very good, Miss Corrales. I'll see you next week.'

They left the six ivory shawls at the front of the room, each one identical. Each one colourless as the rain outside.

*

By the time classes finished, everyone was keen to go to the common room before dinner. 'The cove', as it was called, was probably the Fallow's most pleasantly designed room. Not only could you collapse onto the squashy settees, but it was high enough up in the building to provide a sort of hidden eyrie, away from the lower dormitories and all the worries that brewed there.

'So. Any more news from Foxe?' said Rhos, flashing a sly smile at Catrin.

'The ordinary kind,' replied Catrin, cagily. While she hadn't become any less acerbic over the course of the week, Magda and Muriel were beginning to tolerate her like a thorned rose in a garden.

'And?'

'He said they'd discovered a new kind of gem down in the mines, one that splits the light into different colours,' she admitted. 'It sounded pretty. I asked him to save one for me, so that I could take it to study when I get back. I wish he wouldn't take so long with replying.'

Alarice laughed. Some people didn't know what it was to have a *real* problem.

'Are you *sure* there wasn't a love sonnet in there somewhere? You know, most girls would've asked him for a necklace.'

'Come off it, he's got no taste with that sort of thing. If it was a necklace I wanted, I'd be better off getting my own.'

A quiet drift in the conversation ensued. This was the gap where someone might crack a joke to lighten the mood, or change the subject entirely. But Magda found herself unable to summon the energy to do either of those things.

'Are you okay?'

She blinked. Muriel was looking at her worriedly.

'I'm just —' Magda lowered her voice as the others picked up a new conversation. 'I was just thinking about home. It feels like ages ago.'

It had hardly been a week.

'Do you think it'll get easier?'

'Probably not,' Muriel sighed. 'I don't think I want it to, though.'

Because that would mean forgetting. That would mean none of it was real; that none of it had mattered. That leaving behind their families had meant nothing.

'I miss them,' said Magda, acutely aware of the hollow pit in her stomach.

A drift of evening rain was coating the windows outside, returning the lantern-light to them like snakes' eyes in the treetops. It seemed impossible to think of this place as home, even a temporary one.

'This won't be forever,' Muriel reminded her. 'Enio and your parents will be beside themselves when they get to see you again.'

'So will your sisters.'

The hope was still there, and they were both trying hard to cling onto it. But it felt so impossibly far away. The threads which should have held their families together were steadily coming unravelled.

Chapter 18

Veridian

It was common knowledge that mangroves needed salt to grow. And while Muriel was not blessed with a warm climate and tropical waters, she did believe the same might apply to people, in a way. Tolerance came with a barb. And only once you accepted the bitter salt in your environment, could you start to strip out the weeds and put down roots.

She glanced over to where Magda was sitting, eyebrows knitted together, gazing out the window. 'What's going on out there?'

'Nothing. I'm just trying to figure out whether our pigeons know we're here or not.'

'Hmm. Hergest was a good tracker, but he wasn't exactly the cleverest.'

'Yours would probably stand more of a chance, then. Pigeon 821, right?'

'She'd still have to fly incredibly high not to get caught,' Muriel frowned. An unsavoury image of a pigeon getting barbecued by the poisoned woodland floated through her mind. 'Do you think Cunning Wood affects birds in the same way it affects humans?'

Magda shrugged. 'There must be a way around it. The crows seem to manage alright.'

It sounded half-plausible. But then again, they'd both attempted to send one to their parents. Neither had been returned. Either the pigeons were getting lost, or something was badly wrong.

'Do you think that home will have changed much, by the time we get back?'

'Who knows,' Muriel stared out the window, as the sky broadened to a pale blue crescent. 'Plover probably won't have stuck around.'

At the very least, she supposed, the house fairies would be glad to have their saucer of milk back. But Isa, who had grown fond of the oversized dog, would be heartbroken. It made her miserable to think of her alone back there. Wildbriar hadn't been an easy place to grow up *with* sisters, let alone without them.

'Seamstresses,' Magda was saying, scrabbling under her bed for a pair of slippers. 'I'm not even good at sewing. Why'd they want us to learn about dressmaking, anyway?'

The peculiarity had stuck with Muriel, too, like a coarse piece of bread lodged in your throat. Anybody with half an eye for coordination could pick it a needle and thread; there was nothing special about these girls. But she could see no point in arguing with the strangeness at present. They were only just managing to keep their heads above water, and asking 'insolent questions' could sink whatever invisibility they'd so painstakingly earned among their classmates.

'I suppose they've got to find some way for us to pass the time.' She picked up her duvet and began to make the bed. 'What I don't understand is why the others didn't tell us sooner.'

'They must have known we'd be confused.'

'Hardly surprising, since the Ethers leave us in the dark at every opportunity.'

'Let's just try to get on with it, then. Until we've found out more,' Muriel sighed. Fiddling with the final corner of the bedsheets, she scooped her mother's quilt up from where it was lying. The darkly inscribed words stared back at her like a swarm of black eyes, hot and feverish and aching with mercy.

One thing you must remember, mi corazón, is that you cannot always trust people's words. Before someone is cruel, they will tell you they are going to be kind. Before they call you beautiful, they will make you doubt yourself. The trick is to know yourself better than they ever could.

She took one last look, then folded the blanket up again. She'd taken to storing it under her mattress for safekeeping, but took a peek whenever she got the chance. Right as she had tucked it back into place, the door clattered open behind them.

'Morning!' grinned Rhos, clutching a small trowel. 'Want to come gardening? The weather's lovely for it!'

*

Outside the air smelled bright with crocuses. Sundays were their one free day of the week, which meant neither of the newcomers had managed to defend themselves with a suitable excuse. At least gardening was a good distraction. Rhos and Alarice were delighted to find their crocuses had germinated — which meant repotting, of course. Even though the red clay stained everything it touched, Muriel found she didn't mind. It was only mud. It felt clean.

'Which is the most poisonous of the lot, then?'

Muriel looked up to find Ingrid peering over their handiwork.

'Well,' she said, slightly suspicious. 'You have crocuses. Daffodils. And cowslips. Over here, there's a small patch of foxgloves that are just putting down roots. Are you going to plant something, too?'

Since her dad sowed their very first garden in Furze, Muriel had delighted in helping wild things grow. But Ingrid was staring into the distance like something else had caught her attention.

'Did you hear me?'

'Hm?' The dark-haired girl looked up distractedly, clearly not having heard a word. 'Oh. Um, sorry.'

'Maybe you should try a cyclamen, they're really good even in cold weather.'

'That's certainly an idea.' Ingrid fiddled with her high-collared velvet cloak. 'Did Rhos say there were spare seeds in the potting shed?'

'You'd know if you'd actually come and joined us last week.' Alarice shot her a pointed look before returning to deadheading. 'But if you're not busy, I could do with a spare pair of hands with these crocuses. Fancy it?'

'Er, I think I'd better leave you to it.'

She turned around and went back up the cobbled path to the North Quad. Muriel and Alarice exchanged a confused glance.

'Don't ask me. She never comes to help us with the gardening,' replied the older girl, throwing a handful of earth over her shoulder. 'Want a go?'

'Sure.'

They sat there for a while, slender fingers pulling apart the clods of crocuses. Dark grains scattering the lawn.

'Did something happen, or what's going on?' Muriel ventured, after a while. 'She seems stressed.'

'It's always hard when people come and go here,' said Alarice. 'Gwern knows it wasn't easy when they took Lissa and Shay. Whoever invented the Progression system must have had a sadistic mind.'

'The Progression system?'

'The Council that says you're ready. By the time you're eighteen, you've got to be ready.'

'Why?'

'That's what Lissa tried to find out. But the Ethers said *Dilys Laire, always gets her way, it's about time she learned a lesson or two.* The next morning she was gone.'

Dilys Laire. The name rang a bell, but Muriel couldn't think why.

'Does it happen often?'

'Only twice a year,' Alarice discarded another clod of loose crocuses, disapproval curving on her lips. 'Ech. Bad roots, those ones. Muriel, can you pass me that trowel?'

Forty minutes later, their task was complete. Alarice and Rhos excused themselves to go and get a snack, and Magda meandered over from whatever she had been digging.

'Did that tree personally offend you?' Muriel laughed, inspecting the lofty brow of lichens that were now clinging to Magda's fringe. 'It looks like you got into a fight.'

'Oh, that! I meant to get rid of it.'

Muriel shook her head and turned back to the selection of plants she'd been arranging. *Crocuses. Daffodils. Cowslips. Foxgloves.* When the ground was less hard, they could plant them out.

'Is that a poison garden?' Magda peered over her shoulder.

'I suppose so.'

'Nice.'

Nice wasn't the first word that Muriel would have used to describe it, but she shrugged it off. It seemed like everybody suddenly had an opinion about her allotment.

'Shame there's no way of knowing how effective it might be,' Magda knelt down to look at the snake-headed foxglove and its velvety petals. 'You could make a decent potion with that.'

'Well...'

'What?'

'Look here.' Muriel pointed to the cowslip. 'This one on the left will have the strongest poison of the allotment.'

Magda squinted at the screwed-up yellow bud. 'How can you know that?'

'It was something they taught us back in Furze. *The last bud to bloom holds the thickest bane*.'

'Sounds like superstition.'

Muriel laughed. 'Want me to prove it?'

'Go on, then.'

It was only a joke, but there was a sudden conviction gripping Muriel's heart. Like a vine twisting towards the flower, she felt herself reaching for the cowslip with her mind.

Little one, how would you do it?

The words came unbidden, and the silence shimmered around them. Her best friend frowned. But to Muriel the flower's voice was clearly audible, a thin, bright ripple through her head.

How would I do what? it asked eagerly.

How would you use your poison?

The cowslip paused for a moment. Then:

I would tear out the tongue and set it aflame,

Wrap scars around his throat,

I would burn the wrists like magnolia,

Turn them into musk-moth wings.

Impressive.

Then she realised Magda was staring at her.

'Am I missing something?'

'You didn't …?' Muriel trailed off. It felt as if she was high up, floating — and only now had she returned to the ground. 'You didn't hear it.'

'No,' Magda gave her a funny look. 'I could have sworn I felt the air turn almost … cold, for a minute there. What did you do?'

'I could hear it speaking to me,' Muriel replied, uneasy. The flower was the same as it had looked before, but there had been no mistaking its words. 'It told me about its poison. Didn't you hear it, too?'

Magda looked frightened. 'Muriel … I know they think we're strange. And I know it's my fault that we're both here. But we can't let the others find out about this. If the Ethers think you're still normal, then maybe they'll still let us —'

'Of course they won't let us go,' Muriel interrupted. 'You really think that now they've got us, they'll let us skip off back home? You heard what Stefania said, about us being *special cases.*'

She thought briefly of the warning that Grimoire had once given them, but this was hardly *powerful Forest magic*. Even if she did have veridian powers — which she definitely didn't — wouldn't it have manifested itself in some more impressive way than talking to a miniscule flower?

'Sorry,' Magda looked down, defeated. 'I just thought we should be careful.'

'I didn't mean to hear the stupid flower in the first place. Come on, let's leave the gardening for another day.'

She tried not to think about all the hidden things that lurked outside the Fallow, in the Forests and beyond. Most of them would gladly eat these girls alive.

*

'So what did you lot get up to in the gardens?' asked Catrin, later that night. The group of them were seated at the high table of the dining hall, and a bright moon was shining outside.

'Plenty of crocuses, and some daffodils. Where were you?'

'I overslept.'

'Lucky there was no post for you to miss,' said Alarice, slicing open an envelope with a purple wax seal. 'The crow only brought mail for me, today.'

'Who from?'

'My sister.'

They watched as she unfolded the inner slip to reveal a dark sheet of paper. It was a deep, rich blue colour, picked out with the white skeleton of a harebell.

'A cyanotype,' Muriel observed. 'How long did that take her?'

'Oh, not long. It's her way of telling me to hurry up and come home.' Alarice folded the sheet back, with a laughing smile. 'Says she's making me a funeral bouquet with a new flower for each day I'm gone.'

They watched as she handed a second envelope to the large black bird which was perching on the back of her chair. Had it been there before? Muriel flashed a worried look at Ingrid, who shook her head and said, 'It's only the crow. They're the least traceable form of correspondence, after all.'

'What do you mean, the least traceable?'

'Come on, Muriel.' Ingrid's voice had tightened. 'The Brenin might think we're special, but that doesn't mean he wants people to *know* about us.'

For the third time that day, Muriel's head ached. None of it made sense. If they were really so gifted and valuable, then why were they being kept like some nasty little secret? As the meal continued, she snuck a glance over at the folded blue cyanotype.

To Allie. From Zaira, with all my love.

She missed her own sisters more than she could put into words. What she wouldn't have given to receive a simple note like that, addressed *To Muriel, with love from Lucía.* Or Isa, except Isa was convinced letter-writing was an old people's hobby from the past.

Either way, it was a fruitless hope. And it was wrong to sneak longing glances at other people's mail, so she went back to taking small mouthfuls of overcooked rice from the cauldron. It was the wrong shape entirely to cook rice; what they needed was an *olla.* Another missing piece in the new, unwieldy tapestry they called their lives here.

'Have either of you gotten any post, yet?' asked Catrin, her eyes bright and curious.

'Not yet,' said Magda. 'It's probably just a delay in the mail system. You know how the pigeons get.'

'I'm sure they're positively overwhelmed with messages from girls imprisoned in faraway institutions,' Ingrid snorted. 'Better to just wait it out. They'll get there in the end.'

'Or maybe they need a bribe to speed things up.'

'Who? The pigeons, or the Ethers?'

It drew a smile to Muriel's lips, but she couldn't join the others in their laughter. Not properly. Because maybe it wasn't money that the Palace was looking for at all: but something rarer, sharper, and more precious.

Chapter 19

Silk and the Sacred Oak

Time moved strangely at the Fallow. The girls' days were all jewel tones — a dark red crease of morning; emerald rain in late afternoon; beetle-black evenings when the storms ceased — and before they knew it, the two girls who'd arrived petrified and rain-trodden from Wildbriar were three weeks into term. Soon they would be seventeen, and there would come the terrifying precipice of *afterwards*... but for now, it was only Monday morning. For now, Magda could stare at the clock on the wall and wish the hours would drip away like mayflies.

'Miss Corrales?' A harsh, coppery voice rang out from the other side of the door. 'Please come in.'

Magda got to her feet, moving reluctantly towards the iron portal.

The other girls had warned her about the nature of the screenings. Each girl was called once a month to have their magical traits analysed, and to monitor any developments in those capabilities. It was, according to Catrin, one of the most unpleasant experiences you could undergo.

She turned the handle and opened the door, before her stomach could churn itself to an even messier pulp.

'Ether Stefania.'

'There you are,' the severe-looking woman continued to write, hunched over a black notebook. A set of tightly scribbled lines covered the page in front of her. 'You may take a seat.'

Wrinkling her nose at the grainy steel chair which had been indicated, Magda sat down. Everything in this office was regrettable. But before she could ask how things would proceed, the frenzied writing came to an abrupt halt and Stefania snapped the notebook closed.

'Let's begin. According to your initial report, you've been experiencing nocturnal visions?'

'It was only a few bad dreams,' Magda tried not to fidget in the chair, which was really very uncomfortable. 'Nothing worth worrying about.'

What she wanted to say was *You hurt my dad. You, you, you.*

She might even have done it, if the warning that Grimoire Malgarty had once given them hadn't loomed large. She and Muriel would be in danger if they didn't keep this hidden. So she held her tongue, even though it took every ounce of strength in her body.

'You're certain it was nothing more severe?'

'Yes.'

'Let's not pretend you weren't brought here for a reason, Miss Corrales.' Ether Stefania fixed her with a hawkish stare. 'We are aware of what happened in the woods the night before we were summoned.'

The silence jarred like too-hot marmalade, thick and scalding. Magda had already suspected the Prices as the ones who'd alerted the Fallow. What she hadn't banked on was Stefania knowing the particulars.

'You mean that —'

'The girl was injured, but is recovering,' said Stefania, evenly. 'You will not be punished. However, you *will* answer for what you have done. You can begin by explaining what you were doing in the woods when the incident took place.'

Of all the people in the world to whom Magda wanted to tell this story, Ether Stefania was right at the bottom of the list. Yet she couldn't help herself. There was that strange sense of compulsion that came when you looked into those dagger eyes, as if her jaw had unhinged itself and started moving of its own volition.

‘That afternoon I went to the bramblings,’ she began, roiling over a wave of nausea. ‘It was because we’d finished our chores for the day. It’s our free time, after lessons, and I —’ she stopped, trying not to recoil at the fresh, horrible memory of it. ‘I saw a girl in a red cloak. Tegwen Price, she’s one of the girls at my school. It looked like she was setting a snare to catch something, a nest of gringelots, I think.’

There was a scrabbling of spiderish white fingers at the clipboard. ‘And?’

‘And I could see them.’ The two younger cubs, poking their noses out of the nest. The mother, frantically trying to distract the girl from her trap. ‘Tegwen was holding something silvery, bright like metal. So I ran out to try and scare her away —’

The words broke off. Magda waited to be asked something else, something easier. But Stefania wasn’t about to let her off the hook just like that.

‘When you’re ready.’

‘I...’ she tried again. ‘I ran out, but Tegwen slipped, and then everything was red — and —’

It was too much, too horrible, and she placed her hands over her ears as if she could block it out. She hadn’t been able to tell even Muriel that part.

‘Thank you.’ Ether Stefania’s pen clicked against the table. ‘This, I assume, was the nature of the nightmare which followed?’

Magda forced herself to take a breath. ‘Yes.’

Far away, the clocks on the wall seemed to have melted to a standstill. Then, after a long moment, Stefania set down the clipboard and raised her head.

'I'll speak with Lorna and Rhiannon tonight, and we’ll arrange your program accordingly.’ A low, leering pause. ‘I hope you appreciate the extent of the Brenin’s generosity in hosting you here.’

Sweat crept down Magda's neck. She knew better than to rise to the bait, but the handful of words echoed like knives.

*

By the time she got to the dining hall, most of the other girls had already finished their lunch. Muriel, who had waited, raised an eyebrow at her friend's state of dishevelment. 'It was bad, wasn't it.'

'Diabolical,' Magda shook her head, reaching for the tray of lavercakes in front of them. 'I never want to go back there again.'

Muriel squeezed her hand. 'I'm sorry.'

'I told you it'd be grim,' said Ingrid darkly. 'Stefania's probably in an even worse mood than usual, seeing as it's almost the Ceremony.'

'The Ceremony?' Magda repeated. 'What ceremony?'

With a pointed glance towards Ingrid, Alarice cleared her throat. 'Technically, we're forbidden to talk about it until the last quarter of each month. It's inauspicious.'

'But you'll see it for yourself soon enough.'

'Well, what exactly happens at this ceremony? Surely you can tell us *something*.'

There was a weighty pause.

'It's a rite of passage they carry out every month,' said Catrin, after it became clear no one else was going to say it. 'Always at new moon. There are preparations to be made on the evening of that day.'

Magda glanced down at the lavercakes on her plate. Her appetite for the thin greenish patties had suddenly withered, along with her patience for the hush of secrets in the air.

'Anything else you'd like to tell us?'

'It's not such a big deal,' said Rhos, seeing the agitation in her eyes. 'You'll get used to it. Do you think they've already chosen this month's Keeper of the Flame?'

In truth, the monthly Ceremony had always terrified Rhos. To say it out loud would make the fear real, tangible, unavoidable; so it was best dispelled by acting as if you couldn't care less.

'I reckon they'll wait until the night itself.' Catrin swept the last crumbs from her plate. 'Come on. Enough doom and gloom for one morning.'

After lunch they made their way to the Gatehouse, a stone-bricked building near the edge of the grounds. Under different circumstances, it would probably have felt like a luxury to attend classes there. Apart from the lack of a portcullis – which was hardly required, given the grounds' inherently defensive location – the bluestone engravings gave every impression of Gothic grandeur.

Ether Lorna was waiting for them at the entrance. 'Come on, girls. We can't have you getting rained on before the afternoon's even begun!'

A slew of autumn sleet was thickening in the sky above. Ducking under the slate-roofed gables, the girls took their seats in the inner chamber.

'That's better,' Ether Lorna moved neatly to the front of the room. Draped over her shoulders was the usual glittering overcloak, crowned by a chestnut-coloured necklace. 'A moment's silence, now. For silk and the sacred oak.'

'For silk and the sacred oak.'

The briefest silence twinkled, starshot. Then the Ether dipped her hand into the bag of Artifice which was fastened at her hip: with one swift motion, a handful of the powder flew into the air, plunging them into shadows. It spread like midnight ink across the ceiling of the Gatehouse, until a series of constellations began to appear amid the darkness.

'Today, we raise our hands and voices to the skies. Who can tell me why today is so auspicious?'

Ingrid raised a hand. 'It's the turn of the third quarter.'

'Correct, Miss Leyshon.' Ether Lorna crossed the room, footsteps slow as unstoked embers. Above the place where she now stood, the Artificed air shimmered with a giddy speckling of silver. 'In just a matter of days, the stars will be at their very brightest.'

Magda shivered. There was less than a week until the new moon. A mere matter of days before the Ceremony, if Catrin had been true to her word.

'Is it true there'll be a ritual at the end of the month?'

'Every month, the necessary preparations must be made. All students are expected to partake.' Ether Lorna handed them each a square book. 'I'm afraid I can't explain in any greater detail at present. For now, please read page seventy-two of the Vellum.'

Magda studied Lorna's fingers as they passed over the holy book, each movement made with mercenary precision. These were hands that did not fail. Hands that exacted nothing less than what was asked of them.

'What happens if we're not able to attend the Ceremony?'

'All matins are important, but the Ceremonial rites cannot be missed.'

Matins. The morning song of the birds: that was its most pure meaning. Before the Rift, some religions had used that word to denote a service of prayer. The truth, however, was that matins would always belong to nature. There could be no goddess older or crueller than the earth beneath your feet.

'So it's compulsory.'

'Let's not stray too far from today's service, Miss Corrales,' Ether Lorna's voice had grown a shred tighter. She stepped back and gestured to a cluster of stars covering the top corner of the ceiling. 'We raise our blessings to Cyfan, the crux of justice. Her starlight will guide the way for the lost heir to return.'

Cyfan's constellation was a shining ring of stars. Absentmindedly, Magda wondered how long they'd been wishing for the lost heir to return. If she dared to speak her mind, it seemed whoever heard those prayers had turned a blind eye. She knew it was wrong to think such things. Wrong to doubt the goddess. But for once, Magda was grateful for the darkness of the room, hiding those impious thoughts along with her cynic's tongue.

'We bless the goddess and the threads with which she graces our lands.'

She tried very hard to concentrate on Ether Lorna's words. The Great Weaver Gwern came first and foremost, as the one who had woven these lands from the very fibres of the earth.

'*Silver braid for Tarren Mawr. Coarse kelp for Abergwyll.*' The prayer wound and wove around the room like a slipped knot, a fine skein of lace in which they were dancing. '*New linen for Dauglyn. Fairest lambswool for Porthdeilio.*'

As Magda recited the words back, the painted walls and tufted carpets began to fall away around them. Once you forgot the strange new circumstances, the words were as they always had been: because this was the mythos in which she believed. Each word, each rhyme, rich and round as a bell. It was like hearing her mother back in Wildbriar, reading the prayer aloud for the very first time.

*

That night in the common room, there were new tides adrift. A crash of intrigue sang high in the eaves, and below it, Muriel could hear the rip currents of gossip circulating. Even before they'd set a foot downstairs, her shoulders tensed at the sound.

Neither she nor Magda had fully shaken the feeling that they were in some strange dream: one from which they might wake up at any moment. Sure, the Fallow had trapped her here for three weeks. But the ache in her chest hadn't grown any duller. One step through those double doors, and the kaleidoscope might contort in any direction at all. Inside, outside, all the way back to a sunny vision of Wildbriar.

She glanced sideways. 'Are you sure you're feeling better?'

'I'm over it, I swear,' Magda insisted. 'Don't worry. I won't let Dagger-eyes get to me again.'

The staircase tripped and complained obligingly as they made their way down to the cove. With each descent, their heels clicked like shimmery, shiny fish on the crick-backed steps.

'There you are!' Rhos beckoned the pair of newcomers in eagerly, the door already open. 'You did hear, right?'

'Hear what?'

There was a sound of clanking porcelain at the back of the common room. Three figures were crowded around the table. Somebody was muttering a string of curses, while the two people beside them were cheering around what appeared to be a ceramic teapot.

'I don't understand.'

Rhos looked almost offended. 'You mean you didn't see the parcel?'

'What's so special about a parcel?'

'Well, it's really a —'

'Merrick, stop spoiling the fun!' Alarice was waving them over to join the table of chaos at the back of the room. The curled ends of her braids, which began in flat rows along her scalp, shimmered under the lamplight. 'Why don't you get over here and see for yourselves.'

'It's your parcel?'

'No, it's mine,' said Ingrid, the last cuss dissolving between shadows. In one hand was a teacup; in the other, the remnants of wrapping paper. 'My parents sent it.'

In contrast to the jubilance she should have felt, Muriel's sense of optimism was dying a slow death. She hadn't received a single letter from her parents. Nothing from her sisters. And not a sausage from any of her friends. Instead of trying to muster up a half-hearted congratulations, she moved closer to the table. Sitting proudly on a neat green tablecloth was the subject of all this commotion.

'A teapot,' she stared blankly. 'Well. That's ... nice of them.'

'It's not any ordinary teapot; it's an Everything Teapot,' said Alarice, as if it was common knowledge. The dainty white teapot stood in the middle of the table, with five wildly unmatching cups set out around it. 'Scurlock. A demonstration?'

With a shrug, Catrin picked up a mug and poured out a measure. A deep, smoky aroma rose settled over the teapot. 'Let's see... Ooh, hot chocolate.'

'That's not fair. Mine was only nettle tea!'

Setting down the cup, which was now filled with a velvety brown beverage, Catrin gave a triumphant smirk. 'It just shows I've got better taste than you.'

Meanwhile, Muriel's gaze hadn't moved away from the teapot itself. She'd seen many interesting contraptions before, but never a kettle which could brew multiple drinks at once. 'What else can it make?'

Ingrid smiled. 'Just about anything, and everything.'

The empty shell of the brown paper still lay on the table. *To our dearest Ingrid. With love from Ms Honoka Leyshon & Mr Taren Lightwater.*

'Where on earth did they get it?'

'Probably one of my dad's latest finds at the antique shop. He goes every weekend, they've got all sorts of trinkets and gadgets in there.'

'Tell her about the time he found a self-cooking pie dish,' urged Rhos.

'That was one of his less successful culinary endeavours,' Ingrid admitted. 'The timing mechanism wasn't exactly perfected, so the sweet potato pie ended up closer to chargrilled than baked.'

'Do you think he double checked this one?'

'Only time will tell. Want a go?'

Muriel surveyed the artefact carefully. It looked perfectly unassuming with its red terracotta exterior and chalky polka dots. 'Er, how does it work?'

'It's easy: you just let your mind wander. And when you pour the teapot, it'll fill your glass with whatever you desire.'

'Anything?'

'Anything.'

So Muriel tried to let her mind go blank. It was harder than she'd expected; there were too many thoughts that jostled for place. Half of them were tinged in crimson and green, colours that seemed to seep through every waking moment...

'Ready?'

Muriel blinked. It was Ingrid who'd spoken, and she was still standing there clutching the teapot like a total lemon.

'Yeah. Let me see,' she lifted it and poured, watching as a clear orange liquid came streaming from the spout. 'Ah, it's iced clementine. Just like my dad used to make it.'

She took a sip, not expecting the bittersweet feeling that hit her in the gut. The tartness of the fruit cloyed with notes of elderflower, tapa de dulce, and nostalgia. You couldn't deny it: memory was a most difficult thing to deny.

'I wish I'd gotten something better,' Alarice was still lamenting, from the other side of the table. 'It must be biased.'

'It's probably worn out!'

'Then perhaps we should let it rest for the night. I do have something else we could investigate, as a matter of fact,' Alarice paused. She reached into the pocket of her skirt, an elegant piece made from geometric Ankara fabric, and brought out a shiny piece of jet. It sat in her palm like a mammoth's tooth: black, smooth-edged, and about the size of a quince. 'Look what I found in the orchard earlier.'

'Is that a hagstone?'

'It's rare, that's all I can say for certain.' She tilted the rock in her palm, and it shone between her fingers with a degree of relish. 'It was just lying among some mosses near the north cutting, so I scooped it up during Botany. Thought it might be of use.'

'Can I see?'

'Sure.'

As they inspected the stone, Muriel caught sight of a set of letters which were engraved into the base of the rock. 'Not just *any* hagstone. That looks like a Telling-stone to me.'

'Wow, you're right. We should go and test it out!'

Telling-stones were a special kind of pebble which were sometimes used to divine the future. Their accuracy was a subjection of contention, but certain folk swore by their predictions.

Others warned that Telling-stones were the work of witches.

'We could go to the edge of the woods, since it's darkest,' said Ingrid, still admiring the stone. 'It'd be the ideal conditions for divining!'

There was much jostling and general clamouring of agreement. But while the sudden excitement had half the room in thrall, the two new girls remained silent. There was a second side to this thrill: one with a rusted metal edge. Muriel tried to catch Magda's eye, and failed. While her best friend would usually have been raring to go, Magda now seemed caught in a distant grey haze.

'So, is everybody coming?'

'Wouldn't miss it for the world.'

'Same here.'

'And you guys? You're coming too, right?'

All eyes turned to face them: pinning them to the spot. Muriel scrambled for an answer, surprised by her own daring. 'Yeah,' she nodded, fighting a pang of nausea. 'I'll come, if everyone else is going.'

There was no *real* rule forbidding the expedition, provided they didn't go outside the Fallow grounds. She glanced hopefully towards Magda.

'Alright,' said Magda, relenting. 'I'll come, too.'

*

'This is the worst idea you've had in ages.'

'How was I supposed to know it'd be freezing out here?'

'Next time my money's on staying indoors with that teapot,' Ingrid muttered. 'I'm sure it could have been convinced to make more hot chocolate, if you'd tried a bit harder.'

'Oh, shut up.'

The night air clung to their bones, whipping fabric into torrents of billowing linen as they walked. Added to the dampness of the grass, it made for an unpleasantly chilly experience, which some people would have probably called *bracing*. The only thing Muriel could call it was a mistake.

'Are we nearly there?'

'Almost.'

The clouds of their breath pierced the air as they stalked through the shadows, into the night. Beyond them lurked Cunning Wood, and it seemed like tempting fate to joke in the presence of such fearful surroundings.

'Is this good enough?' Muriel stopped, pausing for breath. Magic was best worked at liminal times and spaces; if they walked much longer, they'd be over the threshold of twilight and into the true dusk.

'It'll do,' said Catrin. 'Pass us that rock, will you?'

'Give me a minute,' Alarice hovered, digging the little rock out of her pocket. She bent down to place it on the ground, making sure it was settled in the earth. 'Okay. Has anyone got a question?'

There was a conspiratorial murmur.

'I have,' said Rhos, with a knowing smirk. 'When will Catrin's boyfriend send another letter?'

'Has anybody got a *serious* question?'

'Come on, no need to be a killjoy!'

'Fine,' Alarice relented. 'We'll ask it.'

From its half-buried position in the soil, the chunk of coloured glass began to sizzle with a strange light. A Telling-stone always had to be in contact with the earth to work. They watched as the hole through its centre grew brighter and brighter, struck with a liquid incandescence until it was too bright to look. And then — so quickly you could have blinked and missed it — the light fizzled out altogether.

Scooping up the stone, Alarice squinted to read the writing which had etched itself across the base. 'The Telling says: *fear the winged messenger.*'

'What's that supposed to mean?' Catrin snatched the stone, frowning. 'Sounds like nonsense.'

'Maybe it's a riddle of some sort?'

'Or a false reading.'

Neither option was a very satisfying answer.

'We could try another question,' said Magda quickly. 'Maybe a less personal one?'

'Yeah, can't really blame it for not wanting anything to do with romantic affairs,' said Ingrid. 'How about we ask it something serious. Like, is there *really* a sunken kingdom off the West Isles?'

Everyone groaned.

'You and your sea monsters,' Alarice sighed. Dormitory Six had been decorated with Ingrid's sketches for months now, ever since she'd developed an interest in cartography.

'They're a classical feature of seafarers' maps! You can't just ignore them, they must have been guarding *something.*'

'Hang on, it's changing!'

The stone had begun to glow again, and Muriel bent down to observe it more closely. *Something* was changing inside it, morphing to generate that light — but what *was* it?

Before she could get a better look, the effulgent glow went out altogether.

'Right.' Ingrid grabbed the stone, turning a more critical eye to the inscriptions this time. 'It's changed. That's weird, though. It says: *lost girls seek the sunken hollow. The house beyond the woods.*'

Catrin rolled her eyes.

'Seems more like a crossword puzzle than a fortune teller.'

'More likely it's a counterfeit, or something from the Selvedge. Shame. The real thing could've been useful.'

With both spirits and cloaks dampened by the rain, they left the little rock discarded where it lay, still warm against the earth. As they trailed back to the dorm rooms, Muriel noticed the pensive expression on her roommate's face.

'Mags. Is everything alright?'

It was as if Magda had been underwater, and only snapped back to the surface when a cautious hand was placed on her shoulder.

'What?' Magda blinked. 'Oh, yeah. I was just ... thinking about things.'

'That was some Stone, huh.'

'Pity that it didn't work like they were hoping.'

They walked back to the dormitory through snippets and locks of idle conversation, but Muriel got the feeling that things had been left unsaid. Back in the dormitory, the familiar glow of the lamplights was upon them. It was the kind of warmth that should have meant safety.

Chapter 20

Shades of Gold

Breakfast was a quiet affair. Muriel was infinitely glad to be back in the daylight, because in the darkness everything contorted itself to terror. The mirrors especially. Some part of her secretly feared she'd find another face staring back, peering over her shoulder, but she shook the thought from her mind.

Downstairs in the dining hall, the porridge was still hot. The morning was unstirred, dense and carotid, but no ghosts tapped at the windows. She took a spoonful. Surely you couldn't eat *and* feel sad at the same time.

'What's wrong?' Rhos nudged her. 'Don't tell me they undercooked the oats again.'

'No, they're edible.'

Ingrid peered over the other end of the table. 'Pass us the sugar, will you?'

Muriel caught sight of the silver dish, which had been gradually depleted throughout the last couple of days. 'Sorry. The dish's empty.'

'Oh. I suppose marmalade will have to do, then.'

Right as they were about to tuck in properly, an imperious voice boomed into the dining hall.

'Miss Silvana?'

Muriel felt a sinking feeling in her stomach. Oh, stitches, she couldn't have forgotten, could she?

'Your screening,' repeated Ether Stefania, one hand on her hip. 'Now.'

Muriel got up from the table, her cheeks burning with embarrassment. No one attempted to make conversation as she was escorted out of the room, and Stefania led them swiftly down a series of narrow corridors until they reached the office that Magda had described. It was the crowning misery on a week that had absolutely nothing to say for itself.

Breathe. Just keep breathing. It's only one tiny meeting.

As the door clicked open, Ether Stefania gave a frigid smile.

'Shall we?'

Muriel nodded, wondering if this was how an armadillo felt in the moments before the ocelot sank in its teeth. Waiting, frozen, helpless.

'Let's see. According to your initial report, you may be liable to minor symptoms of botanical magic. Could you tell me more about that?'

Muriel shifted in the cold metal chair, her gaze fixed on the desk. 'Not really.'

'Are you quite sure?'

Annoyed by the woman's insistence, Muriel made the mistake of looking up. This time, Stefania caught her eye and didn't look away. The cogs of something deep and moss-covered began to shift, itching at the corners of her mind.

'I never …' she broke off. The full sentence wouldn't form. Something was holding it back, like a dam barring a river. 'I don't know what you want me to tell you.'

'Only the truth.'

The cogs turned once more, painful and rusted.

'The forest,' said Muriel, through gritted teeth. The words had wrenched themselves from her without asking permission. And then, all at once, they were tumbling from her lips like sleet. 'I can hear the forest, but the voices get … blurred. Amongst the storms.'

Stefania made a note on her clipboard. 'And have you experienced any ability to draw the poison from plants?'

Muriel was still reeling from the woman's previous question. Why on earth had she spoken? She had told the truth, but it felt as if Stefania's dagger glare had a way of prying whatever she wanted from you.

'No,' she answered, at last. *But the cowslip. The cowslip.* 'Sometimes I can *hear* the poison in them.'

Stefania scribbled down another note. 'Thank you. For future reference, this will be easier on you if you don't, well, *resist* so much.'

Muriel's cheeks flushed with embarrassment, and shame. The woman's audacity was astounding. What kind of an interrogation was this, anyway?

'It's alright,' said Stefania. 'I only warn you that it is in your best interests to cooperate here. We seek to aid your chances of joining His Majesty's division.'

'I understand.'

The room snowed itself silent.

'One more question. Have you ever felt any kind of hostile urge when you tapped into the Forest's power? And if so, might I ask who was the subject of this urge?'

The question took Muriel by surprise. She shook her head resolutely: this was absolutely off bounds. If Ether Stefania thought she deserved to know her innermost fears — well, she was badly mistaken. Sidonie Silvana had been quite clear in her opinions on misplaced trust: *do not reveal yourself to anyone,* anyone, *until you're certain they are worthy. Pain is far more intimate than joy.*

Stefania flipped over a clean page of her notebook. 'You'll receive instructions from the head office next week. Rest assured; this is strictly confidential information.'

Muriel almost laughed out loud at that. The Fallow girls lived in such close quarters that almost everybody knew each other's business.

'Is there anything else?'

'Not for today. Thank you for your cooperation.'

Muriel couldn't get out of the room fast enough. She hurtled down the first hallway, ducked beneath the narrow staircase, and skirted around the corner. A sick feeling was cramping her stomach painfully, and refused to budge.

Not only that, but she realised she was no longer alone.

There was a blurred silhouette beneath the doorway ahead: a person whose back was turned, meaning they hadn't seen her, but who looked like they were waiting for something. Would it be Alarice, with her quietly commanding presence? Or Ingrid, with her disdainful stare? As Muriel deliberated, the figure moved.

It was the hair she recognised. There was no mistaking that hair anywhere — not the messily woven plait, and definitely not the woeful straggle of black ribbon.

'Magda,' she waved, relieved at the sight of her friend. 'What are you doing here?'

'Hey, you're out already!'

'You didn't think I'd hang around in there, did you?'

'I didn't know how long it would take,' Magda looked bashful, then began fumbling in her pockets for something. 'Here. I thought you might need this. You know, in case it was bad.'

'Aw, thanks,' Muriel grinned at the bag of rocky fudge which was being offered to her, and picked out a chunk. Her unconquerable sweet tooth revelled in the warmth of a good confection. 'Where'd you get that?'

'The back of the kitchens. Someone left a bunch of biscuits in one of the cupboards, and I think this is a suitable occasion.' She paused. 'Dare I ask how it all went in there?'

'I think Ether Stefania would make a good prison warden.'

'Isn't that what she is?'

'Yeah, but it was like she got you to talk even if you didn't mean to. That was the thing,' Muriel admitted. They passed beneath a low archway, crossing the courtyard to the North Quadrant. 'Something was different this time. *I* felt something different.'

'What do you mean?'

The feeling had no name; it was a low curdling in the blood.

Veridian.

Forest-weaver.

Those unsightly and forbidden strands of magic.

'Um. You know the things that Grimoire said about me, back in Wildbriar?' Muriel hesitated, afraid of what Magda would say. This was the theory she'd been scared to consider, to even contemplate, since the little things had begun changing. It bit back every time she tried to silence it, and her hands were too bloody to fight any longer.

'Yeah?'

'I think ... I'm beginning to think those things might be true.'

There was a long moment between them. The idea had grown, subtle as a vine, between the mornings and the long, silverblue nights. At one point, she'd dared to hope those feelings would go away by the time her screening rolled around.

They hadn't.

'You mean...?'

'Yeah.' Muriel felt paralysed, waiting for one of them to say something that made sense of it. The beat of her heart was not hers; it belonged to somebody else. Somebody who was a veridian. Somebody who knew what to *do* with those feelings, for Gwern's sake. 'Are you angry with me?'

'No, of course I'm not angry.'

Magda looked like she was about to say more, then gave the tiniest inclination of her head. The wind whipped at their ankles, as they stood there in that stupid courtyard with its patch of flocked green grass.

'I should have said something sooner. I kept trying to convince myself it was nothing, but...'

'Muriel,' Magda shook her head. 'I'm the one who should have spoken sooner. I've been wondering about what Grimoire said, too. My visionary capabilities, and all that.'

The blood pooled in Muriel's lungs. 'What?'

'I was thinking the same thing you are. Except I'm not as brave as you, and thought it was better if I just tried to pretend.' There was a rueful expression in Magda's eye, one that didn't give away the whole story. 'We can't all be heroes, after all.'

'But you've done nothing wrong.'

'And yet here we are,' said Magda, simply. 'I wish I could be more like you. You're the valiant one, the trustworthy one. I'm just a rotten coward.'

Muriel couldn't believe this. Couldn't believe that her best friend held herself in such low esteem. 'If you're serious about this, Magdalena Corrales, I might have to murder you.'

'Don't threaten me with a —'

'No, I'm *not* going to indulge such a bloody great lie as you being some sort of deserter! Where'd you get that crap from, the pre-Rift archives?'

At least that elicited a laugh. But Magda was still standing awkwardly, the pair of them halfway down a path that seemed to have doubled in length. 'I'm sorry.'

'It's okay.'

'I just didn't want to cause you any more, well, problems.'

'You mean the thing in the woods?' The words died on Muriel's lips. They both knew exactly what Magda was referring to. 'It's okay, you know. You don't have to punish yourself over things that weren't your fault.'

'That's what everybody says.'

'And the nightmares,' said Muriel, slowly. 'Is there anything I can do to help? If there's anything you need, say the word.'

'I will, if you will, too,' Magda gave a tired smile. There was a sprinkling of mud over one shoe, which slid free as she paced from foot to foot.

'Whatever you need, you can ask me any time. And I don't mean that in a half-soaked *please-don't-take-me-up-on-it* kind of way.'

The wind whistled, blowing green and grey as they stood still in time.

You never were a one to do things by halves, thought Muriel, and didn't say it.

'Come on. Let's get somewhere inside.'

They moved back into the corridors, marble arches and slit windows casting a web of amber light between each pace they took.

'What made you think that Grimoire was telling the truth?' asked Muriel, one shoulder painted auburn by the hazel sun.

'The other night with the stone.'

They walked on through the colours, the rays painting them in and out of the shadows. Grey. Copper. Cast-iron orange. A full three shades of amber went by before Magda elaborated further.

'When we were out there in the orchard, I thought I saw something.' They passed beneath the great rose window, spilling gold like filaments through a spinneret. 'I think it was a premonition.'

Muriel thought back to the group of them, huddled around the Telling-Stone as it churned and sizzled with molten colour.

'What did you see?'

'It was sort of ... shadowy. I'm not sure what it was, really, but I could have sworn ...'

Muriel waited.

'Never mind,' said Magda, after an agonising pause. 'It had a certain presence, whatever it was. Like how you'd feel a chill if you opened up a chest freezer.'

She looked so forlorn that Muriel couldn't stand it any longer. As they stood there in the failing light, it was impossible to say which of them initiated the hug. It simply happened, like a pebble being carried by the tide.

'It's going to be okay,' said Muriel, her voice muffled. 'It will be, I promise.'

'I know.'

They sat with the fear, watched as it settled beside them, its long shadowy arms spilling across the floorboards. It was an eldritch guest but not an unkind one, and they let it be.

'I hate worrying about all this stuff,' said Magda, after a while. Her cheeks were red and blotchy. 'If Enio was here, he'd never let me hear the end of this.'

'If Enio was here,' Muriel retorted, 'he'd be too busy trying to win over the entire North Quadrant to listen. That boy thrives on attention and bad music.'

Their laughter scattered across the hall like a flight of birds, until they were themselves again. Ochre, marigold, deepest bronze. More shades of amber, streaming through the window with unseemly temperance.

'We should have a plan for what to do next, shouldn't we.'

'If Grimoire was telling the truth about our powers,' Muriel reasoned, 'then she must've meant it when she said to keep it a secret, too. This has got to stay between us. Just me and you.'

'Right.'

'Not forever,' she added, wishing there was a better solution than this. Magda looked so *deflated*. 'Just until we're eighteen. Once we're out of here, they can't hurt us.'

Chapter 21

Nocturne

That night, Magda stared into the sky. It was crackling dusk, and it had left the horizon streaked with careless red. More oppressive than the colour, though, were the thoughts. She cracked open the window to let in the whirling breeze.

'Mags, aren't you cold over there?'

'I'm fine,' she lied. 'You should try to sleep.'

'You, too. Get some rest.'

If only it could be so easy. The things that Muriel had told her earlier, that *she* had told Muriel, had come swirling to an eddy in her head. Could they really face the parts of themselves that they'd held down for so long? The penny-bright lilt of their memories was now tricked through with ink: for there was comfort, and there was relief, but there was fear, too.

So much fear she couldn't breathe.

Just what did it mean, to be a visionary? She resented the fact that Grimoire Malgarty had known more than she had, let alone named a part of her she wished was non-existent. It wasn't fair, and there was no guidebook, no roadmap, to navigating this.

Now she had to face her beastly dreams alone.

Rolling back over onto one side, the thin linen duvet creased her shoulder with its striped imprint. If she closed her eyes, perhaps it wasn't so different from her old bedroom: the slivered corner of moon peeking over the foot of the bed, and a chorus of silver birches rustling outside.

What she had said was true. She really *did* wish she could be more like Muriel: kinder, more understanding, and more compassionate towards herself. The night of the Telling-Stone had troubled her in more ways than one, not least for what she'd seen. The vision had fallen lightly, like a veil, in a way that could not be mistaken for dreaming. A flash of light. An image so strange and momentary it couldn't be real. And then, mercifully, she had come back to reality.

This time, however, Magda could feel the visions lurking beneath her bed, waiting to drag her into something deeper. She tried to stay awake. She tried to think of home, of any place more comforting than this. But sooner or later, the dreams got their way as they always did.

The clocks struck midnight.

That first, fleeting vision had been swift, so transient it was almost possible to brush away. Now Magda felt a kind of lightness that lifted her off her feet. She was standing up, and walking down the hallway — lightly, so lightly — then she felt the soft click of the lock, and was padding barefoot up to the edge of the orchard.

Visionary, echoed the memory. *It's true, it's true, it's true.*

Heat and humidity blurred the edges of the dream. Magda searched for the moonlight as she stepped onto the grass, aiming in a direction which made little sense. The north orchard. Across the far lawns. And towards the edge of the Fallow grounds. She wasn't really here: but something else was, and she could feel its gaze searing into her back. Where could it be hiding?

That was when she saw it.

There, at the very edge of Cunning Wood.

Two bright canine eyes were looking out from the hedgerows. For a moment Magda stood paralysed, caught in those furnace eyes. They burned like no fire she'd ever seen, but fear clung fast to what it knew best, and she knew this creature's name like a second heartbeat.

It was a gwyllgi.

Everybody knew the great wolfish beasts were portents of death: after all, this was a spirit who her mother had made her promise to avoid at all costs. She had glimpsed it once before, in the briefness of the premonition two nights ago, but now she was certain.

It was following her.

'What do you want?' Magda whispered.

Such an animal couldn't be in Cunning Wood by accident. The legend of the Forest's poison was so prolific, she felt that even the creatures should be avoiding it. These woods meant danger, and men did not come here because they were afraid of that poison. Skin burned away from contact with noxious plants; feet blistered from running over envenomed moss; arms lacerated by vines that grew out to touch you.

But though its eyes were flaming red, the gwyllgi didn't look scared. If Magda didn't know better, she would have said it looked calm, utterly composed. Like it was nothing more than a gigantic puppy with an uncharismatic aura of violence.

In spite of every instinct that screamed against it, she took a step forward. The dream melted around her.

'I'm not going to hurt you.'

The red-eyed wolf flickered. It seemed to hover in and out of existence, as if it was no more flesh and claw than a reflection in still water. As if it hadn't decided whether to approach, accept, or attack: and had decided on none of the above.

Then there was a sudden crash, and lightning split the sky.

Whatever the opposite of a shadow was, thought Magda, *this was it*. The illumination cast its electric eye over every tree and flower for miles around. It picked out every insignificant detail, from the bones of the orchard to the lowest blade of grass, and lit them up in full-colour glory.

The lightning itself she could have tolerated. What it illuminated, far in the distance, was the thing that made Magda's heart stutter.

A building, deep in the woods.

She saw it for mere moments: a slanted rooftop, jagged grey tiles, and a skinny weathervane, just poking out from above the trees. But it was enough. Although the building vanished with the white-hot flash of light, Magda knew she wasn't mistaken. The whole outline was the spitting image of the old, ramshackle library back in Wildbriar. Except this building was tucked away inside the woods, and looked sparkling new.

It was only a vision.

Nothing but a trick of the light: and already, the image was vanishing before her. The red eyes were gone, too, although a sound like wolfish laughter echoed in the distance.

'Wake up,' she turned back, uneasy. 'You need to wake up.'

*

'Corrales? Coming for breakfast?'

Magda jolted awake to the sound of Ingrid's voice, trailing down the hallway. She was back in her bed. The memory of the vision was foggy, but the image of the library burned in her mind. It was only a dream; she had to remember that. Visions were not reality, and they couldn't hurt you.

'Magda?'

'Coming.'

She sat up and brushed a stray twig from her hair. Stupid. She should've closed the window: the cold draught had done her no good, and blown in half of the Forest besides. Thank goodness the dawn made things look so much more ordinary. As exhausted as she felt, the morning had given her the grace of good natural lighting. She pulled on a pair of boots and began to make her way downstairs.

Yesterday's revelation had probably been a long time coming.

Neither she nor Muriel had quite expected it, and neither of them had wanted it, but there was an element of a fever, finally breaking. Slowly, the strangeness of their new surroundings was sinking in.

For one, Magda no longer had to kid herself that nothing was out of the ordinary. She didn't have to curse each step she strayed into the unknown; didn't have to hide her feelings like rotten apples that might contaminate the barrel. For the first time since they'd arrived, she took her seat at the breakfast table without feeling guilty.

If Muriel could accept her for who she was, then maybe she could, too.

'Did you hear about Ether Rhiannon?' Catrin whispered, as they bit into the crumbly loaves that had been laid out. 'Rumour has it she's got a secret lover outside of the Fallow. Somebody saw her riding back through the woods early this morning, with only a charmed cloak to protect herself.'

Muriel looked exasperated. 'Is this the only kind of news you get here?'

'It's all the others will be talking about.'

Part of Magda was intrigued to know how everybody ended up in these amorous affairs in the first place, but there was no way of asking outright. At school, boys had either looked at her like she was a walking textbook, or like she was a threat to them on the sports field. Neither option was screaming *romance*.

'I'd better be getting the post,' Catrin stood up, searching her satchel for a pair of reading glasses. 'I can't believe I forgot.'

'Someone already beat you to it,' laughed Rhos, while the other girl's expression turned sour. 'Look what I found on the window ledge!'

A letter was dangling from her right hand, torn open like a battle trophy.

'Give that back to me. Right now.'

'Alright, alright, no need to panic.' Rhos flipped the envelope to show a bright green seal on the reverse. *To Rhoswen Merrick. Love from Dad.*

'Try that again, Merrick, and you'll regret it.'

'Ah, nothing like a good altercation to brighten up the morning,' Alarice took a leisurely bite of her toast. 'Where would we get our entertainment otherwise?'

'Who knows. Do you think the Ethers get time to send post to their families, too?'

Magda hadn't even considered that the Ethers really *had* families. But somehow, as grudging as she was to admit it, even Ether Stefania might have someone out there who cared about her.

'They're probably too busy to write letters,' said Rhos. 'When they're not teaching, they always seem to be running around on errands. Attending business in Helygen. Or doing site maintenance to stop this whole place from falling down. Ether Stefania used to work as a farrier, once.'

'Really? How'd you know that?' asked Ingrid, suddenly interested.

But nobody seemed to hear her comment, and the group returned to picking the breakfast table clean, demolishing toast and marmalade like a pack of starved wolves.

That was, everybody except Muriel.

'Not hungry?' asked Magda, casting an eye over her friend's plate.

'Less than usual.' Muriel picked up the knife and scraped a thin line of butter over her toast. 'I have a feeling we're going to need a strong stomach this evening.'

'Oh. That.'

Tonight marked the new moon, and their first Ceremony together.

'Surely it can't be that bad. They're probably overreacting.'

Muriel gave a weak smile. 'I know. But I'll still feel much better once it's over and done with.'

At that point she was cut off by the rowdy chatter of the other girls, which had suddenly become much louder.

'What do you mean, you've never kissed anyone?' Alarice was saying, her eyes wide.

Rhos glared back at her. 'We're not exactly spoiled for opportunities here, are we?'

'Let me read your palm. Maybe it would have something to say about your romantic prospects.' Catrin reached with thin, birdlike fingers to Rhos's freckled hand — but Rhos snatched it away.

'That's none of your business! I can find out my own romantic prospects for myself.'

Ingrid rolled her eyes. 'Don't know why you're so hung up on boys, anyway. Waste of time, if you ask me.'

There was a clamour of indignation, but the conversation was cut off by the bell for morning prayers. Nobody contested it. Really, love was too delicate a thing to scrutinise by the harsh light of day.

*

The afternoon saw them hacking up the weeds from the borders of the kitchen gardens. *Before the frosts set in, and the ground turns hard as nails,* Ether Lorna had advised them. It didn't make the task of digging up acidic soil any more pleasant, even if it was a virtue to rid the plot of ragwort and creeping thistle.

'I don't think I was cut out for this,' Ingrid wiped her brow with the back of her hand. Botany had never been her favourite class, but she rarely felt this extent of physical remorse for it. 'Anybody want to swap spades?'

Magda glanced over her shoulder. 'You can try mine, if it's any sharper.'

'Oh. Uh, thanks.'

They returned to digging.

Suddenly, Magda's shovel collided with rock. Something hard and jagged was buried there among the weeds, and she struggled to unearth it.

'What's that?' Rhos moved over, curious. 'I always wondered if there was treasure buried here!'

'I don't think it's treasure, but...'

She reached down to smooth away the crumbly black soil. The thing that had been lodged in the earth was a piece of porcelain, light purple and yellow, painted in faded swirls like a sunflower field.

Don't play twp, I already saw you break that vase!

The memory slipped, and so did the porcelain fragment: falling from her fingers like glass. She had been eight, and Enio, ten, when the big violet vase in their kitchen had gotten smashed.

'Shame the rest of it's all broken,' Rhos mused, moving back to her own plot. 'It might've been worth something, once.'

'I doubt it,' Magda turned away. Scraping the patch of earth aside, she began to dig with new vigour. Anything, everything, to distract herself from the memories that she needed to bury. *Clot:* the shovel sank in. *Thunk*: another heft of earth, weeds and all, went flying.

After a few minutes Muriel sidled over to inspect her work, having finished her own plot. 'Anyone would have thought you were trying to murder something with that shovel.'

'It's probably the lack of sleep.'

'Didn't you get any rest last night?'

Magda stopped digging, and leaned over the handle of the spade. 'Not really. I thought ... I saw something strange.'

'We can shut the window, if it's making the curtains flap about too much.'

'No, I had a vision.'

'What?' Muriel lowered her voice. 'And did you ...?'

'I can't remember all of it,' she ran a hand over the back of her neck, reluctant to recall the eerie scene. 'There was something. Something in the woods.'

'That's not possible.'

'I know,' Magda said, and didn't elaborate any further.

The simple fact was this: English was the wrong language to do the explaining which this required. There were legacies of everything in the languages they spoke, and she missed hearing her dad's rambling string of curses at the onions he sliced for dinner. Onions had always made him cry. Las malditas cebollas y sus malas mañas.

So Spanish was like a bell, bright and rich, that rang between casual inconvenience and hearty warmth and soft melancholy. It felt like too precious a thing to open up in such a place as the Fallow, and she often wondered what Muriel felt about the words they'd once shared.

'I don't know if we should talk about it here,' she admitted. 'Sorry.'

Perhaps what she needed right now were not words at all; but acts. A hug would have worked wonders. Yet the pair of them stood frozen, trespassed by some impassable tract of ocean.

'Well, if you do want to talk about it, at some point later ... you can tell me anything, you know.'

'Thanks,' Magda picked up the shovel again, unable to make the smile meet her eyes.

English was the currency of grief. Its slow, sunken words were pits and hollows, but Spanish was a language that rippled with memories. It was musical like Welsh, but without the heaviness of those earthy consonants and rolled, guttural sounds.

Here, there was no warmth to the bloodless sun. Here, there was no place for that old familiar world, and it had dug a deeper pit in her heart than any of the garden's.

Chapter 22

Ceremonial

The summer she turned nine, Muriel had crossed an ocean for the first time. She had loved Costa Rica long before she set foot on the tarmac runway, but every summer since that first visit she had awaited their annual trip with anticipation.

Her parents knew she adored the city. If you picked the right day, you could get exactly what you were looking for at a fraction of the regular price. But you had to go early. It was already dripping hot by nine o'clock, which meant your best bet was getting ahead of the crowd. Once you arrived you'd find grocers selling manzanas de agua, caimito, and steamed pejibaye, jewellers with shining wooden ornaments, or artists displaying their finest prints to the marketgoers. After they got home it was time to wash and store the goods in the fridge, lest they spoil in the intense heat. The rice went on to cook; peaceful clouds passed by the window. And afterwards, when the triumphant lunch had been eaten, she scrubbed the pans clean with the hard little cake of dish soap, pale turquoise and grainy as clay.

On one of the early years, Lucía had picked out a charm locket for the three of them. A matching sprig of mango blossom, cut in silver, threaded through a loose black string of a necklace. Luz had guarded hers jealously, and so had Isa: but Muriel had let hers slip. It had been years since she'd seen the silver locket in years, now. And even though it was just another little piece of driftwood, flotsam in deep waters, Muriel could feel that tide dragging at her ankles more fiercely than ever.

Break, it ushered her. *Splinter into threads. Turn to silver, jade, and granite.*

But she refused to dissolve like that.

By late afternoon, classes were over, and she stared down the Eve of the Ceremony with defiance, if not spite. The hours were dark blue satin: winding and turning, guiding them to the feast in the dining hall, and Muriel tried not to dwell upon the vision that Magda had mentioned.

Dreams of the woods didn't bode well. There could be anything in there: acidic sap, virulent lichens, boiling brooks. But it was useless to question it further. Whatever places her friend went to by night, she could not follow.

Rhos gave a sympathetic glance as they filed out into the dark. 'Nervous?'

'Sort of.'

There was an empty pit in Muriel's stomach. At dinner she could hardly look at the food on her plate, let alone contemplate eating it. All she could think about was golden cloth that now covered her skin: for tonight, they wore the same ghostly robes as the Ethers.

It unnerved her.

'Will it be over quickly?'

'The Ceremony always finishes on time.'

'Okay,' Muriel walked on, her head lowered. 'That's good.'

Beneath her bare feet — shoes were forbidden for the Ceremony — she could feel the tug of the grass straining towards her. *Wait*, it seemed to say. *Danger*. She still struggled to accept the phenomenon of hearing those voices at all, for these were still forbidden arts. But Grimoire's warning wound its way beneath the skin. If her experiences could be explained by veridian magic, then at least it meant she wasn't going crazy.

'I'm glad you're not too freaked out by the whole thing,' Rhos muttered, oblivious. 'After tonight, you'll probably get used to it.'

It was a bad lie. Even the earth seemed to prickle with fear; with the knowledge that something was coming. Around them lay a circle of standing stones, and above them was the blind night.

Muriel glanced across the circle. There were the six of them from the North Quadrant, and a huddle of younger girls who looked even more petrified than she felt.

'Welcome, takers of the Ceremony.'

It was Ether Lorna, striding towards the centre of the circle. A high, arched headdress concealed her hair behind thick gauze, and the warmth of her usual attire was replaced by cold starlight.

She didn't look happy to be here.

'Each student of the Fallow has been selected carefully for her prowess, or potential, in the magical arts. It is a marked privilege to practise such arts. One which must be acknowledged in kind.' There was a stilted, hollow pause. 'This leads me to ask, who will accept that blessing this month?'

'We will, Ether Lorna,' murmured the circle.

'And who will be our Keeper of the Flame?'

'We will.'

Muriel's eyes darted anxiously, waiting for an explanation of some kind. But no context came. Instead, Ether Lorna began to walk with eerie precision from girl to girl — touching each one on the shoulder. Inhaling as if she were scenting the air. Her fingers felt warm as death against your skin, and Muriel froze when they pressed into her shoulder.

Not me. Anybody else but me.

Before she could utter the silent plea again, Lorna had moved on to the next girl. Misshapen planks of wood lay at each girl's feet, but the woman moved around the circle with an impossible deftness, before finally settling on her unfortunate victim.

'Miss Leyshon. You have been chosen as our Keeper of the Flame for this Ceremony,' she beckoned Ingrid towards the centre of the circle. 'It is with great honour that we take you in our arms tonight.'

Ingrid didn't move. All eyes turned on her, and Muriel wondered if there was any rhyme or reason to the selection process. Why her, of everybody? Then she remembered Ether Stefania's ominous tone during their first Ardracy lesson.

I'll see you after class, Miss Leyshon.

Back at the centre of the circle, Ether Lorna had knelt down and placed both palms upon the bare earth. Her brown knuckles brushed against the grass, and for a moment it might have been just another Botany class. When she gazed up, her eyes were filled with cold white starlight.

And when she spoke, it was in a voice that sounded nothing like her own.

'Elder spirit, we summon you. Let your soul burn through the night. Let your daughters rise to hear you.'

They watched as Ingrid walked towards the centre of the circle. Seven towering monoliths, rich bluestone, crowded around her to cast their long shadows. The middle of the ring was piled high with wood, and a flicker of alarm twinged in Muriel's stomach.

This had to be some kind of strange test. Not the other, more frightening thing, which hovered just beyond her vision.

'Elder spirit, be merciful,' Ether Lorna bowed lower, her hands sinking into the soil. 'The sisters of the Fallow beseech your blessing, for the New Moon, and for the Ceremony.'

There was a high keening sound in the distance, like a sparrowhawk. It was very far away. Ingrid came to a stop, dew clinging to her ankles, and the wind whipping through her hair.

'Miss Leyshon, are you prepared to help your sisters?'

'I am.'

All eyes were fixed on the pair of them. Muriel hardly dared to breathe, lest she disturb the magic that was oozing into the ground around them. She could feel it rising beneath her feet.

'The two goddesses will protect you,' muttered Ether Lorna. 'In Gwern and Eila's name, let her not burn.'

Muriel tried to move, and found she couldn't. It was as if her legs were now rooted into the ground. And why would no one meet her eye?

Something. Someone. Anyone.

But the others stood iron-faced as statues before that terrible silence.

'It is done,' said Ether Lorna, in her normal voice. Then, with eye-watering calm: 'Miss Leyshon, please step onto the pyre.'

Muriel felt her stomach drop. All too late she understood what the instruments on the ground were intended for. Ingrid stepped forwards like a ghost, moving as if she had no choice in the matter at all.

'You may light your torches.'

The other girls leaned over to pick up the rough lengths of wood at their feet. Muriel's piece of torchwood was carved carefully with glyphs of fire and ash; it had been made to burn. She wanted to yell, but her throat was frozen. And at the edge of her peripheral vision, she could make out Ether Lorna's silhouette: far, far away. Avoiding their gaze altogether.

Muriel didn't understand why, or how, but her feet seemed to move of their own volition. There was something unnatural in that circle; something that made you want to drop everything and do as you were commanded. The ring tightened. Darkness fell as they moved towards the centre, towards the place where Ingrid was sweating — from the heat of the crackling wood, or fear, they couldn't tell. There was darkness, and then there was light.

'*Now.*'

The pyre tore into a mountain of burning flame.

PART III

Interlude

Three Weeks After

Just like every other despicable day, Isadora Silvana woke up home alone. Salt and green ice shone through the sunlit window. Her head swam. It was a horribly lurid time of year, drowning in excess and scarcity, and they had a dozen sprigs of mistletoe but no fresh potatoes in the cellar. Worse, every shop in Wildbriar insisted on selling garish leftovers from Invernal: you just couldn't walk anywhere without being assaulted by a hideous pair of stockings or a novelty fleece. And you especially couldn't walk anywhere without being subject to the smiles of happy families, obliviously blissful in their cocoon of undeserved joy.

Isa tried not to think about last Invernal. The year before, and every other year before it, their family had everything.

That was before her little sister had been taken.

Kidnapped, if she was being blunt.

Vanished off the face of the archipelago, if she was fearing the worst — not that the archipelago particularly seemed to care. With nothing but an earmarked page, the world had glossed over Muriel's disappearance like it was a penny dropped in a well.

A sharp splash, then undisturbed ripples once more.

Some mornings, Isa managed to get up without the hideous dread sinking into her bones. She swung one leg over the side of the bed, onto wooden floorboards, and forced herself to go downstairs. Mornings like that were a rare reprieve. She found herself waking earlier and earlier, a little more bloodshot, a little less agreeable, before the red flesh of day broke properly. Most nights, she still heard Plover shivering outside the door or barking in the distance.

It wasn't real, of course.

The wolfhound was nothing but a trick of the light; a wishful shadow.

'Sweetheart, are you up there?' Her father's voice, calling from downstairs. There was a shuffling sound as the front door clanged shut. 'We're back.'

'Coming!'

Hastily, she made her way down to the hallway hastily, where her parents stood with a dripping umbrella. The long-awaited meeting at the Town Hall had finally taken place.

'So what did they say? They told you where she's been taken, right?'

'No, love,' her father gave a long sigh. 'They've said they're working as quickly as possible to find new leads, but it's taking longer than expected.'

Isa wanted to scream.

'It's been three weeks. How can they *not* have any further information?'

Once upon a time she'd wished for this: perfect solitude. For some space away from her eldest sister, so confident and headstrong, and some time to grow outside her youngest sister's sparkling shadow. How would it feel to be the only, the one everybody looked at and admired?

Lonely, was the answer.

'I'm going to get the stove on,' said her mother. 'Do you want something hot? I picked up some groceries, maybe we could do a vegetable guiso?'

She nodded, feeling strangely numb. 'I'll get the table ready.'

Those eyes are so unusual, a distant aunt had once cooed over her, right around the time when Isadora started to get taller and ganglier than either of her sisters. *Eyes like green charcoal. Serás una rompecorazones, chiquilla.*

Those eyes hadn't changed much, even now, although Isa knew they'd been looking more weary than usual. She pulled out the tablecloth and let it unfold over the wooden counter, watching as it cloaked the smooth oak. Every embellishment was a testament to the years it had been loved: there were various patches covering wear, rips mended with tiny slipstitch, and a trim of scallop shells stitched neatly around the fraying edge.

'They'll find her, Isa,' her father patted her shoulder, moving towards the staircase. 'It can't be much longer now.'

Isa said nothing, waiting for him to go. Maybe her aunt had been right, and she really would break hearts one day. But right now it felt like the only heart breaking was her own.

*

Nobody ate much that night. The food cloyed in Isadora's stomach, leaving her cramped up and uncomfortable, so she drank more coffee instead. It didn't ease the gnawing hunger. When it got bad, she chalked her jittery, irritable attitude down to stress.

On nights like these, she couldn't even blame Plover for staying away. Tragedy spread like ink through water, poisoning everything it touched. She gazed out the window towards the place where the shaggy grey dog used to lurk, waiting patiently to clear up the leftover vegetable scraps.

'Where do you think he went?'

'Oh, Isa,' said Sidonie, her heart aching. 'I think Plover must've got a fright just like the rest of us. It'll be safer for him somewhere else. Try not to feel too sad.'

I'm not sad, Isa wanted to shout, *just empty.*

'Do you think we should send a message to Lucía yet?' asked her father, his voice low. 'It's getting to the point where —'

'No.' Sidonie was shaking her head. 'She'll be back here in a flash, you know that. And things are only going to get more dangerous. You saw the way that woman looked at this town,' she hissed. 'Like she wanted to roast it on a spit.'

There was a harsh jangling of cutlery against plates.

'I'm going to bed.' Rafael didn't meet his wife's gaze. Then he turned to the other chair at the table. 'Isa, I'm sorry to be in such a bad mood lately. We love you very much, you know that?'

'I know.'

They sat there wordlessly as the table grew colder. A hundred menaces burned in Isadora's chest, slowly eating away at her. *It should have been you*, they said, *it should have been you and not her. You're the older sister; why didn't you do anything to stop this? You should have stopped it, it's your fault, it's –*

'Stop it,' she whispered, her eyes bright with tears.

'Isa?' Her mother cast her a worried glance. 'Who are you talking to?'

Isa looked up too quickly. 'Oh, it's nothing, Mum. Don't worry.'

She got up and started to clear the plates away from the surfaces. Sketched over the countertops were a patchwork of painted flowers from another time: long strands of fairy-flax, tufted wood anemone, and a scattering of white bryony.

Chapter 23

Triolatry

Later, Magda would think of the Ceremony as just one night of terror among many. But the first instance twisted like a thorn in her side. She couldn't get the image out of her head: the circle of approaching figures, and then Ingrid's body. Wrapped in scarlet flame.

Burning and burning and burning.

She hadn't slept, much less dared to go outside afterwards. The idea of another nightmare was intolerable. Besides that, the fresh horror of the Ceremony was only another chip on a block of torment, one which danced visions of red behind her eyes. All too often it turned to a pair of crimson eyes in the dark, and a building behind the woods.

'Why didn't you tell us?' Muriel glared across the breakfast table. 'You all knew. You knew what was going to happen, and you said nothing!'

Nobody dared to answer for a moment.

'There's nothing to be gained by knowing,' Alarice's voice was heavy. 'You wouldn't have escaped it, even if we'd told you. It would've made things worse.'

'Worse than walking in clueless?'

'They prey on fear, Muriel. If you knew what was coming, they'd have sensed it in an instant.'

Magda couldn't reply. That was one of the things that had unnerved her the most: that it could have been her. It could have been Muriel. And she would have been powerless to stop any of it from happening.

'Like I said, the flames can't actually burn you. That's the point of the blessings. They work as a kind of protective charm.'

'Well, I'll try and remember that when I'm next stuck in a bonfire,' Muriel retorted. 'From where I was standing, it looked like it hurt.'

'It did,' said Ingrid. It was the first she'd spoken all morning, and the words dragged like rusted steel. 'They don't burn you, but they don't let you get out unscathed, either.'

'So what's the point of it?'

'I don't know. Some kind of power play, maybe. *Look at how much we could hurt you, but we are merciful.*'

Magda didn't like the sound of that one bit. She couldn't argue, though, not while all the elements pointed in the same direction. A sacrifice; an honour; a mercy.

'It's not the only reason,' Catrin tried to reassure them. 'They said the ritual's supposed to represent purification, remember? Fire creates ash, and ash fertilises the land.'

Ingrid gave a scornful laugh. 'Tell that to the next Keeper of the Flame.'

'Is there anything we can do?' asked Muriel, carefully.

'It's fine. I'll live,' said Ingrid, stabbing a forkful of laverbread with murderous intent. 'But Ether Lorna won't, not if she ever tries that again.'

In the Old World, there had been a name for fire that didn't burn. *Ignis fatuus*: foolish fire. These flames, on the other hand, didn't sound foolish in the slightest.

They sounded lethal.

*

All morning Magda tried to focus, but the beginnings of a headache were gnawing at her temples. Ether Stefania's Ardracy lecture drew all the joy out of a topic she'd once been fond of, and it cost her the eyes in her head to even maintain a semblance of interest. What she really wanted to do was pick up the constellation sheet and send it sailing out the window.

'Did you get that?' Alarice nudged her, as they turned to a new set of maps on the following page. 'Look sharp, or she'll pick on you.'

'I'd look a lot sharper if she wasn't making it sound so dull,' Magda muttered.

But the last thing she wanted was to draw Ether Stefania's attention, so she leaned forwards to study the star charts. Tenebris, the Black Star, was a hidden jewel surrounded by five white dwarf stars. It was Muriel's favourite, and had been ever since they'd watched their first meteor shower one June. With it went an old rhetoric: *there is beauty in the things we cannot see.*

Now Magda couldn't stand to look at it.

'I'll be back in a minute,' she got up, while the others pored over intricate diagrams. The headache was getting worse, and a power nap might be just the thing for it. 'I, er ... I need to pick something up from the dorm room.'

'Okay,' shrugged Rhos. 'See you in Triolatry.'

Magda turned down the corridor to the North Quadrant and glanced up as a young Black woman swept past her. She had long crinkled hair and quick footsteps, and she wore the glittering cloak of an Ether.

'Got lost on the way to lessons, did you?'

'Oh.' Magda blushed, realising. 'Are you Ether Rhiannon?'

'The very same. I suppose it's my Triolatry class you were about to skive off?'

Sheepishly, she followed Ether Rhiannon back down the corridor. It was the first time she'd spoken face to face with the mysterious third Ether, and she would've given anything to have made a less clumsy first impression. She was hoping the others might not have sat down yet, so she could avoid causing an embarrassing fuss as she waded between desks to find a seat.

No such luck.

'Good afternoon, everyone,' Ether Rhiannon pushed open the door and stepped neatly into the classroom. She wore a skirt which was creased with knife-sharp pleats, and pendant earrings that shone with yellow opal. 'I trust the Ceremony hasn't left you too shaken to continue with your studies?'

A nervous ripple of laughter fluttered around the room.

'Well, I'm glad to see you all under happier circumstances. Miss Corrales, please take your seat.'

There were a couple of chuckles as Magda made her way across the room to join them, but they were mercifully short-lived. The chair scraped against the floor with a metallic *shriek*. At the very least, she was no longer the most conspicuous thing in the room.

Meanwhile, Ether Rhiannon wiped the last remnants of chalk from the blackboard, and began to etch new letters in their place. 'Triangulation,' she finished, stepping back from the lonely white syllables. 'Can anybody tell me what that means?'

Catrin stuck up her hand. 'It's a research method. You approach the subject from three different angles, to ensure the most accurate answers.'

'Very good,' Ether Rhiannon picked up a copy of the book that was laid out on each desk. 'There are many things which we cannot afford to get wrong. And if we can triangulate with research, then why should we not with history?'

Magda peered inside the cover of her own book. The pages were illustrated with different textiles, patterns, and designers: some brightly photographed, others sketched in black and white ink. Unfortunately, trying to pick apart the miniscule text only made her headache worse.

Inhale. Exhale. Breathe.

'This,' said Ether Rhiannon, 'is a material history. We either scrutinise each thread, or we allow others to pull the wool over our eyes. Let's begin with page 137.'

Magda scanned the first paragraph of the chapter. *A woman's cloak, circa 1940*, read the note. Beside it was a picture of a dark blue draped shawl. *Made from sheep's wool, woven at a mill in north-west Wales, and dyed with woad. Lined with sea silk or byssus, spun on a narrow loom, and trimmed with a beaded edge.*

'My first question for you, girls, is this. How many hours would you say went into making this cloak?'

A hush fell over the room. They considered the core and fancy yarns; the frogspawn-glimmer of beadwork; the narrow snare of its collar.

'Forty hours?'

'Sixty?'

'Over two hundred hours went into this piece,' replied Rhiannon. 'See here, at the trim. Those beads have been applied by hand. It's impossible to understate the care that has gone into this item, and the cloak was valued at a sum of six thousand plovers.'

'But who bought it?' asked Magda. 'I've never heard of a garment that expensive.'

'This is not your average high-street purchase,' said Ether Rhiannon, 'but in every piece of textiles there is hidden labour. On market day, many sellers will put buyers' demands above fair recognition of their employees' hard work.' She let the book fall shut. 'Which is why this cloak only sold for two thousand plovers in the end. A fraction of its real price.'

Magda looked back at the image: so delicate and faded. Who owned the cloak now? Did they wear it to fireside gatherings with friends, or out on horseback in midwinter? Did it gather dust in the back of someone's wardrobe, or had moths long since eaten it to pieces?

'If you are to succeed as artisans for the Brenin,' Rhiannon said sternly, 'promise me this. That you will never, ever undervalue your work.'

They turned to the next page, which was covered with intricate illustration. Magda followed the feather-green ink trail from one edge to the opposite corner.

Marram grass, read the entry. *A uniquely flexible fibre which was once collected by villagers to weave mats and fishing nets in Wales. The plant itself grows in sand dunes, where its root system helps keep the beach from eroding.*

Copying down notes was the easy part; ignoring the nagging headache was Magda's real challenge. She debated the wisdom of asking to be excused, but it seemed a shame to leave such an interesting class so early.

'Ether Rhiannon?' Alarice raised a hand. 'I read that Tarram Swamp had a new subspecies of marram grass growing there. Have you ever seen it?'

'Regrettably, I've never been to the further western provinces.'

'Oh.'

'That's not to say I don't have my favourite haunts this side of the Channel,' Rhiannon gave a quiet smile. 'I've a soft spot for the Spindle Isles. They're a marvellous breakwater, and you get all kinds of seagrasses in the reef. Purple laver, eelgrass, twisted wrack...'

Magda decided that she liked Ether Rhiannon. Like Ether Lorna, she spoke with precision and didn't cut corners. And unlike Ether Stefania, she appeared to regard the girls as people rather than test subjects.

By the time the class was over, she had learned more about marine ecology and plant dyes than there was room for in her notebook. It had unexpectedly taken the edge off an otherwise cutthroat morning, and she made a mental note to bring extra paper next time.

'Thank you for your hard work, everyone,' Ether Rhiannon smiled. She looked really, genuinely pleased. 'It's good to be back on Fallow ground. I'll look forward to seeing you all next week.'

*

That evening, Magda hoped it would be easy to disguise the redness in her cheeks. She hoped her bitten-down nails would go unnoticed, that the raw edges would be less stubborn, and she pleaded with whatever life force governed the Fallow for her eyes to look clearer than they had done earlier.

She'd told Muriel she wasn't hungry, when in reality she felt a hunger of vast proportions. She craved not for food, but for company. She longed for people who she could not see. There was only one thing for it — one way to kick her putrid hopes in the guts — and that was to go downstairs.

Downstairs it would be harder for her thoughts to linger where they weren't wanted, at the very least. Up here, they twisted themselves into a bandage that wrapped around an open wound, one that didn't bleed and didn't clot with pus.

Dad? Dad! Get up, please, get up.

She had seen sheep with flystrike, and knew the way those parasites tormented the flesh. They would crawl right beneath your skin, if you let them, and so she couldn't allow herself to think it. She refused to even entertain the possibility that her father had not recovered from his injuries. But in the corners of her day, the moments between real places, those fears came straggling back.

Ether Stefania's silhouette, and the sound of horse-hooves down the drive.

A darkening gash. Her father's arm torn open.

A hollow.

Enough was enough. Without bothering to pin back her hair, Magda trampled down the staircase, away from the swarm of terrible fear, and towards the dinner table where everybody else had already gathered.

'Corrales. We thought you'd never make it in time.'

Seven pairs of eyes grazed her skin. They seemed to pierce the fabric covering her shoulders, seeing all the way through to her ribcage and the ragged heart that was pulsing underneath it.

She pulled out the chair, forcing a smile. 'I had a change of heart.'

'Well, tuck in.'

She was grateful when the others returned to their conversation, something light and pretty that eluded her entirely. A cloud passed the window. Some small bird pecked outside the glass. These things she could count, one by one, as they congealed into the soupy violet night.

'Ingrid's okay, you know?' Muriel glanced over, picking at her food. 'The Ceremony, the fire, all of that ... it didn't do her any physical harm. It can't harm you, either.'

'I know.' Magda pushed uselessly at a piece of potato on the plate. It had been boiled so long it was soft and saltless, but she couldn't eat. 'It's not that. I don't know what's the matter with me right now. Everything just feels wrong.'

'Do you want to talk about it? If it's more nightmares, or visions, or —'

'I don't want to discuss it.'

Muriel looked hurt, but it wasn't enough to make Magda regret the words. She was not always the person she'd have liked to have been. As they ate the rest of their dinner, she felt herself sinking closer to the other thing that had been worrying her all day.

The wolfish creature at the edge of the woods.

It was still lurking in her memory. Every time she thought she'd forgotten, it edged closer, those piercing eyes burning red in the dark.

Chapter 24

Green Wednesday

Somewhere between the shades of dawn, Muriel woke up angry. She hated feeling this way, and hated that she was not able to control the feeling. Why did her body have to choose such stupid times to get like this?

All because Magda had stopped talking to her.

She would get over it, in the end. She knew this because she had gotten over it before: in fact, it was to imagine a worse situation than the one they'd been in on that first day. A stilted carriage rattling through poisoned woodland, utterly alone, with nothing homely but the quilt in her arms. There had been no shred of closure for them; nothing to grasp onto, and she suspected the same doubts troubled Magda often enough. But they didn't talk about it. The most vulnerable conversation they'd had was about Grimoire Malgarty's warnings, which had been necessary, but which had also opened a new can of worms altogether.

Now they had to play the charade of fitting in here. Since their arrival it had been a cartwheel through meeting all the other girls, avoiding Ether Stefania's attention, and keeping their own cards close to their chest. The weight of the effort was crushing. And none of it felt quite true, either: because where was the call of the herring-gulls that meant hometime? Where was the slanting road up the hill, and the sound of the biscuit tin after school? Where were all the things that had used to mean home?

In spite of her best efforts, Muriel resented what had happened in Wildbriar. *She* wasn't the one who had made a mistake. She hadn't gone into the woods and caused some calamity, and if Magda would only talk to her, she'd probably find out it hadn't been Magda's fault, either.

In the meantime, she was fighting the urge to ask questions.

Since crying was a waste of energy, one which would be better directed towards making a hot drink, Muriel went downstairs to the cupboard of tins and powders. There was a little kitchenette below the dormitory, although nobody used it much. It had coffee, which sometimes helped, but she eventually found the label she was looking for.

Siocled poeth.

Pouring out a cup, Muriel breathed in a lungful of steam and tried to gather her thoughts. Hot liquids would suffice, although what she would really have liked was a hot bath. They only had miserable showers here, whereas her old house had had a great big tub where you could swim for hours on end. She wondered if maybe baths were something else that was magical, and therefore outlawed, or what Grimoire Malgarty would have to say about that.

The thought of the mysterious woman had been playing on her mind more often, these days. Did she still go to visit Wildbriar? Did she still keep her grimalkins, and offer strange but ominous warnings to girls who weren't even old enough to understand yet? She'd once hoped that not thinking it, not talking about their magic, would make it go away. But slowly, surely, it had found its way back to them. It was a hand-me-down that nobody wanted; a too-big cardigan that neither girl knew how to fit.

But that was a worry for another day. Fishing behind the kettle for the tin where biscuits were kept, Muriel managed to retrieve a slice of day-old tiffin. The crunch of chocolate and glossy ledge of pecans were a far cry from the deep, glittering sourness clenched around her heart, and she watched the quiet minutes tick away.

Another day, they would figure out how to handle their forbidden powers. But not right now. Chocolate in hand, Muriel crept back to bed. It was almost six o'clock in the morning.

*

'Did you get the invitation?' asked Rhos, in the bright sunlight of a green Wednesday.

'What invitation?'

The three of them were walking down the corridor, having spent the morning sewing gloves for the southern market towns. The grain of the crushed pile had stayed on Muriel's hands. That was the thing: velvet never sewed the way people expected it to. Even when you cut it, there was none of the smooth, slinky sound you expected; instead it sounded grainy, like chalk or sand.

'Catrin's seventeenth,' Rhos reminded her. 'The party's next Friday.'

'That's a burgundy day,' replied Muriel, without thinking. Monday was blue; Tuesday was red; Wednesday was grass-green. It had always been that way, since Muriel could remember, because of the dark emerald 'e's. 'Who's going?'

'Everyone, probably. It's set to be the event of the year.'

Muriel contemplated the invitation. Did alligators usually invite fish to their social gatherings?

'I'll think about it,' she decided.

'Don't worry, you'll enjoy it,' Alarice smiled. 'And so will I, as soon as I've managed to find an outfit.'

Muriel cringed internally at the thought of her meagre wardrobe, with its selection of garments from Wildbriar. There was nothing in it that could possibly pass for a party dress, and she thought longingly of the velvet from their earlier class. 'I wish she'd told us sooner.'

Right at that moment, the door swung open behind them. It was Catrin, looking uncharacteristically awkward and out of place.

'Scurlock. I thought you and the others were going to Ardracy,' Alarice turned to face her. 'We were going to catch you up!'

'It got cancelled. Stefania's on urgent business in Helygen.'

'What happened?' asked Muriel, concerned. 'Are you okay?'

The blonde girl's eyes were red and raw. Even worse, her face looked both irritated *and* inflamed: two conditions which she'd sworn to avoid at all costs. She glared straight past Muriel.

'Alarice, have you still got that Telling-stone?'

'No. We threw it out, remember?' Alarice frowned. 'What's wrong?'

'It's —' Catrin hesitated. 'It's nothing.'

From the corner of one eye, Muriel could see a shred of paper tucked into the girl's front pocket. It was scrawled with writing, although the ink was blurry in places.

'If there's nothing better to do this morning, maybe we can help you to get ready for your party?' said Muriel, hoping to dispel the simmering tension. 'It sounds like quite the event.'

'Yeah,' Rhos nodded her agreement. 'We can help you get stuff organised. Music. Decorations.'

Catrin's expression seemed to soften a little.

'You mean ... you'll all come?'

'Of course we will.'

*

With the passing of the morning, things moved slowly back towards the normal. Catrin carried herself with her usual grace, Rhos had found the latest shred of gossip to dissect, and Alarice smoothed over a dozen almost-arguments with a handful of choice words. Yet the uneasy feeling in Muriel's gut did not shift. She hadn't seen Magda anywhere, and didn't trust herself to look too closely. If anything, there was a crack in the porcelain that was holding the Fallow together.

'This would be a perfect night for ghosts,' sighed Rhos, putting down the string of fairy lights that she'd hung from the rafters. Each one glowed with soft bioelectricity, pulsing a faint greenish glimmer. 'I wish one would come and visit us.'

'Me, too,' Ingrid nodded sagely. 'Ghosts don't give you any of the stupid crap you get from people.'

'Like what?'

'Well, like loads of things. Have you ever met a ghost who's tried to make small talk? Or who's wanted to share your chips?'

'If it was bothering you, you could've just said,' Rhos muttered, and went back to decorating the side of the cove. 'How long have we got til next class?'

Muriel looked at the clock. 'Maybe half an hour.'

'Lucky that Stefania cancelled when she did. We'd have had no chance to get this sorted otherwise!'

It was certainly a relief to have avoided another earful in Ardracy. But what Muriel couldn't help but wonder was why there was such an erratic schedule in the first place. What could possibly be so serious that Ether Stefania needed to go riding down to the capital? Couldn't the Brenin just send a pigeon, or was he above such correspondence?

'Those banners look like overkill,' Alarice cast a discerning eye over a set of silver streamers that were covering the doorway.

'They're elegant,' Catrin retorted. 'It's my party, anyway.'

'Fine, fine. But don't blame me when someone gets tangled up in them.'

Muriel laughed. The unfinished silver banners reminded her of a spider's web, and she imagined Catrin hovering at the centre: the most glamorous spider of them all.

'What's so funny, Silvana?'

'Er… Nothing!'

'Go on, tell us the story.'

For a moment, Muriel was tempted. She loved stories, and could have told a good one, but it felt wrong to enjoy herself too much without Magda.

'I was just thinking about something back home,' she lied. 'Don't worry.'

'Oh, but now you've got to tell us!'

It couldn't hurt, could it? Just a little tale. Nothing grand or serious.

'Fine,' she relented. 'It was a foggy night, and the snow was thick on the ground. There was this spiderweb over the gate, you know when they get all frozen and craggy?'

'Right.'

'And at the very centre, was this big golden spider.'

Rhos looked intrigued. 'Did you give it a name?'

'I should've done, now you mention it. You know who it reminded me of?'

Behind her, she could hear Alarice beginning to chuckle.

'Brilliant story,' Catrin rolled her eyes. 'Got any tales where I'm *not* the butt of the joke?'

So she gave in. Stories with no place to go made holes in your heart, and over the passing weeks there had been no one to listen to Muriel's ramblings. Isa and Lucía and all her friends from school were far, far away. Magda was nowhere to be found. And Plover, who knew her stories best of all, was lamentably absent.

First she told them the Legend of the Missing Cakes. It had been her mother's story first, and the other girls listened in good spirit. A smattering of mirth broke out at the end, as the platter of stolen rock cakes was returned to its rightful owner.

Next she told the Tale of the Broken-down Tractor. That one had been Isa's favourite, but there was a certain thrill to telling it alone, now. Both her elder siblings were both natural storytellers: everybody fell under their spell so easily, like falling into deep water.

This time it was Muriel in the spotlight, alone and shimmering.

The third and final story she told was a new one altogether. She didn't mean to choose it, or perhaps the story had chosen her, but it came unravelling thicker and faster than a bundle of roving. There was smoke in the air, a ramshackle library at the town's edge. It was an image that had been burned into their minds from a young age: because everybody knew what happened to the girls who strayed outside after dark.

'The old women back in Arianydd used to frighten us with those tales,' said Ingrid, quietly. 'They always said they knew a girl who'd burned to death there.'

Rhos looked deeply unsettled. 'It happened to one of the girls at my school. Lucie Trellis.'

'You saw it?'

'I never did. But everybody heard about the fire. It was like a great red beast with too many tongues. They never did find her body.'

There had been no shortage of horror stories, floating from school to school, which was enough to deter all but the most stubborn rebels. But even the handful of disbelievers didn't dare put the theory to the test.

'The abandoned library,' said Alarice, returning to Muriel's story. 'Was it true? Could you really get there just by skirting a few fields?'

Before Muriel could answer, there was another voice behind her.

'Yes. I wouldn't recommend it, though, unless you fancy risking your neck crossing a ditch or two.'

Muriel turned around, mortified. She hadn't even heard the latch swing open. 'Magda. I didn't mean to ...'

'It's Weftwork in five minutes,' replied the other girl. 'We'll all be late if we don't get over there soon.'

The conversation faltered after that. It was as if they were all guilty of a nameless crime, leaving the room and leaving the story behind like a slain beast. Muriel couldn't believe she'd been so stupid as to let her guard down. Making assumptions about her friend's whereabouts. What must Magda be thinking now, seeing her swanning around like that?

That she didn't care, or didn't want to know. But she had done this to herself, hadn't she? The feelings tangled, nebulous and impossible to convert into words that could make things better.

You're the valiant one, the trustworthy one.

I said I don't want to discuss it.

Oh, Magda. We tried our best to keep you safe.

Chapter 25

Cyanotype Girl

It was late when there was a knock at the door of Dormitory Eight. Alarice was still awake, burning the midnight oil with her trusty sketchbook, but she was surprised to find Catrin still up. The girl had been in a whirlwind mood today, swinging so quickly from happy-go-lucky to dejected, that Alarice didn't know what to make of it.

'Sorry,' said Catrin. 'The crow didn't come back til later than I expected.'

'Did somebody die?' Alarice returned to the canvas where she'd been painting lilies-of-the-valley. 'I don't know what's going on, Cat, but you seem upset.'

'It's hardly anything life-threatening. It's just ... Foxe said something than made me feel, I don't know, angry. Maybe I should stop opening all the letters.'

Just as she'd expected. Alarice set down the paintbrush, contemplating the ethics of sending a minor hex via carrier-pigeon.

'Should we be plotting ways to make him suffer?'

'He's probably suffering enough already, what with the Sickness out there.' Catrin's eyes darted back to the letter in her hand, doubtful. 'Anyway. It doesn't really matter, when all's said and done. At least we're still friends.'

She tucked the letter into her bedside drawer. Though Catrin insisted there was nothing between her and Foxe, Alarice had her suspicions. Was it wise, she wondered, to feel so deeply for someone who you couldn't see? She infinitely preferred the letters she got from her friends back in the Wolds, full of city gossip and the latest scandals.

'You know what we should do?' Alarice raised one eyebrow. 'Cyanotypes.'

'But it's nearly midnight.'

'And? We can use the sunlamps to cure the solution.'

'Alright,' Catrin looked hopeful. 'I'll get the boxes.'

As they turned on the lowlights and got out the painting equipment, Alarice hummed a fragment of a song under her breath. It was an old favourite, *Cyanotype Girl* by Julia Saez. In her opinion, the world would be a better place if there was more Julia Saez in it.

Oh, I'm so blue
Like a cyanotype girl
Waiting here til nightfall
Hiding from the sun

'Please,' Catrin made a face, as they unfurled a spare bolt of linen. 'My ears.'

'As if you're the world's finest singer!'

Once the fabric was laid out and the solution prepared, Alarice took a paintbrush and placed a stencil over the corner of the canvas.

'That looks about right. Ready?'

Art of one of the reasons why they'd become friends in the first place. *Painting's like an exhalation*, Catrin had said once. *Something you have to get out of your system, whether you want to or not.*

Alarice agreed. When she was alone with her paints, most worries shifted into blissful oblivion. They painted and painted until the fabric was covered with blue, and fine, mossy white tendrils.

'This must have been what it looked like during the Year of the Eternal Storm,' Catrin peered outside, where rain was battering the windows with silver. 'No sun, no light. Just rain after rain.'

'An endless tide.'

'Weird, isn't it.' Catrin dipped the brush back into the pungent-smelling liquid, painting another panel of white fabric. 'That there was always magic, even in the Old World. But it took the seas rising up and a great flood for it to wash over the land again.'

The term *Tidal Folk*, after all, came from the ocean. It was widely believed that the magic had flooded Wales again because of the water that rose up and swamped the lands, before the New World emerged. Not everywhere had survived the flood: the low-lying country to their east, which they called the Sunken Isles, had been entirely submerged. The rains had also destroyed most Old-World technology, leaving only the waterlogged remnants floating at sea.

This was the place where the New Worlders had built their homes.

*

Several hours later, by the time the sheets were hung and dried, and Alarice's skin was stained with the sour-smelling chemicals, she stepped out into the corridor to get some water from downstairs. She hoped none of the dye had gotten onto her skirt — but maybe if she sped up, it would be possible wash it out.

That was when she bumped into Muriel Silvana.

'Sorry, I didn't see you there,' spluttered the bright-eyed girl, visibly out of breath. Her hair fell in a loose plait down her back, but there was none of her usual poise. 'I... I don't know what to do.'

'What's wrong?'

Muriel bit her lip. 'Can you come with me? It's Magda. She's in a bad way.'

***

Three summers ago, Magda had been watching dandelion clocks blow over the coast of Abergwyll, out towards the west.

It was a school trip. They'd brought brown paper bags containing squeaky cheese sandwiches, they'd learned about the fallen pre-Rift architecture that had once covered the valleys of the North, and at the end of the day Mrs Sachar had uttered the angelic words 'it's time to visit the bakery'. Many things had been lost when the Old World fell, but people's fondness for hot, crispy baked goods was not one of them.

Do you think they have secret recipes here? Muriel had asked, her mouth full of bara brith. *Those dulce de leche pancakes looked amazing.*

Not as good as your dad's. Did you get anything from the gift shop?

The last tin. Isa's going to be so happy.

That memory now belonged to another world altogether. It was one that Magda wanted to inhabit so badly, it hurt. Because in that world, no one had been taken from her.

This world had pitched a wound clean through her chest.

'Mags?' Muriel had asked her, after they'd turned out the lights in the dorm room. 'Is something wrong?'

She had pulled her knees into her chest, worrying at the thought like a loose tooth. There was nothing to say. Nothing she could say. 'Cold, isn't it.'

'Yeah, I suppose so,' Muriel was perched awkwardly on the end of her bed. 'But you seemed quiet, and sort of ... upset. Sorry if I've got it all wrong, but it just seemed like ...'

'Honestly, it's nothing. I wasn't trying to avoid you, I just needed some time.'

'Time for what?'

She couldn't answer. Muriel was right; things *had* been weird lately. It felt like the control dial on her emotions was in perpetual flux.

'I needed time to figure out what in Gwern's name we're doing here. I don't even know what we *should* be doing.' She took a deep breath, trying not to let her voice crack. 'It feels like all the right answers have gone out the window.'

'It's been a lot for me, too. I don't want you to feel like you're alone in this.'

'I know.'

Then there was a gentle hand on Magda's shoulder. She didn't mean to flinch, but by then it was too late.

'Sorry.'

With a slightly hurt look, Muriel drew back.

'If there's anything I can do, just tell me. I can try and fix it, or I can —'

'Yes, I understand,' Magda cut her off, hating how terse she sounded. 'And I appreciate your concern. But I think it's best if I handle this myself.'

An almost imperceptible shift swept through Muriel's expression. 'Okay. I'll leave you to it.'

Magda watched her friend draw further away. The damage was done; she knew she should let her go to sleep. But a small part of her, one that was spiteful, spoke first.

'By the way, you don't need to look at me like that.'

'Like what?'

'Like I'm in need of pity.'

The second the words were out, she knew it had been the wrong thing to say.

'Is trying to be a good friend such a bad thing?' Muriel's voice was quiet, dangerous. 'Goodnight. I'll see you in the morning.'

The cruel part of Magda thrilled at the reaction, even though it was far from what she wanted. *More hurt. More venom*, it seemed to urge her.

Muriel was at the door now, pulling down the fleecy dressing gown from its hook.

'I'm sorry,' Magda called after her, too late. 'I didn't mean it.'

The sound of footsteps paused.

Then she felt the blinding flash of pain in her head. The ground came crashing towards her, white-hot and blurry. Suddenly images were racing like ash before her eyes: a starless sky, a fur cloak, a pair of white hands against the earth –

'Magda?'

She needed to slow down. Things were moving too fast, but her legs felt strangely fuzzy. It all felt like something bad had –

'Magda, can you hear me?'

Yes. Yes, she could hear her perfectly well; it was her damn *vision* that was the problem. This wasn't the first time something strange had happened without warning. But it was worse than she was used to, and right now she felt paralysed by the echoing heat of her blood.

'Magda, I'm going to get help,' said Muriel, somewhere far away. 'I'll be back, I promise I'll be fast –'

Help? What did that mean? Not one of the Ethers, surely? Magda clutched her temple as another wave of pain rolled through it. Things weren't making sense, and she needed her mother and she needed her father and she needed people who weren't there, who weren't –

'Magda.'

She blinked. How much time had passed? Muriel was back, thank the Weaver, this time with the slender girl called Alarice. Magda tried to reach towards them, but only indistinct voices seemed to hover above her.

'Has this happened before?'

Another voice surfaced, shapeless as water. 'Not like this.'

Just moments ago, Magda had felt like all she wanted was to be alone. Now she wanted to collapse into somebody else's arms. Someone, anyone, to drag her out of the nightmare that was clawing at the edges of her vision –

'Magda, what can you see in front of you?'

The clear voice cut through the edges of her failing vision, and she clung to it. *The window ledge. The cool wooden floor. A hollow moon.* She clung to the girl's voice.

'Can you name three of them?'

Slowly, Magda's thoughts became words again. Her head hurt, but at least she could think clearly. Even if it stung to look into the brightness of the hallway, the rush of cold air, the shadows it cast.

'Tell me what you can hear.'

The birds. The sound of footsteps in the corridors. And something else, a young girl's voice over running water.

It took a long time for the dull ache to subside, for her limbs to feel normal again. Little by little, the pieces of her were settling back into place. She didn't understand the spectral illusion she'd just seen, or what it had meant; all she knew was she was out of it now.

From the look on Alarice's face, they had some explaining to do.

*

'I get these ... visions, sometimes,' Magda began. They were sitting coldly in the dorm room. It didn't feel like much of a weekend any more. 'They're not exactly dreams. But it's not quite reality, either.'

She waited for the other girl to laugh, or screw up her nose in disgust, but Alarice's expression had barely changed. One eyebrow was raised slightly, and her soft brown hands were crossed over her lap. 'Are they a regular occurrence?'

'It happened to me earlier this week. The other night, just before the Ceremony.' Magda paused, wondering how they'd managed to go through with that awful ritual and then proceed as if nothing had happened. It had blindsided them both, leaving no time for grieving. 'During that vision, I saw a building in the woods. It reminded me a bit of the old library near Wildbriar. The eaves, the roof, even the shape of the chimney was the same.'

Muriel's expression shifted. 'You never told me that.'

Not even Magda was sure of the reason why. She wrung her hands together, thinking of the fearsome vision. She'd tried to forget all about it. Yet the wolfish silhouette of the gwyllgi had been stalking her for days.

'I didn't ... I guess I didn't want to think that any of it was real.'

'At least it's only a building,' said Alarice, not quite convincingly. 'I can think of much worse things to have found there.'

'There was something else, too. Something alive — an animal, with big red eyes. I think it was a gwyllgi.'

At that, Alarice fell into a contemplative silence. It was possible that she didn't believe a word of it. Or maybe she already knew about visionaries, and had drawn her own conclusions about that kind of magic. Would she alert the other girls? Or worse, the Ethers themselves?

'You can't let them find out,' Magda said quickly, sounding far too desperate for her liking. 'We might be in danger. Well, more danger than we're already —'

'I wasn't going to,' said Alarice, flatly. 'So you're saying you saw some kind of apparition. A prophecy, right?'

Magda shot Muriel a sideways glance. Did they throw caution to the wind and explain the whole chronicle? Or was this straying into dangerous territory?

Tell her, said her friend's expression. *We can't keep this a secret any longer.*

'It was a prophecy,' Magda nodded. 'You see, the reason Muriel and I came to the Fallow is a bit ... complicated. We used to live further north, but one day a physician came to our school. Except, she said we had the makings of, well —'

'For scrim's sake, Mags, get to the point.'

'Okay, okay.' The words danced like hot coals on her tongue. 'A physician named Grimoire Malgarty came to assess our aptitudes. She told me that I was a visionary.'

'And that I'm a veridian,' said Muriel. Her cheeks were tinged with pink, as if she couldn't believe what they'd just admitted out loud. 'I'm sorry for, um, springing this on you.'

They waited for Alarice to screw up her face in disgust, horror, or run for the hills. That was what would happen; what *had* to happen, because there was no possible response to this news that could be good.

But instead she gave a thoughtful nod.

'That means the Telling-stone was right. It told us to seek a house beyond the woods, remember? And that's what you saw.'

No recoil.

No immediate repulsion.

'You're not surprised,' said Magda, unable to think of a suitable response.

'Sorry, was I supposed to act shocked?' Alarice cocked an eyebrow. 'I think we've all seen and heard far worse.'

Nobody asked what those things were. The implicit quiet was a knowing in itself, the knowing of where to carefully draw a conversation closed. Stepping over the invisible chalk line was a foot into no one's grave.

'So ... the stone.' Magda thought hard. 'You think it gave a true Telling.'

'It's not impossible.'

'Shame we left it out in the orchard, then. It could've been useful.'

'But in the meantime,' said Alarice, 'we've got you. If you're a visionary, we've your dreams are the real deal.'

'Well, yes, I suppose. But it's not something I can exactly control.'

Outside, the rain was humming a new tune. Muriel pulled at a loose strand of her fluffy green jumper. 'Either way, it'd be good to go and get the Stone back. What if one of the Ethers finds it?'

Magda hadn't thought of that. She didn't like to imagine such an artefact falling into the wrong hands.

'It's a good idea,' Alarice agreed. 'And besides,' she nodded to Magda. 'we've got no guarantee of how often you'll be having visions. For your own sake, I hope it won't be frequent.'

'How about I go and look tomorrow evening, while everyone's at dinner?' Magda suggested. 'That way the Ethers'll be distracted while I search the orchard.'

'Are you sure you want to go alone?'

'Positive.'

Muriel shook her head. 'I wish you'd show some instinct of self-preservation.'

'No risk, no reward,' Magda attempted a smile. The quagmire of the night was slowly drifting clear, and she was relieved to be in calmer waters once more. Things weren't quite back to normal yet, whatever that meant. But it was closer than she'd felt in days.

'If you need help, just say.'

'And if you can find the Stone, maybe we could ask it some questions about both your magic,' said Alarice. 'I know a little bit about visionaries. But I wish we knew more about *your* condition, Muriel. Back in the Wolds, they treated veridians as more of a local legend than reality.'

'Well, what can I say. I'm just a miracle of nature.'

At least that elicited a laugh. Nonetheless, Magda hadn't completely set aside the thought of her visions, and what the next one might hold. After she got the Telling-Stone, there was another business she had to attend to. And if she succeeded on that front, then maybe they'd get some of the answers they really needed.

Chapter 26
The Deathlies

'And where exactly have you been?' Ether Stefania's face had turned an interesting shade of puce. 'This kind of behaviour is an embarrassment to our institution. If you keep it up, you'll never be selected for Progression.'

'Sorry. It won't happen again.'

In return for their lateness to her nine o'clock class, Magda, Muriel, and Alarice were placed on sweeping duties in the sewing rooms. Of course they all made an effort *not* to look as tired as dogs, but being up half the night had taken its toll. Secretly, Magda was relieved. While sweeping was an unpalatable task, it was infinitely preferable to attending class.

A series of inquisitive looks met them when it was time for mid-morning break in the common room.

'Where were you guys earlier?'

'Overslept.'

'A complete accident, I'm sure,' Ingrid gave an approving nod. 'I've got to give it to you, you're craftier than the last girls. It was months before Lissa and Shay could even look old Steffie in the eye.'

'Hey, leave them alone,' Rhos nudged her. 'They were nice girls. *And* they had an interest in the natural sciences, unlike some people.'

'By the alder, Rhos! The less interest in nature, the better. You'd better not bring home any more creepy crawlies from the orchard.'

'Norbert is a hexapod invertebrate, actually.' Rhos's chin was tilted up in defiance. 'And the only animals I found this afternoon were fireflies. They were far too flighty to bring home, unfortunately.'

'Where on earth did you see those?'

'Just beyond the north fields. I thought I'd go back tonight to see them after dark, if anybody wanted to come with me.'

'Sorry, we can't.' Muriel hung her head. 'We're on sweeping duties. Stefania says the South sewing rooms need tidying.'

'Oh, okay. Maybe next time.'

Nobody doubted that Rhos would have found a new menagerie of animals by whenever *next time* came around. But for now, the afternoon stretched ominously before them. It was possible that Magda might have dragged her heels on the way to Ardracy. She felt just a teensy bit sorry for herself, and it looked like it was going to be a long one.

*

'Bwgan magic,' Ether Stefania gestured towards the ceiling of jewelled stone, as if the answer was hiding there. 'Mortal arts. Rhithcraft. There are many names for what we are going to discuss today, but you may refer to them in shorthand as *The Deathlies*. Dead, dying, or dead: that's what these Folk deal in.'

It sounded suitably jolly for Stefania's liking, and Muriel unfolded her textbook to take notes. Some of the corners were stuck together with a thick unctuous liquid; others tarred with scorch marks. She decided not to question the stains. She wasn't sure she wanted to know what — or who — had put them there.

'Can anybody tell me what gifts an arvaress might possess?' Stefania paced forwards, her haunted eyes following each girl around the room. 'No one?'

Catrin stuck up her hand.

'The power to raise the dead.'

'Correct, Miss Scurlock. Legend has it that these individuals can imbue the unworldly with new life, through the touch of their hand. Many centuries ago, their powers were highly sought after by the bereaved. A skilled arvaress might have made a tidy living from her arts.'

Magda paused, her pen in mid-motion where she'd been taking notes. 'You mean they could make someone immortal?'

'Not exactly,' replied Ether Stefania. 'There is always a price to pay.'

With a soft and unceremonious *plonk*, she began to place magnifying glasses on each of their desks. The metal handle tapered in the shape of a lizard's tail, with the bronze lizard perched on top of the bronze rim. It wore a grin as smug as buttered bread.

'If you turn to Chapter Seventeen, you'll find a copy of some miniature engravings,' the pale woman flicked through the pages. 'One way in which an arvaress may draw her power is through metalwork. A ruby engraving, or a stamped piece of gold. Whatever is needed to temper a soul.'

From the front of the room, Alarice put up her hand.

'If they could really bring someone back, what would happen to that person? Would they know that they'd been dead?'

'No. But others would perceive it.'

'Why?'

Because the horror is exquisite,' Stefania set down the book, as if she was contemplating something soft and deadly. 'Because those souls are never the same, afterwards. Only the desperate would seek an arvaress; only the wretched return. They weigh no more than an ounce of sugar, and they sing with the loveliest venom.'

The room settled into uncomfortable silence. Magda didn't think she had ever seen such a thing, and she most fervently hoped she never would.

'Please begin with paragraph sixteen, ladies. I'll be right back in a moment.'

There was a solid click of the door. A few girls began to leaf through the pages with gusto, while others looked like they'd been put off their dinner.

'Cheerful stuff, isn't it.'

Among the dozens of miniature designs were tiny skulls, leering out at them with hollow eyes, tastefully circled with miniature blood droplets and various anatomical organs. Muriel decided that the one she liked best was a skeleton holding an umbrella, even if the still-rotting flesh was peeling from her face.

'Lovely,' Alarice shook her head. 'This looks like something you'd see in the death metal corner of the record shop.'

'You think she's a fan?'

'It wouldn't surprise me. Frankly, I don't see how anyone can teach Ardracy without developing a taste for death.'

By the time their guardian returned, they'd long since finished the readings and had begun doodling designs of their own in the corners of the pages. The door clattered open with a jarring *clang*.

'Thank you for your patience, ladies.' Ether Stefania hurried into the room, pulling open a drawer in the front desk and shoving in a pile of papers. 'It's a pity there isn't more time for us to discuss the other variants of the mortal arts today. It would be remiss of me not to mention such Folk as greylags, scarps, and ...'

'Shades,' said Rhos, her voice a fraction colder. 'An unlucky kind of magic, don't you think?'

'Quite the contrary. A shade's power is true and terrible, for she may bestow the touch of death upon any living creature.'

'Yes. A pitiful power indeed.'

Something in Rhos's eyes made Magda think of the gutted house all those years ago, of the Skelbrights and the implacable sense of loss, even though nothing had been taken.

*

It was late in the sewing rooms and yarns flew across the room. The afternoon had been unpleasant, whereas tonight's chores required mercifully little concentration. It was hot, airless work sweeping stray threads from under the desks: soon Muriel found her elbows were covered with harlequin filaments, jade and copper tangling together.

'Mags, I need to sweep down there. Will you budge over?'

'Hang on. You'll have to wait a minute.'

Meanwhile, Alarice was clawing at the fine moss of wool fibres that had coated her knees. 'Urgh. It's like a dog moulted down here!'

Muriel hid a smile. The tightly-crimped protein fibres were long and unwieldy, and faintly reminiscent of the silvery fur which had always trailed in Plover's wake. They went on sweeping for another twenty minutes, before a wicked idea came to her.

'Hey. How about we say ten more minutes and we're done?'

Alarice paused. 'You don't think she'll come back to check?'

'If she's that bothered, she can finish it herself.'

Magda, who had hefted her bucket out from under the desk, looked all too eager to agree. 'Sounds like a plan.'

With a final unceremonious *wrelch*, the three of them gathered up the brooms and brushes, dumping the contents of the buckets into one thick carrier bag. An impressive array of coloured threads was gathered there, like the nest of some kaleidoscopic bird.

'Who knew threads could be such a nightmare,' muttered Alarice, stooping under the desk to retrieve her cardigan. 'Too many of the damned things.'

Muriel paused to catch her breath. There were things they'd left unsaid last night, and she didn't like to leave them. 'Alarice ... I'm sorry we dragged you into this. I didn't mean for you to get caught up in all this mess, you know.'

'Oh, don't worry about it.'

'Are you sure it's alright?'

Magda hadn't spoken. A troubled expression crossed her face, like she was watching a bank of storm clouds rolling over the horizon.

'It could have happened to any of us,' said Alarice, getting to her feet. 'And it can't be easy being a veridian, or a visionary. Anyone would struggle with having a power that they couldn't control. I'm glad you felt like you could tell me.'

'Thank you. That ... that means a lot.'

'Yeah. Thanks.' Magda's voice was strained. 'I think we should get going, now. Before anyone comes by to check.'

Alarice gave a nod. 'Fine by me.'

Chapter 27
The Sunlight Zone

From the highest bunk bed in Dormitory Six, Ingrid Leyshon was sitting cross-legged on the mattress and contemplating the tree-lined view from her window. One of the peculiar pains of being an older sister was having to watch every hurt you'd ever gone through, approaching like a loose wagon, and trying your hardest to stop it in its tracks.

Knowing it would shatter over you. Knowing you'd get hurt in the process.

But that you'd try anyway.

Months ago she'd watched that wagon come straight at her little brother, and it had left a bruise. Worse was knowing that she couldn't be there to help any more. There was no justice in it, but coming to the Fallow was her only way of keeping Tomren safe.

She would do the same again, and again, and again if it came to it.

'What are you reading?' asked Rhos, from the opposite side of the room.

'Oh. Just some old papers.'

We miss you, Ingie. Will you be home by Invernal?

She folded the letter away quickly and tucked it back into her bedside drawer. 'Let's see that dress, anyway. I didn't come here to watch moths all night.'

'But they're pretty,' Rhos protested, setting down the jar of lace-moths that she'd caught earlier in the day. 'I've decided to name this one Leopold.'

'Where did you even get them?'

'Down by the patch of scarlet pimpernel. Muriel told me where to look,' smiled the red-haired girl. 'She said to avoid the cowslips, though. They're poisonous.'

'She seems to know a lot about that stuff.'

'It's probably because her mum kept a book about useful plants. She said she's got the thing memorised, including which ones to avoid. It even had a bunch of recipes at the back — nettle soup, laverbread, the lot.'

'Well, I wish she'd brought it with her.'

The food at the Fallow was tolerable, but not excellent. Perhaps the thing that kept most girls from using the little kitchenette was the resignation of it. Ingrid could have cooked perfectly well if she'd wanted to; it just didn't feel the same this far from home. She tried her hand at the occasional dessert. But there was no neighbourhood cat to poke his head through the big window, or prowl over the recipe book as they fended off pawprints on the window sill.

Rhos, too, seemed more pensive than usual. 'I can't believe it's been a whole season since I left Caer Madoc. Do you think the snow finches will still be by the harbour? I hope Dad hasn't forgotten to feed them.'

'The finches'll still be down south,' Ingrid reassured her. 'I doubt they'll fly back until it starts to get warmer.'

Unlike the snow finches, who could take wing and shelter from the hardest frosts, summer seemed far away from the girls at the Fallow. If happiness was like sunlight, filtered carefully through the layers of ocean, Ingrid's old home had been basking in pelagic waters.

The Fallow felt like the depths of the benthic zone.

Suddenly, there was a sound of hangers clanking and the soft *thwump* of clothes landing on the dormitory floor. She sat up, staring in disbelief at where her roommate had begun to rifle through the wardrobe.

'Merrick, what's gotten into you?'

'It's okay, I've almost found it!' called Rhos, disappearing between a bunch of old coats. 'Give me a minute.'

The wardrobe began to quake as the hangers clanked together. It looked possessed.

'I can't see a thing.'

'Don't worry, I've got it now!'

With a final *yank*, Rhos pulled out a ruby-coloured dress with a floating asymmetric hem. The silk had been fluted to create a thin ripple, which reminded her of seaweed. 'What do you think?'

Ingrid gave an approving nod. It was an elegant choice for Catrin's party, and suited Rhos down to the ground. 'Some red gloves and shoes to match, and you'll be on your way.'

'Well, I'll certainly try my best.'

Her roommate was one of the few people who Ingrid would trust with choosing an outfit. Nonetheless, she had been trying to delay any discussion of the party for as long as possible.

'You still haven't chosen an outfit, have you?'

Ingrid glanced away. 'It's not until next Friday.'

'Better get your skates on, then.'

It was no secret that Rhos was the more extroverted of the pair. Mostly that was a good thing, but this time there was a niggling feeling of suspicion, one that made Ingrid wary at parties. People who became *merry* soon lost their filter. And when people got sloppy, they asked all kinds of questions that had no business being answered.

When she glanced back, Rhos was turning circles in the mirror: blissful and ignorant. 'I'm so excited. Wait til I show the girls next door!'

Groaning, Ingrid laid back on the bed and stared up to the ceiling. Although she wanted to like the new girls, Muriel and Magda, she got an uncanny feeling when she met their eye. The way they spoke betrayed a certain cautiousness: like they were treading on eggshells.

Like they were scared, too.

'Rhos,' she called over to the door. 'When you were talking to Muriel about the flowers, she didn't ask you anything untoward, did she? Anything ... unusual?'

'No,' the other girl frowned. 'Why?'

'You know why.'

Pouting, Rhos looked younger than her sixteen years. 'Stop being such a spoilsport, Ingrid. Are you scared I might actually make a friend without you?'

'I'm only trying to be careful,' said Ingrid. On the day she'd left Arianydd, she'd made a promise to keep her family safe. Now she was here, her friends were the closest thing to family that she'd got. 'We can't afford to take risks.'

And you couldn't really know a person until it was too late.

'I'm going downstairs,' the other girl stood up, gathering her satchel. 'Have fun with your papers.'

Without moving, Ingrid glanced over to the picture which she kept pinned by the top of the dresser. The people in the photo were laughing: the mum and dad in formal attire, the grandmother in her *geta*, and two young children with wide smiles. There was an aching tug at her chest.

She was so tired of having to be older than she really was.

Chapter 28

The Raven Queen

Friday morning hovered falcon-eyed and hawk-tailed, and Muriel couldn't seem to escape its sunless glare. Weftwork had been a quiet couple of hours, most of which she'd spent focusing on the intricacies of satin stitch.

Smooth linen. Embroidery floss. The thin glint of the needle.

Ether Rhiannon's voice was like waves lapping against a shore, slow and peaceful. And although she hadn't left a spot of untidy sewing in sight, Muriel felt exhausted by the end of the class. It was heavier, much more difficult than sewing had ever been at home: as if the needles were weighted down with lead. Or perhaps it was simply nerves. Everyone, it seemed, was on their best behaviour in anticipation of tonight.

Muriel could hardly believe she was looking forward to Catrin's seventeenth birthday party, either. But winter nights hugged the buildings close, like blankets pulled around cold knees, while the scant hours of daylight waned towards the edges. Each morning was a morning further away from Wildbriar. Any distraction was a welcome one: and slowly but surely, this day, too, would darken like fruit turning into wine.

'Hey, Muriel! Are you coming?'

A scattering of voices beckoned her down the corridor. Several girls were heading straight to the cove after classes finished for the afternoon, but Muriel was reluctant to join the crowd just yet.

'Sorry, I can't right now. Catch you later!'

'Looks like I'm not the only one hoping for some calm before the storm,' Alarice shook out the scarf around her shoulders, closing the classroom door behind them both. 'I don't suppose you've got a free minute?'

'How come?'

'I may or may not have finished making my dress for the party. And if you're not busy, I could do with a hand sewing on some sequins.'

As they made their way to the dormitories, Muriel wondered what everyone would be wearing. Almost all of the girls seemed to have elaborate garments tucked away from their past lives. Meanwhile, she and Magda had been frantically darning the closest things to 'formal' garments they had saved from Wildbriar.

'This is it,' Alarice reached into the wardrobe. 'Do you think it's too much?'

Muriel could only stare. The long gown had the rich, rippling colour of an opal, and was accompanied by a high-collared velvet cape.

'It's beautiful.'

'Well, I can't have Catrin showing me up. Shall we get these sequins on?'

As they began to stitch on the iridescent, taupe-coloured glass beads, Muriel's mind drifted. The sky was threatening a pink winter sunset outside, and she knew Magda had a tendency to sleep off her worst moods. It unnerved her a little. The quietness, the stone-still torpor, and not least of all the visions.

She tried to convince herself that it would all be okay again by tonight. The rest of the girls were in the cove, where Magda would likely join them. They would smile in their finery and marvel at how pretty the others looked. It would be a party, and quite frankly Muriel was in need of some light relief after the week they'd had.

'There!' Alarice set down the needle and thread, beaming. 'That looks so much better, doesn't it.'

'I'm sure you'll look stunning either way.'

'Thanks, Muriel. You're a star.'

After Alarice's sequined dress was finished, she rifled through her own wardrobe for something to wear. There was only one garment that seemed fitting. Which meant it was time to dress the part.

*

At eight o'clock Muriel tiptoed down the corridor of the North Quadrant, gown ruffling behind her. How many people would even be at this party? She hadn't thought to ask. The entire cohort of the Fallow was not large, only twenty or thirty girls altogether, and their dorm group were among the eldest. But since Catrin was a social butterfly — or more accurately, a social hawk — Muriel reckoned that anyone who was anybody would be coming.

'Muriel?'

A voice shimmered in the darkness as she turned around. If Ingrid had looked striking by daylight, then by burnished candlelight she was devastating. Her glossy hair was swept back into a low bun, and she wore a flattering dark brown jumpsuit.

'I love your jacket,' Muriel admired the gleaming golden buttons. Unlike the thick, hard-sheened leather that you usually saw in shops, the jacket looked soft and faded, like the leather of a worn notebook. 'Where'd you get it?'

'Nowhere special. It's been sitting in the back of my wardrobe for too long,' Ingrid admitted. 'How about yours?'

'It used to be my sister's. Naturally, I thought it looked better on me.'

'That sounds about right,' Rhos laughed, joining them in the hallway. 'It's very elegant, though.'

She was looking at the purple-black lengths of taffeta brushing Muriel's ankles. Isa had kept it plain, but a little embellishment had done the dress wonders. A jewelled brooch here, a handful of cowrie sequins there, and the garment looked brand new.

'Did you get the cowries locally? There's a good market near Porthdeilio, I'd really —'

'Rhos,' Ingrid rolled her eyes. 'Let her keep some secrets, for goodness' sake.'

The conversation flitted to twilight, and Muriel began to hope they would stop hanging around soon. It was getting to the time of night where mosquitoes would be queueing up to attack her ankles. 'Where are we actually supposed to meet?'

'Oh, inside the cove. It'll probably be starting now.'

Once they reached the common room, it was clear the party was already well underway. Snippets of music drifted out from between the cracks in the wood. The occasional screech of laughter burst out alongside it. With her heart hammering her throat, Muriel gave a push at the door.

'Merrick! Leyshon!' called somebody from within. 'Who's that you brought with you?'

'Let us in, Serena!'

The cove yawned wide before them. Realising that many of the girls outside the North Quadrant would have no idea who she was, Muriel hung back and scrutinised the spectacle from a safe distance. In contrast to its usual understated decor, the current scene within the cove was riveted with laughter and illuminated by burnt orange shadows. They chased each other like loose embers.

'We're not supposed to be encouraging our magic without proper guidance,' whispered Rhos. She was looking towards the centre of the room, where Catrin was stood on the table with something bright and wicked in her hands.

It was fire, Muriel realised. Pyromancy.

That was Catrin's gift, and why she could stand there with flames dancing in her hands. It flashed in whirls of tawny light, making Muriel's stomach turn a giddy flip. That fine, golden hair. Those unnaturally bright eyes. This was what the Ethers were trying to train out of her.

And here she was, flaunting it.

'Has she always been able to do that?'

Rhos only shrugged. 'Rarely this extravagantly, or the North Quad would have burned down a long time ago. Catrin Scurlock doesn't do things by halves.'

Speak of the alder, thought Muriel. The flames had suddenly suspended in mid air as Catrin slipped down from the table and sidled towards them.

'Muriel. Rhoswen. Fashionably late, I see.'

'Sorry to interrupt the fun,' laughed Muriel, watching as a flock of girls from the East Quadrant floated past. They were paradisiacal in madder-dyed linen, dark blue nettlecloth, and willowish grey voile. 'I had no idea so many people were coming.'

'Birthdays are a big deal around here,' Catrin replied. 'Enjoy it while it lasts.'

It seemed like just about everyone in the Fallow was packed into the room. As the birthday girl returned to her tabletop showcase, Muriel picked out the faint lyre music that was coming from somewhere.

'Hey! Muriel, is that you?'

A girl from one of the other dormitories crashed into Muriel from amid the dancing. She had a vaguely familiar face, but it was impossible to place. A stranger. Or someone she had lost long ago, back when everything was different.

'From Furze! I'm Brionne, remember?'

She was a slender girl with pale skin, black hair, and amber eyes blown wide. The two syllables of her name moved in slow motion beneath the lights: she looked exhausted from dancing. Meanwhile, Muriel felt frozen. Brionne was a girl from way back — before she'd even moved to Wildbriar. What on earth had she done to end up at the Fallow?

'I, uh, think you've got the wrong person,' she faltered, hoping her expression didn't betray her. 'Are you okay? Do you want to sit down?'

'What? Of course not!' the other girl grinned. As she span, her hair flew out in wild curls. 'This is the best party ever!'

'Yeah, I get that,' sighed Muriel. 'But are you ... you know?'

If the Ethers caught them having a party, they'd be in big trouble. But being caught intoxicated — that would be worse.

'What?' Brionne looked offended. 'Of course not! I only had some of those cakes to eat, you should try one.'

Muttering a string of curses, Muriel went to investigate the spread of food towards which the other girl had gestured. There was a glorious array of all the best things: nook-and-cranny pastry lattices. Trifle with fresh custard. Aromatic bread dusted with cinnamon and black pepper. Surely just one bite wouldn't hurt. But as she was about to take one, someone grabbed her hand.

'Don't,' said a familiar voice. 'It's charmed, I think. Everyone who's eaten them has been acting funny.'

'Magda,' said Muriel, surprised. 'I thought you weren't coming.'

'I wasn't planning to.' Magda looked down. 'But I thought we should talk about yesterday. I'm sorry for causing all of that mess in the first place. It was ... I shouldn't have gotten you and Alarice tangled up in all of this.'

'It's okay, seriously,' said Muriel. 'It wasn't your fault.'

'You're not mad at me?'

'Come on, Mags. Something was going to happen sooner or later. And it'll be alright, even if doesn't seem like that right now.'

Magda smiled awkwardly. 'Thanks. And I'm sorry for, well, disappearing.'

They surveyed the scene, its painted colours of copper and rose. The room smelled of autumn night air and simmering fruit, like someone had left a pot of elderberries on to boil.

'You certainly picked a good place to disappear tonight,' Muriel leaned back against the table. 'It's so crowded, you'd think the entire county had packed itself into one room!'

'Indeed you would. Who's that?'

Muriel turned too late to see Brionne come whirling towards the pair of them. She was going too fast to stop, too fast even to avoid them, but Magda didn't seem to have realised the impending threat.

With an almighty crash, the pair collided and toppled to the floor.

'You idiot!' scowled Magda. Over her fine lace sleeves, there was now a slash of bright red from Brionne's glass of punch. 'Look what you've done to my clothes!'

'Sorry, sorry,' protested the younger girl, staggering to her feet. 'Let me help.'

'No need,' Muriel cut her off. 'We'll take care of this ourselves. It should wash out... You just leave us to it.'

It was only when Magda stood up that they saw the full majesty of her gown. She wore a robe of grey gossamer whose overlay of black lace dipped and rose like tendrilled vines, or snowflakes.

'A spider's web,' Muriel realised, staring at the impossible fabric. 'Where on earth did you get that tailored? It's incredible.'

'Thanks,' Magda muttered. 'It's also ruined.'

At that point a smattering of applause broke out from across the room, thankfully not directed towards them. Its glowing recipient was Catrin, but it looked like she was about to take a break from her fire display.

Muriel's guts twisted as their resident pyromancer made her way directly towards them.

'Magdalena.'

'Catrin,' Magda inclined her head, extending a hand to hide the stained sleeves. 'Happy birthday. I trust you're enjoying your night?'

'I am,' Catrin gave them a smile so winning, that Muriel wondered if she ever practiced in the mirror. 'What about the rest of you?'

Muriel glanced from Magda to Brionne. Neither of them looked very happy at all, but she nodded before it became too obvious. 'Oh, yeah, absolutely. I mean, how did you get all of this planned without the Ethers figuring it out?'

'It took a little trickery. But that's nothing I can't handle,' Catrin stretched her arms as if the ease of it all bored her. The sleeves of her dress seemed to stretch, too, dripping with an oilslick of black feathers.

'I like your outfit,' said Brionne, absentmindedly. 'You look like a raven.'

'Very apt,' added Magda, her eyes lingering over the draping wingtips. 'Highly intelligent but ruthless. It suits you wonderfully.'

Catrin stared. 'You have the nerve to come to *my* party, and insult me —'

'Magda's just had, er, a little too much to eat, I think.' Muriel gestured over at the food, hoping it really was charmed. 'I'll take care of these two.'

Catrin didn't look impressed. 'Well, the food's only there to help people relax — loosen their inhibitions. It's not my fault if it makes a brat out of her.'

And the raven queen swept off without another word. For someone who was not tall, thought Muriel, Catrin did a good job of looking down on people.

'What was that for?' Magda elbowed her, as soon as she was out of earshot.

'You've got to watch your tongue, or we'll end up with more enemies than friends! There won't always be a convenient excuse to save our necks, either.'

'Sorry. I thought this was a party.'

'I'm not saying you didn't have a point,' Muriel admitted. 'She's acting particularly vulturish tonight.'

The three of them laughed.

'Hey, there you are!' Alarice tapped them on the shoulder, appearing from among the crowd. She was dressed to the nines in the glittering sequin gown, but sounded out of breath. 'Sorry I'm late, if it hadn't been for these bloody *shoes*. Stupid things.'

'You missed nothing,' Magda replied, wearily. 'Except a narrowly avoided argument.'

'Shame,' the other girl laughed. 'An argument with Catrin Scurlock? Guaranteed entertainment.'

'Alarice!'

'Muriel!' Alarice teased, with a flicker of amusement. 'I don't know about the rest of you, but I'm hungry. Has anybody seen any food that *isn't* charmed?'

'I think the hot chocolate's safe.' Magda pointed over to a towering fountain. It was overflowing with rich, dark liquid. 'We could give that a go.'

'Thank goodness. I was beginning to think we'd starve all night.'

For the next hour they stayed by the fountain, taking slow sips of the melted chocolate. Girls were giggling and tripping over their feet. The dancing was wild and uncontrolled: red and black and purple and purple and black and red. All of it, this bright-eyed revelry, and Catrin in the centre with her flames, dancing and dancing like some burning goddess.

Chapter 29

The Vespertine Library

The morning after the party was a wreck. Some miraculous clean-up operation had been performed on the common room, although everyone was struggling to pull themselves together.

'I can't believe you were dancing on the *table*.'

'You were the one who bet I couldn't!' Rhos blushed furiously. 'I only did it to prove you wrong.'

'You were having fun,' Ingrid grinned, tearing into a loaf of something that smelled like nutmeg and tea. 'Don't try to deny it.'

'Is that bara brith?'

'Yep,' said Ingrid, still chewing. 'I asked if we could get some this morning.'

'I thought we only got special requests on feast days.'

'It's almost Invernal, isn't it? Make hay while the sun shines.'

'We would, if you'd only leave some for the rest of us!' Alarice nudged her. 'Pass it here.'

The comforting mixture of dried fruit, candied peel, and spices helped lighten the mood, and Magda was hungrier than she'd realised. For the first time since they'd left Wildbriar, she felt ravenous. Sating that appetite was pleasant enough to distract her from the bad thoughts, which drifted by without quite managing to cloud her vision.

Nonetheless, there wasn't much time to rest. With midwinter so close, there was maintenance work to be done on the grounds: and due to the

Fallow's remote location, Magda and Muriel were delighted to discover that none other than the girls themselves were responsible for its upkeep.

'Come on, you lot, it's only a bit of grass! It's not going to hurt you.' Ether Rhiannon looked positively exasperated by her students' lack of enthusiasm. 'If you'd worked a day in your life at a stable, you'd not be complaining.'

Ingrid, who most certainly *had* worked a day in her life at a stable, had never grown accustomed to the ammonia smell of bunking up straw. They were near the Gatehouse, in a barn where horses were occasionally kept overnight, for when the Ethers had business in the capital. To her great disappointment, they spent far more time cleaning out the bedding than with the horses themselves.

'I'm tired,' Catrin leaned against her rake. 'Can we have a break?'

'You'll have a break at the same time as everybody else, Miss Scurlock. Your seniors never struggled half as much with this! I never heard young Dilys grumbling about a bit of dirt.'

Magda, who was struggling to carry her own load over to the wheelbarrow, was beginning to wonder just how much they hadn't been told. The names of old girls passed through conversation like ghosts who hadn't quite left.

'Catrin,' she lowered her voice, turning to the blonde girl. 'The day we got here, someone mentioned a council. Some sort of event, for the oldest girls who are ready to leave. What did they mean by that?'

'Oh, the Progression Council?' Catrin tore off the pair of gardening gloves and bent down to grab a trowel. 'It only happens a few times a year, so it won't be a while til you see one. But each time they choose from the eldest girls, to decide who'll be transferred to the Brenin's workshop of artisans. It's a great honour to be selected.'

'Is it?'

'That's what they say, yes.'

With that, the brown-eyed girl began weeding the undergrowth around the barn's outer walls, reluctant to linger. An unspoken stalemate.

'What about the girls who don't get selected?' asked Muriel, moving in to join them. 'What happens to them?'

Catrin tore up a handful of weeds with a violent *rip*. 'The Council's the deciding call. By the time you're eighteen, you have to be chosen. There's no one here who's older than that.'

Slowly, all too slowly, the pieces slotted together.

'Have you ever seen where they go? The ones who don't get chosen?'

'I'm not sure what you're getting at.'

'Ether Lorna said the same thing, back when we first arrived,' Muriel explained. 'She said that by the time we're eighteen, we have to be ready.'

'Well, yes.'

'But you only get chosen if you're good enough.' A pause. Muriel turned to check that Ether Rhiannon was out of earshot. 'What happens if you're not?'

The sound of straw-covered rakes cloyed like rotten fruit.

'Well?'

'We don't talk about that,' said Catrin, her face closing up. 'You'll be fine. We'll all be fine.'

Magda saw the other part, the thing that had been left unsaid. *We'll get through this, because we have to.* Because there was no other way.

'Are you sure that it's not —'

'Please.' Catrin shrank back towards the undergrowth. 'Please don't talk to me about this right now.'

It was the first time that Magda heard her sound vulnerable. Perhaps all the girls here were just as frightened; they only hid it better.

'I'm sorry,' Muriel drew back, as if she was a hunter who'd shot a rabbit and found it alive, still limping in the bushes. 'I didn't mean to upset you.'

Beyond the horizon, the winter sun lay grinning like a viper's tooth. The girls knew better than to mistake it for beauty. Not in this season, not in the cold consolation of their existence here.

*

By dusk the sky was a different beast entirely. The wind tied knots in the treetop, and tangled ribbons of memories that kept Magda from ever properly drifting off. *Sneak out the window*, hissed one voice. *Steal a carriage*, whispered another. *Forget the others. Save yourself.*

'Oh, piss off,' she muttered, rolling over.

'You're still awake?'

Cringing, Magda caught sight of a lamp flash on from the other side of the room.

'Sorry. I was just trying to... Never mind.'

'I don't blame you,' Muriel shrugged. Her own duvet looked crumpled and weary in the cold wash of moonlight. 'These pillows are awful, they're wrecking my curls. I should've pinched a silk scarf from Isa.'

'She'd have your guts for that.'

The other girl gave a half-hearted smile, but the lack of sleep betrayed her. 'It's weird, thinking it's just Isa at home right now. Everything's weird. I keep thinking we'll wake up and walk down the hill to school each morning.'

'Yeah,' Magda shifted uncomfortably in her bed. Her own parents had hated having an empty house, and it was bad enough when Enio left. Now there would be nobody, nobody there at all. 'It's like trying to imagine Invernal without snow.'

'Magda ...'

The wind breathed lightly, almost enough to mask the sudden difference in Muriel's voice. Magda pretended she hadn't heard it.

'I'm sorry for asking this.'

Her voice was a lost ember in the fire, one that Magda could put out now if she wanted to. She could cut the question off before it was asked, leave nothing between them but quiet, beautiful, silent distance.

'Did you kill Tegwen Price?'

All the air left the room. This was not a part of her that Muriel could know about. There was no defensible answer she could give which would make things okay, no words she could utter that wouldn't carve a marked path. She couldn't be that person, and Muriel's best friend, at once.

'I never meant for anything to happen that day,' Magda tried to say. The moon had hidden its face behind a cloud, cast over by ivory smoke. 'Tegwen got hurt. But I didn't ... I never did that.'

But I almost wanted to.

'Okay,' said Muriel, sounding relieved. Magda hated that she could be so easily reassured, and hated herself more for thinking it. 'Okay, Mags. I was just worried. Get some sleep, okay?'

'You, too.'

It took a while for the sound of snoring to rise softly from Muriel's side of the room. She should have known that things wouldn't have been solved just through one conversation, no matter how much of a relief it had been. But if it was a visionary that the Fallow had come for, it was a visionary they'd get.

She'd become exactly what they expected.

And worse.

Peeling back the covers, Magda crept outside to the hallway, then down the stairs. Only days ago she'd promised Muriel and Alarice that she'd go to look for the Telling-Stone, and there was no time like the present. Once she reached the edge of the orchard, however, a sudden sleepiness drew over her.

Surely it wouldn't hurt to sit down for a few minutes. There was a fluffy bank of moss just ahead, sheltered by the canopy of a stocky alder tree. Alders were a good omen in the eyes of the goddess. And although a few spots of starlight dappled through the foliage, it was dense enough to cover Magda entirely.

Just a few minutes, she thought, nestling on the downy moss bed. *Just a little while.*

Unconsciousness lodged itself like a hook in her throat, and pulled her under.

*

She felt the vision more acutely than the last. This time it was vivid, real, as tangible as the ferns curling over her feet. Because that was what it felt like to be inside Cunning Wood, didn't it? The Forest clawing you home. Without a lantern, it was hard to even see the mossy floor — but she was there, no doubt about it — and she was standing up in dark cotton robes she'd never seen before.

Who else was there? Who was watching?

In her dreamlike trance, Magda peered between the trees and rocks, over the horizon, and into the woods. There was a silhouette on the horizon.

She knew instinctively that it was the gwyllgi.

The black, burning-eyed dog was waiting there, shimmering with the vigour of a live coal. Cunning Wood was dark and deadly. But though the hound hovered between the grass bank and understorey, no harm came to it. For some reason, Magda felt certain that no harm would come to her either. Dreams were strange creatures, after all: and so, letting go of her inhibitions, she stepped forward towards the forest. One pace at a time, over and over, until the woods closed around them.

It sent a shiver down her spine. The Fallow was placed in the heart of Cunning Wood for one reason alone — to make escape impossible. Who needed guards when you had the protection of a deadly Forest on all sides? Had this been anything other than a vision, the potent toxins would have destroyed her in a matter of minutes.

But the dream-version of Magda followed on, picking her way through the woods. It was clotted with tufts of temperate vegetation, the ground a maze of moss, rosy saxifrage and ivy-leaved bellflower. She had to chase faster and faster to keep up with the wolf, which ducked with ease through the undergrowth. After an unknowable amount of time, they came to a clearing.

Moss dripped. Insects clicked. They were standing in a place that Magda recognised. And at the centre of the glade was a broad, imposing building. Its arched exterior was covered with thin tendrils of ivy, as if the Forest hoped to claim the brickwork for itself one day. Through the thinnest circular window, she could've sworn she saw a shelf of books.

It was a library.

As impossible as it seemed, the silhouette she'd once glimpsed among the treeline was now standing before her, in full brick and mortar. This was the place she'd dreamed of: the library in the woods. Picking her way down the front path, she gazed in wonder at the great grand door. Tall letters were chiselled into the smooth white chalk. It was a word – no, a name.

'*Vespertine*,' Magda read, except her voice didn't come out right. That was the problem with visions: they warped even the slightest thing. When she tried the door, it wouldn't budge. '*Let me in*,' she attempted to say. '*Let me ... in...*'

As if in answer, a smaller, circular door, swung open. The edges peeked with a pale gold light, like the smallest bonfire was kindling inside. Slowly, dreamishly, she took hold of the handle and pulled.

Inside the library was not a tidy place.

Unkempt stacks of books littered the floor, and a thick layer of dust coated most of the surfaces. Nonetheless, the hanging panels and dark wood shelves gave the impression that it had once been carefully curated, whorled with the shapes of lost centuries. It felt like the kind of place that ached with secrets.

'*Hello*?' Magda tried to call, the vision fragmenting her voice. '*Is anybody there*?'

There was no reply. Her attention fell to the large earthy book which lay on the front desk, where a receptionist might have once waited. It had been bound with mulberry-coloured leather, and the title was embossed in a golden monogram.

Welcome to the Vespertine Library, read the inner cover. *Please sign this entry book if you wish to speak with a librarian.*

She turned the page. It was blank, although she now noticed a pen that hadn't been there before. Nobody preceded her entry; nobody followed it. She took great care in carving the only relic of a person on the page, ink swelling from the low sweep of the *l* to the hissing secret of the *s*.

Magdalena Corrales.

When a new line began to appear underneath it, she dropped the pen in shock.

Welcome, Miss Corrales.

The book. The book was writing back to her.

What are you looking for? continued the foreign handwriting, in swirling umber script. *The Library prides itself on its many specialties and extensive archive.*

Feeling numb, Magda picked up the pen again. The nib had split. Whatever she wrote was going to look about as sophisticated as a toddler's scrawl.

'Have you got any texts on the Tidal Folk?' she asked out loud. She doubted any more responses would appear, but kept hold of the page just in case.

For all literature concerning the Tidal Folk, please see Aisle Seven.

Peculiar indeed. And yet, sweeping peculiarity aside, Magda followed the instructions to scour the aisles. The long hall seemed to transform before her, unfolding like a book itself: there were towering bookcases and tumbling velvet curtains, cold plaster and soft fabric that murmured with warmth. Each circular windows had fine black grilles in the shape of a spider's web, and a smell of ancient paper rustled the air.

Still, she couldn't let herself get distracted. This was an unprecedented opportunity to uncover new information. A book about visionaries, veridians, or both — that was what they needed.

The lightest current of wind tilted one book out towards her.

'*Blank*,' she opened it, disappointed. It was blank. What was the point of a blank novel? Worse, when she returned to the front desk and its all-knowing entry-book, she found the pages there were equally void of ink. Was it possible that she'd imagined writing her name just minutes ago?

I need some advice, she inscribed, more carefully this time. *Veridians. Visionaries. An encyclopaedia of Tidal Folk, or something like that.*

An answer seeped through the paper like blackberry wine, slow and delicious.

Have patience.

Then a gust of wind snapped the book closed.

'Thanks a lot,' she grumbled. For all of their two minutes' acquaintance, she'd hoped the book might have a more helpful answer for her than that. The floor was cold but not uncomfortable, so she sat down to think. 'Wait. Did you say this place had a librarian?'

Only the wind howled in response, a lonely wail.

When she stood up again, however, there was a new book sitting on the desk. It was lime green and wrapped with brown paper, like a long-abandoned gift, and Magda eyed it with suspicion. Either some hidden person had placed it there in lightning speed, or this vision was playing tricks on her.

A Treasury of Oceanic Gifts, read the title. There was no author to speak of, and Magda opened it greedily. Would it be another self-writing journal, or a long-lost history? Would it be filled with ancient folklore, or brimming with modern knowledge? Were the two the same thing?

The book did not reply.

Unlike the first, it was published in the more usual fashion of printed text: everything was already in its place. You got none of the spontaneity of a spoken folk tale, but it suited her purposes, and Magda began to search the glossary for the section marked 'V'. *Varathor. Vastra. Vedrinnet. Veridian.*

'Veridian,' she flipped through the pages, relieved to have finally landed upon something useful. 'Let's see.'

Veridian, read the first line. *One with an innate affinity for the natural world. Powers tend to mature as the individual approaches adulthood, though minor traits may begin to manifest sooner.*

Magda tried to commit the words to memory, but they fluttered like moths, scrambling faster the harder she tried to cling on to them.

Veridians are able to communicate with plants, tap into their power, and manipulate biological matter; for example, they may cause plants to grow, or decay, unnaturally swiftly.

'What about visionaries?' asked Magda, feeling the weariness warping her voice. Soon, she somehow knew, it would be time to wake up again. She had to get the answers before it was too late. 'Please help me. I haven't ... got long.'

To her surprise, the book was kind.

Visionary. One whose dreams, sometimes known as visions, have prophetic qualities. Often, what visionaries see is what comes true in the future. However, they may also become fixed on the past.

Most of Magda's visions were too horrible for words, and there was no question of fixating on the past. Some days the past was the only place where she could bear to exist; other days, she would have given anything to escape it.

When she tried to turn the next page, she found the book had clammed itself shut. It knew she couldn't stay here. It was warning her to leave.

'Thank you,' she muttered, curling beneath the velvety pool of those beautiful curtains. She felt tired, so tired, and the curtains were so wonderfully warm. 'Thank you.'

Chapter 30

River

Ingrid didn't like to recall Raglan's face, but she remembered the clothes he wore. Hard clothes. Soft clothes. Clothes like armour, that weathered the seasons.

She remembered wearing his jacket, the one she'd torn a hole in and promised to patch up. It was dark green and made of denim that changed colour with the seasons, patched with pieces of linen every colour under the sun.

Here, she'd smiled, one morning. *I fixed it.*

That old thing? Sweet, he folded it up. *I'll have to keep it with me, to remind me of the good old days.*

To remind you?

Come on, Lacey, I already told you. They said it could be any time now.

Oh, her stomach had dropped through the floor. *Oh. So it's really happening.*

Yep.

And you're... You're going to go.

I have to.

You don't have to. Just tell them the truth.

There was a harsh, ragged laugh.

The truth? Oh, that is *a good one. I can't think of anything they'd like to hear less.*

She didn't move. Didn't feel that she could, with the weight of the world pulling her apart at the seams like this. She'd always thought they'd have at least one more Invernal together, before everything went to shit.

Hey, don't give me that face. We both knew this day was coming. You knew it right from the start.

I know. I just thought...

That you were different? That I'd change my mind?

I thought you cared a little more. I thought this meant something to you, after everything we've been through.

She didn't say that last part. Just let him leave, and take the stupid jacket with him. She never wanted to see it again.

*

'Ingrid?' asked Rhos, looking at her worriedly. 'Are you okay? You look like you're on another planet.'

'Huh?'

It was only then that Ingrid realised that she was in the dining hall. She was not, in fact, on a cold riverbank somewhere near Arianydd. She glanced back at Rhos. 'Oh. I was just thinking about Invernal.'

'You're right, it's about time we started decorating.' Rhos's face lit up. 'We could do *garlands*.'

'Yeah,' she nodded, smiling faintly. 'Yeah, we could.'

Once, a long time ago, Invernal had been her favourite time of year. The winter holiday was rich in splendour, followed by the springtime festival in the warmer months. But while the latter came for long and balmy days, Invernal thrived on jet skies that were flooded with stars. And Ingrid lived for the night.

'D'you think it'll snow this year?' Rhos kept saying. 'Ooh, think if we get to make snow angels on the lawns!'

If only that excitement was contagious. Whatever Ingrid lacked in enthusiasm, Rhos made up for, and she was glad. It dwindled every time she thought about the river and all the things it carried away each year. Firefly lanterns, reeds, people.

The truth was that Raglan wasn't the one who broke her heart; he was the one who'd made sure she would never get her heart broken. It itched beneath her skin, so much that she wanted to peel back the layers until she was the girl she'd been last year, and the year before, and before. But how deep did the wound go? That was the question she kept asking herself. Was there even a person left beneath it all?

*

They walked down the hallway to classes quietly. Although the corridor between the North Quadrant and the dining hall looked unassuming, Ingrid knew the Fallow had its fair share of hiding places. First there was the old potting shed behind the House of the Lyre (most of them had known about that since their first month of arrival), and then there was the little cellar in the South Quad (she'd hidden there the day after her sixteenth birthday), and then there was the conservatory at the back of the Glasshouse — not so good when it was cold, but ideal for gossiping in the summer.

What Ingrid hadn't expected was for their own dormitories to become a place where hidden things were kept. She'd forgotten to pack tapestry needles in her bag for Weftwork, and doubled back to the dormitory to collect it: which was when she heard the voices in the room next door. They were hushed, whispering, flitting from girl to girl like fireflies swarming the air.

Ingrid knew she should have knocked.

She should have announced her presence, allowed the occupants of the room to resume their discussion another time, and go. Or she could even have just left them altogether; borrowed someone else's tapestry needles when they finally got to class. Once upon a time, she would have done the noble thing.

But that part of her had withered up somewhere between the flagstones of a burning street, and the edge of a cool woodland glade. Hardly daring to breathe, she knelt beside the door and pressed her ear against the wall. The voices crept out like a fine skein of silk, and she was slowly teasing the threads towards her.

'I found it.'

That was Magda's voice.

'When? Last night?'

'Yeah.' A shaky breath. 'I saw the wolf again, it led me to this clearing in the middle of the woods.'

'You went into *Cunning Wood*?!' cried someone else. Muriel.

'I told you, it was only a dream! Of course I couldn't have gone inside otherwise... but it felt so real.'

'What did you see in there?'

'That building ... It's called the Vespertine Library. There was a voice inside, it sort of — *spoke* to me, I can't describe it. Like it was writing back to me, except there wasn't anybody else in there.'

'Interesting,' mused a third voice. Alarice. 'What did it say?'

'It seemed to know what I was looking for, but when I got the book, it was unreadable. The only way to read it was to wait.'

There was an exasperated huff. 'Don't suppose you'd like to spill the secrets?'

Yes, thought Ingrid, bristling with anger. *Why don't you go ahead and share? Since you obviously trust us all so much.*

'It wasn't exactly cheery,' Magda warned. 'It said that veridians have powers which will develop as they approach adulthood, but minor traits might show sooner. As well as the affinity with plants, they can manipulate biological matter, leading many to become healers or herbalists ...' She hesitated. 'If I were you, I'd be careful. It seems like a conspicuous kind of power.'

The Ceremony. The screenings. Ingrid could feel the flames licking over her skin, shielded only by the barest bones of magic, and wondered if they were thinking the same. It was all a dance with fire, wasn't it?

'You think they'll figure it out,' said Muriel, slowly.

'It'll be okay,' Magda tried to reassure her. 'We won't let them find out anything like that. We'll make sure of it.'

'You can't,' the second girl's breathing was shallow. 'You can't promise that.'

Still crouched outside, Ingrid tried to process the rest of it. Muriel was a *veridian*? Blessed threads, no wonder they'd kept quiet during Ardracy. And if Ether Stefania got wind of it ... She didn't even know what the protocol was for that. It couldn't be good.

'I asked about visionaries, too.'

There was more? thought Ingrid. She strained closer, desperate. For now, it was possible to ignore the guilt of eavesdropping.

'It said that visionaries may experience visions of the future — but they can become fixated on the past, too.'

'That would explain those nightmares you used to get,' said Muriel. She sounded only slightly calmer than before, her voice a fraction steadier. 'Thank the goddess that it *is* the past now.'

It's only the past. Except it wasn't, thought Ingrid. The past was a living thing that leapt and thrashed at the edges of its cage, with total disregard for your desire to put it behind you. The harder you pushed back, the bloodier you got.

'At least we're safe for now.'

'But what happens as we get older?' said Magda, her voice oddly chipped. 'It might be a little obvious if our powers become fully-fledged overnight.'

'The Ethers can't know.' Alarice's voice was flat, brutal. 'It's a rare gift; they'll want to interrogate you both. The best thing is to lie low, keep it hidden as long as possible.'

There was a pause.

'What if we got out of here first?' said Magda, tentatively. 'You're saying we're sitting on a time bomb. But we're only sixteen. Think how much more time there might be before any of Muriel's powers develop. Before mine develop any further.'

'That's true,' Alarice considered it. 'When she's stronger, those powers could come in useful. They might be enough for us to make our escape through Cunning Wood.'

'Through Cunning Wood?!' the two other girls exclaimed in unison.

Ingrid was inclined to agree. What on earth was Alarice thinking?

'Cunning Wood's toxic enough to kill any man who sets foot into the Forest,' she began. 'But if a veridian can wield such power over the woodlands, don't you think she might be strong enough to fight that poison?'

The other girls didn't reply.

'Think about it,' Alarice urged them. 'If Muriel will reach her full power by the time we're adults, couldn't she use it to protect us?'

'To neutralise the poison in the plants,' said Magda. 'So that we could escape through the woods.'

An astonished hush fell between them.

'So we just wait it out. And keep the Ethers from suspecting.'

'Do you think we should tell the others?'

Ingrid felt sick.

'No,' said Alarice. 'Not yet.'

Chapter 31

The Red Beauty

On the third Weftwork class of the week, Ether Rhiannon unveiled a pile of brightly dyed fabric. 'I hope you've brought a sharp pair of shears, girls.'

Magda raised an eyebrow, wondering what they'd be cutting from the stack of boiled wool on the table. 'It's very, er, yellow.'

'The colour of madness,' Alarice remarked. 'Tasteful.'

'Yellow is a perfectly respectable colour, Miss Gosselin, one which represents the nobility of our ruler,' Rhiannon reprimanded her. 'Today we'll be making mantles for the northern districts. May the Weaver bless your work.'

'I'm sure we'll manage just fine without the Weaver,' Ingrid muttered, reaching for the cloth weights and fabric shears. The pattern was for a high-collared coat with a layered cape at the neckline. It looked much warmer than the garments they'd been accustomed to wearing. 'Which town are they for?'

'Ciltraeth. Their barley crops failed this autumn, which has led to their present hardship. It's the least we can do to spare an act of charity.'

'Could we send food, too?' Catrin cut in. 'I'm sure the coats are helpful, but they must be hungry.'

'I don't know how much you girls have been told of the situation,' said Ether Rhiannon, a glimmer of concern crossing her face. 'The Sickness across our lands has been harsh. As such, there are only limited resources to go around.'

And they'll stay firmly where they are, thought Magda. The Brenin could spare a coat, but he would never give up a meal. The others could go on struggling, as long as it was conveniently out of sight from the Palace.

'We could check the storehouses,' Muriel suggested. 'Have we got anything to spare?'

Ether Rhiannon straightened her cloak, which hung over a dark blue linen dress embroidered with golden-white owls. They ducked into the folds of fabric as she walked, then hovered as she stopped at the front desk to pick up a pile of fabric. 'I think it's best if we do not dwell on matters that we can't change.'

The reluctance across the room was palpable, but nobody raised another complaint. Rhiannon's message was clear: *get back to work.* They used thick tapestry needles to tack the pieces of wool together. The cloth was dyed yellow from turmeric, which would fade over time, but that was the issue with most plant dyes; they weren't always lightfast. What would this fabric look like in a year's time? Ten? Twenty?

'Match the notches carefully,' Rhiannon held up two sleeve pieces to demonstrate. 'Like this.'

Magda made every effort to replicate the movement, but her stomach was starting to rumble. It was highly distracting: probably because the yellow fabric was the exact same shade as soft, buttery torrijas. She pinned the pieces with an aggressive *stab* and tried to focus on lining up the notches.

The sound of fabric shears scoring through cloth were initially soothing, but all the while they sewed, she could feel a strange straining in her fingertips. It was as if the weight of something was seeping out, somehow being absorbed into the fabric. Her head felt lighter, oddly hot, in a way that didn't make much sense.

She was just hungry. That was all.

'Got it?' asked Muriel. 'Mine's gone all wonky.'

'It's certainly a one-of-a-kind piece.'

'You mean I've engineered a work of bespoke tailoring?'

'Interpret it as you wish.'

They laughed, but something else was on Magda's mind.

'Muriel,' she lowered her voice, before Ether Rhiannon returned to their corner of the room. 'I know we didn't talk much about this morning.'

'And?'

After her escapade at the Vespertine Library, all they'd had time for was a quick discussion between classes. But the guilt weighed on Magda. She'd dumped a tonne of information on Alarice and Muriel in one go, and there'd been no time to ask questions. It was a constant race to get from one place to another, sew garments, study magic, all of it, that each day they were stretched thin enough to shatter.

'I was just ... you know, yammering about libraries and dictionary definitions. Sometimes I rush off thinking I've got all the answers, and I didn't really ask how you were doing at all.' Her voice was very small. 'I should have been a better friend.'

There was a moment before Muriel spoke. Magda wondered if she had to run a mental draft through her head before speaking, too, or if she was one of those people who could trust themselves not to blurt out something stupid.

'The last few days have been really hard,' she said eventually.

'Sorry. I'm really sorry, Muriel.'

'I'll be alright,' Muriel sighed. 'There've just been so many changes to get used to. I don't think I've got there yet. And I know it's not your fault, but I think we both know things have been, well, off between us.'

Magda shifted uncomfortably. There was the rift that formed slowly, subtly, creeping wider each time they pretended things were fine. A gap between their unspoken words and the reality.

'I'm sorry,' she replied, at last. Useless words for a coward heart. 'There are just ... so many bad memories, it feels like I'm drowning in them. I didn't see the point in burdening you with that.'

'It's not a burden, Mags. I'd like it if you felt like you could talk to me about those things, too. We're friends, aren't we?'

That's what we've always been.

'Okay. I'll try.'

They shut up as Ether Rhiannon walked past. She cast a critical eye towards the nascent works of sewing on their desks, where the front panels lay like a fractured iceberg. Abandoned on the other side of the desk were the sleeve pieces and half a dozen pins.

'Those coats aren't going to keep anybody warm like that.'

'Sorry, Ether Rhiannon.'

'Less chatting, and more sewing, perhaps?'

'Yes, Ether Rhiannon.'

It took a while for the angular pieces of yellow fabric to start looking like a garment, but it was satisfying work. Layers became joined. Linings were put in place.

'You know,' Muriel held up the collar piece to turn the corners through, 'it helped, the other day.'

'What?'

'Talking to Alarice. It felt like a weight was gone after we told her, don't you think?'

It did. Magda couldn't be certain what would have if they hadn't had that discussion, but it had been oddly comforting to welcome somebody else into their inner circle. Alarice was kind, and wise, and if they had told her without the world imploding, then perhaps there might be some shred of hope for everything else after all.

'Maybe Grimoire Malgarty wasn't right about everything.'

'No. I don't think she was.'

They picked at the remaining stitches in the overcoats, and Magda was grateful for the silence. Mostly she was made of pieces: some shining, and others worn, like driftwood scattered at sea. In spite of that, there were certain moments that made her want to cling to those gold-touched fragments, the ones which floated so slenderly among the rest.

'Only one more hem to go now,' said Muriel, to nobody in particular. 'It's too good a day to waste sitting indoors.'

A distant mote of dust crossed the room as they picked at their remaining work. The others, who seemed to sense the collective urge to leave, had also sped up sewing: threading and stitching and threading and stitching until the bell rang, and class was finally dismissed. They sprinted down the corridor, their laughter echoing brightly as a chorus of doves in the eaves.

The deep relief of it sank through Magda's chest like a red-hot sword: burning, holy, and then, inexplicably, healing. After days of being on edge, something had finally given; the wound had cauterised. Magda had been afraid that that thing would be her and Muriel's friendship.

Now there was light pouring in through all the jagged edges, and the sun had yet to set.

*

Later, after day had mellowed to soft red shadows, the girls were languishing in the common room. There was an aura of still air, held-back rain and drooping flowers. Some girls were half-asleep; others busily reading or listening to music.

'I wish Stefania would stop setting us readings on the history of Wales,' Rhos grumbled. She sat reading in the alcove of one window, curled up like a baby bird. 'Who cares how long the Brenin's been ruler, anyway?'

'I'm amazed they even bother to teach it,' said Alarice. She was putting the finishing touch to some watercolours, which had taken her all week. 'You'd think they'd avoid anything that might go giving us ideas.'

'Well, there's plenty of other stuff they could teach instead. I'd love to hear what they think about Aurelia Madreth, for starters.'

Magda looked up. 'Who?'

'You know, Brenin Elisdair's wife?' Alarice stared, as if she was forgetting something very obvious. 'They called her the Red Beauty. The one who was there from the very start, before all this mess.'

'Oh,' she lied. 'I forgot.'

It had unearthed a faint memory, of a time where she knew the name that lined history books around the isles. Somewhere, deep down, she'd never really wanted to look into who had come before the Brenin. Whatever she might read, the Red Beauty was a figure who now belonged to the past; her golden brown smile and flowing tresses, the stuff of legends. It hurt too much to think about what kind of a life they might have had under different circumstances.

'What did she do to get that kind of nickname?'

'The hair, obviously,' grinned Rhos.

'You wish,' said Ingrid. 'It's because she was like fire. Impossible to look away from, harder yet to leave.'

Magda thought of a castle, towering and turreted. In the morbid curiosity of her mind's eye, a woman's auburn hair tumbled over the ledge of one window, all the way down to the river below. Her flaming locks were generous as summer blood, drowsed among the waterweeds. It might have been a story she was told, long ago, but she couldn't be certain.

'Aurelia was the one who left,' Magda remembered, suddenly. 'She fled the Palace.'

'Yeah, well. No one knows exactly how it happened.'

Alarice sighed. 'I think the aftermath speaks for itself.'

The aftermath had lasted nearly ten years. Magda understood that a change had taken place after the Brenin had come to power, of course she did, but she'd been too young to pinpoint exactly what it was. It had settled like ash over farmland: almost traceless, but omnipresent. It was there, in the eyes of her parents over the breakfast table each morning. She had swept it under the rug as they got ready for school. She had looked out of the window instead and seen pigeons, bright-eyed and beady, ready to carry whatever careless merriment she could think of to her friends.

'If only she'd stayed,' said Muriel, unmoving. Her mouth was set in a hard line. Had she always looked this serious? Had that blunt edge always been there, that rancour hissing just that close to bubbling over?

'I wish she had, too,' one of the other girls nodded. 'Then we'd never have had that wretched Mandate.'

And we'd still have our safety, thought Magda. Because that was when the Palace laws had changed, and the country had changed with it. Something vital had been lost along with the Red Beauty herself.

'What about their son?' asked Rhos. 'I don't see why he couldn't have taken over.'

'I guess he was too young. And then he was gone, wasn't he.'

There was a lull in the conversation, while the sky outside took to casting long blue shadows over the room. Magda picked up a square of paper and began to pick at the edges, teasing it into tiny shreds that scattered like confetti over her knees.

Congratulations! You've earned: a lifetime imprisonment in a poisoned forest.

As she picked at the paper, the story twisted like a moth-eaten tapestry in her head. There were gaping holes where the important details should have been. Why couldn't she remember? And why couldn't she bring herself to ask any of those most perilous questions out loud?

She looked across to the sofa, where Alarice had gone back to her watercolours. The paintbrush made thin, careful strokes across her canvas, now a light, silvery purple.

'What are you painting?'

'Home,' replied Alarice. She held up the sketchbook, which was flooded with a painting of dark water. 'We used to live right by the coast.'

It was one of the things that Alarice missed most, being close to the sea. Her parents' house back in the Wolds was a tall, proud building just off the east beach. When she thought of summer, she thought of the view from her bedroom window: a glittering ocean, all of it strung with gossamer-fine threads of gold. This was her closest form of escapism, the reminder that such places did still exist, even if she couldn't set foot on those sands in person.

'Did you ever get bioluminescent jellyfish?' Catrin peered over, curious. 'We used to get floods of them floating up in the winter, from the West Sea.'

'It was the same for us. Zaira always loved them.'

The jellyfish were one of those rare things that weren't magical, but might as well have been. When the tides drifted in colder currents, hordes of the fat, shiny creatures glossed the shores with a fluorescent glow. It was a phenomenon that Magda had often hoped she'd see one day.

But tides would come and go without her; jellyfish would breathe and flounder and return to the sea, without her ever being there to bear witness. Whole chords of the ocean would change, leaving no mark upon the beach and no footprints in the sand.

'Maybe it's not such a bad life, being a jellyfish,' said Rhos. 'Just floating along, without having to think about anything.'

'You can't be serious.'

'At least jellyfish don't get set assigned readings,' Rhos waved the textbook again, reluctantly returning to her page. 'And I haven't heard them complaining.'

The others laughed, but Magda remained trapped in her sea-pool of thoughts, a tireless eddying whirl that tossed her like a pebble across the shoreline, over and over again. Aurelia Madreth had left, and there had been uproar. The Mandate had struck, and there was terror.

But stitches frayed; threads came loose.

Surely there was only so much a country could take before it splintered.

Chapter 32

Seer

That night, Magda dreamed of a beach.

Its vast, white sands stretched wide around her, like the arms of an immeasurable snowman. She was walking on fine powder, the wind lacing cold fingers through her hair.

There was something buried here: something, and she did not know what. Only that it needed to be retrieved, lest it sink beneath the sands forever.

'*Are you there?*' she whispered, the words stolen away on the wind. '*Tell me where you are.*'

Over the sandbanks, the marram grass grew in coarse compliance. Clumps of it hung in thick drifts, like the fur of a shaggy dog, barely covering the hide of the beach. Further down the shoreline was a cave full of stalactites, but she didn't dare to step towards its two laughing jaws: hanging open and full of malice.

Oh, how the wind howled. Oh, how she longed to be sheltered from it.

'Are you there?'

Her words got lost again, and the ground had begun to hum, each tiny grain of sand shaking with a primeval tremor.

Come out, come out, wherever you are.

She woke up before the earth could tear itself to pieces. Without digging her shovel into the sand, without finding the buried treasure. A sinking feeling hacked at the back of her throat: the storm-swept sand should've scratched her all over, left her ankles blistered and aching. But it wasn't real. None of those night terrors could really touch her, even if she was crushed within their grip.

*

For the next few mornings Magda floated vacantly, the waking hours merely a distraction between long and lightless trenches of night. She saw the way the other girls regarded her: the miraculous shades of concern, curiosity, fear. She brushed past them as if they were paintings in a gallery, a parade of human inquisition.

'Hey, have you seen my sketchbook anywhere?'

'Your sketchbook?' She looked up, embarrassed. She hadn't realised that Alarice was talking to her. 'I haven't, sorry.'

'Never mind, then. Hopefully it'll turn up soon enough.'

One Triolatry class, she thought she'd seen a ghost. When birds crashed into windows there was a white powdery substance left on the glass panes, leaving a perfect relief of the bird in question. Sometimes it happened with nocturnal birds, startled by the shimmering lights within.

She had recently begun to feel like that: as if she'd crashed into a window and left the imprint of herself clinging there. The real Magda had fallen far below, stunned and stinging in the shrubbery below.

'I like your plaits,' said Muriel, as they walked over to the House of the Lyre. 'Where'd you get the ribbons?'

'Just the remnants stash from the haberdashery.'

The answer came easily, which surprised her. She wasn't sure if it was from the congeniality of their conversation, or from the fact that they had actually carved out a life here, in the weeks and months that had passed. They were Fallow girls too, whether they liked it or not. Theirs was the haberdashery from whence a person might filch ribbons to decorate their plaits, and theirs was the weight of the responsibility for those ribbons.

'They're nice.'

'Thanks,' said Magda, wishing she could think of a compliment back. Muriel's hair looked lovely, but it always did. So did her green corduroy skirt, and her brown leather boots. What else was there to say? 'I brought you some cashews from the kitchens,' she said in the end. Muriel loved cashews. She had been meaning to pass over the little jar for ages, and had forgotten until now.

'Aw, thanks.'

She watched her friend reached into the jar and picked out a handful of nuts. They crunched between her teeth with satisfying chaos; they were a noisy and therefore interesting kind of crop.

As for Muriel, who still remembered the first time she had seen cashews growing in the wild, the gift was a double blessing. She had been simultaneously bemused and scandalised to learn that such a pedestrian-looking nut could grow in this elaborate manner. To be bright red and curved in the shape of a question mark, as if they were asking something. She had never deciphered quite what that question was.

'Mags?' she began, hesitant.

'Yeah?'

The question that had been on the tip of her tongue eluded her, too. 'Actually, don't worry. I'll tell you later.'

*

By the end of the week all thoughts of classes and notebooks had ebbed away entirely. There was one thing which came back to Magda's mind, itching like clockwork, no matter how hard she tried to dispel it.

The prophecy of the lost prince. Because that was the thing nobody could answer, wasn't it?

Precisely what had happened to the Brenin's son.

According to her parents' account of the story, the boy had gone missing almost six years ago. In the beginning there had been search parties, inquiries, questioners — all of which came to dead ends. Eventually, even those last efforts waned and faded altogether.

Maybe he'd died. Perhaps he'd gotten lost, or fled the archipelago entirely. It would be difficult to trace someone who didn't want to be found.

Yet for every day of his absence, the Five Forests grew sicker and sicker. It distracted Magda at every step, kept her from concentrating in and out of lessons, or even making conversation like a normal person. Since the night they'd talked about Aurelia, those thoughts had plagued her ceaselessly. The Red Beauty had left a son who should've saved their country, and instead he had condemned it.

How could you do that? How could you abandon your kingdom when it needed you most?

If they ever found this prince, she'd be the first in line to give him a slap across the face.

Selfish bastard. Royal coward.

Trying to push down the last of the wrathful thoughts, she rolled over in bed for another night of bad dreams. She tossed. She turned. Eventually, her eyelids drooped closed out of exhaustion, if not somnolence.

*

She didn't know how she'd arrived here.

The softly shrouded feeling of a vision was folded around her: every shadow was blurry-edged. Curtains rippled in and out of colours; trees swayed with wilful reluctance. She was standing on the outside lawn, for some inexplicable reason, in a purple dress she'd never seen in her life.

In front of her was the orchard. Its silver lawn was bordered by thick-canopied lime trees, the grass faultless as fabric fresh off the mill. It would be comfortable to lie down in. She could avoid this vision altogether, if she really wanted to. But at the edge of Cunning Wood, a shadow was stirring in the gloom.

A thickening shadow, with four legs and two dark red eyes.

Watching.

Waiting.

Anybody sensible would have turned back. The cloisters were not far away, and anywhere inside was a step further from the spectral hound across the lawn. But the cloisters were cultivated solitude, and what Magda craved was a loneliness so loud it roared.

It didn't make much sense, when she stopped to think about it. Maybe it was better if she didn't. Things between her and Muriel were better; the visions were a distraction which she could mostly cope with, and classes were their usual variety of educational suffering. And still there was this. Why now, after the long-warranted breakthrough? Why now, the underlying sense that it couldn't last — that something worse was just around the corner?

She moved across the lawn, the dewy grass dabbling her toes with cold. Sharp, spacious, green. Closer to the treeline now, the canine silhouette tilted back its head and let out a high-pitched howl. It was looking particularly sorry for itself after the evening's rain, which had glued its wiry fur to its skin, and its big ears stuck up like a fox's.

Something told her that it hadn't wanted to come here.

It needed to.

By now, Magda stood mere paces away from it. Its breath rose in clouds above the smoky night, reminding her of someone, or something, from years ago. Its eyes were such a deep red they looked almost brown. They were the kind of eyes that remembered everything.

'*You look like somebody I knew*,' she tried to say. The vision jarred her words, and a muscle twitched in the creature's shoulder. '*You look … familiar.*'

The wolf didn't make any motion to indicate its assent or dissent. It got to its feet and turned towards the Forest, nose in the air, as if it had scented out some other more entertaining way of spending the night.

'*Wait,*' Magda scrambled after it. 'Wait for me!'

If the gwyllgi heard her pleas, it disregarded them. Sooner or later, it must have known, she would learn the quick-footed way of the woods. Soon she would be chasing along rather than being dragged. Every now and then she caught glimpses of its expression: leaping high to cross a stream, or wiggling over a patch of rotting ferns. Undeniably, and quite unashamedly, the creature looked happy.

By the time they eventually reached a clearing, she was out of breath. It was not wise to grow fond of visions, especially not ones like this, but the exhilaration of running had made her careless. Right now she felt weightless, skyborne as the æther.

'Thank you,' Magda breathed, trying to gather her thoughts. 'I thought...'

But the wolf had already disappeared. She was standing alone, she realised, before a building that she now knew by name.

The Vespertine Library.

*

Somewhere within that magnificent carcass of a building, thought Magda, it was quite probable there were books that she could make use of. But that task was made mighty difficult by its condition: it was as higgledy piggledy as things could get, and stumbling through its circular door-within-a-door was wearing off as a novelty. Stepping over the threshold felt more like being a neighbour with a spare key. Her footsteps were awkward, clumsy, in a place where she didn't quite belong.

'*Is anybody there?*'

The words echoed baldly. It hadn't gotten any tidier since she'd last dreamed of this place, and she had to step around a stack of unsorted books to reach the front desk. Sitting in pride of place was the familiar purple entry-book, a thin layer of dust adorning the cover.

Welcome to the Vespertine Library. Please sign here if you wish to speak with a librarian.

If only the librarian would care to make an appearance, thought Magda. But she signed the book anyway. To her amusement, a new line scrawled itself below her name, each letter rolling with flippant ease.

Good evening, Miss Corrales. How may I help you?

Perhaps it shouldn't have been surprising. The book had written back last time, though it seemed improbable for a miracle to work twice. She scribbled down a reply before it could vanish again: if her handwriting looked sloppy and rushed, she didn't suppose an incorporeal assistant could complain.

I need to read about Telling-Stones, she wrote.

For texts concerning prophecies and charmed artefacts, please see Aisle Four.

It was an odd feeling, being here. Like an oasis of calm tucked within the storm that was Magda's life, recently, and a place in which her old life and her new life seemed to exist within equal reach of each other. If she walked this way, she'd be back at the Fallow. If she turned the other way, Wildbriar would be lurking just over the hill.

She couldn't go home, of course. Not like this; not yet. But still, the unspoken promise of home being out there was comforting.

In the meantime, there was a task at hand. Since she had arrived here without choosing to, it seemed prudent to make the most of the opportunity to find the Telling-Stone. The library parted around her as she searched, turning through shelves in kaleidoscopic fashion. Even though the shelves seemed to strain under the weight of hardbacks, paperbacks, and clothbound special editions, she got the impression that there was always room for one more.

At last she chose a book from Aisle Four: one with a rough, stoney cover that reminded her of shark-skin. Returning to the front desk, she set the book down carefully. 'Will this one do?'

This is a library which relishes the obscure, came the entry-book's cursive reply. *The book you've chosen is called Gathering the Future: A Seer's Handbook.*

'Excellent. I'd like to read it, in that case.'

A warning, Miss Corrales, said the entry-book. *Most of this Library's visitors do not come here to read.*

That's fortunate, thought Magda. If they did, the library probably wouldn't have much business. To even find a book was challenging, let alone to read it: and to her dismay, the *Seer's Handbook* proved more cryptic than it looked. The only lines that she could make out were vague and scratchily carved, and nothing to do with Telling-Stones at all.

One line began: *Our fate is in the palm of your hands. Knit them together, and all is ruined. Unravel them, and all is saved.*

Disappointed, she returned it to its shelf. Her skirts mingled with loose papers as she walked, skirting the floorboards like tumbleweed in a bad Western film. Someone was clearly neglecting their duties as caretaker.

'You really need to get a new librarian here,' she told no one in particular. 'This place is a mess.'

There was a loud rustling sound.

She froze, watching as the pages of the entry-book fluttered open with an aggressive breeze. Curiosity soon got the better of her, and once it had stopped flapping about like a stranded goose she went over to investigate.

Beggars can't be choosers.

'I wasn't talking to you,' she stared at it, wondering if she was imagining things.

Pity, the book replied, in thin curling ink. *Perhaps you should have listened to all those warnings, you know. The library by night is not what it seems.*

Magda felt her pulse quicken, but she refused to be reprimanded by someone she couldn't even see. It was only a vision. It wasn't real.

'What do you know?'

You wade so comfortably into your visions, that you think nothing of whose dreams you've invaded. You don't even imagine they might see you right back.

'Wade into visions,' Magda repeated, clutching her head. It was pounding. 'I'm sorry, I don't know what you're getting at. Is this some sort of joke?'

Jokes rarely outlive their welcome. Unlike certain people.

The insult smarted. Enough was enough: she wasn't going to stand here and get taunted a book, especially one that didn't know what it was talking about. She shouldn't have followed that dog. She shouldn't have come here. It was nothing but a trick of her mind, pulling together fragments of distorted memories. Distressed, she stepped back, searching for the door again. Where had it gone? Why was her vision getting — fuzzy?

If you want answers, stop taking the coward's route. Keep your eyes open, Magdalena Corrales.

Magda wanted to speak: truly, she did. She wanted to ask what in the Weaver's name she had gotten herself into, and why the words now eluded her entirely. She wanted to ask a dozen other things, except the world was rushing back —

And the library was vanishing before her eyes —

And —

She sat up, gasping for breath.

The dorm room was quiet. It was just before dawn.

Chapter 33

Still Waters

If there was one sound that Muriel hated, it was the sound of stilettos pacing behind the door. Specifically, the sound of Ether Stefania's stilettos: because it was harsh and jagged, like everything else she did. It grated at her mind. Made her want to run, and froze her to the spot. Last time she'd come here, there'd been little hint of what came next.

'Miss Silvana?'

'Here.' Muriel's stomach flipped unhappily. 'Should I come in?'

'Please do.'

This time, she stepped inside the screening room knowing just how dangerous the dagger-eyed woman could be.

'Good morning,' smiled Ether Stefania. A reptilian black notebook was already open on her desk, pen poised idly in one hand. 'I trust you've found your feet here over the last few weeks?'

'I think we've made do as we can.'

'Well, I'm glad to hear you're settling. And I think we both know the purpose of today's review.'

The words felt thick in Muriel's mouth. 'What do you need to know?'

'Well, first things first. Has there been anything new to report? Any changes, or developments in your previous experiences?'

Muriel shook her head. The less Stefania found out, the better.

'And how would you describe the traits which you mentioned last time?' The Ether hovered over the notebook, white fingers waiting to carve like chalk. 'Your ability to discern botanical poisons. Your feelings of connection towards the plants.'

'It's stronger than it was.' The words took Muriel by surprise, because they were true. She looked away quickly. 'Not that it was, um, that bad in the first place.'

'That must have been a challenging experience for you.'

'All I meant is that — it's harder to distinguish between the voices lately. That's all.'

Stefania looked suspicious, but scribbled something down in the notebook anyway. 'Remind me how old you are?'

'Sixteen,' said Muriel. Not seventeen, like the girls in the top dormitory. Still too young for more frightening powers to develop, or so she hoped.

'And since last month, I don't suppose you've had any kind of premonitions?'

'Um... no?'

'Not to worry, then.' Ether Stefania closed the notebook. 'It's a requirement that we ask, in such cases as your own.'

'I thought my case was unremarkable.'

'So we are led to believe. That leaves us with just one last protocol for today —'

'I've been keeping up with all my work, and taking notes in Ardracy.'

'I should hope so,' smiled the Ether. 'We'll be extending the syllabus in due course.'

The smile was a lie. They didn't trust her. Didn't trust any of them, or why else did they need all this monitoring?

Stefania was already turning to the next name on her list. 'I'll see you next month, Miss Silvana.'

*

'What happened?' asked Magda, when she returned to the dining hall. The smell of overcooked pie wafted out from amid a hefty soup tureen. 'You were ages.'

'Oh, nothing,' she lied. 'I just got a bit caught up with things.'

'It never does get easier with that old bat,' Alarice took a solemn bite of her lunch. 'Are you sure you're okay?'

Magda's face fell. 'It was your screening today?'

'It's fine.' Muriel grabbed the plateful of pie that had been saved for her. 'What did I miss?'

'Well, I was just telling Alarice about last night. I would've told you sooner, except you were already gone when I woke up,' Magda glanced around to check no one else was within earshot. 'Did it go okay with ... Well. You know?'

'It was nothing unusual,' Muriel chewed the forkful of pie slower than was strictly necessary. The miscellaneous vegetable filling had the consistency of glue, although it wasn't the reason why her throat felt so tight. 'What happened last night?'

'I had another vision,' Magda sighed. 'It started with the big black dog again, this huge shadow across the lawn. Just at the edge of the orchard. So I followed it into the forest, and ...'

'Seriously? You went after a gwyllgi?'

'It led me to a clearing,' the other girl explained. 'And it was only a dream. We got to this big white building, all ancient chalk and ivy. It was the same library from before.'

'The Vespertine.'

Muriel envied Magda's ability to find strange, beautiful secrets like this. The story was mystifying, bordering on impossible. Yes, she was scared enough for them both. But she was also faintly jealous of not having seen the abandoned library for herself.

'You went inside, right?' asked Alarice, half-yawning. She looked tired, and Muriel wondered just how many of them were spending their nights in fitful sleep. 'I take it nothing had changed dramatically.'

'Only one thing.'

Muriel listened as Magda told them both about the library's warning. That, and the lines from the *Seer's Handbook*:

'Our fate is in the palm of your hands. Knit them together, and all is ruined. Unravel them, and all is saved.'

'That's a bit ominous.'

'Yeah. They don't seem all too keen on saying things how it is.'

'What about that other part, Mags?'

Her friend shivered. 'It said that the things I dream of can see me right back. I don't know if it was some kind of a joke, but it sort of ... put me on edge.'

They were quiet for a moment.

'Do you think it was a riddle?' Muriel wondered. 'It said to keep your eyes open. Maybe it's trying to warn you to watch out.'

'For what?'

The words reran like a tickertape: too fast, half blurred.

'*If you want answers, stop taking the coward's route*,' Magda repeated. 'I think it was telling me to visit the library, for real. With my eyes open.'

Alarice stared. 'If it were a real place, there'd be half a poisoned wood between you and the clearing! You can't be thinking of going in to look.'

'Who's to say it's not a real place?'

Muriel held her tongue. Of all the unlikely things they'd come to believe, this one was far from the strangest.

'Whether it is or it isn't, please don't go getting yourself killed,' she said in the end.

There was no way through Cunning Wood without a protective charm, or you'd be ripped to shreds. They'd dared to hope her magic might protect them from that poison, but it still seemed a faraway fantasy. Muriel was all too aware that her magic was weak. The person they were relying on to save them was someone older than her, wiser than her, stronger than her.

She set down the pie fork, her appetite gone. 'Maybe you should wait a few days before you go back there.'

'Fair enough,' Magda shrugged. Then something curious flickered across her face. 'It was too cocky for its own good, anyway. That'll teach it a lesson.'

'Teach it a lesson?'

They were cut off by the sound of the bell ringing, summoning them to the Gatehouse. It was time to pray that the Great Weaver had been merciful.

*

'Welcome, everyone,' said Ether Lorna, while the ceiling shimmered darkly above them. 'Let us raise our hands and voices to the skies.'

Muriel craned her neck towards the high arches. It was as if a handful of new stars had been woven into the fabric, cloaking them with safety. Other times she had despised that buffering layer of sky. Now she was grateful for it.

'I'm sure you're all looking forward to the longer days of springtime,' said Lorna. 'But while the flowers lie dormant through this winter, I thought it would be fitting for us to sing the Canticle of the Blossoms.'

Moving around the circle, she handed out copies of the Vellum to each girl. Muriel unfolded the pages gently, as if it were her first time holding the sacred book. The entire thing was written in brown ink, and two brightly gilded endpapers peeked out from beneath each cover.

'We have to sing?' somebody muttered.

A disconcerted murmur spread around the room.

'Come on, girls, that's no spirit!'

Reluctantly, they began to recite the canticle: slowly, and not much louder than was required. Muriel thought back to a time when singing had been fun. They'd put on the radio in her dad's old car, a shiny green jewel of a vehicle, and belted out the lyrics to Ivor the Bard's latest hit. *Still waters*, people often said about her dad. Not that it mattered, any more. The world of singing through long road trips was now a pale and distant vision over the horizon.

Back in the Gatehouse, she realised that she'd forgotten the words to the song. The chorus had petered out, and other girls were glancing between each other awkwardly. Everybody hoped that Ether Lorna would brush past it.

Instead the Ether stood frozen to the spot, as if some invisible creature was peering over her shoulder. It could have been a *duende*, thought Muriel, remembering the unseen spirits who her grandparents insisted could be as capricious as they were troublesome.

'Would you like to continue with the second verse?' asked Ether Lorna, suddenly returning to her usual poise. Whatever spell had fallen over her was broken, and her sharp-eyed gaze narrowed. 'Here. There's a copy of the lyrics for those of you who aren't familiar.'

So they began anew. The song dragged on, lasting several minutes before finally dying a death, at which point everybody returned to companiable silence. At last it was time for the closing prayer.

'Silver braid for Tarren Mawr. Coarse kelp for Abergwyll. New linen for Dauglyn. Fairest lambswool for Porthdeilio. Let the Goddess never fail us, let the thread never break.'

Muriel found it curious how most people never spoke the name of the second goddess aloud. Gwern was the Great Weaver; her sister Eila was the Great Destroyer. One could not exist without the other, for it was Eila who wove the threads of the dead back into life.

'Alarice?' said Ingrid, quietly. 'What are you —'

Muriel could hear feet shuffling at the back of the room.

'Leave it.'

That was when she noticed it: the unmistakable chill in the room. It was coming from the back, as if someone had opened a window and let in a cold draught. She turned around to look, then wished she hadn't.

In the row behind her Alarice was visibly sweating, fingernails tightly clenched against her palms. A thin trickle of blood ran down the side of her neck, adorning the soft hollow of her ear lobe, and vanishing beneath the collar of her top.

'What happened?' Muriel tried to catch her attention, ignoring the alarm in her chest. The sight of blood was the least worrying part, compared to the harrowing expression on their friend's face. 'Do you need something? I can get some water and a dressing, if you want.'

In response, Alarice merely shook her head.

'Don't be stubborn,' Ingrid nudged her. 'Let us help.'

'I told you to leave it.'

The rancour in Alarice's voice took Muriel by surprise, although she could understand why. It was embarrassing to discover a spontaneous injury, let alone have to be excused to attend it. With malaise came a bizarre quality of the celebrity: everybody wanted to see, to help, to be there with you. And Alarice wanted none of it.

By this point, lamentably, it was too late. Several others had begun to cotton on to the fact that something was the matter.

'Allie?' asked Catrin, her eyes wide and childish.

'Sorry,' the other girl stared at the rug. 'It's nothing, honestly ...'

'You look like you're about to faint.'

'I am *not* going to faint.'

'Ladies, is everything alright?' Ether Lorna made her way over to where they were sitting. She stopped in her tracks at the sight of the girl in the back row, sweat dripping down her brow, each breath more ragged than the last. 'My sincerest apologies, Miss Gosselin. May I help you?'

'I don't want your help,' Alarice looked annoyed. Her voice sounded torn, laboured, like a bird whose wings were snagged on barbed wire. 'I just need a moment to ...'

Her sentence broke off with a choking sound, harsh and horrible.

The room asked itself, *what do we do now?* The girls turned to each other asking, *what's the right way to help?* The problem was that nobody knew what the protocol was for a friend in distress, who was refusing help, and who looked like she might collapse at any moment. The blood had now trickled down onto the carpet, dyeing it in dark red droplets.

Meanwhile, Ether Lorna hovered but did not approach. 'I'll send for Ether Stefania immediately,' she decided, as if this was a sentence of great comfort. 'She'll know how to treat this.'

Unable to speak, Alarice glared daggers at Ether Lorna's back. Muriel read the message in her eyes clearly: *I'll never forgive you for this.*

'What if we —'

'I'll be right back,' Lorna assured them. The door slammed behind her, and they heard footsteps racing down the pathway outside.

The change in atmosphere was immediate.

'I need you to shut the windows,' said Alarice, something quiet and warning in her voice. Her dark, coily hair had stuck to her forehead with sweat, but the blood on her neck was beginning to dry. 'And the doors. Now.'

'What?'

'I need you to close them all.'

Muriel exchanged a puzzled glance with Catrin, Magda, Ingrid, Rhos. Wordlessly, the five of them got up and began to pull the high awning windows shut. Each one clattered into place as they swung the latches shut.

'Is that better?'

'Thank you,' said Alarice. Closing her eyes, she sank back against the wall and pulled her knees into her chest. From a distance, it looked like she was dreaming.

*

The sun was low in the sky. In a minute or two it would be gone entirely, but for now they stood haloed by copper light: that middlemost of colours. It was the colour of the shingle as dogwalkers combed the beach back home; it was the colour of faded walls in Wildbriar's town centre, buildings slightly past their prime; and it was the colour of the end of the world. This was the sunset they had chased all the way down to the West Quadrant, where the medical bay was held.

'She can only see two of you at a time,' said Ether Stefania, appearing at the door.

No one moved.

'Let us in,' said Ingrid, in a voice that brooked no argument. For once, the woman looked too stunned to refuse.

They were led to the back half of the room where a series of beds lay. Long curtains were drawn around two of them, and an unnerving quiet coated the hall. It was the shell of a living place: an empty husk.

'Alarice?'

No reply.

Catrin tilted her head. 'Maybe she's resting.'

As they walked closer to the row of beds, Muriel puzzled over the mystery of the entire afternoon. Nobody could be certain of what had caused Alarice's sudden ailment. All they knew was that she had to be okay.

'You've got ten minutes,' Ether Stefania gestured to the bed in the corner, moving away to allow them space. 'She's just in there.'

They moved closer, uncertain, new silence falling. There was a shuffling from within. Then the curtain yanked itself to one side, to reveal Alarice peering out between two white panels. 'What's going on out there?'

'You're awake!'

Alarice turned to face the group, stood there for a moment, then plonked herself back down on the bed. 'You all came to see me?'

'Of course we did. Thank the Weaver you're alright.'

'You look terrible.'

'Consider me flattered, Scurlock,' Alarice rolled her eyes. 'Like you'd look your best after sitting in a hospital bed all afternoon.'

What happened? Muriel wanted to ask, desperately curious. But it was an insensitive question which would have to wait: the girl had barely been awake for a minute, for scrim's sake.

'What happened?' asked Ingrid, with no hint of apology. 'We were all scared stiff for you.'

Reaching over to the bedside table, Alarice picked up a cup of something that smelled like herbal tea. 'It was my own fault,' she took a long sip, wincing at the hotness. 'It's not a mistake I'll make again for a while. But I don't think it's wise for us to discuss it here.'

Muriel didn't understand. How could it possibly have been her fault? And why, she wondered, had she wanted the windows closed with such urgency? A part of her suspected it was not the first time something like this had happened. But that was none of her business, and out of respect for Alarice's privacy she decided to try and change the topic.

'Have they given you, er, anything to read? You know, to pass the time.'

'To read?' Catrin shot her a withering look. 'It's not a leisure centre.'

To both girls' surprise, Alarice cracked a smile. 'I could do with a decent novel, actually. I think I'll go mad if I have to stare at this wall for any longer.'

'Then we'll bring you some books,' nodded Rhos, wringing her gloved hands anxiously. 'Or anything else you want.'

There were dark smudges on Rhos's gloves, which Muriel noticed had been a different pair each week. She had assumed it was a precaution against the cold, but it seemed a little odd to wear them with such diligence.

As if it were impossible for there to be a silence longer than four seconds, Catrin gave a small cough. 'I'm glad they seem to have helped you recover from the afternoon. They have they been giving you enough fluids, right? And whatever medicine you need?'

The light cast feathered tendrils over Alarice's cheekbones. 'Don't worry, they've been most attentive. It would probably look bad if one of us dropped dead on Fallow grounds.'

'You shouldn't joke about that stuff!'

There was a weak scattering of laughter.

'I'm fine, I promise,' Alarice sighed. 'Sorry for scaring you all. My head still hurts, and that's about it. None of their painkillers seemed to do the trick, but it's hardly the worst of problems.'

An idea clarified in Muriel's mind.

'Give me a minute.'

She made her way out of the curtained-off area, back to where Ether Stefania stood over a paper chart and a pair of scales.

'Miss Silvana. Can I help you?'

'I wanted to ask if you've administered any kind of potion to help alleviate Alarice's headache? I'm no expert, but there was a recipe my mother once used. They say that it could —'

'The things your mother believed in are of small importance,' replied Stefania, without looking up from her inventory. She had begun to weigh several ounces of red powder into a jar. 'Even if she was the most skilled herbalist in the archipelago, I doubt she'd be able to help in a case like *this*.'

The words sent crawler lightning through her chest, and it took every ounce of Muriel's strength not to send the jar and its contents crashing to the floor.

'Alarice is our friend.'

Stefania went on spooning red powder into the jar.

'If you would let me try, I'd be most grateful.'

After a long pause, the Ether cleared her throat.

'Ardracy is the study of magic, of learning about yourselves. Part of that education comes in lived experience.'

Oh, thought Muriel. *Oh.*

'You knew that this would happen?'

'We did not know,' replied Stefania. 'But given the circumstances, it seems like Miss Gosselin did not take the precautions which she might have done.'

All the words in her throat seemed to have dried up.

'Could you have stopped it?'

'Magic is as cruel to bear as it is to wield,' was all Stefania said. 'And if you do not learn to harden your heart, then it will be broken.'

Acid pooled in Muriel's stomach.

'If we've finished our learning for today,' she began, fighting to control her tone, 'then I would like to make a suggestion. Do we have access to the ingredients for a Curd of Ambergris?'

Stefania raised an eyebrow. 'Yes, Miss Silvana. I believe we do.'

Curd of Ambergris was a powerful antipyretic. Even if it couldn't completely neutralise the headache, then at least it might relieve the worst of Alarice's symptoms. It had to be better than nothing. When Ether Stefania returned from the pantry next door, she brought a heavy mortar and pestle. On the table by the bedside, she laid out the precious powders and — to Muriel's amazement — a tiny chunk of waxy rock.

'Perhaps you should be the one to prepare it, if you are aware of its potency.'

Muriel didn't trust herself to answer. All too aware of how Stefania's cold eyes were following her, she took the first powders and began to blend them. She crushed the chunk of ambergris and added it to the mix.

Chapter 34

Perennials

'She's already doing better,' said Ingrid, her words running over themselves. 'By the alder, Muriel, I don't know what you put in that potion, but it really did the trick.'

'Have you always been this good at healing?'

From across the breakfast table, Magda couldn't help but think of what the voice in the Vespertine Library had told her. *Veridians are able to tap into the power of plants and manipulate biological matter, leading many to become skilled healers or herbalists.*

Healers. They were natural healers.

'Don't you think a decent night of sleep might have done Alarice some good, too?' she tried to sound offhand. 'It must have been exhausting going through all of that in one day.'

She tried not to sound as if that day had dragged her back to her senses, too, after a week of sleepwalking. That certainly couldn't be normal. It had taken one of their friends falling violently ill to remind Magda that she wasn't the only person in the world, and that suffering did in fact exist outside of her own personal sphere.

'Of course the sleep will have helped,' Muriel agreed. 'In fact, I think that —'

'How did you even know what Curd of Ambergris would do? I've never heard of it,' said Ingrid, ignoring them both. 'I wish *my* mother had kept recipes on potions. All those plants must come in useful sometimes.'

Muriel laughed nervously. 'Oh, it was only some old notes. Nothing special.'

'Well, I'm glad you tried it. Stefania obviously thought there was nothing more to be done.' Ingrid paused. 'So either you knew more than they did, or there's something they're not telling us.'

'Why would there be something they're not telling us?' said Magda, faintly. She couldn't be imagining the way the dark-haired girl's gaze was lingering on her. Her smile was suddenly harder, more catlike, those dark eyes pinning them to the spot.

'Wish I knew,' said Ingrid. 'The sleep probably helped, too, although a nocturnal preamble never hurt anyone. You'd know all about that, wouldn't you?'

That was certainly too specific for Magda's liking.

'I'm sorry, what exactly are you getting at?'

'She only meant that your bed is right under the big window,' said Catrin, setting down her coffee with a smirk. 'You've got the cold draught to contend with *and* Rhos's snoring next door. I'd say that a good night's sleep would be a miracle for someone in your position.'

*

Whatever ease had come with breakfast was quickly burned off like the early morning dew. Magda tried to focus on peaceful things, largely memories, such as the dull craw of the seagulls back at Wildbriar. She looked for remnants of those places in the fresh breeze, the grey-cobbled stone walkways: absent, of course, of old ladies with pencilled-in eyebrows, but still faintly familiar. Anything to remind her that this was not so far from home as the Ethers made them feel.

In spite of her best efforts, the morning's classes soon turned rabbit-eyed and restless. Everything perched precariously on the edge of fright, and Rhos was the jumpiest of them all.

'Did anybody else cross through the East Quadrant earlier? I could've sworn I saw something in the bushes.'

'Merrick, you're always seeing things in bushes.'

'No, but this time it was fast! Like a blur, or a wild animal.'

'Maybe it was the wind?' offered Muriel. She repositioned her satchel over one shoulder. 'Or some kind of insect. Didn't you say the ladybirds were migrating around this time of year?'

'It wasn't a ladybird.'

'Then don't worry about it,' Ingrid focused on the path ahead. 'Right now, the most important thing we can do is watch out for each other. Let's just get through the rest of the day and discuss it once Allie's back.'

'But I only wanted to –'

'Please, Rhos.' There was a tight nerve coiled in Ingrid's voice. 'I don't know how much patience any of us have got left today.'

'Okay,' Rhos sighed, kicking at a leaf which had stuck to her shoe. 'Did anybody do the set readings for Triolatry? I'm so behind, I forgot to take notes this week.'

Magda avoided her gaze. Her head had been so full of half-dreams and fantasy, that she had forgotten to even remember there was reading due. 'Which chapter was it again?'

'The Witching Tradition. We were supposed to be researching the history of weaving magic into cloth, and ritual sewing.'

'You can copy mine,' Catrin replied. 'Come on. We'd better hurry up, or Rhiannon will want to know what took us so long.'

*

To everyone's relief, Alarice was out of the medical bay by late afternoon. The group was careful not to ask too many questions, and instead chose to fill her in on the events of the day. It wasn't even February, but the purplish-white sprigs of eyebright were already forming in the planters just outside the dormitories.

'They're not *that* remarkable,' Catrin snorted. 'Anyone with taste would agree that lily-of-the-valley is prettier.'

The flowers blew in the wind, their white skirts high as a bride's. After returning to their dorms, it would have been tempting to just sit and watch the beautiful flowers. But Magda was too tired for any of that, and took an accidental nap instead.

By the time she resurfaced, the sky had turned the colour of ruby wine. Muriel was sitting across the dormitory, an amused expression on her face.

'The sleeping beauty awakes.'

'Shit,' she sat bolt upright. 'I didn't mean to fall asleep. I meant to do so many things...'

'Calm down, it's only been an hour or so. The others went to get ready for dinner, so I thought I'd better wake you.'

'Thanks. I'll be down in two minutes.'

The clock on the wall gave a *tick* with faceless eyes, as if waiting for something to snap. The scene should have shifted like a set change as the two girls stood up, gathered their belongings, and trundled downstairs. Instead, the pigment remained inexplicably static. Neither one of them moved.

'What's wrong?' asked Magda, eventually. Perhaps she had snored particularly obnoxiously during her nap.

Muriel was still chewing her lip. 'I was thinking about earlier. About what you said at breakfast, when everyone was asking questions.' A pause. 'The others can tell that something's up, right?'

'You mean Ingrid?' Magda cocked her head, surprised. 'I'd hardly call that a majority.'

'But she noticed. She's not stupid. And after yesterday, she's going to be watching us a lot more carefully.'

Magda began to fiddle with the lace at the edge of her sleeve. 'So you happened to brew a botanical potion, and it happened to help out our friend in need. How does that make us the ones in the wrong?'

'Magda,' Muriel's eyes were wide with anguish. 'It's not about innocence and guilt. It's about trust.'

'That's the first thing we should have realised back in Wildbriar. People can't *be* trusted.'

'Maybe not those people, but we need these girls to trust us,' Muriel insisted. 'It's a two-way exchange. If we're giving them nothing, then why should they want to be our friends?'

The hour chimed a little colder, and Magda got unsteadily to her feet.

'I'm going to get changed. I'll see you at dinner.'

'Don't act like this.'

'I'm not acting like anything.'

'You are,' said Muriel. 'What I was *trying* to say, is that I think we should tell the others what's going on. Right now they're starting to guess, and make assumptions. That's going to do more harm than the truth ever could.'

Magda wanted to laugh.

'More harm than telling them about everything Grimoire said to keep secret? Because that worked out so well for us last time.'

'You said you felt better after we told Alarice!'

'Yes, but a whole group isn't the same as one person. How do you know this won't make things worse?'

'I'm not trying to freak you out,' Muriel sighed, 'but I think there's no point in trying to hide it any more. We need as many friends as we can get here.'

Magda sat down again. She felt like a miserable sack of stuffing, lonely and abandoned by the roast dinner that would have made it whole.

'From what Ingrid said this morning, she's already onto us.'

'Exactly,' Muriel nodded. 'And if we let her keep poking, she'll probably dig up a lot worse than what she needs to know. That's not even to mention the Ethers.'

The Ethers. They were always lurking insidiously at the edges of the girls' consciousness; never quite tangible, yet always threatening.

'So what do we do?'

'If we tell the others, then they could help keep us safe. No one outside the North Quadrant dormitories,' Muriel met her eye carefully, 'but you know what they say about safety in numbers. A group could help us keep the Ethers on their toes. If we *don't* tell our friends, then the Ethers might find out first. Then we'd be really screwed.'

Magda mulled the words over. As usual, Muriel had a point: a really bloody good point, at that. But the thought of sharing their secret frightened her more than she cared to admit.

'Are you sure about this?'

'I'm not scared of what they'll think,' said Muriel. 'Not after everything we've been through. And I think we're going to need as much help as we can get if we want to make this escape plan possible.'

A smile tugged at the corner of Magda's lips. The idea was simultaneously terrifying and thrilling: it crashed over her like a wave in a reef. 'So we're really going ahead with this. The almighty prison break.'

'We're not calling it that.'

'But we'll tell them?'

'Yes.' Muriel took her hand and squeezed it. 'Tomorrow night?'

Chapter 35

The Fell

Dormitory Eight had weathered many a storm in its time, but none so pitilessly freezing as that year's midwinter. The rain came in icy sheets, and forked lightning scorched the ceiling of their room as the girls hurried back from the dining hall.

Catrin didn't like it one bit. During lilac season, she would have been glad to have the bed nearest the window: the sweet fragrance of the flowers would waft up from below, and the balmy sun would flood the whole room. But this was a miserable time of year to be right in the eye of the hurricane.

'Do you know if we've got any hot water downstairs?' asked Alarice, chucking her shoes underneath the bed. 'Ugh, these are soaked.'

Catrin shook her head. 'I'll go and boil some. Hot water bottle?'

'If you don't mind.'

They had all been worried about Alarice's sudden ailment, even though everything seemed to be back to normal now. Even if something was the matter, Catrin doubted Alarice would have told them. *Stubborn as a rock*, her mother would have said. Then again, Vienne and Hallux Scurlock found a turn of phrase for just about anything that displeased them. *Ach y fi, this one's messy as a crayfish! Dotty as an otter!*

'Spiny as a fish,' muttered Catrin. By the time she reached the kitchenette, the winds outside had begun to pick up. Someone had raided the stash of hot chocolate, but the kettle remained, so she cleared it out and put a pot of fresh water on to heat.

When she eventually returned to the dormitory, Alarice was looking sheepish. 'You didn't have to go to all this trouble.'

Yes, I did.

'You've still got a high temperature. And don't act like you weren't dozing off in Triolatry earlier.'

'I'm just tired.'

'Which is why you need to rest,' Catrin set down a cup of tea. 'Try this. It'll help you get to sleep.'

Alarice looked at it reluctantly for a moment, then drank the tea. 'If the others knew we spent Friday nights drinking tea indoors...'

'That's why we don't tell them,' Catrin laughed. 'We've got a reputation to maintain.'

'Oh yes, the wise elder residents of the North Quadrant!'

With a smile, Catrin poured out another cups of tea. If the younger girls thought that she was aloof, more fool them. A stony exterior was key to gaining the respect of strangers. But although she'd developed a thicker skin since leaving Tarren Mawr, sometimes she wasn't sure she knew how to take it off again.

'Hey, Cat?' called Alarice, rearranging her blankets.

'What?'

'Bags not on cleaning rota this week.'

'Fine,' Catrin quirked an eyebrow. 'But only if you let me listen to that new phonogram you've been banging on about. What was it called again, Hill Music?'

'*Fell Songs*?'

'That's the one.'

'Interesting,' said Alarice. 'I didn't realise you were into that stuff.'

'That sounds like a thinly veiled insult.'

'You think? If I was going to insult anybody, I'd make sure they knew about it.'

Catrin gave a tight smile, wishing she could believe the false bravado. 'Get some rest, you.'

It took a while for the storm to ease. But by nine o'clock, the sound of her friend's snoring was finally replaced with stillness. At that point Catrin got up, feeling a pang of remorse at the sight of her reflection in the mirror. Since last week, Alarice's hair had been styled in a thick crown braid. It suited her. Catrin, on the other hand, couldn't help but feel the weeks were running away from her, and that she looked more unkempt every day.

She knew why. But to acknowledge the fact she was trying to stretch out the passing time would be an admission of defeat, and an admission of the thing she couldn't quite bring herself to face. Foxe's letters sometimes came late, but they were never *this* late.

There was only one thing for it.

She took a seat at the little desk in the corner, close to the wall. That was what snakes and lizards did, she seemed to recall, because something about small spaces made them feel safe. But what on earth was there to like about being cramped? Snakes were stupid, and so was she, because unlike the snakes she was still waiting for something that was never going to arrive.

Hasty, she fumbled with the lock to the envelope drawer, her fingers too cold to get it open on the first try. The bad feeling trailed back to the letter he'd sent her the week before her birthday: a week that should have been perfect. The letter should have come full of hope, and good tidings. Instead it had been marked with a sense of fatigue, and something else, unnameable.

Remember that summer we said we'd both save up and move to the West mountains, and raise a goat farm? I thought of it the other day; it made me smile. I just wish things were still that easy. This winter's been harder than ever, especially with the Sickness. Even the Milliners had to sell up last month... To tell you the truth, I don't think moving is the worst thing they could have done.

She tried to understand how Foxe was feeling. By the alder, she hated how *she* was feeling. They had always been good friends. Best friends, even. But now things were changing so fast it felt like she was being left behind altogether.

At least one good thing's come of it. Lilavati Gower asked if we could help them move some cattle to the lower fields, and in return they'll help us restock the log piles through the season. It's good business, and it'll help us get ahead before the spring. That's the perennial struggle, Cat. I've got to think of my future.

That was the part she'd never seen coming, the real sucker punch. Lila Gower was the prettiest girl in the village. And whatever Foxe might have claimed about their business, Catrin was certain he had no idea how she felt.

'Idiot,' she muttered under her breath. 'You idiot.'

She should have known better. She should have realised what it meant when their lives had been ripped away from each other. Not even the best friends could stay as close as they had been, when the factors stacked against them were insurmountable. She should have known better than to hope for more. But stitches, she'd tried not to feel it, fought that battle for so long, that his blissful ignorance hurt the most.

I'm going to help out at the Gowers' farm for the rest of the month. If you don't hear from me in a few weeks, try not to think too much of it. I'm sure you've got plenty of celebrations planned yourself over Invernal.

She resisted the urge to tear the letter into tiny little shreds. She didn't tell him the half of what went on at the Fallow, for fear of putting him in danger. But what did he think they did here, really? Braid each other's hair and throw parties? The infuriating paradox of Lilavati Gower was that she was impossible to hate. All she'd done was be there, when Catrin couldn't. A sweet smile, kind eyes, a friendly face.

Nobody here, of course, knew quite what was going on.

She'd sooner die than let her friends realise their casual jokes had hit their mark: so she kept those rumours at bay as best she could, with her laughter that said *I couldn't care less, and no, he's not my boyfriend.* What Catrin wanted right now was not friendly banter, or even rational advice, but boundless commiseration — the one thing she didn't deserve. For all the months of denying what was going on, she could hardly ask for sympathy now.

I've got to think of my future, Cat.

Only now that the rain was pouring down in thick ropes of silver, did her head begin to feel clearer. She waited for the storm to condense. Then, taking out her reading-glasses with the pearl temples, Catrin reached into the desk for a blank sheet of the most expensive parchment.

Dear Foxe, she began, *I hope you're happy.*

Chapter 36

The Thinning of the Year

As the January sun crept through the windows, Magda thought of their old car, light glinting off the bumper.

She found it astonishing how humans would do basically the same thing over and over again, no matter how stupid, given the simple distance of time. Even before the Rift, there had been plenty of trouble caused by cars. Crashes, contamination, congestion, infrastructure meltdown: before finally, the big kaputz. And what had people done in the decades and centuries afterwards, when the tides had long since wrecked their old motors?

They reinvented them. Admittedly, there were significant changes to the way they ran — namely using kelp-generated bioelectrics — but the premise was the same. Box on wheels. Long straight road.

What more could humanity possibly ask for?

Enio used to joke that when they were older, he'd sell their mum's beaten-up blue truck and buy a real carriage and a fleet of horses instead, like the one the Davis family had in town. As if they'd had the money! He was always having far-fetched ideas like that: most of them much further-fetched, and considerably more ill-advised than the horses. But in spite of those ideas, Magda missed her brother. She missed the way that big things seemed possible, even if they weren't. And she wished she had the courage that he would've had, when faced with the task that befell her tonight.

The plan was simple: she and Muriel would break the news about their magic, clear the air, and launch themselves into a new era of closeness and mutual respect among the Fallow girls.

That was the theory, anyway.

As they closer they edged towards the evening, her stomach clenched itself into a tighter and tighter ball.

'Are you sure you're okay?' Muriel looked over, worried. 'If it's too much, we can wait another night to tell them.'

'I think I'll be sick if we wait any longer. Let's get it over with.'

Perhaps she was only imagining the eyes that seemed to be watching her from the hallways all day. They lurked all through Ether Lorna's Botany class, Triolatry with Ether Rhiannon, and Weftwork with Ether Ffion, but the invisible watcher was nowhere to be found.

'Everything alright?' asked Rhos, at lunch. 'You look as if you've seen a ghost.'

'Oh, I'm fine,' Magda gave a bloodless smile. 'Nice pasta, isn't it?'

*

Even if the springtime festival had come four months early, it would have been hard pushed to match the noise levels inside the cove that night. There were screams, shouts of excitement, and irritated squawking. Magda tried to ignore the nausea rattling her stomach while personalities clashed left, right, and centre across the games table.

'Ingrid Leyshon, that is the worst move I've ever seen you play!'

'Bit rich coming from you.'

'Has anybody seen my hair pins? I could've sworn I left one of them down here somewhere...'

'Stop staring like an afanc, and take your turn!'

A pile jewel-coloured cards lay discarded at the centre of the circle. Someone had decided it was a good idea to play Sleight, but it was also an amazingly quick way to start an argument.

Ingrid slid a pile of cards across the table, looking glum. 'Best of three?'

'You're on.'

'Is anybody else feeling a bit warm?' Magda glanced sheepishly towards the window. 'Maybe we could, er, open the shutters for a few minutes. Let some fresh air in.'

The rest of the girls exchanged perplexed looks. Alarice, who was wearing a dark yellow turtleneck, adjusted the cashmere collar so that it sat a little higher. 'It's freezing out there, Magda. Are you feeling alright?'

'Oh. Don't worry, we can leave it.'

'Actually, I could do with a break, too.' Muriel cut in. 'This weather's miserable. Should we get the kettle on?'

'Rhos'll hear none of it,' Ingrid shook her head with a smile. 'All week she's been going on about how much she loves wintery weather.'

'Well, where is she? For someone who loves the cold, she's taking her time in joining us.'

Magda cast a wary glance around the room. *That* was what had set her nerves on edge. Somebody was missing.

'Maybe she stopped at the pantry for a snack?' asked Alarice. 'She told me and Catrin she'd catch up with us.'

'A snack, or a banquet?'

'It's only been twenty minutes. She probably got distracted by a stray animal or something.'

Muriel tried to smile. A single vein fluttered at the side of her temple. 'If we've got a little time to kill, there was actually something Magda and I wanted to talk to the rest of you about.'

'Something juicy?' Catrin looked up. 'This weather's bumped off whatever appetite I had for anything serious.'

Magda locked eyes with Muriel across the circle.

'I suppose it's more of a proposition, to be precise.'

'A proposition,' Ingrid repeated. 'What exactly were you wanting to ask?'

Magda tried to think of how she would word it. Her cheeks were hot already; she hated everything about this, but it was too late to back out now. 'I don't know what the protocol is for new intakes to the Fallow, or how any of this usually works. But I can, er, understand if you've had your reservations about us.'

'And if you wondered why we were brought to the Fallow,' Muriel added. 'Or why we didn't tell you anything when we got here.'

The winter's gale whistled outside, a passive onlooker. It felt as if each word was coated with ice: harsh and abrasive.

'It's okay,' said Alarice. 'There's really no protocol, since we all ended up here in different ways.'

Catrin nodded, staring vaguely in the direction of the window. 'Don't get me wrong, I love a good story. If you don't want to talk about it, it's fine, though.'

'But I'm sure we'd all be curious to hear,' said Ingrid, louder.

There it was: the trace of suspicion. Magda ignored the tightness in her throat. 'Ever since we began school it's been the same, as I'm sure it was for you. We were warned never to trust the Folk, warned how dangerous they could be. So, when everybody found out what we were ...'

The room had gone still. She tried not to feel the sweat beading her brow. This was almost it; the moment where it could all go wrong.

'It was a Thursday morning,' she stuttered, suddenly unable to string together a coherent sentence. 'There was a knock on the door.'

Outside, the wind danced like it had done on that day. Magda had not seen the figure riding up the hill, all cloaked in gold, until it was too late. The storm had seized their house with a nightmare grip, shaking it until it tore free of its hinges.

'Was it Stefania?' asked Catrin. 'I remember the day I got taken. We all thought she was some kind of murderous ice-witch to start with, coming to strike us down where we stood.'

'Close enough.'

'She came because someone had spread rumours about us,' said Muriel. 'Somebody knew, or suspected, our magic. Before that, a physician who visited our school had warned us to keep it hidden. But we couldn't keep it from everyone.' There was the lightest pause. 'And after that ordeal, I don't see the point in hiding it from any of you, either. I'm a veridian.'

Magda watched as those words tumbled into the frosty air. She couldn't tell whether the others felt shock, fear, or admiration: for a stunned silence had fallen upon the group. In those strange frozen moments before time picked up its skirts and hurried on, it was all blue oil and malachite, palatial revelation.

'A veridian?' whispered Ingrid. Her fingers worried at the sleeves of her jacket, dancing over slub yarns like sparrows on a branch. 'But that's... an elder magic.'

'It's really not such a big deal.' Muriel tried not to flinch. 'It's more of an affinity for nature: flowers, trees, mosses. Manipulating biological matter. And it's useful for healing, too, although that wasn't my intention the other day.'

The other girls shared a nervous glance. There were whispers now, a soft chorus that rose and sank with the hush of a tide.

'So that's that. And I'm a visionary,' said Magda, abruptly. Everybody turned to look, discomfort writ loud across their faces. Her clumsy interruption was the postscript to an already uneasy conversation: but if she didn't say it now, she knew her nerve would fail her. 'It's to do with the dreams I get some nights. Uncanny visions, prophecies, that kind of thing. That's what we wanted to tell you.'

She drew back, her breath coming shallow. She was awful at giving any kind of speech. But the truth was out; now they only had to see what kind of chaos would unfold.

'Stitches,' murmured Catrin, frozen. 'I think we're going to need something stronger than tea to drink.'

Behind her, they could see Alarice smiling, the blue shadows tangling with the indigo dye of her skirt. 'Those are certainly rarer magics than most. Was there some special sign when they first started to manifest?'

'Not really. It's been gradual,' Muriel ran a hand over her forehead, relieved for Alarice's grace in navigating the whole conversation. She glanced back to Catrin and Ingrid. 'And you're not ... angry with us?'

Catrin gave a tight smile. 'Believe it or not, most of us have been there and done that. Sudden magical developments, bad omen, crippling fear of it being discovered. You fill in the blanks.'

'Besides,' said Ingrid, drily. 'If you've made it to the Fallow, then the worst has already happened.'

Magda felt all the devastating irony of her words. What more could the Ethers do to her than what they'd done in Wildbriar?

'However you might feel about this place,' Muriel warned, 'Promise us this: that nobody outside the room can find out. None of the girls from any other quadrant, and certainly none of the Ethers.'

Magda observed the faces of the other girls; their friends. They were *friends*, no longer *acquaintances*. Because this was the kind of thing you did not tell just anybody. Everybody realised the kind of deal that was struck made here, the kind of stakes that desperation bred. It was as good as handing over a box of matches and asking the other person not to strike a flame.

'If anyone here wanted to sell you out, we wouldn't have waited two months to try.'

'Way to put them at ease, Cat,' Alarice rolled her eyes. 'She means your secret's safe with us.'

The remark was a soothing balm, but not enough to calm the scalding waters of Magda's mind. She couldn't help but feel something else was itching, waiting to pounce. Their newfound acceptance was pockmarked with things that could still go wrong.

For one, Ingrid didn't look convinced.

'That's the thing that you wanted to tell us?' Her cheeks were spotted with high colour, as if she was embarrassed she'd even asked the question. 'I just ... I don't understand why now. What could you possibly have to gain from telling us?'

'We trust you,' said Muriel, simply. 'That's about it.'

'Oh.' The other girl looked even more embarrassed. 'I see.'

Magda's heart was pounding now, impossible to ignore. Everything they'd kept closely guarded was spilling out, and the sickly thump of blood in her chest was all too much to bear. 'There's something else, too.'

'Is there?'

'Well, my dreams are prophetic. So I was thinking, maybe we could use them to gather information. Work together to form a plan,' she continued, painfully aware of how brash it sounded. 'And Muriel's powers will be even more useful: because one day soon, she could have mastery over any Forest in the archipelago. Maybe even the entire woods.'

The wind crackled outside. If anyone had looked towards the window, they would have seen the strangest sight at the edge of the lawn. But nobody looked, and nobody wondered why the lanterns seemed to flicker before returning to their solid, vacant stare.

'Mastery over the woods,' Catrin's eyes widened. Her eyes had a faded look to them, like this was a hope that she had long since given up on. 'Not just any wood. Cunning Wood.'

'Exactly,' Muriel said slowly. Extending the invitation. Daring to voice the possibility. 'The crux of it is this: we've got a plan to get us out of here.'

'To get us out?'

'An escape plot, if you will.'

'We wait until the new moon, when it's darkest, and when Muriel's strong enough to defuse the poisons in the woodland. Then we make a break for it.' Magda waited for the idea to sink in. It was terrifying even to her, to voice such a thing aloud. 'With the right work, it should be possible to temporarily disarm the things that make Cunning Wood so dangerous. We could break the spell.'

'But that's impossible,' Ingrid was shaking her head. 'Walk through Cunning Wood and emerge unscathed?'

'Well, run through Cunning Wood is probably more like it.'

Outside, a cloud passed over the moon. The pale shadows gave it a soft chalky edge, like someone had tried to draw the sun, given up, then erased everything but the ashes.

'Are you sure this magic will be enough to protect us?' asked Catrin.

'It will be, soon enough. And by the time we're out of this place, the Ethers will regret having ever brought us here. That's the idea.'

The words hung in the air like sparkling fruit; a sugar-plum of a promise. Magda wondered if they would take it, or whether the sweetest fruit would turn to rot in an instant.

'I say it's worth a try,' Alarice nodded.

Catrin, too, gave the tiniest inclination of her head. 'I can't believe I'm agreeing to this. Never thought you two would be the ones to raise a rebellion.'

'Me, neither,' Ingrid's expression was unreadable. 'Wait til Rhos hears about this.'

'So are you in?'

There was a short nod. 'I'm sorry I doubted you. We'll help you, all of us.' A pause. 'Just don't make me regret it.'

A slow smile rippled through the room. They had voiced the most terrible thing, only to discover that perhaps it wasn't such a terrible thing after all. The others were on their side. All they had to do now was piece together an escape plan.

'Thank you.' Magda's chest ached with relief. 'Thank you for trusting us with this. We won't let you down.'

Right at that moment, the bell began to ring.

Everything paused to listen.

It was a light, musical sound, one that might have announced an ice cream van or some other cheerfully unimportant event. The look which was exchanged between the other girls told Muriel and Magda that it was not.

'Quick,' someone whispered. 'Get the lanterns.'

'What is it?'

'Follow us.' Ingrid was already on her feet and leading them out of the room, Alarice and Catrin and Muriel, in a long line of hands clasped tightly together.

All of them except Rhos.

What's wrong? Magda wanted to ask again, knowing somehow that it was the wrong question, that it would have all kinds of answers that she didn't want to hear. She didn't doubt the knowing. Some things spoke louder than words. The tension in Catrin's fingers, laced tightly between her own, spelt out terror that didn't dare to breathe its own name.

'This way,' Alarice tilted her head towards the arched hallway that marked the passageway beneath the courtyard.

The bell was still ringing, louder now, fiercer and more high-pitched. To Magda it sounded like the smallest, angriest god, who had played his favourite game and lost.

'What in Gwern's name are they doing?' Muriel hissed behind her.

They were arriving at the Ceremonial Grounds. Palely, but unmistakably, the silhouettes of all three Ethers were gathered in the distance, glittering cloaks and tall, hooded moonlight.

'They warned us this might happen,' was all Catrin said. The blood had drained from her face. 'That bell. I remember that bell.'

'Where's Rhos?' asked Muriel, her voice trembling. 'Does she know everyone's out here, Catrin?'

They were almost there now, reaching the place where everyone had assembled, right at the edge of the north orchard. Every girl and every Ether was gathered there. The forest of limbs made it difficult to see what they were actually looking at, until they got closer. Closer, and closer, and suddenly all too close together.

'Blessed threads,' someone murmured. 'The poor thing.'

Oh, was all Magda could think, *oh mercy* and *oh the weaver* and *oh, please, save us all.* Every hopeful thought had pitched itself clean out of her head and was draining down into the moon-sodden soil. Because right at the edge of Cunning Wood, one ankle over the threshold, was the body of a girl who looked a little like somebody they knew.

She was still in a way that was not sleep. Her softly curling red hair looked a little like Rhos's, except Rhos's hair had never matted and clumped in a thick, liquidy way that seemed to bleed into the earth. Her skin looked a little like Rhos's, except Rhos's skin had never wept the greenish red colour of mildew in the grass, had never torn itself in loose pockets and welded into craters in other places. Her mossy suede gloves, which lay discarded on the floor, were Rhos's, and those alone.

That pitiful body belonged to somebody else.

Paralysed, Magda cast a glance round to the other girls. Someone had to know what was going on, to understand whatever this frightening scene meant. It was Ingrid who moved the least, and who looked the most terrified.

No, said Ingrid's eyes, but her lips didn't move. *Is it this, is it really, is it is it is it. Rhos, Rhos, Rhos.*

That look was a plea with somebody who was already gone.

'We have gathered you here,' said a voice, Ether Stefania's, 'because your world is full of dangers. Here at the Fallow, we will keep you safe. But we can only protect you from them as long as you protect yourselves.'

The gloves were so clean, thought Magda, stupidly, unable to look away. Each panel of fabric was mustard-yellow and blemishless, jarring horribly with the rest of the sorry scene. It was unthinkable. Impossible. And yet there it was, laughing at them all.

'These are the perils of Cunning Wood,' said Ether Lorna. No blood touched their cloaks; no drop of red clouded their skin. But the woman looked tired to the bone, as if these lines were familiar and ancient. 'This is what happens to girls who stray from the path that has been so bountifully laid out for you here.'

There were plenty of books where girls and women were described as beautiful in death. But all the Fallow girls saw in it was horror. Death was not beauty, and death was not freedom from the evils that pursued them.

'She will be buried far away from this place,' said Ether Rhiannon, her voice strained. The tears streamed freely, but silently, down her cheeks. 'Somewhere quiet. Somewhere where she will be at peace.'

Peace, thought Magda, unable to move. The tears had all dried up in the storm. If peace had ever been an option for girls like them, she doubted they would find it now.

'She's — she's not —' Muriel took her hand, choking through sobs. 'I can't look, Mags. Tell me it's not her.'

Only minutes ago, the possibilities of escape had seemed so boundless. Now Magda wanted to gouge away the eyes of the night, put out that handful of stars that dared to shine over such a scene. The motionless body. The gloves. And the strange echo of feathers, brown and blue and white, that lay just beyond the orchard's edge.

It was a scene that Magda had witnessed before.

Unlike Tegwen Price, Rhoswen Merrick did not clamber to her feet and run screaming for her parents. She did not wring the water from her skirts or threaten they hadn't heard the last of this. But there was the same hurt in Muriel's eyes. The aching betrayal. The deep injustice of it all.

You're not the only one who has bad dreams, Magdalena Corrales.

PART IV

Interlude

Three Months After

Deep in the woods, the stone clocks ticked.

Cinnamon. Suet. Mace.

Nobody had ever promised the life of a witch would be easy, but it was a cautionary hazard which Grimoire Malgarty was prepared to take. She weighed out the ingredients without looking to the recipe, without needing to, before beginning to mix them in the heavy bowl.

Nights like these brewed bad storms. And being a stickler for the proper preparations, she'd already made sure the fire was roaring: one blue-grey grimalkin curled up in front of it like a living shadow.

'Gio!' she swatted at the second feline, who had brazenly ascended to the kitchen countertop. 'That is *not* for you.'

The gold-backed grimalkin ducked away haughtily. He didn't like it when things didn't go his way. That, thought Grimoire, makes two of us. Or three, if she were being pernickety.

The memory of Aurelia often came to her unbidden.

As she was mixing batter to make amber pudding. As she was lighting a fire. As she watched the storm dance outside the window. The same wild, curly hair as her own, except the colours shifted: bright copper and burnt green eyes. It was possible to leave behind a friend, or an old flame, but it was damn near impossible to forget a sister.

'Maelstrom?' Grimoire turned back to where the grimalkins were snoozing. A rich, savoury aroma was wafting from the oven, which she could only assume meant the rabbit was cooked. As much as she enjoyed it, she had never particularly excelled in savoury cooking. 'Rabbit's ready, pet.'

The response was immediate. Eyes wide, soft bushel of fur slinking down from the settee and appearing at her feet. She pulled the tray of meat from the oven with a thick tea towel, uttering a string of curses when it spat hot oil at her.

'There we go.'

Maelstrom was not a dainty eater, but there was a certain leopardish thrill to watching him dissect a rabbit. Caravaggio, who seemed to have renounced any predatory lineage in him, waited for her to dish up the rabbit into his bowl instead.

For all their caveats, she really was grateful for the grimalkins. They were the best company she had, most days, although she supposed that much had been her own doing. Hadn't she come here for that precise reason? To get away from what being Aurelia's sister meant?

She could still remember those last words they'd exchanged, clear as day, before everything changed.

I love him, Grim. Can't you be happy for me?

'Happy for a partridge on a shooting range,' she scowled, mixing the bowl of batter more violently than was strictly necessary. 'Happy for a heifer in a slaughterhouse.'

It was the same way she felt about all those girls, the ones who got chosen, because they were special. They hadn't learned yet what it really meant. That it was a dagger, cloaked in the disguise of mercy. Did the last two girls from Wildbriar know was it was, now, to be truly afraid?

The worst part was that she had not been able to save them.

'What's that, Gio?' She looked down to where the burnished golden grimalkin was trilling around her ankles. 'Something's wrong?'

The Fallow, he seemed to say, tangling urgently around her legs. *The Fallow needs your help.*

'You know I hate that place.'

But Caravaggio only kept staring at her with those big puppyish eyes. It wouldn't do to ignore him, especially with the sixth sense that her feline companions seemed to harbour.

'Fine,' she glared. 'I'll be back.'

She went to put on a cloak. It was her favourite: the spiderwebbed black silk one. Then she closed her eyes and envisioned the place she needed to get to. One, two, *three*.

Quick as a wink, new ground came tumbling beneath her. She stepped neatly onto a dewy lawn, slipping out of the shadows. There was a neatly picketed orchard, grey stone steeples, and a high rose window to the main building. In truth, the Fallow looked no worse for wear than she remembered: except this time there was a lingering scent of decay upon it. Green ash, or alder. The scent of burning.

If any of the Fallow girls realised what she was, thought Grimoire, they probably wondered why she had never come to their rescue. She would have done, if there was anywhere to go. Anywhere that would be safe. Any way she could do so without being found out, hunted down, condemned.

After all, Grimoire Malgarty knew what the Brenin did to those who wronged him once. She did not like to think of what he would do to those who wronged him twice.

When she reached the edge of the woods, it became clear what her grimalkins had sensed. Beyond the lily-of-the-valley was a hollow, a pocket of dead space, where there should have been a green tangle of undergrowth. She stopped. Knelt down. Inhaled once. It was enough to tell her that Caravaggio had been right, and it just about broke the witch's heart. Whoever had fallen here was young. She could still sense the outline of their laughter, the echo of a skip in their step: all of it juddering horribly, miserably, to a halt.

She could only hope they were with Gwern and Eila now. Taking a shaky breath, and feeling none the steadier for it, the witch got to her feet again. This new world hurt. She yearned to go back to a life that was as easy as cinnamon, suet, and mace.

Chapter 37
Elsewhere

Some years ago, Muriel had learned what it was to grieve a life some people didn't even see. She'd waited at the bus stop, rucksack over one shoulder: it was the snap of a new season, a crisp stroke of orange blotting the sky and pavements with honeyed leaves.

Then there was the badger.

It was nosing through the gutters on the other side of the road from her, unobtrusive in the morning sunlight. It snuffled with bright eyes in the leaf litter. Perhaps it had found something good to eat. And then, before she could even cry out, the broad-wheeled van came clattering past and wiped the little creature flat. What had been happily trundling through its day was suddenly guts, red and shiny, against cobblestones. The driver had not swerved. The driver had not slowed down. The driver, if she could bear to think it, had sped up.

As for Muriel, time stood paralysed. She crept on board and paid her fare; hoped nobody could see her red eyes and wet cheeks. Couldn't explain why she was crying when she got home.

A long while afterwards, she wondered if the grief of girlhood had always been this heavy.

It wasn't like human deaths, which were a different kind of awful: with those, months went by and all you had left were photographs. It was like that when her grandmother passed away. Printed pictures, everywhere. Nobody could bear to tamper with the gaunt image of the past, and Muriel couldn't even look it in the eye.

There was nobody for the crushed badger. No one who would lay a wreath of flowers, or tell its children what had happened. For people, bouquets gathered at the door for weeks afterwards, until the house stank with grief. Even the bins were soon overflowing with petals from people who hadn't come to visit in years.

Last time grief had come right at the crust of the season, a peaky sunrise too early for spring to have properly softened yet, and long before the butter months of April and May. This time hurt so much worse. This time it was Rhos who had been crumpled out of existence, their lovely friend with her bright voice, with as many hopes and dreams as all the rest of them, and Muriel couldn't move. Couldn't speak. Could barely believe the thing that had happened, even had a name.

That didn't stop the Ethers from giving it one, because between death and a funeral there was a crucial window of time. It was enough, they knew, to close the gap between rumour and report. Enough to silence speculation.

For rumour's sake, Rhos's death had been a tragic accident. A mishap from a girl who strayed too close to the poisoned forest, and learned by brutal example what it was to cross that threshold. Muriel didn't want to hear any of that. Instead she clenched the memory of Rhos's smile into the deepest, safest, place she knew.

Snow forgot, and earth forgot, but she would remember.

*

'Nobody's going to say it, are they.' Alarice's fingernails had etched deep lines into the table. The food on her dinner plate was untouched. 'She didn't just wander into the woods and die.'

'Don't,' warned Ingrid. 'Don't say that.'

'Everyone's thinking it, whatever they're pretending.'

The table went silent. Two weeks had passed, and nothing felt real.

'We all miss her, Allie,' said Catrin, softly. 'Hypothesising won't bring her back.'

'That's not what I'm doing.'

'But you're in mourning. Your brain's just about saturated with grief and terror and all kinds of things you should've never had to deal with. It's impossible to think straight right now.'

'That's exactly what the Ethers want us to believe,' said Alarice, grimly. 'They want us to mourn so hard that we neglect to look closely, that we let them sweep it all under the rug and forget this ever happened!'

Muriel leaned forward. 'You think it was the Ethers who did this?'

'Is it really that unthinkable?' Alarice stared. 'You said it yourself a few months ago. The Progressions happen twice a year, when the eldest girls get selected for transfer. What happens to the ones who don't make the cut?'

By eighteen, you must be ready.

'That's not for ages,' said Magda, alarmed. 'Besides, it's nothing to do with this. They can't just randomly attack teenagers because they weren't good enough at sewing.'

Deep down, though, she wondered if they could do far worse. It was the unspoken edge to each class, like the unsightly back face of an embroidery hoop. There were things that none of them wanted to see; the simple solution was to not look.

'You've got a point,' said Catrin. 'Something wasn't right.'

'That doesn't mean they killed her!'

'Everything seemed, well, stilted.'

'And the gloves,' Muriel considered. It felt wrong to contemplate these things so baldly, as if they were discussing furniture arrangements. 'I never saw her take them off before.'

They sat there for a while, unable to answer. It was better if you didn't inspect the details too closely. If you kept the separate elements in isolation, a piece of distorted skin and flash of bloody bones didn't constellate to form a person who had once laughed and joked with them at this very table.

'I hate this.' Ingrid looked like she was on the verge of tears. 'I hate talking about her like she's some kind of puzzle piece. She was our friend. Can't we focus on that, before we try to dissect how she died?'

'I'm sorry,' Muriel faltered, as if it made the slightest bit of difference right now. *Sorry* meant nothing without action. *Sorry* was a coward's excuse.

'It's too soon for this,' said Ingrid, and she left the table.

It was too soon. Muriel couldn't have agreed more, and yet the days gathered like lace around a set of pins. Slowly, but surely, the lace was being made, the bobbins floating over and under, and the tapestry of their life grew inch by inch around the gaps.

'We can't go back to how things were, can we.'

'I don't think so,' Alarice poked at the soup in her bowl, which had long since turned cold. 'Something happened to Rhos, and we have to find out what.'

A pang of shame stabbed Muriel in the stomach. If one of them had only gone outside, had looked for Rhos instead of talking on that night...

'Those things we said. About us, and a way for us to get out of here,' Magda looked down, wracked with the same guilt. 'I'm sorry for bringing it up. But I can understand if you've changed your mind.'

'This isn't your fault,' Catrin was shaking her head. 'It doesn't change the agreement.'

'But things are different, too,' said Alarice. She ran an anxious hand over the back of her neck. 'That plan's more important than ever. If we don't get out of here fast, then the same thing that happened to Rhos...'

She didn't finish the sentence. She didn't have to.

Now that the threat was out there, no one was safe.

*

Seven more days went by, and the girls of the North Quadrant perfected the art of looking Elsewhere. They would look anywhere but directly into the other person's eyes. At the walls. At the carpets. At the grass, which grew a subtle shade greener. And when the time came to finally change into the ceremonial robes for the end of the month, Muriel felt numb.

Something hollow had made its home inside her chest. The slow, creeping recognition that the Fallow was caught between two worlds: the temperate north, and the ancient south. She knew now that strange things happened in the cut-between places.

'Are you ready to go?'

Catrin was at the door, having managed to make the ceremonial robes look almost glamorous. The gold of her hair reflected in the dull fabric, but she didn't smile.

'I will be soon,' Muriel pulled at the ill-fitting cloak. 'Are the others out already?'

She tried to distract herself after they filed into the corridor, focusing hard on the girl in front of her. If she didn't look away from Alarice's silhouette, then maybe the world beyond it could stop existing. It worked, for a little while. Only once they reached the clearing, a feeling like cut glass slivered between her intestines.

'Welcome, takers of the Ceremony,' announced Ether Lorna.

She wore the same arched headdress as last month, one side of her face illuminated by the glow of the main building. Each movement she made was like a river towards the sea. Deceptively strong, and sinuous.

'Who will be our Keeper of the Flame tonight?'

'We will,' replied the circle.

For not the first time that day, Muriel wished the ground would wrap itself around her and swallow her into the dark earth. It was as intolerable standing here as it would've been to walk a bed of hot coals. More than that, she couldn't reconcile this version of Ether Lorna with the one who taught them Botany and read them star charts in the daytime. Where was that kindly mistress now? This person was a stranger: someone who picked for weakness among the Fallow girls and, when she found it, scraped at the decay like an abscess.

It was difficult not to flinch as the cold fingers inevitably brushed past her shoulder. Then, to Muriel's relief, the Ether moved along to the next girl. The younger students remained frozen, watching as she settled on a meek-eyed girl whose ceremonial cloak was far too big for her. She could only have been eleven or twelve. Barely old enough to call a kid.

'Tabitha Penry, you will be our Keeper of the Flame for this Ceremony. It is with great honour that we take you in our arms tonight.'

On the left-hand side of the shivering girl, Ingrid lowered her eyes. Maybe she felt the grace, and anguish, of being spared just as much as the rest of them did.

'Elder spirit, we summon you,' Ether Lorna placed a palm against the ground. Her voice was unrecognisable. 'The sisters of the Fallow beseech your blessing, for the New Moon, and for the Ceremony.'

Unable to protest, Tabitha began her small, shaky journey towards the middle of the circle. The towering standing-stones cast their shadow over her, bluestone against grey night, almost as still as the circle of girls around her.

Muriel could feel the grass beneath her bare feet. It was angry, scratching at her ankles like it was willing her to do something. Anything but tolerate it.

'Miss Penry, are you prepared to help your sisters?'

The girl didn't speak; only gave a near-imperceptible nod. Perhaps it didn't matter if she agreed or not. She had been chosen by forces that she couldn't hope to contest with.

'In Gwern's name, let her not burn.'

The pile of wood at the centre of the circle seemed to loom higher than ever, and the familiar trill of fear soured to acid in Muriel's stomach. She couldn't have moved then even if she'd wanted to.

'Miss Penry, please step onto the pyre.'

Now it was too late, and they were saying the words.

The words that always got said right before they –

Before nothing. Muriel struggled to control her breathing. *This was not death. The girl would not be harmed.* Still it felt like torture watching their chosen Keeper of the Flame stepped forwards, face turning pale as she ascended the pyre.

'Ladies, light your torches.'

She bent down and picked up the rough length of wood at her feet. The torchwood, carved with its elegant glyphs of fire and ash, should have been a lovely thing. But some sweet things were meant to flourish, and others were destined to burn. She walked in a daze, her feet obeying commands that weren't her own.

'*Now.*'

Hours later, after the fire had long since burnt to ash, Muriel would try to get the smell of smoke out of the fabric. But it was no good. The scent had already traced itself across her skin.

Chapter 38

Evergreen

'It doesn't make sense,' said Catrin, over her bowl of porridge. 'That was no ordinary fire.'

'Didn't you notice her cloak? They're saying she added something to the fabric, sewed it into the underlayer.'

'Like what?'

The breakfast table hummed with conspiracy. What nobody could understand was exactly how a scrap of a girl like Tabitha Penry had managed to leave the pyre not just unscathed, but glowing. Instead of its usual coppery colour, the flame had turned a shimmering green hue the moment it touched her skin.

Chartreuse, thought Muriel. *That was the word.*

'The cloak burns, but the girl remains unharmed.' Catrin. Her nail varnish was chipped, raw nail peeking through the bitten-down edges. 'It's always the same sequence of events.'

That was what made it a Ceremony, after all. What set it apart from every other day: a sky the colour of gristle, an even stormier atmosphere, and the thick cloak of fear that overlaid everything.

'Except this time, something stopped it from working.'

Muriel watched without speaking. She felt like a silkworm, tangled in the lacy pink shadows of the morning. She wanted nothing more desperately than to scrape the remnants of last night from her skin. To step out of the confines of this conversation — of its sphere of relevance.

But she and Magda were as much Fallow girls as any of them by now, and the news stuck fast.

'Do you know what it was that she embroidered there?' she asked, giving in to curiosity. 'Was it a witch-rune, or some kind of protective glyph?'

'It was just a common chain, stitched onto the hem.'

'Huh. Well, that girl must have a gilded needle.'

The table mulled to quiet again. Almost everyone had deliberately spread their plates and belongings a little further apart, so that the new space wouldn't glare at them so starkly.

'Pass us the ladle, will you?'

Steam hissed spitefully as Muriel replaced the pot lid. Just weeks ago, the same cauldron had been filled with fresh cockles: but since the Sickness dipped its fingers beyond the coast, tides turned to tempests. These days the fisherwomen came back empty-handed, if they came back at all.

'A gilded needle,' Alarice said slowly. 'Maybe there's something in that.'

'How do you mean?'

'The method. She could have found some way to imbue the stitches with Tidal magic.'

'But how?' Catrin shook her head. 'She must have learned somewhere. There's no such art.'

'What if there is?'

Muriel glanced sideways to where Ingrid had spoken. It was the first thing she'd said all day. 'You think there's something in the stitches?'

'There could be,' Ingrid reasoned. 'When we've got time at the cove, we could share notes to see if there's a pattern.'

'I thought you wanted to wait until the end of the week?'

'That was only if nothing else happened.' She hesitated. 'This is something.'

*

Outside, the February frost lay hard upon the ground. The trees shivered like knives: long shadows and cold white bark. But the medlars needed to be harvested.

Muriel reached between the boughs with new vigour, because at least it was something to do. She was under no illusion that they forgot their remorse while picking the fruits: but at least they could act as if they weren't drowning in that remorse. It was an exhilarating masquerade in which they pretended this was just ordinary life, and these their ordinary tasks.

'You can bring the wheelbarrows over here, girls.'

As ever, seeing Ether Lorna after the Ceremony was a jarring experience. She was a lean-looking woman with an eye for precision, and Muriel didn't suppose those toned forearms had come from sitting around and letting the Fallow orchard overgrow. As they were rapidly learning, maintaining those orchards was hard bloody work.

'Blasted things,' Alarice looked displeased by the time they'd emptied the fourth wheelbarrow of the hard brown fruits. 'My wrists hurt.'

'This barrowful's going to be the end of me.'

'I'll hear none of that, Miss Scurlock!' Ether Lorna called back. 'Those medlars aren't going to gather themselves.'

It took almost an hour to pick the hard leathery fruits from the trees, tumble them into the wheelbarrows, and fill the storehouse with stacks of brown and olive pomes. Stone fruits reminded Muriel of the summer, of long, blushing dusks. These medlars would take several weeks to soften. Then, after they'd bletted, they'd be rich pickings for sweet jelly and all kinds of curds.

She picked up the wheelbarrow again, suddenly resentful. Medlar tart had been her dad's favourite. But medlar tart belonged to another place now, a softness that had long waned. Her parents might as well have lived on a different continent, for all the Ethers cared.

*

The prophecy and its fickle temperament grew starker hour by hour.

Everything we're storing will come in useful down the line, the Ethers reminded them. *You just don't know how long anything's going to last these days.*

Muriel didn't deny it. Yet the strangest part was how the Fallow girls never quite saw any of it. Everything worth knowing seemed to happen just outside of their reach. And so, she supposed, it was a relief when a knock came at her door. Three sharp taps, the signal of someone else existing out there. Of being a little less alone.

'Hello?'

A set of neatly-manicured fingers curled around the side of the door and pulled it open. Each nail was painted a uniform emerald, with a dark red flower at the centre, and Muriel could only think of one person who would go to the trouble of such a painting.

'Alarice. What's the matter?'

'What are you and Magda doing up here?' asked Alarice. 'The others were beginning to worry.'

She looked tired: or rather, empty. All the light had fled her eyes.

'I thought the meeting was ...'

'Tonight,' the other girl fixed her with a reproving look. 'Starting ten minutes ago.'

'Oh, crap. Sorry,' she went to gather her belongings quickly. 'Mags, let's get going.'

'What?'

'It's tonight.'

Perhaps they had forgotten the meeting, because of all the effort it took not to think about the other thing. It had been a tacit agreement; an accord not to disturb those troubled waters unless somebody else brought it up first. But it rattled through the bones of the building at every corner.

Gone.

Rhos was gone.

Every step they took, every plan they made, or meeting they held, would now be stained with her absence. When they finally reached the door to the cove, the tall arched windows swam with stars.

'Silvana. Corrales,' Catrin nodded to them. 'Glad you made it in the end.'

The conversation lasted an indeterminate period of time. Ghosts, instead of words, swam around her. Muriel could have been half-asleep, for all the others cared. All their talk of defiance and escape turned to paper houses, blurring in the rain.

'The patterns in the sewing,' somebody was saying. 'You think it was a secret rune?'

'I think there was something she knew, and we didn't.'

'Maybe they did,' Ingrid rested her head in her hands. 'Either it's very well hidden, or it's very obvious, and we're just not seeing it.'

'Either way, it protected her.'

The medlar of Muriel's own heart clenched itself tighter. Rotted a little deeper. In the dormitory above them, Rhos's bedsheets would already have been stripped clean; her clothes-draws gutted for parts. A flock of favourite posters, torn from the walls. She was only just realising these things, weeks after the collision.

'Magda, didn't you have something else to tell us?' asked Alarice, hoping to change the subject. 'About a vision.'

'I mean, only if the others wanted to hear it,' Magda looked uncomfortable. How hollow the words sounded. How futile the possibility.

Catrin nodded *yes*. 'Go on.'

'So ... I had this dream, about the library in the woods. It started with a shadow across the lawn,' Magda began. The tale unfolded like a map: here was the path through the woods. Here, the ivy-ridden library. Here, a shelf of moth-eaten old tomes.

'But that's impossible,' somebody was saying.

Outside, the pit of winter was hissing like hot oil. Muriel fidgeted. She had been a fool to come to the meeting in the first place. Every word was the wrong word; every line, the wrong line. She waited for the story to end, and for the book to snap shut.

'What's that supposed to mean, "Come back with your eyes open"? Either it's messing with you, or you've got a death wish.'

'I'd argue the latter.'

'Do you think it's a bad omen, to be dreaming about libraries at all?'

'It's only a vision,' said Catrin. 'Whatever the legends say about those places, I hardly think dreaming about one is a crime.'

'So it's not a real place?'

'It shouldn't be,' Magda deliberated. The unwritten words were there, hovering at her lips. *But what if it is?*

And what, then?

What were they supposed to do about that?

Muriel shifted, cross-legged, and decided to speak. 'I don't think the building matters. It's what's inside that we should be worrying about. Somebody, or something, seems to know a great deal more about you than we do about it.'

'The librarian,' Magda met her eye.

People always expected librarians to look a certain kind of way. Short, tidy lady with a neat pair of spectacles and an encyclopaedic knowledge of her shelves. Of course other librarians existed. Of course it was a tired stereotype. But for such a librarian to exist in such nebulous fashion, totally unperceived, and invisible, defied any order of logic that they'd known.

'You need to find out who's behind this, Mags.'

'Well, I'll try my best.'

There was a general murmur of assent. Muriel waited for the fragile hope to condense. It melted, slick as ice, over the jagged edges of her grief.

Chapter 39

The Screamer of the Woods

Tegwen Price had developed a taste for privilege in the way that one developed a taste for butter. Unknowingly, but unmistakably, her life had been coated in it. Seasoned with it. Turned this way or that with a thin skim of grease: the richest, creamiest grease that could be afforded. It was not like oil, which sizzled at a skelter-high heat in the pan, because butter melted. Butter indulged. It dripped from the jaws long after the morsel was devoured.

It left wanting for more.

At least, that was how Magda saw it. Not that it excused her own actions, or allowed her to sleep at night, because it was an excuse of the lowliest order.

If Tegwen Price had been conceited, spiteful, and totally ignorant of her obnoxious nature, then perhaps she could feel slightly less terrible about what she had done.

Rhos's death had changed that.

The day Magda went into the woods and spotted Tegwen by the riverbank, the other girl was watching the nest of gringelots. There were all kinds of things that grew in the forest — tumbledown trees, slate jays, wild hartlets — but the gringelots were Magda's favourite, and this particular burrow was inhabited by a mother with two cubs. They were such quixotic creatures you never knew quite what they'd do: in winter, their downy fur rippled from colour to colour, and their long sleek bodies dangled like ribbons from the treetops.

Tegwen stayed there a long time, and so did Magda. It was the assumption that steered her wrong, in the end. She took the flash of silver in Tegwen's hands for a trap. Silver, shiny, skeletal. And the thought that those hapless creatures might get hurt: that was what drove her to her feet to confront the other girl. Even the village idiot knew gringelots were easy prey.

Magda? What are you doing here? Why are you looking at me like —

She struggled with the memory. The first time Muriel had asked what happened next, it had taken a long time to gather the courage. There was no name for the feelings she had felt. She hadn't known such feelings could exist.

The eldest cub had poked its head out of the burrow, she had told Muriel. *I ran towards the nest, to try and scare Tegwen away from them. I never meant to hurt anyone.*

Now, when she played the memory back, it was Rhos who knelt at the water's edge.

She lost her footing and slipped over the edge of the riverbank. She hit her head, Magda bit her lip, remembering the unreal gush of red that suddenly mingled with the silver stream. *I thought she was... But then she was scrambling in the water down there, and I tried to pull her out. The silver was only a compass, she'd been following an old trail through the woods.*

Muriel had said nothing, only given her the tightest hug. The hug told her it wasn't her fault, that it was all going to be okay. Neither were true.

By the time we got out of there, I should have known it was all over. That her parents would look at me and see one thing.

Rhos's dead eyes stared up at her, floating in the river. Only now did Magda realise they were one and the same. It didn't matter who was the better person: neither girl had deserved to suffer that way. All of them, all of them, deserved better than this.

*

'I'm going out,' Muriel turned to the other side of the dormitory, where Magda sat reading.

'But it's dark.'

'I won't be long. Just need to get some fresh air, stretch my legs a bit.'

Magda glanced at the clock, worried. It was half-past eleven, and the waning moon was washed in pale green light. 'I can come with you?'

'It's alright, you stay and get some rest. I'll be back before midnight,' she turned the handle quietly, 'Don't stay up.'

The truth was that Muriel needed to get outside like a scab needed to be picked. Some bright kernel in her mind had started fighting its way out, and she hurried downstairs with increasing urgency. *El morbo*, as her sisters called it. That unkillable, morbid curiosity. It was the sensation of looking into a dark cellar, already knowing what you would find on the other side. The foot over the doorstep when you knew what lurked behind it.

Here were the facts.

One, Muriel Silvana had crossed the north orchard alone.

Two, she had reached the edge of grass where they'd found the body. A mass of striped blue feathers — a jay's, she was pretty sure — littered the earth, contours split and sticky with damp. The rest of the bird was nowhere to be seen, but Muriel doubted it had escaped with its life: one plume was still attached to a piece of shredded sinew.

Three, she was not as alone as she thought. Somewhere in the undergrowth, a shadow was moving through the dark like tailor's chalk over greige. Only a whisper, barely scraping the corners of her vision, but Muriel knew.

Something was watching her from within the woods.

It was important not to cry out, because any noise would destroy the night's carefully-earned invisibility. Were it not for fear of what lurked in the shadows, however, Muriel would have screamed blue murder. It took a strong will to stifle the terror in her throat. Gradually, her night vision adjusted to the soupy dusk, and by that point the Something in the woods had moved.

All she saw were burning red eyes.

It couldn't be ellylldân, *elf fire,* because the ground was dry and marshless. Water did not flow here; blood did. Nonetheless, Muriel realised with growing concern, it had her in its thrall. She couldn't help but be transfixed by the pale flare of light from behind the trees. Was this what she had come out looking for? Had it known that she would come?

Step forward, those red eyes seemed to sing. A silhouette lurked behind them, tall and vaguely canine, though Muriel had never seen a dog with a glare so piercing. It had to be something else, then. Something strange and wonderful. A mystery that was hers for the taking.

In spite of everything, she inched closer to its haunting glow.

Come closer.

A root caught under her feet, but she ignored it. She was faintly aware of a crackling sound coming from the earth, a rising tremor, but she was so close to the woods, now. Surely it couldn't hurt to investigate just a little further.

Right at that moment, the silhouette in the undergrowth darted to one side, a tail — or a paw — flashing behind it.

Here.

All at once, Muriel was in the dark. That was when the first real inkling of danger struck her: a total absence of illumination. The bright red eyes were extinguished. That, and the silence: for Welsh nights were not like Costa Rican ones. There was no pleasant cacophony of insects to keep you company, not a flicker of softly croaking potoos, or even the shimmy of branches crackling above.

Alone, and unnerved, every instinct called for her to turn back.

So Muriel began to retrace her steps. The sense of Something watching her had not disappeared along with the light: before she could even reach the orchard, a profound gravity had begun to pull her down, down into the ground.

Alarmed, she pulled away. But suddenly her arms weighed twice as much as normal. They were waterlogged bread, drowned loaves instead of flesh. She tried to raise one, couldn't, and felt a tremor of fear run down her spine.

This was no illusion.

Whatever was lurking in the Forest had to be playing a nasty trick on her: or why else would her feet no longer cooperate? She couldn't run; couldn't even curse her luck, because her lips had stuck fast. It was like trying to wade through marsh water as the weeds sucked you down. She felt the lobes of her jaw meld together; a sluggish panic in beating in her chest.

What's happening to me?

If she could only break free of whatever spell she'd walked into. Then, she would have the chance to run back to the cloisters and back up the stairs, back to the North Quadrant and her safe, comfortable bed. Magda would listen to her story in awe, tell her to never get into such trouble again, and they'd both drift off to sleep without a further worry in the world. If she could do that one thing, then the rest of it could wait for another day.

Or, if only somebody looked out through the window. Anybody might have seen her there: but it was late. She had insisted on going alone, for reasons she couldn't quite name, and Magda had respected that wish, even if she hadn't been happy about it.

Nobody looked out.

The presence of the red-eyed spirit weighed heavier.

With each struggle she made, Muriel's limbs refused to budge. The absurdity of the situation almost made her want to laugh. Yes, she'd felt a morbid itch to go outside tonight. Yes, she'd wanted to go for a walk. But what invisible line had been crossed, for her to deserve any of the horror show that was now unfolding?

Come back, hummed the presence in the woods. *Here. Closer. Another step.*

Muriel felt her body twist towards the treeline, like a ballerina in a music-box. Hingelike and mechanical. Of all the Forests' names, she knew, Cunning Wood had the most: the Poisoner's Forest; the Forsaken Land; the Rotted Copse. They had learned each one of them in Mrs Sachar's Geography class. For a moment she held onto those names as lightly as a child holding a balloon, waiting to be lifted out of the maze.

Then the first roots ruptured her right foot.

It was agony like she'd never felt: splintered tendon and lovely white bone smiling for the camera, gleaming back at moonlight they had never seen. Muriel gasped, her stomach turning, as the blood gloated over those sickly roots and drank itself into the ground.

Her breath came shallow. Her knees crumpled beneath her.

It was too late, too late to go back.

Come closer, the shadow beckoned. *Just another step closer.*

She was lying mere paces from the edge of Cunning Wood.

She closed her eyes.

The scene held itself, ink in suspension. It could've been minutes, could've been hours; Muriel wasn't sure she could tell the difference any more. The pain sang until it didn't. And finally, after an indeterminate amount of time, she realised the vicious roots had withered away.

Her feet were free again.

What in Gwern's name just happened to me? she wondered, leaning down to inspect the damage. A grisly delta was blossoming where the roots had pierced her skin. Slow, syrup-thick. A red ring circled her ankle. Muriel knew better than to expect it would hold her weight: but to her astonishment, the bones there seemed miraculously unbroken, and — even more miraculously — functional. Each toe followed her command when she gave them a tentative flex. Every lungful of fresh air was gracious, bountiful beyond words.

'I'll kill you,' she whispered, getting to her feet. 'I'll kill you if you ever do that to me again.'

The woods didn't reply. She'd almost expected a monster the size of a house to come rattling out of the woods, to knock her down then and there. After what had just happened, she wanted something to blame; something to fight. There was nothing but the beat of the wind-flocked grass. The pounding of her heart, like a broken clock.

At long last, like an unexpected party guest, a largeish grey dog emerged from between the trees.

The dog sat back on its haunches and gave a loud *woof.*

Muriel blinked. This wasn't the red-eyed monster that had lured her to damnation. It wasn't even the wolfish beast that Magda had described in her visions, although there was something familiar about it. It had a crooked tail and one ear that was more lopsided than the other one.

It was now staring directly at her.

'You look just like him,' she shook her head, feeling the sudden urge to cry. It was odd how such a thing could make a person emotional. Besides: Plover had been larger, and scruffier, than the dog that was sitting before her.

But still.

You, the wolfhound seemed to say, *You, you, you.*

'What about me?' Muriel raised an eyebrow. 'I've just had a near-death experience, thanks very much. I don't need anything else to be dealing with right now.'

With its large, poignant eyes, the dog gave her a look of utter desperation. It turned back towards the woods with its tail half-wagging, and glanced back over its shoulder to see if she was following.

And then Muriel understood.

*

She didn't know how long they walked for. The hours slipped free of their leash, turning cartwheels through the undergrowth and flaring vicious laughter when she tried to keep up. All she knew was that she had to go on. Each footstep echoed, sweat beading her forehead, until the vegetation thinned to a clearing.

Blessed threads, the wonder of it all.

Each breath ricocheted off the architecture of the new space. Each step was unfathomable, because it was real. The grey wolfhound skipped happily in front of her, moonlight skimming its paws.

'Is this what you wanted?' she asked the dog, as if it could reply. 'You'd better help me get back afterwards, you know.'

In response, the hound began to scrabble at the ground in front of her. They were entering a new patch of woodland, and she wondered what sadistic person had thought to hide such a lovely glen in the first place. Dewdrops dripped. Buttercups glittered with pallid yellow light. This was the kind of grove where you'd imagine unicorns to have drunken, or pixies to have darned their shoes. But nobody darned their shoes here, because Cunning Wood was by definition impenetrable.

Except for her.

For the veridian, whose very blood protected against every toxin that riddled the earth. When the dog had looked at her with those eyes, she finally understood what had happened. And there hadn't been a damned thing she could do to prevent it.

Bones had cracked.

Blood was spilt.

And her magic, her unfathomable magic, had come rising up to protect her. Faintly, Grimoire Malgarty's words scattered through her mind: magnolia leaves on the breeze, bright white and blinding.

In many parts, veridians are considered the most powerful among the Folk.

Before Muriel had had the chance to ask questions, though, the wolfhound had begun moving. If she hadn't pursued it right then, it would have slipped away entirely. Which, all things considered, perhaps wouldn't have been such a bad option.

The thing about magic was that it came at a price.

'Wait for me!' she'd yelled after it. 'Wait.'

The creature had showed no signs of slowing down. It was now or never, because this was her chance, and —

Was this what had happened to Rhos?

The thought had almost stopped her, almost made her hesitate.

And what was she thinking? There was no way she could do this, not with her friends waiting for her back at the Fallow, and her family waiting for her back in the North. She couldn't risk it all on such a chance assumption.

But the heat of her magic burned in her blood. It was a knowing, and for Muriel Silvana, the price of magic was knowing. The regret of *what if* would torment her, and she had been unable to bear it any longer.

She'd kept her eyes shut. There were some powers that screamed to be obeyed, and so she followed the silent command to walk forwards, not stopping until the shadow of the forest had closed around her.

When she opened them again, the blood was gone from her feet. Her skin was smooth, brown, and unblemished.

And she was inside Cunning Wood.

*

Inside the tall white building, a book lay open on the desk. The floor was crowded with papers; the halls of the cavernous building high and shadowy. It was exactly as Magda had described, if not more so: because who kept seventeen copies of the same paperback, for goodness' sake? And why couldn't they be bothered to shake the dust from their curtains?

Welcome to the Vespertine Library, read the cover of the entry-book. *Please sign the entry book if you wish to consult a librarian.*

Muriel took a deep breath.

Then she said, 'I know you're in there.'

For a moment there was nothing, except the smell of damp wood and faded leather dustjackets. There was a shuffling of papers, like the lightest breeze crossing the room.

Impatient, she cleared her throat. 'I haven't got all night, you know.'

'Haven't got all night?' replied a voice in the dark. It was golden and cursive; rippling of burnt sienna. 'Not often travellers come to this neck of the woods.'

The voice was an arrow, landing on its target. The voice was the thing that had to be seen to be believed. And the voice was proof that Muriel wasn't crazy, wasn't as absolutely delusional as she'd feared moments earlier.

A flicker of a smile played on her lips. Not even a vision could have been this strange, if Magda's visions had ever been just that.

'So you do exist,' she ventured, aware of the awkward silence that she'd left hanging.

'Exist? I should certainly think so.'

'And this. It's all real, isn't it? A library in the woods.'

'Your friend was brave enough to dream it,' replied the voice, cold and elusive. It seemed to come from behind the chalky stone, then it shifted to the trees, and then away again. 'You were brave enough to find it.'

Chapter 40

Small Hours

There was a quiet peace in repairing things. As Alarice knelt over the piece of cloth in her hands, the needle darted in and out of the fabric. Soon it would be time to go. But until then, she could snatch a few minutes' sewing. A tear slipstitched closed. A loop pulled back through its ladder.

This was the imperceptible act of salvation.

Often, the work reminded her of a surgeon's. The glamour of a curved needle that sutured wounds; the gore which coated it. For a surgeon, though, it was a matter of life and death, whereas she was only fixing the cuff of a jumper. It had snagged on her favourite charm bracelet: the silver slipper's heel had pierced a hole in the knitted fabric. Somehow, fixing the small abyss didn't feel like a lesser task. Clothes weren't everything, but didn't people wear their favourite garments like a second skin? They covered the things you wanted hidden. They kept you safe.

As she moved along, the stitches settled. A little more tension here, an invisible knot there, and it would be done. The only thing distracting her was a song that was stuck in her head, which Catrin had been humming the previous day. She was always doing that. It was one of Alarice's few regrets that she could never join in.

It was somewhat regrettable, too, that she could let Muriel and Magda trust her with their secret, while she couldn't trust them with her own. It scared her, that oldest scar. It hung around her neck like a spiderwebbed necklace, so bright and glittering that you could almost forget about its weight.

She set down the piece of darning.

Then she heard voices outside her door, and knew that it was time to go.

*

'Where were you?'

Alarice observed the sharp clang of the door to the breakfast hall as it closed behind Muriel. She looked alert in a way that was not well-rested, closer to a rabbit's eyes, all whites and twitchy vigilance.

'You were gone all night,' Magda repeated. 'They had us up at dawn, Muriel. I thought Stefania would ask questions. We'd have had no idea what to tell them.'

'I came back as fast as I could,' said Muriel. Something hard and agrestal hovered below the words, like a sparrowhawk waiting to dive. 'It took longer than I was expecting. I'm sorry.'

'Didn't you think we'd get concerned?'

'You're the one who used to go sneaking off into abandoned libraries!'

'That was different,' said Magda. 'That was ... A long time ago.'

'I told you I'd be careful. And I was.'

'You missed the dawn Invocation,' Ingrid's eyes were stones. 'Maybe you should have thought about that first.'

The Invocation had been mercifully short, but numbing. It was the funeral rites which had made Alarice's stomach turn. The things they'd said about Rhos, as if she could really be folded away so neatly beneath the earth. As if this was a sorry nightmare that had everybody regretted to have witnessed. Unlike a bad dream, however, there was no waking up on the other side.

'What?' Muriel faltered. 'I ... I had no idea. I thought the custom was to wait a few months before any of that.'

'They're probably in a hurry to cover things up. And who can blame them? The quicker it's done, the fewer questions we can ask.'

'I'm so sorry,' Muriel's voice was very small. 'If I'd known, I would never have ...'

But what was there she could say? That she'd have dropped everything and returned to a sad and lonely graveside, as if her presence could somehow cheer the room? She'd already grimaced alongside them through the worst of times; the Invocation was merely the charade, the condensation of grief which was permitted before everybody decided *that was quite enough of that.*

'I'm sorry.'

'It wasn't nice,' Ingrid sighed, the tension suddenly leaving her voice like a spring gone slack. 'Maybe it's best you didn't have to see it.'

*

Over the sleek curve of afternoon, the predators circled. Merlin, sparrowhawk, and kites hovered several hundred metres above the crest of desert noon, their skies miles beyond the gardens of the Fallow.

Pigeon 821 felt terribly out of place among them all. She really didn't want to be there, if she was honest, but she was carrying a vitally important message with her. It had to arrive. There was no contingency plan for her failing to deliver.

Back in the heyday of Wildbriar, she had been among the best of her ranks. It had been a sorry descent since her Messenger Human had vanished: because what was a pigeon to do without someone to bring them post? To entrust with their most precious words? Pigeon 821 had searched far and wide, but the girl had vanished off the face of the earth.

At least, so it had seemed until this morning.

Now the scroll weighed heavy in her claws, and she flew faster. Lower, too, than the hovering mealy-eyed raptors, who she most fervently hoped would turn elsewhere. To her relief, the scenery soon began to change: high, frost-cragged mountains turned to lowlands and valleys, and the River Vesper shone into sight. It was her most familiar beacon. For a little while it seemed that the Fallow was not so far away; that her message would reach its destination as they'd hoped.

She didn't even see the falcon dive.

From the edge of the Glasshouse, if one of the girls had looked up just slightly, they might have seen something like war on the horizon. Had they peered into the far skies, the clearest view of the skirmish would have unfolded before them. Really, it was quite a sight to behold: the blue-cream speckles of the peregrine, tangled against the indignant squawking of a valiant pigeon. It was the kind of odds that nobody bet on, because there were no two ways about it.

At the heart of her misery, Pigeon 821 felt the most remorse for the girl who'd trusted her with her words. She'd known it was a long way to go. But she also knew that Pigeon 821 had never failed at such a task before. And this? This was a betrayal of the worst kind.

As they fell, she caught a glimpse of a girl inside the Glasshouse with dark braids and burgundy nail varnish. She was distracted, carrying flowerpots from shelf to shelf, but there was no mistaking her. The first thing that Pigeon 821 had ever learned of this place was that this particular girl sometimes left crumbs for the crows and pigeons on the window ledges. It seemed ironic to only realise the location's significance too late, after her Messenger Human's whereabouts had been belatedly identified. And there she was now: standing right beside the kindly stranger!

Still falling, Pigeon 821 gave a squawk that she doubted Muriel Silvana would hear. She was so close, and all too far away. She hated not to be able to convey the handful of gratitude that was surely due her friend. And she wondered, as they plummeted towards the ground, if anybody would know that she had tried her best.

Without warning, the light slipped loose entirely. A dozen amber clouds snuffed themselves out, and, strip by strip, the letter dissolved on the wind: torn away by that cruel, hooked beak.

Slowly, silently, the scattered pieces of Lucía Silvana's handwriting rained down, like snow over the isles.

*

'I'm sorry I got angry with you this morning. It was just the Invocation, it really threw me.'

Muriel didn't look up, and continued to study her plate of potato curry. 'You've got every right to be upset.'

'But I shouldn't have —'

'We're not upset,' Catrin placed a well-meaning hand on Ingrid's shoulder. 'Just concerned.'

They were sitting at the dining table, picking at an early dinner since the afternoon breeze had heightened to a tempest. The hours of the day stretched out before them, long and languid, like nylon being pulled from its solution. Nobody wanted to think of what to do next. The evening obliged by lengthening into red and purple shadows.

'If you don't mind me asking, where were you last night?' Alarice directed her gaze towards Muriel. 'Magda said you'd stepped outside for some fresh air. We were worried when you didn't come back.'

The corridor, half-empty. Then the breakfast table, glaringly absent.

'I didn't expect to be gone so long,' Muriel glanced away furtively. Alarice noticed then that her arms were scratched with briars, and that several stray twigs had woven themselves into her long dark hair.

'You saw something, didn't you.'

There was a pause. Muriel's brow was furrowed, as if she couldn't remember it clearly. 'You don't understand. It wasn't like I went out looking for it.'

Across the table, Alarice saw the panic in Magda's eyes. Heard it in the careful tilt of her voice. 'Looking for what?'

'At the edge of the orchard. There was something in the woods, just near the place where...' She trailed off. 'It was moving. And it had these burning red eyes.'

Magda shook her head, incredulous. 'You should've told us. You should've come back.'

'But I couldn't look away,' Muriel insisted. 'It was mesmerising, like some kind of enchantment. And then it changed altogether. It was as if something overcame me, and I lost control of ... of everything.'

The fear burned, slower than wood. A fire beyond the glade; a phantom in the woods. Nobody wanted to piece it together, for fear of what that answer would spell.

'Maybe it was a marsh fire,' said Catrin, after an agonisingly long silence. 'You know how it gets over the bogs in winter.'

'It wasn't a marsh fire. It looked like some kind of animal, to be honest.'

'What kind of animal?'

'I don't know. A wolf, or a dog, maybe.'

Alarice knew what Magda would be thinking, because she was wondering the same. It was too similar; too uncanny. It was exactly as she'd described in her last visions: a gwyllgi at the Forest's edge. How far, she wondered, did those torrid dreams grow?

'I tried to move away, but my legs wouldn't move. I couldn't go back. It wanted me to come forwards, to step closer, closer to the woods.' Muriel grimaced, remembering. 'I thought I was going to die.'

'You what?'

'It hurt so much. And then ...'

Muriel didn't finish the sentence. Maybe she couldn't.

The girls knew what her silence meant; knew that the wild look in their friend's eyes was the mask of someone who was lucky to have escaped with her life.

'You went in there, didn't you.' Magda hardly dared to breathe. 'Into Cunning Wood.'

A nod.

'Why didn't it kill you?'

'I'm pretty sure it wanted to,' said Muriel. 'It was like the forest tried to tear me to pieces, before everything healed over again. It must've been my magic that did it.'

Alarice didn't like to imagine the extent of those injuries. The things they had not seen were things they would never know, but in her mind they painted tall, lurid colours of gristle and bone. Red and brown and white.

'Your powers weren't supposed to get stronger for a long time.'

'Well, it seems they've decided otherwise.'

Stronger, and deadlier, too. If the Ethers had ever caught wind of this, Alarice dreaded to think what might happen. Veridian magic could manipulate natural forces for the better, but with every gift there came a spindrift silver edge: one that dripped with ichor.

Meanwhile, Ingrid was still staring. 'If you're strong enough to shield yourself from Cunning Wood, can you protect the rest of us, too?'

'I ... don't know.'

The girls exchanged wary glances. For all their talk of escape, no one had expected such a thing might become reality so soon. Now, with their confidence trickling like honey down the drain, everybody hoped that someone else might speak first.

'We can't assume it will work like that,' said Magda, eventually. 'If we try to rush things, Muriel could get hurt. *We* could get hurt. It's not a risk that we can take right now.'

'As opposed to the risk of getting murdered in an orchard?' Ingrid folded her arms. 'I know which chance I'd rather take.'

'Cut it out, you two.' Catrin silenced them. 'Let's not get ahead of ourselves. Muriel, what happened after you went into the Forest?'

Muriel looked far away, like something she'd dropped in the woods had stayed there and taken root. 'Hmm?'

'I know it must have been frightening, once you got in there. But is there anything you can tell us about what you saw?'

'It wasn't so frightening, not once I was inside.'

'But it's a poisoned wood.'

Muriel remembered sharp stones bloodying her feet, and a clear brook that sang with relief. 'When I got to the middle there was a clearing. A lovely little thicket with ivy covering the walls.'

The hairs went up on the back of Magda's neck.

'The walls?'

'Of the library.' Muriel's dark brown eyes were wide, full of wonder. 'It's real, Magda. The place you dreamed of, it's all real.'

***

The smell of blood was on the wind. Alarice wasn't sure what direction it was coming in, but it unnerved her. It was a darkening cluster on the horizon, probably some poor rabbit or toad had crossed the threshold, and there was nothing they could do to move it. The scent of its must would now wind its way through their corridor of Forest, until the woods claimed it entirely.

She should have realised what had happened to Muriel sooner. At breakfast the girl had looked a certain kind of way — and too much that kind of way — for it to mean anything good. Although, she supposed, the development in her magic was supposed to be a good thing. It meant that

Muriel was growing closer to that power, and leaning into it. It might even mean they'd have a way to escape.

Assuming that no harm came to their friend in the process.

For them to get through those woods unscathed, a great source of energy would be required. Nothing came without a price, Alarice knew that too well, and she didn't like to see it happen to someone she'd grown fond of.

She picked up the jumper she'd begun to repair. Spotting the place where her earlier work was coming undone, she began to weave the loops together again. Golden threads laced back in place. A smile sewn shut.

At the heart of it, Muriel Silvana was a sweet girl.

The trouble with bad things was that they liked sweet people.

*

'A sunny day,' Catrin muttered, as they sat around a box of biscuits that evening. 'Who has a funeral on a sunny day, for Gwern's sake?'

Alarice took a scallop-shaped shortbread from the pile. It seemed an inappropriate occasion for biscuits, and the crumbs mashed uncomfortably against her teeth. But if nobody partook she feared they'd sit there in silence, which would be infinitely worse.

'If only the weather had been the worst of it.'

'Nothing we can do about it now.'

The group of them had gathered in the cove after the impossibly long day, weary but running on adrenaline. Morning already felt like several lifetimes ago, and nobody had wanted to end the day this way. But Muriel's discovery had stirred up new and troublesome waters: ones that threatened to sweep away everything else. An invisible, ticking part of them knew it would be worse to put off the other, unspeakable thing. And with the road that lay ahead, Alarice wondered if they'd ever get the chance again.

'Who wants to start, then?'

'I will,' Catrin raised a mug of insipid tea. 'I'd like to say a word for her gardening on Sundays. Never did enjoy digging up beds myself, but ... it was always nice to see the hellebores and daffodils after she'd finished. Even the winter aconite brightened up the place a bit. I hope she was proud of them.'

There was a soft murmuration between the group. It was a fond memory, a quiet piece of mosaic to the courtyard, whose lack would grow all the more conspicuous as winter turned to spring. The ground would melt but no pink-cupped trumpets would unearth themselves. No youthful shoots would crow in the new season: except for the daffodils, who'd bloom again and again even in the absence of their gardener. Alarice didn't know which was worse.

Then she realised that the others had gone silent, waiting for her to speak.

'I'd like us to remember her letters,' she said quickly, aware that her cheeks were getting hot. Was it too personal an observation? Should she have given some other, more generic eulogy?

'Yeah. She was a good writer.'

'Not the content of them, as such,' said Alarice. 'I mean she was a person who always wrote back, and quickly. I think that counts for something.'

She thought of the care and painstaking detail that went into each missive, the shining glee whenever Rhos had received something new. It didn't matter whether it was her father, some distant relative, or a friend: Rhos treated them all with the same level of reverence.

Across the circle, Ingrid looked like she was going to cry. A stab of anguish jolted through Alarice's chest. Why wasn't *she* crying, too? Why were none of them able to shed the tears that boiled within them?

This had been a bad idea.

This had been the only idea.

Somebody needed to speak. Someone, anyone, please.

'I think she had a great sense of humour,' said Muriel, to Alarice's surprise. 'Not many people can live in a place like this and find little things to smile at.'

The balloon of panic in Alarice's chest began to deflate again. Those were the things she could hardly bear to dwell on, with the insanity of their being gone. They would never replace them — would likely never even try — because it was less painful to press on with their gaping wounds than it was to apply the stinging salve of remedy. But they had been there, those good things. Rhos had found the brightness in the corners of the evenings. She had laughed at the patches of grass bleached yellow in the sun.

Meanwhile Magda, whose fingers were clenched into tight fists, looked overcome with emotion. The room had turned to her for the next comment in line. It watched. It waited. Not patiently, but with an endurance forged by hardship.

'She was kind,' said Magda, after a long moment had passed. 'We shouldn't forget that.'

The words listed like sunflowers in the breeze, or a boat on a summer tide. But it was undeniable: in deeds more than mere words, Rhos had shown her generosity. Through invitations to come foraging, gardening, firefly-hunting. Three hundred and sixty-five days a year, she'd subjected the lot of them to her enthusiastic ramblings and questions of worldly intrigue.

Of course, Alarice knew, it was easy to praise the dead.

She was also beginning to understand why people did it with such urgency, in spite of the many imperfections in a person. It was a desperate plea for them to hear, for them to not yet quite be gone, for them to take your words and hold them in their hands.

Forgive me, I should've given you these earlier.

The lamplights flickered.

Half-illuminated at the edge of the circle, Ingrid drew a shaky breath. 'I'd like to put in a word for all those creatures she befriended. Norbert, and Leopold, and Frederika. Hexapod invertebrates and everything else in between.'

There was a ripple of mirth.

'How'd you remember all their names?'

'Because she never shut up about them,' Ingrid smiled, in a way that looked close to the opposite. 'It didn't matter that they were small, or puny, or only had a lifespan of three weeks. She believed in every single one of them.'

All those dreams she had, thought Alarice. In their minds, there had been boundless swathes of time: to be plucked from the trees, fished from the oceans, and found hiding underneath the bed.

Now every last minute had dried up. It was a bad joke, one that Rhos would surely pipe up and laugh at: *I'm not dead, stupid.* But she was nowhere. There were many things that Alarice wished they'd told her, so much sooner.

***

For many light sleepers, the ocean was a thing of terror. Shipwrecks; natural disaster; deep-sea leviathans, drowning — you name it, and somebody had a fear of it.

For Alarice Gosselin it was the opposite. In her worst nightmares she saw not endless waves, but dry land. Deserts so parched they charred her throat. Earth that split and cracked. A hundred years without rain.

What she desperately needed was deep water, and the Fallow was no place to find it.

'Cat?' she croaked, out of instinct. Stumbling awake, the murky dusk had not yet solidified around her. Only when she stubbed her toe on a wooden pallet, wincing, did she realise she'd sleepwalked into the corridor.

It wasn't the first time it had happened that week.

Except: last time she'd dreamed of the Wolds, it had been a glittering ocean on their doorstep. The roar and crash of loose tides. Pockets of water, heated by the sun, and the languid inhabitants of each rockpool. This time it was a nightmare version where the sea had all dried up. She had wandered into a version of their city where nothing remained but scorched earth.

I miss you, she wrote back, every time Zaira sent a letter. She missed the view over the shore, the waves breaking over the dock. And she missed feeling clean.

Here at the heart of the woods, every stain stuck: the blood on pillowcase, the saltwater sap of grief, the slightest criticism from the Ethers. All of them clung to her skin, and what the rain could not dislodge sank in. There was nothing, truly nothing, like the oceanic relief of a tide. A great grey blanket, where she could cry and not be seen.

Chapter 41
Midwinter

In Magda's opinion, there were three kinds of winter. First came the snowy, delicate eider variety, which trod just lightly enough to announce its presence, and disappeared before you could greet it properly. Second was the stalwart grey-eyed wayfarer, hobnail-thick and here to stay. It lingered long after it was welcome, did its due, and kept a comfortable misery of sleet on the ground at all times. Third was the final kind, the one that robbed the other two at gunpoint and left them to bleed in a ditch.

That was the winter who'd come knocking this morning. And after the heavy sorrow of the evening before, Magda was beginning to wonder if it was worth getting out of bed for class.

'Ether Lorna had a letter from a secret admirer this morning,' said Catrin, as they dug into their breakfast. 'A sprig of dried flowers in the envelope, if you can believe it.'

'How'd you know that?'

'Mix-up with the crows,' Catrin shrugged. 'Don't worry. I made sure it reached its intended destination.'

Magda scanned the table. The air felt somewhat cleared by the break of dawn, although the return to business as usual seemed a little forced. Presumably, everybody was keen to set the past behind them. *Snap*, and the butterfly's wings folded together: two painted faces closing towards each other in perfect mimicry. With every wingbeat the butterfly lifted a little higher over their heads, a little less terrible to consider.

'What's got your goat, Corrales? Anyone would think you'd sat on an ant's nest.'

'It's probably something she got in the post.'

'Oh,' Magda laughed, awkwardly. 'No, nothing to speak of.'

She tried not to think about the last letter she'd tried sending home. There had been no reply, no acknowledgement of receipt, and Muriel's attempts hadn't yielded any better luck.

From where her roommate sat, peering over a mug of dwindling coffee, Magda must have looked like an old photo: somewhat lost, and desaturated.

'D'you think they're okay back there?' she asked, when a louder conversation had established itself downwind.

'They must be,' said Muriel. 'There's probably some issue with the pigeon office, that's all.'

It didn't sound too convincing. Public transport back in Wildbriar was crap, but the pigeons were always reliable. They were pretty much the only thing in the town that ran on time.

*

After breakfast, they trailed outside for Botany. Thick clouds were covering the sky like an angry grey moss, but it refused to rain. It was somehow both cold and humid instead, which Ether Lorna was keen for them to view as *refreshing* instead of *miserable*.

'So,' said Ingrid, pulling on her gardening gloves. 'Are you going to tell us more about that library, then?'

Magda glanced over her shoulder to where Muriel was tending the raised beds. The matter of the library had been hastily set to one side since yesterday afternoon, as if everybody knew that to discuss it further was to go down a road of no return. So, in spite of her burning curiosity, Magda had resisted the urge to ask questions all morning. She'd left that pit distinctly unperturbed.

Trust Ingrid Leyshon to put her foot right in it.

Shifting to one side, Muriel began pulling up the thin scattering of weeds that coated the borders. 'I already told you what I know.'

'About the building.'

'Well, yes.'

'But you were gone for an entire night,' said Ingrid. 'What about the librarian?'

The librarian was a point that Magda had forgotten to consider altogether. In the haze of fear for Muriel's safety in the woods, and for the sake of her own sanity, she'd not dared to ask what else of her vision matched up with what Muriel had seen.

'I don't know what you're talking about.'

'You're saying you spent an entire night in the woods with nothing but a pile of books for company?'

By this point everybody else had turned to listen. For reasons unknown, Ether Lorna had gone to check the storehouse, and Magda was eternally grateful for her absence.

'If you must know, I thought I heard something.' Muriel slung the pile of weeds into the empty wheelbarrow, where they landed with a brash *clod*. 'But it's not like you think.'

'So there *was* a librarian.'

'I don't know what it was! It was just a voice in the dark.'

So far, all of Muriel's descriptions had matched Magda's visions: the spiderwebbed windows with their thin leaded solder, the lush purple carpets, and the hanging valley of bookshelves. The layer of dust over the furnishings, even the lingering scent of damp paper throughout the library.

The abrupt introduction of a *voice* was where that familiar tracing diverged.

'Someone else was there?' asked Magda, hollow. 'You could've mentioned that yesterday.'

'Yesterday was already bad enough.'

'So this person ... this librarian...'

Setting down her trowel, Muriel gave an exasperated sigh. 'Like I said, it was just a voice. No body, as such.'

'You mean you could hear them, but you couldn't see them?'

'That's about right.'

'Hmm. It could've been an elaborate invisibility charm,' Catrin suggested. 'Or some kind of recording.'

'Who'd bother to record something for an abandoned building? And besides, how would they get it there?'

'Maybe it's from before the woods turned.'

'But that was centuries ago. There's no way a building like that would've survived the Rift.'

Magda felt her stomach turn to tepid soup. 'This voice. Did you talk to it?'

'It was the strangest thing, Mags. I think it knew who you were.'

***

In an effort to rid her clothes of the stink of kitchen gardens, Catrin Scurlock had excused herself for a stroll in the grounds. This was better, she supposed, now that evening had slid the bolt across and barred out any possibility of light. Now nothing could shine that might expose the truth of her feelings.

She'd thought she had this together. Wasn't she acing every one of her classes? Wasn't she handling it so well, sleeping through each night, and nodding in all the right places?

It was a perilous masquerade, a mask that threatened to slip with each step she took. The thing she was really trying to be rid of was much harder to shed than the faint whiff of marjoram. And the faster she walked, the closer it breathed down her neck.

A visionary and a veridian in their midst.

How had she not realised sooner?

How had she not seen the signs, far before now? Like everybody else, the new girls had been afraid of their own magic. And Catrin knew too well how that felt.

It no longer gave her grief, to feel the spark of pyromancy in her veins. *Hotshot*, Alarice had laughed, the first time she'd dared to demonstrate. *I wish we could show Zaira, she'd have been all over this.*

Well, you'll just have to tell her next pigeon.

Don't flatter yourself, Cat. You're not the only shiny thing around here!

That certainly was the truth. Except this, this was burgeoning with something new. It wasn't fear; it wasn't jealousy; it was a simmering tension that she didn't have a name for. Her magic was no longer the talk of the town. Her magic paled in comparison to the things that Muriel Silvana could do, might do, or might one day hesitate over. The eyes of the Fallow followed what bled the brightest, and that person was no longer Catrin.

Now that she thought of it, she couldn't be sure it ever had been.

Unlike the other girls, quiet and assured, she had always set out to prove a point. If they were subtle, she'd be garish. If they were reserved, she'd be explosive. It had worked, in the short and dizzying experience that was her life, up until the point where everything came unravelled.

The fabric had slipped suddenly, like pins pulled out before the stitches were placed. First, the revelation. Then, Rhos. Now, this new discovery of a library in the woods. It made her head spin just to think about it: this new reality couldn't truly be hers, could it?

She stopped.

Took a deep breath.

She'd come to the place where everything dissipated to shadows, searching for the icy cold comfort that leached from such a place. The Ceremonial Grounds were vast and unearthly by night; the huge ring of standing stones, coldly foreboding. *From above*, thought Catrin, *this was a perfect circle. A perfect centre*. She now stood at the eye of a needle.

And who was to say they couldn't be happy here? Only the Ethers had decided this place should be a prison, when it might otherwise have been picturesque. It was all in the branding: institution for the gifted, jailhouse for the supernaturally inclined, secluded retreat in a pastoral setting. Your choice.

Under the pale hood of moonlight, Catrin slumped to her feet and leaned back against one of the standing stones. Well-placed shadows were a tricky business. They'd only ever assembled here at new moon, and on this brighter evening many things stood out that Catrin had never noticed.

First of all were the remains of last week's pyre. The firewood was burned down to cool white ash, which looked more like sand in the beachy wash of the moon. In a different life she might have made a sand castle, picked up a bucket and spade, knocked it down again to rebuild tomorrow. She might have taken Foxe here, and they might have looked up at the stars together. She might have taken Rhos here, and they might have laughed about how stupid boys were in the first place.

Might.

In this version of her life, she had no might at all. The weakness ached in her belly, where it rankled like a piteous howling infant. It couldn't even find the words for what was wrong. And worse, she didn't know what would take away its pain. She sank her hands into the dead ash of the bonfire, and watched it sift between her fingers. She reached out to clasp another handful, feeling an oddly scratchy texture at the base of the pile, then stopped.

Beneath the circle of dead ash was something harder, something unmistakably solid, and her fingers had brushed the edge of it. They scrambled to find it again, scooping aside bits of dead branch that had blown there since last Ceremony, and scraped a gap in the place where the pyre had lain.

At the centre of that hollow was a bright edge.

An etching, carved into the chalk. As strange as it was barren. Cut into the earth itself.

For a moment Catrin stared at it, wondering if this was a precursor to some whirlwind experience like the one Muriel had experienced in the woods. But the chalk carving only sat there, inert in its crumb coat of white rock. The peculiarity of its being there struck her more than anything else.

Who went around carving symbols underneath ceremonial pyres?

And why did she feel that irresistible compulsion to reach out and touch it?

In spite of everything, she hesitated. If the chalk carving was some kind of signpost, she didn't have a map. If it was a rune, she didn't have a translation, although she had a cursory knowledge of enough witch-runes to try that. She studied it again, the odd curves and river-like swirls of the etching. That was why it had been so imperceptible: the milky rock disguised itself perfectly between layers of brilliant ash. And the fire that burned above it each month, blinding white and petrifying.

Turn to stone.

That was what the word meant, after all. And that was how Catrin felt: immovable. The rock was holding her there, long after it seemed sensible to linger in the open grounds, and she wondered if this was the part where something bad would happen. Perhaps it would be the standing stone that would fall down and squash her flat. *What a pity, her guts made such a mess.* Or maybe lightning would strike her for staring with such insolence at the barefaced carving, pale and exposed there on the lawn. *She never did know when to stop looking.* Perhaps her own good heart would fail and clot itself to misery, leaving her stranded like a beached whale.

What she had not been expecting was the fourth, unprecedented option.

Fire: summoning itself from her veins.

Fire: as a spark's ascension to a blaze.

Before she could even think what she was doing, Catrin leaned forwards and put her hand to the chalk carving. The flame caught greedily. Then, as she held her handful of fire shimmering over that dim chalk carving, the cogs seemed to slick into motion. Now the strange marks were shifting; now the patch of grass seemed elusive as velvet.

Turn to stone.

And it did. The fixtures of the chalk carving began to hiss with steam, like metal doused in water. They bent sideways, solidified, and melded into new shapes altogether.

Distantly, Catrin was aware of her aching hands, but she did not move away. All she could look at was the transformation. Soon the crumbly white chalk was chalk no longer, but a new surface of morphous grey rock. There could be no mistaking its form: a circular grey porthole with a chiselled grey handle.

She was staring into the mouth of a trapdoor.

*

'There you are,' Alarice turned to where the door to the cove had creaked open. 'We thought you'd never come.'

'Want a scone?'

'No, thanks,' Catrin gave a tight smile, taking her seat in the huddle that surrounded a game of Teller in the cove. Her hands were still trembling, but nobody noticed. 'Who's winning?'

'Me, of course.'

'Don't count your chickens.'

The antler-shaped piece that Ingrid had been holding hovered in mid-air. On the next go Magda moved her own piece, a chunk of quartz carved in the shape of a conch. The object of the game was to dig out the traitor of the pack — the Teller — before your own secret got rumbled.

'You're quiet, Scurlock.'

'Am I?'

'*Suspiciously* quiet,' Alarice paused, then cleared three marble pieces off the board with her own. 'Did you come across any handsome strangers out there?'

'Are you really asking that?'

'Sorry, sorry.'

'Let's stay focused on the game,' Ingrid nudged her. 'Some of us have got a stake in the matter.'

So Catrin tried. Or didn't try, but pretended to be enjoying the game or be present in the game or be anywhere, anywhere else than where she had been an hour ago.

Eventually, though, they were left with a cluttered board, a Teller, and the inklings of a stomach-ache.

'Bloody scones,' Ingrid muttered. 'Why do they have to be so moreish?'

'It's like that joke, what's the fastest cake? *Scone*.'

At that point an argument broke out about how *scone* was actually pronounced. Catrin's stomach was aching for entirely different reasons, but she didn't think it wise to eat when such a peculiar tightness was wracking her abdomen.

'Hey, is everything alright?' asked Muriel. 'You seem a bit ... glum.'

'It's just the time of year. It'll be easier when it stops pissing down with rain every other day.'

The others mumbled their agreement. Wasn't it chilly, wasn't it grey, didn't it look like sleet was coming. Inane comment after comment that made her brain itch.

'Maybe they'll have to cancel the next Ceremony on account of the inclement weather,' someone joked. 'Two hurricanes and a thunderstorm, no thanks.'

'It's the Ceremonial Grounds that are the problem,' said Catrin, the words finally slipping free. Sickly and green, they gushed forwards like bile. 'There's something there. Underneath the earth.'

'What are you talking about?'

Catrin hated this. She could feel the stupid, hot tears pricking at her eyes. Everybody was looking at her, but it was for all the wrong reasons.

'I found something. It's right in among the ashes, where the pyre used to be.'

Chapter 42

A Spider's Web

'A portal,' Magda let out a low huff as they walked through the tall wet grass. 'Do you think it's true? It just seems...'

'Far-fetched?' Muriel squashed a dandelion beneath her foot. 'No more so than the other discoveries we've made. By the alder, you were the one who used to go sneaking into abandoned buildings back home!'

'Yeah. I suppose it could've been worse.'

Whether Catrin's discovery was far-fetched or not, Muriel knew that they couldn't rest until they'd gone to investigate further. They were digging themselves into a hole: that much was undeniable. But perhaps that hole might be the tunnel they needed to escape.

'This is the place, right?'

They looked down. The chalk carving was exactly as Catrin had described, faintly lit by the first dregs of colour in the sky. Carefully moving the damp logs away from their cover, Muriel fixed the twisting curls of white with a curious gaze.

'It looks like those dragontails you used to make.'

'It does not!'

'Come on, that's the exact shape of the jam spirals.'

'We come to investigate an important ancient artefact, and all you can think of is food?'

'Sorry,' Muriel laughed, unable to quite distract herself from the fleeting similitude. 'I just ...'

'Home,' Magda realised. 'You were thinking of home.'

Muriel hesitated, one foot hovering above the chalk engraving. 'It feels like we're never going back there.'

'It might take a little longer than we were hoping. But we'll get there.'

Bringing the box of matches from her pocket, Muriel knelt down to base of the pyre. According to Catrin, it was fire that had caused the carving to change in the first place: there was surely no shortage of kindling, given its location. But since the morning rain all that remained of the firewood had been turned to damp ash. A thick scent of wet moss filled the air.

'Do you think it'll catch?'

'Hope so.'

She struck the match, watching as the meagre flame took its first breaths. At first there was nothing. The matchstick fizzled out with a subdued cough, spluttered once, and gave up.

'Maybe we should —'

'Look out!'

Suddenly, as if she'd lit a fuse, the chalk carving began to turn — no, *warp* — in twists that shifted and glowed before their eyes. Muriel jumped back, wide-eyed.

The patch of ground was yawning itself open.

Half terrorised, they watched as the carvings melded into new shapes, whorling like a Catherine wheel in the earth. Anything could have been sizzling away down there. For all Muriel knew, there was a pot-bellied dragon underneath the crust of the earth, who might plunge a claw through the surface at any moment.

Magda shot her a sideways look. 'We could always go back.'

'We could.'

Yet they stayed there, waiting for the earth to stop turning, until the molten rivets had cooled again. A chiselled grey door was staring back at them: smooth-grained, and perfectly circular. It had no business existing, let alone looked about as appetising as a gwyllion's lair, but Muriel knew they were both too proud to walk away now.

'Maybe it's prettier on the inside.'

'All I ask is that we don't get stuck down there.' Magda took one glance over her shoulder, then walked ahead to inspect the portal. 'I'll go if you'll go?'

'Fine.'

It took a great deal of effort to pull the trapdoor open. As she swung her legs over the edge of the precipice, Muriel wondered how in the world they were going to get back out. Would it still be nighttime when they emerged? Would the first dregs of dawn be waltzing the horizon?

'Hurry up, will you! I can't see a thing.'

Fortunately, time didn't exist underground: and the only way was down. She held her breath for those first steps, blind air and red, claggy soil, before gradually the tunnel gave way to steadier ground. Whoever had put this doorway here had taken no chances. Not with interior design, and not with the fates of hapless strangers. Only a doggedly determined traveller with a healthy lack of survival instinct would be able to find their way down here.

For the third time that week, Muriel hoped she wasn't about to get herself killed.

'Wow,' she heard, metres below her. There was the sound of solid ground, and the faintest glow of something like candlelight.

'What is it?'

'Just get down here already.'

Intrigued, Muriel descended the final rungs of the ladder at record speed. Shaken, sweaty, and more than a little bit scared, she dropped to the floor of the tunnel with a soft thud. Only then did she understand what her friend was looking at.

'Wow.' Muriel's breath whistled in the stifling earthy air. 'It's beautiful.'

There was no mistaking what this underground cavern had been built for. Before them was a tunnel that opened out into a room: and it was magnificent. Over a maze of red-carpeted gildwork, there were shelves stacked high with book after book after book. Enough pages to warrant a lifetime's reading. And no one around to read them.

Why, Muriel wondered, *had everything impossible decided to happen in the space of one week?* She tried to picture how the others would react when they got back: Alarice, with her discerning eye; Catrin, who had been out of sorts since yesterday evening; and Ingrid, who she still hadn't quite figured out.

The boundaries of what had seemed possible had gone slack, like elastic, over these last few weeks and months. If she hadn't felt so utterly rattled, it was possible that Muriel would have laughed out loud.

'No way have we been sitting on top of an underground library for six months.'

'Your guess is as good as mine,' Magda tiptoed forwards, so lightly she might have been walking in a fairy-ring. 'Maybe it's something to do with the Ethers.'

Unable to reply, Muriel surveyed the scene before her: a mislaid pile of atlases, a worn-out ladder, and another towering bookcase. At the edges of the cavern, the shelves melted into soft brown rock. Perhaps the sheer size of the underground hollow should have been daunting. Yet out of all the libraries she had seen, this one had the most peculiar charm.

For one, it changed the complexion of books. Muriel had always seen them as inert, lifeless objects: things that could be considered and then set down without much care for what happened next. In contrast, the books here seemed infested with life in a way that was both thrilling and unsettling. Muriel felt that to reach out and touch one was to risk its tendrils sinking into you.

She forced herself to maintain a safe distance. 'Surely it can't be the Ethers. This place is too vast; it'd take them years to explore even half of it.'

'Who, then? Who else would go to the trouble of hiding a doorway underneath the Ceremonial Grounds?'

The walls bore no answer. Muriel thought of all the doorways she'd ever known: of the portcullises and wooden cottage doors, of the double-hinged swing windows and high, arching gateways.

'Who'd go to the trouble of organising a Ceremony at all?' she wondered out loud. 'It can't be a coincidence. This place, this very spot. Like it's the epicentre of some ... scheme.'

If fire was the key to the gateway, then each time the girls built a pyre, the portal would become active: concealed ever so lightly beneath the flames. The clockwork carving would melt into the familiar stone doorway. But if that was the case, then why hadn't they ever seen it?

'New moon,' Muriel realised. On the darkest night of the month, those shadows could hide a multitude of sins. 'It's deliberate. It has to be.'

'You think they're using the Ceremony for the fire?'

'It's the only way to activate the portal.'

Magda looked like she'd been slapped across the face. 'Every month. Every month this door has been opening, and we never even noticed.'

We never even thought to look.

'But that can't be all the Ceremony was for. Can it?'

'I don't know,' Magda studied the rows of books, which glistened in the damp earth like brawny-backed toads. 'It must serve another purpose, or why not just use a match? If it was fire they needed, they'd hardly require a whole pyre to do it.'

All those girls, thought Muriel. Terrified: every one of them. Holding their breath, while the flames licked at their heels. And what was it all for?

To open a stupid door.

To get into an underground library, full of books that nobody could read.

Her blood boiled.

'Maybe we should be getting back soon,' said Magda, looking slightly taken aback by the thunder in her face. 'The others can't keep watch all night.'

'Just one more minute.'

There had to be something else that the Ethers needed here. Something that only the Fallow girls could help them access.

'People don't just put tunnels in the ground for no reason,' she lifted out a book from one shelf, which creaked and complained as she folded it open. 'What if it was here first? What if the Fallow was built around it?'

'How old do you think this place is?'

They tried to picture it: the trees being cleared, architecture built brick by brick, a ring of bluestone monoliths left standing guard over the whole thing. Muriel still didn't understand how the charm that protected the clearing worked. But a part of her wondered if some element of that power came from the ancient rock itself, veined deep below the earth.

'There's something here,' she hovered by the bookshelf, a narrow rack against the wall. 'Some kind of gold mine. We're sitting right on top of it, I swear.'

'So we'll come back to investigate another time. It's too late in the day to be philosophising.'

Muriel sighed. 'Okay.'

But when she tried to put the book back in place, it wouldn't fit. Perplexed, she tried a different angle: then another, and another, until she finally found the right position. There was a shallow crackling sound, like an ancient hinge that badly needed grease, and the book slotted into position against the wall.

To her astonishment, the entire shelf moved with it.

'Er. Mags, did you see that?'

'What is it?'

'Look.'

They both watched intently. With the pressure of the book that Muriel had shoved into place, the bookcase had suddenly retreated by about half an inch, receding into the wall itself. It was a landslide that hadn't happened yet; an avalanche waiting to cleave itself free.

The creaking sound was growing incrementally louder.

Muriel had never heard a glacier split, but she knew instinctively not to approach. 'Any minute now,' she held her breath. 'Almost.'

'What do you mean, *any minute now*?'

Suddenly, like a tearaway sheet of ice, the rectangular bookcase veered away from the wall altogether. Large, proud, and labyrinthine, it swung on burnished gold hinges.

It was a magnificent mess.

'Another bloody door,' Magda shook her head. 'I don't believe this.'

'But isn't it amazing?'

'That scared the life out of me!'

'Sorry.'

It looked like something out of an old picture book, or an antique shop, with its curling woodwork and façade of jacketed books. But while a layer of dust had settled around certain parts, the handle was squeaky clean.

Muriel peered through the crack that had yawned open.

Magda shot her a look of alarm. 'Er, maybe we shouldn't ...'

'It's fine, I'm only looking.'

She knew it would be a bad idea to venture through a doorway without knowing where it led. A truly terrible idea, really: the kind that Lucía or her father might have suggested. And yet, what adventure!

'Look,' she peered down in wonder. 'There's a little spiderweb engraved on the knocker.'

‘That’s not funny, Muriel.’

But she barely listened, because here was the door.

Here was a way out.

All she remembered was stepping forwards into darkness.

Chapter 43

Variations on a Theme

Lorna Daven slit open the letter with shaking hands.

The week after the Ceremony was a jittery time, and Stefania only made things worse. She knew exactly how to set the South Quadrant's teeth on edge, not least by her overpowering presence in all places where she wasn't wanted.

It was one of the Fallow's small comforts that Rhiannon understood what she needed at such a time. Peace, quiet, and for the love of the goddess, please no loud music. Hands steadier now, she set the envelope on the desk.

My dearest Lorna, the letter began. It unfolded as in its usual rambling pattern, and she followed the lines of curled script one by one. You could never quite predict which way the 'r's would slope, or how the 'i's would be dotted, so Lorna took to guessing. The ending stayed the same, though. *Yours always. G.*

Hoping that her candle would last long enough to scratch out a reply, Lorna reached into the drawer under her desk for a fresh sheet of parchment. She couldn't think of anything to say, but it didn't matter. With Gretta her mind always found the words.

She wondered what it would be like when she got back.

Would they be able to resume life as it had been, like taking a hard-frozen pizza out of the ice chest? Would it be so simple?

Hi, darling. I've done some terrible things, hope you don't mind, but I'm back now so let's forget all about it.

She couldn't imagine what Gretta would say if she knew the half of what went on here. She suspected that was why those questions were never asked, not specifically, anyway.

Lorna often wondered how exactly it had come to this. She'd spent the first twenty years of her life like a frightened rabbit, jolted from this place to that place as she struggled to understand what she needed or wanted from her brief existence on Earth. The first half of her thirties had passed in comparable felicity, with that rare combination of enough time to do things and enough money with which to do them.

Lamentably, it wasn't to last.

She put pen to paper, trying to think of what to say, when there was a knock at the door.

'Hello?'

The door creaked open. It was Rhiannon, holding two mugs of coffee.

'Kettle's just boiled. Thought you'd like one.'

'Thanks, Rhi.'

The other woman smiled, surveying the crumpled paper which Lorna was still holding in one hand. 'More letters from your wife?'

'Just the one. She's a busy woman, you know.'

'Clearly,' Rhiannon shook her head, still smiling. 'Lovesick teenagers, the pair of you.'

Blushing furiously, Lorna returned to her desk and sat down to write. This time, the words would come. This time, everything was going to be perfect.

***

It hadn't even occurred to Muriel that she might be lying on the ground, or that Magda might be sitting in a crumpled heap beside her. But, as she came to her senses, it was clear she was staring at the ceiling from a perfectly horizontal sprawl.

She twisted to one side. 'Magda?'

Nothing.

'Mags, wake up. You're squashing my arm.'

'Hmm?' A vague grumbling finally emerged from where the other girl was lying. 'Ow. Ow, that hurt.'

'I know,' Muriel winced, sitting up. 'I don't think that was a regular door.'

'Nothing is a regular anything any more.'

She paused, staring at their surroundings. The pair of them had landed in a room that was not only awash with a veritable tide of papers, but stacked with yellowing books that nobody had bothered to sort. Half of them were piled in front of empty shelves, others had made it partway there and now hung suspended in mid-air, like the insides of a snowglobe.

'Oh, no,' said Magda, getting to her feet. 'It can't be.'

Muriel said nothing.

It really, really shouldn't have been.

But neither girl needed to look outside to recognise the familiar cut and arches of the building. They were standing in the Vespertine Library: sure as silk was silk.

'I knew this was a bad idea,' Magda rubbed her head. 'This is exactly why you shouldn't walk through unmarked doors without knowing where they lead!'

'It's not so awful,' Muriel surveyed their surroundings. A crooked lamp, a wonky shelf, and the empty front desk. 'At least we're somewhere familiar. And look, the door's right there if you want to go back.'

As if in response, there was a sudden ripple of wind towards the place she'd gestured: unnaturally cold and lofty. *Someone must've left a window open*, Muriel told herself. But even that thought wasn't entirely comforting, because then there was the question of the Someone.

She scrutinised the shadows.

'Is anybody there?'

Silence.

Had Muriel stepped outside, she would have heard the roar of the winter's gale in all its glory: it was a dog's howl, a blood moon, a thousand forestly things combined into one solid gulp. But from where they stood, shivering in the foyer, it was oh so quiet.

'Is anybody there?' she called again.

'Stop doing that,' Magda hissed. 'Come on, let's get out while we still can.'

'But we can't leave yet. Not before we've found that voice.'

'Muriel, this is horror story material!'

'Just let me try one last time.'

'Fine.'

'Well?' Muriel beckoned to the empty air. 'What have you got to say for yourself?'

For a moment it seemed that they were the only two people in the world. They were silent visitors in a museum: every ornament and item of furniture a piece of still life, placed there for their enjoyment. For that languid, dreamish moment the Vespertine Library was nothing but an amusement park for wandering tourists.

And then: a voice in the dark.

'I see you've finally taken the shortcut.'

*

The candles sweated with oil, thin and waxy rivulets down to the table. Muriel wiped her brow as she jotted down notes in her pocket notepad. There was something faintly comedic about the whole scenario: an interview with a ghost. The disembodied voice darted, like pollen drifting on the wind, with each question. It never seemed to stay in one place for longer than a few moments.

'And you've been here for how long?'

'Long enough to know that this is the best way between libraries.'

Muriel paused, glancing sideways. Magda's current complexion was the same colour as the candles, and for the last twenty minutes she'd only spoken in monosyllables. Muriel supposed she could hardly blame her. There was a first time for everything, even being confronted with an incorporeal voice in a library.

'Right,' she flipped the page casually, as if the whole scenario were some run-of-the-mill press conference. 'And you're saying we came in through that door?'

'I call it the spiderweb gate. Easy to get into, so long as you don't become entangled.'

The voice gathered itself, then scattered like leaves. The absence of a face, let alone a body, became no less unsettling with each iteration. Out of the corner of her eye, Muriel could tell that Magda was growing impatient: her brows had knitted themselves together with more than their usual exasperation.

'It's going to be alright,' she tried to reassure them both. 'So, mystery voice, have you got a name?'

'Not one that's worth knowing.'

'Fantastic,' Magda shook her head. She set down the mulberry-coloured entry book, which had sat in her arms for a good couple of minutes, like a disgruntled ginger cat. 'First light can't be far off, Muriel. Remind me why we're still wasting time here?'

'Because we need to gather as much intel as we can!'

'It's a shame the librarian can't be more obliging,' Magda muttered under her breath. 'There's a bloody *door* between this place and the Fallow, and it didn't think we'd like to know sooner?'

The voice chuckled.

'Don't worry, you were quicker than most of the others.'

'Quicker than the others?' Muriel suddenly felt a pulse of panic in her chest. 'Who else has been here?'

'I cannot reveal the identity of this library's travellers.'

'Was it the Ethers?'

'I cannot reveal –'

'They must know about it,' said Magda. She glared at the purple entry book, the greedy name-gobbler, which was so much heavier than it looked. 'This library and the library beneath the Fallow are linked, right? And that doorway connects the two.'

'Oh, it's not just those two libraries,' said the voice, gleefully. 'It's all of them.'

Muriel froze.

Had the voice misspoken, or was it toying with them?

'What do you mean, it's all of them?'

'They're all connected. Each and every one of the libraries has got its corresponding gateway, somewhere across the archipelago.'

The knowledge fragmented in Muriel's mind: a sudden mirage of portals, connecting libraries across the country. It shimmered like honey, fractalic and crystallised. She tried to swim through it and found there was nothing to breathe but sweet, cloying liquid.

'Who are you?' she faltered. 'Whose secrets are you keeping?'

'None but my own.'

'Then how do you know so much?' Magda demanded. 'Nobody talks about this stuff. It's has got to be classified information, or something. Hasn't it?'

'The doors have existed ever since the New World began. The knowledge of them, on the other hand, has grown scarce.'

Muriel tried to conjure the image in her mind. Tunnels, no, a labyrinthine rabbit warren, piecing together islands beneath the earth. How deep did those channels run? Did they criss-cross and intersect like some chaotic pedestrian metro? And if every door to the libraries was sealed with a lock, then who held the key?

The voice's words floated, just out of reach.

Then she understood what it was really saying.

'Magic. That's what's needed to open the doorways, isn't it?'

'Somebody's quick off the mark,' replied the voice. 'Now. Weren't you here about a book?'

Chapter 44

Starless

When all was said and done, Stefania MacFarleigh considered herself basically a good person.

She was an exemplary employee who carried out her duties to perfection. She never complained about the work she was set, she never made a promise that she couldn't keep, and the Brenin promised her good things in return for her diligence. Most of all, she did not dwell on things that gave others grief.

Lorna and Rhiannon had both cried when the Merrick girl died. It had been unfortunate, yes, but surely not something worth blubbering over. Everything that happened here served the same purpose, after all. And how had Stefania handled things? She'd held her head high and prevented this entire operation from capsizing. For all the Brenin's generosity, there would be hell to pay if their main objective was compromised — and it would be her head on the chopping block.

In spite of her many virtues, she suspected that her colleagues did not like her very much. Most people did not seem to like her very much, since she'd started at the Fallow. But then again, perhaps it didn't matter, given that the only person whose opinion she'd cared about had been snarled away with the rest of her old life. That was a lost story, though; she didn't love him anymore. Didn't. Couldn't. Wouldn't.

Outside the frost fluttered, and Stefania breathed in its warmth. It was possible she liked the cold because it reminded her of everything that Sam was not. For example, Sam would never have gone riding on a frozen beach in February. Nor would he have thrown her a picnic basket, laughed when she missed, and gone darting off into the sand dunes in midwinter: it was too cold for any of that. The only suitable conditions for Sam's gunmetal blue eyes, his sideways smile, his very existence, were the heat of July. Deep, blistering sun.

She made the mistake of closing her eyes.

Her stomach recoiled at sudden memory of rotting horse flesh. It stung her like salt in a wound, like her farrier's knife and anvil against cream-coloured sand. In that split-second, she saw a torn straw hat and something horribly familiar, strewn out on the shoreline.

A promise she made herself: that summer was never coming around again.

The melting sea rushed away and left her stranded on the dock.

***

'So that's what we found down there. And the Tidal Folk are the only ones who can use the portals between libraries.'

'That's nuts,' said Ingrid. 'Are you sure it wasn't pulling your leg?'

Magda hesitated. She wanted to doubt it, but such an invention seemed unlikely even for an incorporeal voice. 'I don't think it had much reason to lie.'

'It's still weird, though. Who'd have thought there'd be anything down there but molehills and rabbits?'

Catrin, who had been staring intently into the table, finally raised her head.

'The fires. Do you think it's something to do with that?' She paused. 'You know, all the legends about burning to death in the library.'

Magda thought of the runaway tales, and the warnings from adults too old to understand their youthful curiosity. Were they the same adults who had watched, terrified, for their daughters to return home each evening? Did they speak because they knew, or because of what they feared?

'Maybe what they saw was someone opening one of the library portals,' Catrin fiddled with the edge of her sleeve. 'And they must've mistaken it for a real fire. Every portal needs magic to open, right?'

From the opposite side of the circle, Muriel began to nod. 'All they would've seen was a bright light inside a library. And then the person was gone the next morning.'

Enlightenment: that was what they called the acquisition of knowledge. But this felt more like a slow dawn than artificial fire, like it was something that had been coming all along. There was no way to stop it, just as there was no way of hanging on to the long and gorgeous dusk before it.

'That's why they were so afraid,' said Alarice, with a wistful expression. 'They didn't want us to cross paths with the Folk. If we'd gone out there at night, can you imagine the things we might've seen?'

Uneasily, Magda considered what her own mother had once said to her. *Read as much as you like, but never trespass after dark. The library by night is not what it might seem.*

Had she even known what she was warning against?

Had she stood in front of a portal in her own nighttime library, and willed it to open? Or had she watched other Folk flee the town, the bright light opening up and swallowing them whole?

Aisling Corrales, she realised, had made a choice to stay.

'We have to go back there,' said Muriel. 'There must be more to it than that.'

'Than a nation-wide network of magical doors between libraries? I sincerely hope not.'

The circle fell quiet again.

'How big was that place beneath the grounds, anyway?'

'Cavernous,' replied Magda, thinking of the red and gold trellis of bookshelves. It was like trying to describe the contents of a fridge with seventy doors: there were probably ingredients that would never see the light of day, even if she had raided every compartment. 'We didn't have time to read half of the spines.'

'You're lucky that second door brought you to a library that you recognised,' said Alarice. 'And it was nearby, too. Imagine ending up somewhere in the hills of Tarren Mawr!'

There was a collective shudder. Legend had it that the Western mountains were riddled with all kinds of creatures which were best avoided, day or night. Even if the libraries were navigable, great care would need to be taken that nobody got stranded or abandoned in some far-off corner of the continent.

'We need a map, really. A way to chart the libraries in the network.'

'I doubt the Brenin would allow that kind of map to be in common distribution. Let alone here, of all places.'

'But the Brenin doesn't know about any of this.' There was a gleam in Magda's eye. 'That's the beauty of it. And I think I know who we could ask.'

*

Muriel listened to the dark. It wasn't just noise; a sea of sounds came and went like the ripple of a stingray. Voices fluttered like moths between the walls, tangling with the memory of fires they'd discussed earlier in the day. She might have nodded off, except for the unfortunate fact that Magda snored like a goat: loud, and astonishingly dissonant.

For the time being, all Muriel could do was lie awake with a head full of thoughts. Sleep eluded her. And each time she closed her eyes, doors opened in places she didn't expect them to: under the bed, behind the cupboard, at the heart of the Ceremonial Grounds.

What were they supposed to do now? She wasn't certain if she had ever fully believed in the local legends about nighttime libraries, but now there was a certain shred of truth which she disliked. She thought of the Selvedge, and the telltale trail of corpses that wound up there from time to time. There was no denying the evidence in what people saw; it was what they didn't see that troubled her most.

It wasn't fair to be so far from home, thought Muriel, wretchedly. Sidonie Silvana would have known what to do. Sidonie Silvana had probably known a lot more than Muriel had given her credit for, and never thought to ask.

Here, I wanted you to have this. Take it. Quickly.

She hadn't had the heart to look at her mother's patchwork in some time. But now, desperate for some distant scrap of wisdom, she reached under the bed to retrieve it. The ridges of embroidery floss folded like a tiny sierra in her hands, stiletto mountains and a dusting of white lace.

Today was the first day of spring, one square began. *After breakfast your father discovered the wyvern infestation in the attic, luckily they managed to open a hatch for the nestlings. They're so boisterous and fiery! Just like your sister.*

Muriel allowed herself a small smile. She remembered that day vividly: the hissing, the torrent of dark smoke, and finally a stream of brightly-coloured wyverns pouring out from the back of their loft.

Tomorrow we'll be seeing the Brooks for their daughters' birthday. The rest of the entry continued in Spanish. *No sé qué le vamos a regalar, tienen un montón de plata...*

The words were comforting, like waves lapping over the sea shore. Every time she wrapped herself up in the blanket, she felt the shiver of a current like electricity. Something safe; something guarding.

All she needed now was a cup of hot chocolate, and she could rest free of nightmares about libraries or fire-stricken portals. Padding downstairs to the kitchenette would take no more than a few minutes. First was the corridor, then the staircase, and finally the lower landing. Easy.

Or at least, that was what she'd thought.

'Muriel?' came a voice. 'What are you doing here?'

Sitting in the alcove of one window was Ingrid, sketchpad in hand. Her dark red pyjamas flared from the calf downwards, like a sunset spilling onto white marble.

'I was going to make some hot chocolate. You're up late.'

'Sketching,' Ingrid shrugged, by way of explanation. 'The light's better here than in the dormitory.'

'Oh. Right.' Muriel peered outside the window, where a glowing moon hung aloft. 'What are you drawing, exactly?'

'A couple of constellations.' She lifted the paper to show a neatly labelled chart. On the bench beside her was a pebble-coloured compass. 'They say it's the oldest form of cartography, star reading.'

Muriel looked longingly at the diagram. 'It's beautiful.'

'My grandmother taught me.' A shadow of warmth crossed Ingrid's face before she returned to her notebook. Her pen lifted and glided across the paper, seemingly with a life of its own. 'She taught me lots of things I wasn't supposed to know.'

'Isn't that what grandmas are for?'

'Some of them,' said Ingrid, and went back to her sketching.

Far beyond them, the night air had cast everything in shades of silver and indigo. The leaves of the spindle tree were illuminated in shivers of light, through the windows Muriel could see a bush full of guelder-rose berries: fruit that should have been pecked away days ago. Fruit that was now fermenting on the bough.

She looked away from the rotting flesh, feeling queasy. 'Do you think it'll be long before the Sickness in the Forests reaches us here?'

Ingrid's pencil carved a smooth grain across the paper.

'Not long at all, at this rate.'

'And you're not ... scared?'

'The Brenin will find a way to stop the Sickness, eventually. He'll have to,' Ingrid drew in a cornerful of stars, concentrating. 'As soon as it comes to his land and his cattle, that'll be his hour of glory.'

'I suppose you're right.' Muriel took a seat in the alcove beside her. 'It's just difficult not to worry. Magda's so confident we'll figure this all out, but if the prince never returns, and the prophecy is never fulfilled... Then the Forests will just *die*.'

The words sounded horribly final.

'Trust me, the prophecy isn't the be-all and end-all of this archipelago. We'll get through it,' Ingrid hesitated, before adding, 'even if it's ugly and painful and longwinded as a rattlesnake.'

'Sorry, was that a hint of optimism?'

'I can't be a cynic twenty-four hours a day, Silvana.'

They watched the pencil sketch over the paper again. A handful of stars. A cutlass moon. The daytime for reality; the night, for dreaming.

Chapter 45

The Forest for the Trees

On the morning of Ether Rhiannon's Triolatry class, the moon was being obnoxious and dramatic. *Look at me*, the smoky yellow half-crescent seemed to brag, as it dwindled in the low sky. Rhiannon ignored it. If it had any sense, it would quit trying to outshine the real spectacle.

'Good morning, everyone. I hope you've come prepared for some practical analysis.' She passed each desk to hand out a set of square paddles, each with fine metal wires. 'Does anybody know what this is?'

'A carding brush,' said Muriel. 'They use them to detangle raw wool, so that it's ready for spinning.'

'Correct, Miss Silvana. It's very important that the wool is free of dust before it's twisted; there are all kinds of yarns that can be produced afterwards. Slub yarns, loop yarns, fancy yarns... But what most people don't think about so much is the sheep.'

'The sheep?'

'Yes,' Ether Rhiannon nodded gravely. 'The best-kept sheep will produce the best quality wool. Everything about their care will impact the wool: how fine it is, the lanolin, the length of each staple fibre. And besides that, a neglected sheep will be in a rotten mood. Hardly ideal when it comes to shearing.'

At the back of the room, Catrin raised a hand. 'Are there sheep at the Brenin's palace?'

'Only the farmhands are involved directly with their care. But I assure you there's a wide paddock and the finest of pastures for them to graze on.

You'll never find a more tranquil ewe than in the royal acreage,' said Rhiannon. 'After all, the best quality goods begin with the best quality source.'

'I see.'

Silently, Catrin doubted it. No matter how wide and lush the grasses in Helygen were, they couldn't compete with Tarren Mawr. She didn't think she'd ever seen a happier creature than the thick-haired mountain sheep that roamed West Crag.

'Let's go over Chapter Eighteen, shall we?'

As they turned to their textbook work, she stayed quiet. Though Rhiannon's words had been perfectly innocent, Catrin couldn't help but wonder if the Fallow took the same approach to its own students. Were they nothing more than sheep, comfortably fed and well cared for, if only so that they might produce high quality textiles for the Palace?

She glanced sideways to where Alarice was unfolding her own textbook. But while her fingers were clasped around the carding brush, a tightly-wound line had appeared in her jaw. It was the look she got when she had sniffed out something suspicious.

*

An insistent tapping was coming from the window beyond the dining hall.

'Can somebody let that poor bird in?'

'That's the third time this week.' Ingrid peered down the table. 'I wonder who it could possibly be for.'

'Shut up.' Catrin opened the window to snatch an envelope from the crow's claws. 'It's nothing important, anyway.'

'No news from the boyfriend, then?'

From where Magda was sitting, she could just make out the crisp wax seal on the envelope: bright purple and expensive. But instead of opening the letter, Catrin leaned over to the candle at the centre of the table.

The folded note went up in flames.

'Lovers' tiff?'

'It's none of your business.'

'Don't worry, I'm sure he'll be begging your forgiveness by the end of the –'

'Please, Ingrid.' This time Catrin's voice was strained. 'I don't want to talk about Foxe right now.'

Mercifully, before anybody else could offer their condolences, the oak door swung open. Magda watched as Alarice sidled through the doors, a heavy sketchbook folded under one arm.

'Sorry I'm late. What did I miss?'

Ingrid glanced up. 'Who are you planning to impale?'

'No one, for goodness' sake. You and your morbid brain.'

To be fair, Alarice was wearing the kind of boots that could probably puncture a lung if she'd tripped. Black leather, fine silver embellishments, and a glittering heel.

But she didn't trip.

She offered no further explanation beyond taking a seat at the head of the table, with a subtle but noticeable glint in her eye.

'Are those shoes the reason why it took you five hours to get down the stairs?'

'No, they're not.' Alarice plonked the sketchbook onto the table. There were several charcoal smudges adorning the cuff of her sleeves, but she brushed them away before reaching over to the soup cauldron. 'I was late because I needed to make some notes.'

The book's thick brown pages were dishevelled; the leather creased with age. It was the same one she used for watercolours, and one of her most prized possessions. Whatever Alarice had been noting down, Magda reasoned, was important enough to risk bringing the sketchpad into an environment full of food.

Perilous territory for any book.

'The soup's parsnip,' said Magda, without thinking. It was the colour of curdled milk, dusted with an aromatic peppering of nutmeg, and didn't taste of much.

'Oh. Thanks.'

She didn't know why she'd spoken. Perhaps it was because, like the others, she had sensed the sudden tension in the air. Something was condensing, almost imperceptibly: sour as parsnips, or the skim of the milk. And talking about anything else was an excuse to avoid whatever that thing might be.

'There was something I wanted to talk about, actually,' said Alarice.

'Yes,' Magda nodded, desperate. Alarice's demeanour suggested the quiet satisfaction of a cat that had finally tracked down its prey. 'Rubbish weather, isn't it?

'Well, yes. But —'

'Then that's that. Horrible cold, all that frost.' Something, anything, no matter how irrelevant. 'Did you know that there are over twelve kinds of snowflake? You've got prisms, and plates, and dendritic forms and —'

Muriel shot her a look.

'What's gotten into you?'

'We need to talk about what happened this morning,' said Alarice, deliberately. 'In Ether Rhiannon's class. About the sewing.'

The lump in Magda's throat grew tighter.

'Look here,' Alarice opened her sketchpad, to a page which looked remarkably similar to a swatchbook. Pinned to the paper were snippets and fabric samples from dozens of their various sewing projects. Gossamer. Velvet. Silk. 'All of this is part of our education, right? They're training us to be seamstresses for the Royal Palace.'

'The Brenin must have a great deal of clothing,' Muriel studied the miniature squares of textiles, like windows in a picture-book. 'Although it seems like overkill to need *quite* so many tailors.'

'Exactly. And whatever those seamstresses are working on, it's too large a collection to be personal garments alone. What's more, he could hire anyone he liked: but he requests Fallow graduates specifically.'

'The Ethers would probably say it's an act of philanthropy,' Catrin made a face. 'I mean, who wouldn't be flattered to win the approval of a bitter old man?'

'That's not the only thing that's off.' Alarice paused. 'Haven't you noticed the way you feel after a Weftwork class? Tired. Drained. Like something's been leached out of you.'

Magda shivered. She *had* felt that way, but had imagined the other, more competent seamstresses had no such trouble with keeping on top of their work. 'So it's exhausting to keep up with learning new techniques all the time. But we can't do much about that, can we.'

'What if it's not just the sewing?' Alarice pressed. 'What if it's doing something to us, too?'

The stretch and click of a needle. The fabric, like sutured flesh. Glimmering eyes in the form of wooden buttons, a sequined panel whose slick, oily movements reminded Magda of frogspawn.

The clothes they made were beautiful.

Perhaps *too* beautiful to be made of fabric alone.

'Our magic,' said Alarice, turning the page to reveal a set of careful notes. Observations and theories from each day, the neat handwriting growing more scrawled by the line. 'He wants us to make those clothes, because our magic's getting caught in the stitches.'

***

Nothing displeased Rhiannon Mourne quite so much as spilled milk. No point crying, so they said, but then somebody was still left to clean it up, weren't they? She mopped at the edges of the white puddle before it could seep between the kitchen tiles, chastising herself for being so clumsy in the first place.

Things hadn't been quite right since the new moon. Although the Fallow had never been a homely place, Rhiannon had grown accustomed to its patterns in the same way that ivy that grew around a tree. Her knowledge of its various twists and turns was intimate and overpowering — and one day, like the ivy, she hoped someone would finally choke the life out of the place.

She disposed of the milk-sodden napkin with a grimace. Until then there was her darling library, practically the only thing that kept her sane these days. She often spent an evening or so pottering through the shelves for something new to read, or simply to admire the gold-lettered covers and ancient paperwork before it rotted.

It was a pale reminder of her old job, which she had never quite stopped missing. One of the many pleasures of being a librarian was the sheer amount of people-watching you could do: it was hilarious to see old ladies poking their noses through racy romance novels, then hurriedly putting the book down when anybody walked past. Or the middle class businesswomen, who kept piles of eloquent-looking books in their closets, but never had time to read them. The latest emerging category had been youngsters who treated book-shopping as a kind of status game, *who could read the scariest horror novel without getting nightmares!* They shuffled towards the counter without saying much, paid in cash, and Rhiannon usually never saw them again.

It didn't really matter. They were amateurs, the lot of them.

'Rhi?' Lorna had shot her a worried look between classes, as they crossed paths in the corridors. 'I need a favour.'

'What is it?'

Lorna made a vague gesture towards the courtyards. Rhiannon followed her outside. By the time they reached the edge of the grounds, she understood her colleague's concern.

'Is there a way to get rid of it? I've never seen it in my life, I swear.'

The pair of them surveyed the patch of earth beneath the damp ashes of the pyre, and the chalk carving that had been unearthed there.

'It's certainly unusual,' said Rhiannon. It was the only lie she'd told in the history of her friendship with Lorna, which made her feel guilty. But there were some things which she could not compromise. 'Don't worry, I'll make sure Stefania doesn't see.'

'It's probably nothing, right?'

'Most likely it's been there for ages, and one of the storms has brought it up.' She paused. 'But just in case, it might be best to keep this between us.'

'That's what I thought. Stef might blow a gasket if I tell her there's another problem with the grounds. You saw how she got when I told her all the medlars had gotten apple scab... I don't think I can handle another tantrum.'

'I'll take care of it, don't worry.'

Once Lorna had receded safely into the distance, Rhiannon began to pile ash back over the chalk carving. It was clear that somebody else had found out about her doorway, about her library, even if Lorna was oblivious to its real meaning. It was worse than spilled milk, too: because there was no way of easily mopping up the mess and coaxing the carving back below ground.

Those girls, she thought, shovelling another pile of earth over the chalk.

She hoped to the goddess that they knew what they were doing.

Chapter 46
Hex

'You think we're sewing magic into the clothes?'

'It's the only way to make sense of everything,' Alarice replied, her voice low. 'It must be what happened with Tabitha Penry. Her cloak protected her at the Ceremony, because of the stitches she added. And the Ethers: couture robes like that must be pretty hard to come by. I don't think they wear them for the sake of uniform alone.'

Wherever they walked past in those cloaks, Muriel saw a horde of glittering ghosts. From the very first day it had unnerved her. From the very first time she saw Stefania come riding up that hill, she should have known it spelt trouble.

'And Rhos,' said Ingrid. 'Her gloves were custom-made. She wouldn't say why she wore them, only that they kept her safe.'

The image was clear as day: Rhos's empty green eyes, robbed of their spark. Red, curling hair like spilled ink. And the pair of gloves, mustard-yellow, discarded far away from her body.

Muriel swallowed, too upset to contemplate it any further. There had to be some other explanation for this whole affair. 'Maybe there's some connection between our powers and the sewing. But why would the Brenin want anything to do with a load of magical garments?'

Nobody answered. The question stared back at her like a sore thumb. What *wouldn't* the Brenin want? Who knew what could be achieved, with a limitless supply of enchanted cloth?

'Every time we create a new piece, some strand of our powers must get lodged there,' Alarice folded her sketchbook closed. 'So far it's been harmless. All they've given us here is skirts and socks and pretty little scarves.'

The unspoken half of her sentence loomed large. There were other garments, much more menacing than fashion attire, that could surely be conjured from the Fallow's extensive stockpiles.

'Armour,' said Ingrid. Her face had gone cold. 'You think this is for the Brenin's defence forces?'

'He's got an army, and I'm sure he intends to use it,' said Alarice. 'They must have a use for gauntlets. Chainmail. Chest plates and nets. Who can hope to challenge an army that's been dressed to kill?'

No one dared to reply.

Muriel was too busy imagining a scene like the Great Rift, the land heaving itself apart and the water rising up. She imagined soldiers rising up with it, as the water turned scarlet around them. One with a veridian's gauntlet: narrow tree branches piercing dagger wounds through her enemies. Another, with a scendred's chainmail: sending the flurry of attacks ricocheting back at the attacker. And the third, who looked frighteningly young, hurling a pyromancer's net over the masses.

The world did not burn like a candle; it did not burn like a box of matches.

Instead it melted slowly, in one terrible leering flame, swallowing friend and foe as it went.

'That can't be what he's planning.'

Surely it was too gruesome. Too bloody-minded, even for a man who was by nature unforgiveable. Even she struggled to believe in the possibility, with the evidence floating right before them.

'He created the Mandate to destroy people like us,' Catrin steeled herself. 'And now he's found a way to steal our powers. I'd say it's well within his capability.'

'How can we be sure of it?'

'We'd have to test it. By playing him at his own game, of course.'

*

By the next morning, a series of petrel-grey storm clouds were hovering over the Fallow. The menacing sky sizzled like toast left too long under the grill, but no one had much of an appetite. It was overwhelmed by the adrenaline of what was coming after the bell rang.

'Remember, keep your head down.'

'Will do.'

'Okay. Good luck, everyone.'

When they arrived at the Weftwork room, Ether Rhiannon was laying out bunches of thick golden stalks on the front table. It was vaguely reminiscent of wheat, and landed lightly like grain on a threshing floor.

'Morning, girls. We'll be doing some spinning today; just grab a bundle of flax and find a desk.'

Muriel eyed the soft mounds of flax, so pale and feathery. Alarice's plan relied on a series of carefully-embroidered charms: but for that, they would need fabric. The fibres alone were thin wisps, insubstantial as a rumour.

'Ether Rhiannon?' Catrin stuck up a hand. 'I think there's a leftover bolt of nettlecloth in the haberdashery. Should we work with that after we've finished our spinning?'

Rhiannon peered into the store cupboard at the back.

'My goodness, you're right. You can get started with pattern cutting first, if you'd like: it really does need using up.'

Muriel breathed a sigh of relief. Thanks to Catrin's quick thinking, they wouldn't have to wait another week to test the theory. Gathering the pale green material up with shaky hands, she retrieved a paper pattern, and got to work as quickly as possible.

Her pair of shears scored easy lines through the fabric. While she couldn't be sure what these pieces would be used for — she suspected some kind of blouse, or dress, from the shape — it was a smooth, methodical process. Under different circumstances it might have felt meditative. As things stood, it would serve as the canvas for her handiwork; the place where she would aim to weave her magic.

On the opposite side of the room, Ether Rhiannon had begun making the rounds. 'Those look excellent,' she was nodding at work, here and there. 'Just remember to clip the curves properly. And cut your notches outwards, not into the seam allowance.'

The crisp snip of scissors rattled alongside a chorus of shimmering pins, and the heaviness in Muriel's gut grew. But there were still darts to be traced and tailor's tacks to be placed, so she ploughed on and tried not to think of what came next.

Make the mark. Hide the work. Wait.

The needle trembled between her fingers. For a modest weapon of choice, it soon became unwieldy with sweat, and it took every ounce of Muriel's concentration to make the right incisions through the soft, dense cloth.

She'd never cast a hex before.

Thankfully, Alarice had chosen a few simple charms whose effects would be easy to observe. The spell which Magda was working on was *stinging weeds*. Muriel's spell was *split seams*, and Catrin's was *light threads*. With her heart in her throat, she began to stitch in the first line of the hex glyphs.

Of course it was precisely the wrong moment to have chosen.

'How's everything coming along over here, Miss Silvana?'

'Very well, thank you,' Muriel hovered over the nascent glyph, hoping it would be mistaken for tacking. 'I'm just working on some dart markings at the moment.'

'Lovely,' Rhiannon beamed. She loitered for a moment, as if hoping to be asked a question, before realising that Muriel was waiting for her to leave. 'Well. I'll be just over here if you need any help.'

Muriel hoped that the relief did not show on her face. If Ether Rhiannon had moved even a fraction closer, her mutinous stitchwork would have made itself apparent. Then again, who was Muriel to think she held such power? Perhaps their fabrications were really just that: a clumsy handful of seams punched through cloth, made precious only by the Brenin's demand.

Strange memories drifted past her as she made the series of invisible stitches. Her hands occupied themselves with the cloth at her fingers, but her mind wandered far away, into a forest. First there was a fallen-down tree, coated in moss. It was that extraordinarily vivid, almost unbelievable, shade of green — the kind of moss that looked like sumptuous velvet winding round the branches. She'd first seen it many months ago, but the image was warped now: a great antler, furred over with time, wasting forlornly into the soil.

Her memory twisted things like that, sometimes.

Then a second image. Her sisters outside the school gates, both of them smiling. But their teeth were oddly green, a lurid colour, as if they'd eaten key lime pie for three weeks straight. *Isa?* she tried to call after them. *Luz? Wait there, wait for me!* She banged at the gates, which were locked shut for some reason.

Her sisters kept on walking and didn't look back.

It was the third memory that made Muriel's blood run cold: the memory of that night in the woods. The jarring sensation that held her limbs fast, the impossibility of movement. She looked down and saw the light brown skin of her foot, weeping with unfamiliar blood. The blood belonged to her, of course. But the needles of Cunning Wood were rising up like the gall in the back of her throat; roots, merciless roots, rising up to destroy her.

Was this still a memory?

Was she really there at the edge of the forest, pinned to the ground by things she could not see?

'Miss Silvana?'

Muriel looked up, a cold sweat at the back of her neck.

'Your work. Is it finished?'

'Yes, Ether Rhiannon,' she reached out to hand it over. 'It's all complete.'

She could hardly breathe. Partly with the relief of returning to reality; partly with the fear of what would happen next. The Ether moved closer, aquiline elegance caught in those deep bronze eyes.

'Very neat stitchwork,' was all she said. 'You're a credit to the class, Miss Silvana. I daresay I couldn't stitch it better myself.'

Muriel didn't trust herself to answer. The symbol stared back with evil intent; it was a mark that stained the hexmaker's hands. Seemingly satisfied, Ether Rhiannon glanced over to the desk beside her.

'Yours too, Miss Corrales. You've made quick work of that.'

'Um,' Magda's eyes darted away. 'It's not really finished quite yet.'

'It looks perfectly complete from where I'm standing.'

At that point several things happened in rapid succession.

Magda, who was still clinging to the bundle of fabric, attempted to manoeuvre sideways. At the same time, Ether Rhiannon stepped forward and tripped over the leg of the chair. The bundle of fabric went flying, Rhiannon regained her balance, and the nettlecloth landed miraculously in her hands.

That was when Muriel noticed the other sample.

Her sample.

A sour green blush was appearing at the centre the fabric, spreading outwards from the place she'd stitched the glyph. Right as it reached Ether Rhiannon's fingertips, the woman let out a cry of pain – and then the thin ridge in the nettlecloth seemed to vanish altogether.

The hex, Muriel stared, hardly believing what had happened. *Stinging weeds. It worked.*

The urticant properties of the fibre had been rekindled for a split second, and now they had returned to normal. But there was no crowing jubilance to the revelation; no cause for celebration. Ether Rhiannon now stood frozen. Her expression was a close mixture of suspicion and the miraculous.

'Are you... Are you okay?'

'Hm?' There was a pause, as the clouds seemed to clear from Rhiannon's vision. 'How strange. I must have prepared the fabric wrong. I do apologise, girls.'

It made Muriel uneasy to see her at a loss for anything. She wanted to scramble back in time, to weeks and months before any of this, but the world seemed to dry up around her. One by one, she watched as the other girls handed over their carefully stencilled pieces of fabric. They were trapped within a childhood fable, knowing all of the endings. And they were powerless to change a damned thing.

'How many times have I told you to be careful with your raw edges?' Rhiannon looked down in pity at the loosely flapping fabric in her hands. *Split seams*: another successful glyph. 'A little more effort, and this could've been beautiful.'

'Sorry, Ether Rhiannon.'

With each hex the room grew a little dimmer, for a creeping fear had spread its wings over them. It smothered their hopes like the feathers of a great grey owl, with the insult of their newfound knowledge. The skill they'd trained with such pride was just another trick; another weapon to be wielded.

Another string in the Fallow's hypocritical bow.

*

'I say we go east.'

'East? The southwest's our best bet by far.'

'Or the northern forests. They could be useful.'

'Hold your horses, we have to actually get out of here first,' Alarice sighed. A pool of evening sunlight fell over the place where they were sitting, but it felt colder than rain. 'Any suggestions there?'

Of course, nobody could answer.

Scapegoats, thought Muriel, numbly. That was how he saw them. It had all been a careful guise: the special treatment, the exemptions, the training. Once the Brenin had his fabrics, their magic woven into the rivets, it would mean the end to their work. Like any good scapegoat, their most valuable asset was their golden fleece.

All he had to do was spin it off their backs.

'How about Arianydd?' Magda shot Ingrid a questioning look. The world yawned wide beyond the cusp of the Fallow, and few of them had ever been so far west. 'If there's a library you know, then we could try it.'

The doorways between libraries, it had been reasoned, must span the entire network of official bookhouses. If they could only figure out how to navigate the different channels, then they might have some way of getting beyond the perimeters of Cunning Wood.

'I don't think there's much point in going back to Arianydd.'

'Oh. Did your family move away?'

'They'd have been stupid not to.' A pause. 'I suppose Emyr's still there, though.'

'Emyr?'

'My horse. He was a bit of a demon, but he had his moments,' said Ingrid. The dampness in her eyes took Muriel by surprise, and she looked like she was holding back some other comment.

'Well, I'm sorry you had to leave him.'

Ingrid tried to smile. 'It's probably for the best. He'll have a new rider by now, one who can take care of him. What about your town, anyway?'

'Wildbriar?' Muriel repeated. The question caught her off guard, even though she really should have seen it coming. 'Maybe. Although ...'

Although it was possible things would have changed.

Although she was terrified of what had happened to her family, if she would even be able to find them again.

'It's not too close to any of the big cities,' said Magda, tactfully. 'It might be safer to go somewhere with a lot of people. More places to hide, you know.'

'Fair enough,' said Alarice. 'We could try the Wolds?'

'Or Torren?'

Catrin shook her head, a cool red drift in her eyes. 'I'd rather not.'

'Oh,' said Alarice, understanding. None of them had ever met Foxe in person. Despite that, they'd come to know him through the pieces that Catrin carried with her, through fragments of memories that swirled like a snowglobe. 'Say the word, and I'll send him an adder in the post.'

'Allie!' Catrin laughed, in spite of the sadness in her eyes. 'That won't be necessary.'

'What happened?'

The snowglobe shimmered, then shifted altogether.

'I let him go.'

Chapter 47

Doom and Damnation

'Are you sure this is a good idea?'

'Of course not.'

'Urgh,' Ingrid squinted up into the darkness, wafting away motes of dust. 'They need a carpenter and a smith here, not a librarian.'

The underground journey from the Fallow to the Vespertine Library had passed without incident, though everybody was glad to be shot of the unwieldy doors. Catrin and Muriel had stayed behind to keep watch of the portal, which left the three of them alone on their mission into the woods.

Magda was beginning to regret her earlier confidence. While she'd hoped the voice in the Vespertine Library might be able to help them find a map of the network, she had no guarantee whatsoever that it would even appear. And, knowing how capricious it could get, it might not even *want* to help them.

But it was too late to second-guess herself now.

Resisting the urge to sweep up some stray papers, she raised a lantern over a stranded pile of books. Undoubtedly, the pale yellow light was doing the place no favours: but if the library was messier than an autumn wood after a storm, at least it had no structural issues. Those crooked windows and that sturdy oak door were what kept the Forest out. As long as it stayed that way, the entire building was safe.

'Is this the book you were talking about?' Alarice peered over the front desk, holding her own lantern higher. *Welcome to the Vespertine Library,* said the gold letters. *Please sign the entry book if you wish to speak with a —*

'Give me that,' Magda picked it up, slashing her name quickly across the paper. The quiet had made her apprehensive, but there was little she could do to control her nerves. 'Come on. Where are you, for scrim's sake?'

'Hey, it's only an old attic. It can't hurt you.'

She was shaking her head. 'You don't understand. That voice... It's so *infuriating.*'

The three of them surveyed the cavernous building around them. From its thick velvet carpets to its high, celestial skylights, there was certainly a quality of the surreal to the place. Brackish starlight swept the room, dappled by the thick foliage of the wood outside. The outside world echoed like nothing more than a stone dropped into a well.

'Do you think it's gone somewhere else?'

'It's got to be here,' Magda insisted. 'It's always here.'

It had taken a lot of faith to persuade the others to come here; now she must sound crazy. Maybe the voice only came out when people were looking especially desperate. Maybe it would elude them entirely, and they'd have to find a new plan altogether.

'Hello? Is anybody there?' Alarice called, the question echoing into the gloom. Her hair fell in tightly-braided strands, and the silver beads glinted as she moved. 'We need a map.'

There was a ripple in the dark.

'A map? Why, they're a particular interest of mine.'

The three girls froze.

'See,' Magda whispered. 'I told you it was real.'

'It must be an enchantment of some sort,' Ingrid looked a little nauseous, but very much determined not to show it. 'There can't actually be a person living here.'

'Not even visiting?'

The voice was translucent, taunting.

'Not even as a holiday?'

'People don't go to the heart of Cunning Wood for leisure, let alone a holiday.'

'How unimaginative of them.'

Magda ran a hand over her forehead, already sick of the faceless creature. 'We came to find a map of the archipelago's libraries,' she made an effort to compose herself. 'Would you be able to help us?'

'I see,' it mused. 'That's rather unfortunate. You see, most of those maps were destroyed long ago.'

'Should we go?' Ingrid peered cautiously towards the door where they'd arrived. 'If there's nothing to be found here, then we could...'

'Give me a minute.' Magda craned her neck to inspect the rafters of the building. '*Most* of the maps? What about the unofficial ones?'

'Well, Miss Corrales, that's a different question entirely.'

It was the punctilious address that threw her for a loop. There was no justice to its knowing; no rhyme or reason to why the voice sought familiarity when she knew nothing about it in return.

If it had a face, she would have punched it by now.

'I don't get it.' Alarice had picked up the entry book, and was leafing through the pages with a furrowed brow. 'They're all blank. Magda, what *is* this place?'

'I wish I knew. This building seems to have a memory of some sort.'

There was a hollow fluttering at the windows, like a bird trapped behind glass.

'I think we should go,' Ingrid glanced between them, then back towards the door. 'I don't like it here. Feels like something's watching us.'

'Give me a minute. Alarice, can I borrow that book quickly?'

'Sure.'

Writing in careful script, Magda sealed her question in the entry-book. It was a question which seemed irrelevant, one that she was too embarrassed to ask out loud. But it had nagged at the back of her mind for days.

'What are you asking it?'

'Nothing. It's … it's stupid, really. I just thought that —'

'The prophecy? The missing prince?' the voice exploded, as if it was barely suppressing a laugh. 'Haven't heard that one in a while. Sorry to disappoint, but there's really nothing much to tell.'

'That prophecy's a dead end,' said Alarice, not unkindly. 'Look. We're all tired. Maybe we should come back another night.'

'That prophecy is the only way to recover the archipelago's Forests,' Magda replied, her cheeks hot. 'We need to know what to do when we get out of here. How to find somewhere safe, somewhere that's not been ravaged by Sickness.'

'You'd be lucky. Those places are fast dwindling,' replied the voice. 'As for the heir, any hope for the poor fool's long gone.'

The words were like a lodge of ice water. Stunning cold, before the delayed shock.

'He's dead?'

'He can't be,' Ingrid scoffed. 'His return's the only way to make things better. If he's dead, we're going to have a hard time of righting the prophecy.'

'Who said we wanted anything to do with him?'

'I don't know about you, but I'd rather not subscribe to a summer of doom and damnation.'

'Being doomed isn't so bad, actually,' offered the voice. 'You should try it some time.'

Ingrid gave a sigh of exasperation. 'You were right, Magda,' she said. '*Infuriating* doesn't really do it justice.'

There was a small, angry huff, like a mouse in a temper.

'Do you want my help or not?'

'Yes. Sorry. The library map,' said Magda, worn out. 'Your most unofficial edition, please.'

'That'll be Aisle Thirteen.'

***

Five nights had passed since the Vespertine Library, and there was a tiredness in Muriel's blood.

Late winter weighed heavy on the soul. March was a ghost that walked on legs like spindles; it was sharp, and it was bitter. But it was also a promise — no matter how cruel — that things could only get better from here.

The problem was that the reality had not matched up to their hopes quickly enough. What Magda, Alarice, and Ingrid had found in the Vespertine Library mystified more than it resolved: an unfinished map with labels so obscure nobody could hope to read the writing. Half a legend from a nameless voice in the wood. And the final, unspoken fear, which was written so loudly across their faces that even she and Catrin read it easily.

Maybe we'll never escape this place.

In the absence of a saving grace, Muriel sought out the quiet. On those days where her head roared too loud, she slipped out and walked the grounds, allowed the low howl of her magic to cast its shadows. Really, she walked because there was no way back from this. From whatever she had become.

Mujer lechuza, the lawn whispered, beneath her bare feet. *Sees everything. Roams the night.*

'Shut up,' Muriel muttered back. Since when had being a veridian meant suffering the random commentary of anything that grew roots?

She'd taken the precaution of avoiding the others when her powers got too unwieldy, but they often felt like more of an inconvenience than a threat. Not that it made any odds, with how bad morale was getting back in the North Quad. It was better that she kept this to herself.

As she wandered, pieces of the past came shimmering back to her like scales of a fish, sharp and sour salt-smelling. She missed the harbour and its flotsam of little darting fish, sheltering beneath her dad's boat. Did the broad-beaked puffins still squawk on the cliffs of Eirlaw Island, waiting for sandeels? Another year older, and there were so many things she didn't know. She'd turned seventeen almost without noticing it; the one blessing was that no one had done the indignity of wishing her *happy birthday*. Somebody had placed a cluster of snowdrops in a jar on her bedside table, and she was grateful for the quietness of the gesture.

Maybe she'd get back in time to see the sunrise.

Wasn't that what people did at moments of pivotal beauty, anyway? They contemplated things larger than themselves. It was a way to test the depth of that beauty, plunging a measuring stick into murky water. As she made the turn back towards the lower cloisters, droplets of free-roaming starlight condensed in the form of dew. By the time she arrived, however, it became apparent that somebody else had beaten her to the dawn.

'Star mapping again?'

'Silvana,' Ingrid raised her head, both eyes bloodshot. 'You're up late.'

'Or early. It'll be sunrise soon,' Muriel took a seat beside her in the cloisters. 'You look terrible.'

Ingrid set down the notebook she'd been holding, avoiding her gaze. Its pages patterned with stars and sketches of the constellations: a perfect night sky, spilling like treacle across the page.

'Did you stay up all night to do those?'

'The dorm room's all wrong,' Ingrid replied, folding the book shut. 'I can't get used to it.'

They sat there, surveying the few stars that hadn't faded yet. Rhos's absence ran like deep water. Trickling, percolating, into the bedrock of their lives. The furniture remained unmoved, but that half of the dormitory must be staring back at Ingrid like an open wound each night.

'I'm so sorry. I can't imagine how that must feel.'

'Not your fault.' A pause. 'I shouldn't have been so naïve. I thought it would get better, even slowly, but this...'

Muriel tried to think of what she could say. Was there anything that could possibly offer comfort under such awful circumstances?

'I know it seems like it won't ever get better,' she said, gently. 'That's because you cared about her. But if you ever need to talk to anyone, about anything... I'll always be here to listen.'

Ingrid didn't move. 'You know, she'd never have let this happen to me. I should have checked on her. I should have —'

'It wasn't your fault, Ingrid.'

They fell quiet again. The first streaks of dawn were beginning to tarnish the sky, skim milk pouring into a puddle of dark blue coffee.

'I'm just sick of feeling this way.' A deep, transcendental sky. Yellow light at the corners. 'First Tomren, and now this. It's exhausting.'

'Tomren?'

'My little brother. He's been unwell, for a while now.'

Oh, thought Muriel. *Oh.*

Everybody knew that the Sickness had taken a hold of Wales's Forests. But nobody had thought to mention the impact it might have on people, as it spread further and faster through the land.

'I used to think the prophecy was a load of old rubbish,' she smiled, bitterly. 'Stupid, isn't it. Now I can't help but hope it's true. Because that means there's a way back, a way to save him. I can't...'

She broke off.

'You're doing all that you can,' Muriel wished there was something more that she could offer. 'He's lucky to have a sister like you. And he'll know you're thinking of him.'

'There's nothing I *can* do, that's the problem. I can't afford to lose anyone else.'

'You'll always have us,' Muriel reassured her. 'Everyone here, we're cut from the same cloth.'

But Ingrid was looking somewhere else now, her frame suddenly tense.

'Muriel. What's that?'

'What?'

From the left side of the alcove, behind the cloisters, the stairwell was just about visible. In it stood a shadowy figure. Stock-still. Frozen, as if someone had cut its puppet-strings.

'Hello?' Muriel squinted into the gloom. 'Who's there?'

And then there was a violent *crash*.

Chapter 48

The Brightest Hope

The night she dreamed of the golden horizon, Magda knew something was wrong. It floated, just beyond her reach, like a ball of fireflies. Impossible to pin down into one place.

Closer: she could almost reach it. The ball of light danced before her eyes. A great fiery smile, as if it knew she would be tempted towards it.

Closer. Just a little closer, and –

The vision disappeared without warning.

She was awake, alive and breathing in the too-stale air of Dormitory Seven. Her voice was hoarse. The window was blown open, a high wind whistling through the slats.

'Muriel? Are you there?'

Her best friend's bed was empty. It must have been the wind that had woken her up, and the air was thin outside. With her head aching, Magda clambered to her feet and began the journey down the stairwell.

'... the prophecy was a load of old rubbish ...'

There were voices down there. People! Her friends. Blessed threads, she needed them, but they had not seen her yet.

'... cut from the same cloth ...'

She needed to join them. It was like the vision knew she was running, and had sent its rays of light after her. Everywhere she looked were glowing amber eyes. She had to get away from it. She had to get out of that corridor, had to, had to, had to, except –

*

'Magda?' said a voice. 'Oh, thank the Weaver! We thought you'd... cold water, yes ...'

'Who's there?' Magda whispered, trying to see. Waking up was less of a flash and a stab of blinding pain, and more of a slow resurfacing, like being dragged out from beneath icy water. 'Gold,' she murmured, shivering. 'There was a golden horizon.'

'A what?' said a second voice. Ingrid. 'Take it easy, you've been out for ten minutes.'

Magda tried to sit up. Her words were a disobedient flock of sheep, darting away from her before she managed to form a coherent sentence. 'You don't understand. It was so bright. Like a sunrise, all around me. I couldn't...'

'Hang on. You saw something?' Muriel hovered closer, suddenly less blurry.

'I don't know what it meant.'

'Okay. Let's get you some rest before we worry about anything to do with visions.' Her best friend was chewing her lip in the way she did when she got anxious. 'You fell down a flight of stairs, Mags. Anybody would have thought you were being chased by a bear.'

Magda's head hurt. It had certainly felt like she was being chased by *something*, she just couldn't figure out what.

'Do you think it's a bad omen?'

'What?'

'The vision.'

'She said there was a golden horizon,' said Ingrid, picking up the damp cloth that had been pressed over Magda's forehead. 'She seems kind of feverish, though.'

'We should wait. It's too soon to be asking questions.'

'It's okay,' Magda insisted. 'I can talk now.'

'Are you sure it won't, well, upset you?'

She shook her head.

'It was only a colour. Just that same gold, in every direction you turned.'

Muriel looked a little unnerved. 'I'm glad it's gone, whatever it was.'

'Who knows? It could be a sign of something good,' Ingrid shrugged. 'You know what they say about how fire purifies. Maybe it's some kind of symbol.'

'A sign of hope,' Magda repeated.

Yes: that was it.

A crowning glory, so radiant it hurt to look.

It was about time something good came their way.

PART V

Interlude

Three Minutes

The smell of hot earth rose like a crescent moon over Abergwyll. Slowly, surely, like the scent of a spring market-day now that the long midwinter was drawing to a close: except this day was inauspicious. The final Tuesday of the month was a day struck by faeries, beasts, and spirits. If you had any sense, you kept your door locked until the following dawn.

'Do you feel that?' Sidonie rolled over to her husband in bed. Morning light was just beginning to seep through their window. 'It shouldn't be this warm so early. I could have sworn the crocuses were only just starting to germinate last week.'

'No hay que quejarse,' grumbled her husband, still half-asleep. 'Se agradece el calor, y el buen clima...'

'Rafa, I'm serious. You need to wake up.'

Sitting up with a groan, her husband scooped his hair into a low bun and tore back the curtains. 'See? It's nothing to —'

'Look,' whispered Sidonie, faintly. 'Over there in the distance.'

From the third floor of their house, you could see almost the entire view over the hill down to the coast. Languidly, almost casually, a wave of fire was combing its way over the centre of town. Sidonie watched as the sign for Brookit Bridge, Bevan & Trove, and Tanya Okada's began to smoulder, caressed by the wafts of orange flame.

It was almost gentle.

A quiet rupture.

But the smoke was still moving, now beginning to gather at the base of the hill. It swirled like a great grey sea whose waves were filled with strange flotsam.

'Sidonie, I think we should —'

'We're leaving.' She was already out of bed and heading for the door. 'Go and wake Isa, I'll get Lucía.'

'I'll meet you downstairs.'

They didn't waste time on *te quiero* or *stay safe, darling*. The pair of them would need to be fast, to clear the fires. If this was a dance with death — with something whose hunger would not hesitate to swallow them whole — then there was not a moment to spare. And so Rafael and Sidonie began that dance in the same way they'd first fallen in love: each moment was subtle defiance. Every movement brought their pulses racing.

*

Far beyond the outskirts of her old town, Aisling and her son stood crouched in the undergrowth. They carried everything they could in the leather rucksacks, slung low over their hips, but it was getting heavy.

'Let's stop for a bit,' wheezed Aisling. 'Just a few minutes to catch my breath.'

'If you're that tired, then why don't we just go back and take the car?' Enio fixed her with a look. 'It'd be a hundred times faster.'

She shook her head firmly. 'They'd see us.'

'They might not.'

'Sorry, love. We've got to go on foot.'

Enio gave a petulant *hmph* and leaned back, his palms braced against the hard earth. He hated himself for even thinking it, but it was times like these when he missed Eirlaw Island the most. He missed waking up easy and finding bright skies outside his window. He missed working outside all day and coming back to the sound of laughter in the late afternoon sun. He missed –

'Enio, do you see that?' said a voice to his left, very far away. 'Look.'

'Where?' he squinted, trying to locate the thing his mother was pointing at. 'Oh, shit.'

Aisling was staring in the direction of their old town. Or at least, she was trying very hard to. There were tears pricking at the corners of her eyes and slowly, over the crest of the hill, a cloud of black smoke was beginning to rise.

Enio took one look at it and abandoned the rucksack. 'We've got to go back and help.'

'We can't.'

'What are you talking about? Dad's still in the house. He doesn't even know we're here!'

A look of anguish crossed his mother's face.

'Right?' Enio asked again. 'You said we were going to visit Bampi Owain. You said that we were ...'

They stood paralysed, watching the crest of the flames grow higher. This was not a simple smokestorm. This fire was a creature of unnatural flesh, and it was out for blood.

'It's too dangerous.'

'But we can't leave Dad back there!'

'Your father was aware of the consequences of his actions.'

The words landed soft as a bullet. It had been strange, yesterday evening: the *goodnight* they'd spoken oddly subdued, his father's hug its usual inescapable self. But there had been a look in his eyes that Enio couldn't read.

'You knew this was going to happen,' he gritted his teeth. 'You both knew, and you didn't tell me?'

'Please, Enio. Your father and I swore we'd keep you and Magda safe.'

He shook his head.

'You made your decision. Now I'm making mine.'

'Wait!'

For a moment he thought his mother would keep hanging on to the scruff of his jacket, would actually fight him to keep him there. But she let go, bright terror in her eyes.

'Are you sure this is what you want?'

'The Silvanas are still there, Mum. They're family, too.'

Neither of them spoke. Then, before Enio could take the words back, his mother was reaching for the rucksack and scrambling to her feet.

'This way. Quick, we need to go faster.'

They started moving back down the slopes towards the edge of town, their feet tripping over loose rocks like mountain goats. In another life, Aisling Corrales might have been scared. But her son's words had cut her to the bone. This was about family, and the Silvanas had been more of a family to them than anyone else.

She looked back into the greedy eye of the fire, following Enio's silhouette towards the heat. *Our boy. Our beautiful boy.* It was impossible to shake Gabriel's words from her mind, and so she let them ring through her memory, guide them both towards the chaos that awaited.

Wildbriar was burning faster than a wicker man.

Chapter 49

Willowdown

The spring didn't move in; it crept. Like residual heat saved under your skin, the earth became a warm body, one that took longer to cool than the air around it. Some days Muriel felt like they might have been girls anywhere at all, living lives completely untouched by the intricacies of Tidal Folk or the Scarp Mandate. Other days, when the sun strained high above them, she felt the needles of a headache pricking at her forehead.

When moments of peace did unfold, it was like sitting inside a painting.

She saw the sovereign touch of the artist, the pigment across the canvas: smooth, dense, oceanic. Those strange half-dusks made her want to stay clothed in the day, and gave her a sudden aversion to water. There was the unfathomable sense that cold showers might strip the moment, too, from her skin. That she might resurface not as a girl on a clear spring night, but as a different person altogether.

'Miss Silvana,' said Ether Rhiannon, her robes spilling across the floor behind her. The rest of the class was already seated at their tables. 'What an honour to be graced with your presence at this late hour.'

'Sorry, Ether Rhiannon. I ... I got distracted.'

That was the other thing that had been preoccupying her mind lately: Magda's vision. No trace of the vast golden horizon had resurfaced since that night, yet the image set Muriel's teeth on edge. Below the shimmering veil, there was something lurking in dark waters. And it had yet to break the surface.

'I didn't ask for an explanation,' Ether Rhiannon tapped her foot. 'There's still a desk free. Please take your seat beside Miss Leyshon.'

Vaguely, Muriel could feel her headache getting stronger, but she sank into her seat without a further word. Everything was the wrong thing to say. Especially now, with the knowledge of what these classes really meant.

'The Brenin needs skilled artisans, not amateurs.' Ether Rhiannon pointed to the board at the front. 'The Fallow's textiles are finer, and more precise, than most textiles. Like spider silk.'

Except spiders made no pretensions about luring in their prey, thought Muriel. The Brenin had given them no such grace. From the Fallow to the Royal Haberdashery, their magic was a utility: a corrupt, but useful mechanism. It would be tolerated for as long as those enchanted textiles could serve the Palace's purposes, and no longer than that.

The girls themselves were surplus to requirement.

'We'll be embellishing some screens of chiffon this morning, in preparation for the Palace's spring festivities. Each of you can begin with a square of fabric,' Rhiannon gestured to the store cupboard at the back. 'Choose whatever colour you like. And remember to use the double-folded seams that we have practiced.'

The cupboard doors opened like a trove of emeralds. Silks came in all shapes and sizes, and the trilobal prism of the silkworm's filament cast a beautiful lustre. Spiders, however, spun a different kind of silk. Theirs was a filament whose rarity and scarceness made it precious, and not even protein fibres like wool could match its strength and elasticity.

'Oh, stitches,' muttered Ingrid. 'This fabric's too slippery.'

'Yours isn't the problem,' said Muriel, after a few minutes of trying to wrangle the impossible cloth. 'I think I've got mine lined up badly. I can't get the seams to match.'

'As long as you're not planning on maintaining a chiffon-based wardrobe, it shouldn't matter too much.' Swathes of the diaphanous fabric folded between Ingrid's slim fingers. 'Shame we couldn't have used cotton, really. I could've embroidered quite a fetching piece of cheesecloth for the occasion.'

Muriel tried to smile, but it felt as if her head was on fire. The headache was slowly getting worse, aided by the fresh heat of a vicious spring.

'No, no, no. That's not quite right,' Rhiannon stood over Magda and Catrin's desk, across the room. 'The beads need to go in vertical rows, not horizontal.'

'I thought you said the pattern was this way,' Catrin shot Magda a look. 'Are you telling me we've had it upside down this whole time?'

'What do you ...? Oh. Sorry.'

You could have fried an egg on the red-hot silence that followed.

'Ether Rhiannon,' called someone else, across the room. 'Could you check the bugle bead segment on this for me?'

More movement. More talking. More flapping fabric. The colours wheeled, fairground-bright, as Muriel tried to concentrate. She picked up the needle, the metal slipping between her fingers.

'I dare say Miss Gosselin gets it right every time. More attention to detail, and less chatter, the rest of you!'

With every stitch, the room seemed to grow a little stuffier.

'Are you okay?' Ingrid glanced over, frowning. 'You look a bit clammy.'

'I'm fine.'

It was just a headache. It would go away on its own, if she could only have a minute to think straight.

'Since the pearl buttons seem to have caused some problems, I'll demonstrate. Take your thread as so,' Ether Rhiannon continued, back at the front of the room. 'Then get started with the backstitch. The trick is just to —'

Right as she began explaining the next step, something that Muriel knew was terribly, horribly important, a blinding pain shot through her right temple.

' — take your thread back through —'

Now Rhiannon's words were underwater; merging with the air, the vowels losing shape. Why was everything so slow, and bright, and jagged?

'Muriel?'

She blinked. The dark-eyed girl beside her looked decidedly concerned.

'What?'

'Muriel, what did you just —'

'Nothing. It's nothing.'

She swallowed. Tried to remember how to breathe.

'Is it the window?' Catrin turned around from the desk in front of them. 'I can open it, or get some water.'

'Don't worry, I'll be fine.' She didn't want to cause any unnecessary worry, but it felt like her head was bursting. 'Actually ... Maybe we could open the window just slightly?'

'Miss Silvana.' Ether Rhiannon's expression shifted when she turned and saw the sweat beading the girl's forehead. 'Would you like to be excused?'

Embarrassment flooded Muriel's neck. 'I'm sorry, I don't know what's come over me. I'm sure it will calm down in a minute.'

'Very well,' Rhiannon nodded gravely. 'If you wish to visit the infirmary, you need only ask.'

Behind her, Alarice stood up.

'We can take her, Ether Rhiannon.'

Muriel tried to speak, but her tongue felt dull and thick. The words refused to form: instead, they clotted like glue in her mouth. She heard voices ferrying around her as the door was pulled open, and chairs scratched out of their positions.

'Come on,' someone helped her towards the corridor. 'This way.'

It should have felt like a relief, to be out of that room. Muriel's head hung so lightly that it was hard to grip on to the different happenings as they rose and fell around her. She barely perceived the firm hands which settled on her shoulders and carefully, so carefully, guided her out of the corridor.

*

'You need rest, Miss Silvana,' said Ether Stefania, shaking her head as she ran a hand across the girl's boiling temples. 'And something to bring down your temperature.'

'What happened?'

'You seem to have caught a sickness,' said Ether Stefania simply. 'Take this.'

Muriel eyed the flask of steaming liquid suspiciously, but her head was aching so badly that she hoped it would work. 'Is that Willowdown?'

'Yes, it is.'

She watched as Stefania poured out a cup of the potion, catching a faint waft of elderflower and white willow. It was brewed traditionally, as she recalled, with a kettleful of rain. Something to do with its antipyretic properties.

'Urgh,' she spluttered at the hotness. 'It's ... rather strong.'

'A word of warning, Miss Silvana,' Ether Stefania hovered by the door. 'Some patients have reported experiencing unwanted hallucinations after taking Willowdown. It is not a common side effect, but if you see or hear anything strange tonight... try not to worry.'

The door slammed shut before Muriel could formulate a response, leaving her alone and aching. Nowhere left to scratch around. Limbs too heavy to get up. And since the medical bay was hardly a party, she could only lean to one side in hopes of looking out the window.

What was happening to her?

One minute she'd been lucid, and the next she'd been sweating out a fever in the middle of Weftwork. Every girl at the Fallow had been dealt a bad hand: that much was clear. But in the midst of those hardships, they found comfort in sharing their joys.

Now that Muriel was alone, the fever seemed to warp and shrink before her eyes. The solitude. This was the worst part, and it always had been.

Nowhere else to turn.

She tried to reach for the bedside lantern. Her arms wouldn't move.

Nowhere else to hide.

Awful light crept down like a rhizome, sinking its roots into her skin and flooding her mouth with sickly whiteness.

Chapter 50

Oneiromania

A sudden chill, said the Ethers. That was all. It had happened from time to time in the Old World — fevers, mass hysteria, even a dancing plague at one point — but they always passed. Like a field of slash-and-burn, the old crops soon gave way to new earth.

Magda struggled to believe that. The tides could change, and the storms could weep. But since Muriel had fallen ill, the earth stood still. At first she'd thought it would be over in the manner of a short spell of rain; a badly timed forecast. Then it crept in like a long thaw, and didn't leave.

They'd sentenced her to isolation in the medical bay until further notice. With that assertion, more unsettlingly, came the notion that everybody would dust themselves off and carry on with their lives, as if nothing had occurred in the first place. The crows still brought post; lessons went on, albeit slower and grittier than usual. Magda couldn't tell if it was loneliness or denial that had gritted harder. But it was there, salt in the butter, skimming pale yellow margins around their days.

'Remember, girls,' Ether Lorna replied, when they had pressed for details during Botany. 'Your exemption from the Brenin's Mandate comes on the condition that you work hard here to train your skills. I understand your concern for your friend. But as unfortunate as Miss Silvana's circumstances are, you can't be excused from classes.'

Confusion and shame fluttered below Magda's skin. The emphasis always shifted from subduing to controlling their gifts. They had something the Brenin needed, yet he wielded it like a knife over their heads.

'After lunch we've got a free period. Can we go and visit her then?'

'All in good time,' Lorna assured them, throwing a sprig of orange-blossom into the brewing pot. 'Temperance is a virtue. And by the time you leave the Fallow, you will have learned to weather a storm.'

*

'A whole day, and no report? They must think we're stupid.'

'Or desperate.'

'She'll be fine,' Alarice was adamant. 'We've just got to wait it out.'

Magda couldn't bring herself to argue. There were many words in the Welsh language which could describe the uncanny and horrifying. *Dychryn*, for dread. *Afiechyd*, for sickliness or ill health. Even *arswyd*, for terror. None of them quite described the unsettling atmosphere that Muriel's absence continued to foster. First they had been six; then they were five.

Spring had broken with braw, bloody waters.

Now they were four.

'Surely they'll let us go and see her tomorrow,' Ingrid held a sheet of paper up to the light, scanning over a sketch she'd made days earlier. 'It can't be much longer, can it?'

'We don't really know what happened to her, though.'

The tightness in Magda's stomach clenched itself sharply. She should have sensed something was wrong. This was her fault.

*

'Maybe it's a bout of fever.'

'Or some kind of parasite.'

'Or a viral plague.'

The days passed and Magda yearned for something to change. Anything would have been better than the saltmarsh of their routine, its acid burn sucking the plants down into the bog. A burning affection; a corrosive love.

She missed Muriel like walking through the forest. No mossing glade or roe deer shadow: these woods were bare. And in their new absence, the plants shrank back from the hearthstones they had touched.

Maybe years passed before she dared to ask the question.

Can we go to look for a cure?

Can we go to the forest, though we should really stay away.

Can we go back to the house in the woods. Can we? Can we?

'Of course,' said Ingrid, as if she'd asked for a receipt at the supermarket. 'We can go tomorrow night, if it would help.'

The kindness looped around her, shrouding her in words she didn't deserve: but if the other girls pitied her, they didn't show it. Some small part of Magda had forgotten how to feel gratitude, only how to perform it.

'Thank you,' she said, rabbit-lit. She didn't dare to look such kindness in the eye lest it bolted away entirely. 'Thank you.'

*

Under the woods it was dark. The four of them had clambered through the portal at the heart of the Ceremonial Grounds, only to discover that the place was even more lightless than usual. After reaching the bottom of the pit, Catrin gave a cough that echoed around the chamber.

The buried library: a cavern that shouldn't exist.

'Do you think they made it look this way on purpose?'

'Like a hall of mirrors,' said Alarice, moving forward quietly. Its red and gold bookshelves glowed the colour of live embers, smouldering purplish brown. The same view echoed back from every angle. 'Come on, let's keep going.'

They made their way towards the back wall.

'It's here,' Magda gestured to the panel which had led them to the Vespertine Library. Its rows of books disguised it perfectly as part of the wall: almost imperceptible, unless you knew where to look. 'Be careful. It's very heavy.'

This time it opened easier, and Magda wondered if the door had simply been out of use the first time. Like loose cards, they dropped through the portal and into the unknown.

One. Two.

She held her breath.

Three.

On the other side, there was scent before there was vision. Every corner of the place hummed with some peculiar aroma: a forgotten attic, peeling wallpaper, and a damp, brackish scent that filled the air. Wood, or damp paper. It was impossible to tell where the smell of the library ended and the Forest began.

'Urgh,' Catrin scrambled to her feet, dishevelled. 'It's smaller than I imagined. Consider me underwhelmed.'

'It's not the most whelming of places,' Alarice surveyed the run-down furnishings with a critical eye. 'Lucky you didn't come last time, really. You'd have loved the pile of dead moths we found in the corner.'

'I thought you said somebody lives here?'

'A voice, not a person.' Magda sighed. 'You've got to sign the entry book if you want to hear it.'

Catrin shot them a warning look before picking her way across the room. *Don't make me look stupid.*

'This old thing?' She held it aloft from one corner. 'It's practically falling to pieces.'

'That's the one.'

They watched as she fixed the book with a long, hard, stare: then relented, and signed an elaborate scribble of a signature.

The room held its breath. There was the lightest breeze; a kind of mist, if you will. If giants could blow the cobwebs away from an old dustjacket, that was the sort of current you might have felt in the air.

Catrin turned back to the others with a look of trepidation. 'So much for this stupid librarian.'

Something shuffled, with a sound like badly-chosen footwear, behind the nearest bookshelf.

And then: a voice in the dark.

'You know, it's impolite to talk behind someone else's back.'

*

It was a truly odd thing to watch the conversation which took place between the voice in the Vespertine Library and a corporeal body. Magda felt as if she were observing an invisible tennis match, where neither player was quite sure of what their opponent had in store.

'So you're looking for some kind of medicinal text? Or an anthology of healing rites, perhaps?'

Ingrid nodded. 'Our friend's sick. She's been in isolation for nearly a week now, and they won't tell us what's going on. We're looking for a cure.'

The seat behind the desk shuddered faintly, as if a ghost had brushed past it. 'I'm sorry to hear about your friend.'

'You're a faceless librarian,' Catrin observed. 'What have you got to be sorry about?'

'Yes, but I'm also a —' the voice broke off, as if it had reconsidered. 'Suffice to say, you wouldn't be the first to come here with a pocketful of misconceptions about my presence here.'

'Really?'

'I did hear you complaining about the clutter. It's not my fault, you know. But I suppose you take me for some kind of pigeon: stupid, clumsy, fond of mess.'

Pigeons, Magda resisted the urge to interrupt, *were highly intelligent creatures*. Whatever trinkets they collected served a purpose, which was more than could be said for the disorderly stacks of books that filled the Vespertine Library.

'You were listening to us the whole time?'

'It's difficult to avoid it when you talk so loudly.'

'Eavesdropping on a private conversation,' Alarice cast a glance around the empty halls. 'Now *that's* impolite if you ask me.'

'Worse than breaking and entering?'

'Stop arguing, the pair of you,' Ingrid glared. 'We didn't come here to pick a fight; we came to find a book about magical ailments and how to treat them.'

There was a pause. One of the lanterns crackled to darkness, while the drawers behind the desk began to rattle from the wind. If Magda had known no better, she would've sworn somebody was rifling through them.

But that was impossible.

'So can you help us?' Ingrid repeated, uncomfortable. 'The sooner we can get the book, the sooner we'll be out of your hair.'

There was a noise in the rafters.

'In order to find the correct —' some papers shifted '— collection, it will be necessary to provide preliminary information on your —' a window clattered shut '— friend's condition.'

'She's a veridian,' said Magda, wrinkling her nose. The room had wafted with a sudden green scent, like flowers being cut, or moss turning to mildew. 'Everything's been fine up until now, but last week she had some kind of fever and collapsed. A sudden chill, they said.'

There was more clattering.

'Allow me a moment to search. Feel free to, er, converse among yourselves.'

Amusement flashed over Catrin's face. 'Are you sure our conversing won't be too loud for your tolerance?'

'If you prefer, you're welcome to help me locate a suitable text.'

Magda shrugged. It was better than waiting around all night, and so they began to tackle the first huge aisle of books.

The spines were mostly worn and cracked with age. She wondered what percentage of the authors here were dead, how many of them wished that they were, and how many even knew their books were being stored in such a place. Did any of them write with a pen name? Would they have been amused or scandalised to see someone spurn their book? Had anyone poured their soul into writing a whole book — and then gotten cold feet right at the last minute?

For all the books that were out there, Magda would have killed to see the ones that never got written.

'This is useless,' Ingrid sighed, setting down another empty text. 'How are we supposed to tell what's a suitable book when they're all blank?'

Except they're not blank, thought Magda. *Not really.*

'Maybe we'll just know.'

'I wish we would.' Catrin looked equally despondent. 'At this rate, it's going to take us all night to find a cure.'

The voice hovered dubiously. 'I suspect that your friend's sickness is a condition of the lands. And being a veridian, she *feels* the land.' A pause. 'It's in her bones now.'

Magda looked up, trying to pinpoint the location of the sound. 'What do you mean? Are you saying there's no way to cure her?'

'She may just as likely cure herself. Not everything is an affliction, you know.'

But Magda shook her head. This was no good; Muriel had looked like she was suffering.

Hadn't she?

‘We were sort of hoping this library would be able to help.’

‘And it can,’ the librarian assured her. ‘But not in one night. To procure a book of such value, I’ll need more time. Oh, and a token of security will be required to borrow it.’

‘What kind of a token?’

The voice wrinkled into a smile. ‘Something shiny. Something golden.’

Chapter 51
Permafrost

'*Y el jugo de guanábana, de lo más rico. Por acá no tenemos, pero te lo preparo la próxima vez que …*'

Muriel felt her vision fill with harsh light as she came to. Was she dreaming? Was she back in Wildbriar, in a valley of dragonflies, with a house guarded by an old cragged medlar tree?

'Mum?'

The words dried up in her throat when she caught sight of the bed. A dark red braid, dangling over the edge of a thickly embroidered tapestry. Her mother's quilt. And somebody else was reading it.

'Hey. Give that back!'

'You're awake.' The figure at the end of the bed turned to face her, its fingers spider-thin and clammy with rot. 'Wow, the sleep really didn't do you any good.'

The words in Muriel's throat had gone thick. Her tongue felt like a piece of meat, and for a minute she couldn't speak. The girl in front of her – if she could be called that – could not be who she imagined, because it made no sense.

'Rhos.'

The words fell from Muriel's lips, staining the ceramic tiles red.

'No need to stare like that,' smiled the wide-eyed creature. 'Anyone would think you'd seen a ghost.'

'What are you doing here? How are you…?'

'You're a fine one to talk, I've been looking for you all over.' The eyes were the only part that looked recognisably human, but those green irises were unmistakable. 'Stitches, and the weather! Dreadful even for the time of year. I wish the door to class would've opened easier, I had to wait for ages out there in the freezing cold.'

The vision was awful, but Muriel couldn't look away. It had a horrible grasp on her heart: the same deceitful lull that had pulled her out to the edge of the Forest. Out to the follow the wolfhound, all the way to the library in the woods.

It was the one which kept a spare key to all your worst secrets.

'Are you real?' she stared, unable to move. 'Is this because I didn't go to your Invocation? Are you ... am I...?'

'I'm just as real as I was twenty minutes ago,' replied Rhos, indignant. At least, Muriel decided to call the gaunt creature Rhos, even though it seemed no closer to her friend than a paper doll or a straw scarecrow. 'Why didn't you talk to me the other day? No one would let me in.'

'You're not here,' Muriel muttered. 'I'm still dreaming. Or ...'

'Oh, very funny. I've never heard that one before.'

Slow drifts of morning light began to settle on the covers. The figure on the bed was not Rhos as Muriel remembered her, nor Rhos as they had buried her. Somehow she had rotted beyond even that, the remaining skin green and sallow. The flutter at her collarbone was not a heartbeat but the pulse of maggots, and her bracelets hung on bare yellow bone.

'How did you get here?'

'I looked all through the North Quadrant,' said the creature, forlorn. 'I knocked on all your doors, on my old dorm room. No one came.'

'We never heard you.'

'Then I must have done something wrong,' Rhos chewed her lip anxiously. The putrid skin split, and her voice trembled. 'I hope I didn't do something wrong. I'm sorry if I upset everybody.'

When Muriel went to speak, there was a tightness in her throat. 'Nobody's upset with you. We all miss you, so, so much.'

'Then why are you still here?'

Here. Where was *here?* She looked up, trying to get some sense of her bearings, but the last thing she could remember was Ether Stefania offering a potion. Willowdown, that was it. Something must be wrong with her if they were administering medicine, and she needed to find out what.

Sitting up, Muriel found her legs felt strangely heavy. She could move them but only just.

'I wouldn't try it, if I were you,' said Rhos, fiddling with the patchwork blanket that Sidonie Silvana had made. 'You'll upset your arm again.'

With an effort, Muriel reached over just far enough to snatch the quilt. 'Don't go through my stuff again. It's private.'

'I was only trying to help,' the other girl raised a defensive hand. 'If it makes you feel any better, I don't speak Spanish. I just thought maybe you'd wake up, if you heard something familiar.'

'How long have I ...'

'Ages. You've been out for ages.'

And then Muriel saw it.

From the middle of her forearm down to her wrist, a ridge of bright white mushrooms had marched their way down her skin.

'Urgh!' she tried to swipe it away. 'What's that *doing* there?'

'Like I said, it's been some time.' Rhos poked her head over the edge of the bed, where the fungus had continued in a thin line along the duvet and down to the floor. The gills of the white toadstools were curved, like a fan, but dipped above and beneath the earth like the knobs of a spinal column. 'They say the trail goes all the way into Cunning Wood.'

'The trail?' Muriel repeated, eyes wide.

She followed the line down across the floor, all the way to the edge of the woods, and cringed. It was bad enough that a constellation of mushrooms had sprung up on her arm; it was worse they'd somehow linked her to the poisoned forest.

'They can't find out about my magic, Rhos. If they find out, I'm done for.'

'Don't complain to me,' shrugged the decaying matter. 'Complain to someone who's still got a tongue to argue with.'

Muriel stared uncomfortably at the spill of fungi that was blossoming from her arm. No matter how she tried, the wretched matter wouldn't budge: it was as if it had rooted itself deeper than the flesh. The whole thing was eerily familiar, in a way she didn't like to contemplate.

Every girl in Wildbriar knew about faerie rings.

Circles of toadstools were a tell-tale sign of the Tidal Folk, of hidden magic, and stepping inside one of those rings couldn't bode well — sure as silk was silk. But what were you supposed to do when those decaying ganglions decided to make a ring of your own flesh?

'I've got to get rid of these. What else happened while I was asleep?'

Rhos wasn't listening. Her deep green eyes hovered over her own arms, which were in grievous condition. It was as if a spider had spun its web over the girl's wrists: the flesh was tricked through with black lines where veins should have been.

'Rhos,' Muriel nudged her. 'Do you know what happened?'

'Don't you remember?'

'Not much beyond Ether Rhiannon's class.'

One minute Muriel had been sitting in Weftwork with everyone else, and the next she'd fallen off the edge of reality. Unconsciousness was like walking into a lake, the folds of it enveloping her in cool water.

'This trail,' she took a deep breath. 'It goes all the way from here to Cunning Wood, right?'

'Yep. And they're suspicious,' said Rhos, fiddling with a piece of flesh that had come unstuck from its bones. 'Stefania thinks you know about something in the woods.'

'How could I possibly know what's in the woods?'

'She's not exactly the sharpest pair of shears.' A hollow laugh. 'Wait, I know. Perhaps ... Perhaps they're entertaining the possibility that you *planned* this.'

Muriel groaned.

'Hey, at least you've got company. And by the look of things, you'll be here until that starts to heal.'

'What about you, Rhos? Why are you here?'

'Same as anybody else in the sick ward,' shrugged the creature. 'Trying to get better.'

A tear slid down Muriel's cheek, hot and too fast. How did you explain to someone dead that they weren't going to get better, ever?

'You don't mind me staying, do you?'

'Of course I don't mind,' she wiped away the salt. 'You can stay with me for as long as you like.'

Chapter 52

The Ring

Morning slanted like a dove with a blade in its beak, and Magda's limbs were twisted painful. Her sleep had been full of broken memories, but it was the bad dreams that clung to her bones.

Somewhere in that fitful night, she had dreamed of a cat she once met in an alleyway: soft-eyed and skittish, and altogether too slender for the jarring charcoal reality of the street. It was the kind of cat that belonged to a china plate, or somebody's greenhouse. It walked indecisively. Each step quivered with a touch of the surreal.

Alternatively, she dreamed of Grimoire Malgarty and her grimalkins, which swarmed to nightmarish monsters in the darkness. Their ever-piercing glare crept at the edges of her vision, like they were holding back a string of insults you weren't clever enough to understand. It didn't matter that they were not *cat* by name. They were *cat* by nature, and their visceral catness picked you to pieces in disdainful light.

Magda dreamed of a lot of things that didn't have words: only images.

Then there was the tapping outside her room, whose insistence dragged her back to the land of the living.

'Hello?'

'Only me.' Catrin peered around the door to Dormitory Seven, dark circles sketched under her eyes. 'The medical bay's still locked.'

'Oh,' Magda sat back, too quickly. Her occipital bone clonked painfully against the headboard. 'Well, thanks for checking on her.'

'It's no trouble,' said Catrin. But she hovered from foot to foot, like a hesitant ghost. 'Still, I don't understand why they won't tell us what's going on. Surely they must know *something* by now.'

The bolted lock: barring them out.

'I guess Stefania's dead set on stopping us from prying,' said Magda. It occurred to her too late that *prying* was entirely the wrong word to have used. 'We have to hope that she's okay, in the meantime.'

For a moment Catrin didn't say anything. There was a hint of moschatel and wood melick in her hesitation, ancient wildflowers that jarred against the frozen ground.

'What is it?'

'Sorry. I just can't imagine how you must be feeling right now,' the blonde girl wrung her hands together. 'It's remarkable, the way you take things in your stride. How you stay determined. If it were me...'

Magda didn't feel like she was taking it in her stride in the slightest. The dorm room had become a lonely place; certain songs were to be avoided; sleeping was difficult, and rarely restful.

'I think you're overestimating my capabilities.'

'I rarely overestimate people.'

She thought of the string of dormitories, three yellow eyes shining out into the courtyard. They blinked in disjunction, curtains masking their vision with cataracts.

'What was it like, before we arrived here?'

'Before Lissa and Shay left?'

'Yeah.'

She could see the words written on Catrin's face. But she waited for her to say it out loud.

'You know when you've been in a place for so long, that you feel like it will never change?' She looked down. 'And then it does.'

Magda understood her discomfort. She'd felt the familiar tug against her heart, its own neap tide plunging her back into the gloom. The sallow waters turned her skin to a mermaid's, blue-green and bright with minnows.

'You should get some sleep.'

'As should you,' Catrin turned away. 'Breakfast in an hour. Don't be late.'

*

Where a bowl full of tasteless porridge had failed, Ether Stefania succeeded in turning Magda's guts. It was jarring to watch the woman breezing into the House of the Lyre as if nothing had happened at all: as if they had nothing better to do than memorise lines from a textbook.

'It's freezing in here,' Catrin shivered. 'Did somebody leave a window open?'

'I wouldn't worry. Stefania's such a fire breather, I daresay her presence will set things right.'

In spite of their jokes, the cold was wretched. It had them huddled like a pack of rats, fighting to escape frozen shadows, and Magda wondered if summer would ever darken their door again.

'Due to a recent change in our scheduling, we have taken the decision to abridge part of this month's syllabus.' Ether Stefania held out a hefty textbook, which was showing signs of wear. 'Today's class will be on witchcraft, not sea monsters, as we initially planned.'

'Witchcraft? But that's an advanced module.'

'Unfortunately, it has been necessary to make some alterations to the course of your programme,' the Ether replied coolly. 'I'm sure you'll pick it up quickly.'

As each of them unfolded their notebooks, Magda paid close attention to the pinch-faced woman's expression. There were wrinkles that meant mirth or faded laughter, but Stefania's face was smooth of any such blemish. It was as if she had never felt any such emotion: not joy, and certainly not remorse.

'Miss Corrales, is there a reason why you're staring gormlessly into the distance?'

'Sorry. I got distracted by ... a pigeon.'

'A pigeon?' Stefania craned her neck, as if the bird might be looming above her as they spoke. 'I'll have to ask Lorna to take care of that. Nasty things.'

She slid the bolt of the window across. Then, pulling down a blackboard from the storage loft, she began to carve lines across the smooth, dark slate.

Everybody watched intently.

'We'll begin with some basic theory,' Ether Stefania set down the chalk, looking faintly dissatisfied with her work. 'The art of shearing is one of a witch's primary defences against capture. In the blink of an eye, she can transport herself to another place: simply by focusing her powers, and allowing the land to split.'

Magda studied the diagram. The white lines laced themselves together like weft and warp yarns, and a large slash cleaved the centre in two.

As easily as shears through fabric.

'How do they control where they end up?' asked Alarice. 'They must have a destination in mind, right?'

'It's mostly based on how far she can travel,' said Ether Stefania, suddenly sounding distracted. Her neck was tilted at an odd angle, as if she was trying to catch sight of something small and obscure at the back of the room. 'What was I saying? Ah, yes. A witch must draw her energy from a source, but that energy is not inexhaustible. Without it her powers will be weakened.'

Skimming the opening lines of the chapter on shearing, Magda paused over the caption to the first illustration. *Such an art is limited to the higher ranks of witchery.*

'There are ranks of witchery?'

A few sniggers broke out, which were quickly silenced by Stefania's stony gaze. If there had been any doubt in their minds about her mood, it was now pulverised.

'You must learn about these lesser-known crafts, Miss Corrales, if you are to progress to a line of work in the Palace,' Stefania tilted her head with a look of gilded sorrow. 'It is of vital importance that the Brenin's employees are prepared for all scenarios.'

Magda didn't trust herself to reply beyond a nod. More than the impropriety of her comment, some unspoken threat had announced itself in the way Stefania was peering over her shoulder. Hackles up, shoulders low. Her entire demeanour suggested a cornered animal that might strike at any moment.

Somebody, Magda realised, was waiting to ask a question.

'Are you going to keep your arm in the air all day, Miss Leyshon?'

'Not at all,' Ingrid flashed an acidic smile. 'I only wanted to ask where Ether Rhiannon is today. How come she's not been at classes?'

'Ether Rhiannon is attending urgent business in Helygen.' There was that unmistakable twitchiness again, quickly adjusted to a mask of composure. 'There is some correspondence which she is awaiting, as a matter of fact.'

'Urgent business?'

Stefania's eyes darted towards the door. 'It is nothing to trouble yourselves with. Now, if you could read through Chapter Four on the importance of dragons in witching custom, notably passerines ... I'll be right back.'

They watched her get up, with one last, lingering look towards the window, and make a beeline for the door. It slammed shut behind her.

'Finally,' Ingrid got to her feet, practically throwing down the textbook. 'Thank Eila she's gone.'

'What was all that about?'

'There,' she was staring outside, through the narrow slant of the window. 'Look, right there. *Urgent business* my arse. I could tell something was up.'

Magda looked. They had a good vantage point from being so high up, although she'd never much liked the House of the Lyre. But from just the right angle, and just the right posture, it was possible to get a view of almost the entire West Quadrant.

'The medical bay,' she narrowed her eyes, trying to see clearer. 'That's what she was looking at?'

'I noticed it after she started staring at the window all funny.' Ingrid glanced back at the chalkboard, where the remnants of the diagram were still etched into the stonework. 'It had to be something important.'

Magda's heart stumbled. For the last three weeks, the medical bay had garnered new and all-consuming importance: it was the centre of a universe populated by four slate quadrants and an eerily green orchard.

She'd told herself not to hope.

She'd bargained with Gwern, with Eila, and with anyone else who might listen, for Muriel to emerge unscathed from that hidden infirmary. Failing that, she hoped that the version of her best friend who returned would not be like the girls they told stories about at school, the ones who came back half-haunted.

But here was the looking-glass, holding out the fantasy once more. The sweet lie that everything might be just as it was.

'Can you see anything in there?' Magda pressed her face closer to the window. 'It's all blurry.'

'Wait, look. Below the window.'

Magda followed her finger down towards the stretch of damp grass. Beneath the window to the medical bay, there was something white and craggy sticking up out of the ground, a knobbly chain of uneven grafting.

'Are those ... toadstools?'

The forms were paler than chalk, paler than the kind of frost that settled after a heavy snow. The closer she looked, the more distinct they became: a trail of little capped mushrooms, marching their way down to the woods. It was almost like a ring, except it extended both ways. One end creeping up the brickwork, and the other stretching down, down towards the Forest's edge.

'They go right over the window ledge,' said Alarice. 'Is that her in the bed on the corner?'

Perched on one side of the sickbed was a blurry figure, a mass of dark hair coiling down her back. It was Muriel: sitting upright, and facing away from the window. But although they could see her, she could not see them.

'Turn around!'

'Over here, for scrim's sake!'

They leapt and waved frantically, yet it was to no avail.

'I don't get it,' Ingrid stopped waving at last. 'What's she doing?'

Too paralysed to reply, Magda could think only of the Vespertine Library's earlier warning. *It's a sickness of the lands. And being a veridian, she* feels *the land. It's in her bones now.*

*

The empty air carved a hollow between them. A gauze of pale curtains fluttered, obscuring the clear vision across the cove. Every girl in the room knew it, but nobody could dare to say it. The toadstool trail rankled in all their minds: inescapable, unearthly, and impossible to ignore.

'They're going to find out,' said Magda, at last. It screamed like a siren through her blood: *you stupid fucking idiot, you promised you'd keep her safe*. 'They'll think it's because of her powers. They're going to realise what she's capable of.'

'What if it's something else, though?'

Catrin nodded. 'It could have been a facet of the Sickness; you know how it's getting further out beyond the woods.'

The words were well-intentioned, but completely useless.

'You saw it. We all saw it,' Magda held her head in her hands. 'They go right over her arms, like it's leached into her skin.'

For all their best-laid plans and careful concealment, every inkling of magic in these grounds now pointed directly to Muriel. The intangible could be denied; those milk-coloured toadstools, on the other hand, were as solid as flesh or blood. They were magic in its brightest, most unpalatable shade.

With a single decisive motion, Alarice pulled the curtain closed. 'The Ethers might be smart, but they're not superhuman. They can't act on what they can't prove. And as of now, we have the advantage.'

'You think the element of surprise is going to save us now?' Ingrid retorted. 'It's a little late to be playing cloak and dagger.'

Half-heartedly, Magda cast a glance towards the door. How much longer before Ether Stefania stormed in and called their bluff? Was this the last clear view they'd get, before something new and awful reared its head?

If only they could send Muriel a warning.

'Once they figure out what's going on, it'll be too late for us to help.' Alarice paused. 'That's why we need to get her out of there before they realise.'

'And how do you propose we do that?'

In spite of her dejected mood, Magda refused to be beaten down by the baldness of Ingrid's question. Somewhere below the Ceremonial Grounds was the cavern of the Fallow Library, and its elusive doorway to the other libraries. Beyond that doorway lurked the Vespertine Library. And perhaps, for once in its life, the laughable pocket of air that called itself a librarian might actually be able to help them.

'About the escape plan,' Magda hesitated, a dangerous idea dancing on the tip of her tongue. 'What if we could ... well ... fight fire with fire?'

'That had better be a metaphor, Corrales.'

'Just hear me out.' She took a deep breath. 'Whatever that fever did to Muriel, she's going to be knocked for six. There'll be no relying on her magic to keep us safe in Cunning Wood. I don't even know if she'd be able to protect that many people, depending on ...'

Depending on what they've done to her in there?

Depending on if she'd even want to help us, after we let her rot in a hospital for three weeks?

'Depending on the situation,' said Alarice, carefully. 'I agree. We're going to need a backup plan.'

The heavy truth stared back at them with the bright-eyed apathy of a blackbird. *Anything else, anything else to add?* The only person who looked unmoved was Catrin, now slouching against the wall, her glum eyes cast towards the floor.

'So our plan to go through the woods is scuppered. Brilliant.'

'At the moment,' said Magda. 'But we've still got the doors underground, the ones through the libraries.'

'You're not planning on consulting that librarian of yours, are you?'

'Well, sort of. In a manner of speaking.'

She waited for the penny to drop.

'*Oh.*' Ingrid sounded amused. 'Okay. That's a plan I can get on board with.'

'Don't look at me like that! It's not like we've got much choice in the matter.'

'Well, it's Scurlock you'll have to convince.'

'Why have I got to be convinced?'

'Because... you know...' Magda gestured vaguely, hoping she would get the gist. 'You're the only one who can do it.'

Catrin looked like she was about to have an aneurysm. '*That's* your plan? Gwern save us.'

'Come on, it's exactly your style,' Alarice nudged her. 'Drastic. Dazzling. Likely to visually impair someone if they —'

'All right, all right! I get it.'

Magda felt her cheeks turning scarlet. She knew it was a bad idea, she knew it was desperate, and she'd be damned if it was going to stop her. 'That librarian is withholding information. If we sit about and wait for it to play nice, we'll be waiting forever.'

'Right. Remind me, what was that token it wanted again?'

The dare of the words danced before them.

'Something shiny. Something golden.'

Chapter 53

Mercer

Like a sliver of ice against dark water, the moon guided their way. It was the only thing, Magda supposed, which dared to shine a light over such dealings. By now the Ethers would be fast asleep: which meant the clock had started ticking.

According to Catrin's calculations, they had five hours and thirteen minutes before there was the chance of anybody being awake again. They'd observed Ether Lorna's nocturnal peregrinations through the orchard (circa eleven P.M.), then the light flashing on in the South Quadrant kitchens, and the later snap of a lamp going out in either Stefania or Rhiannon's study (Magda assumed the latter, as Ether Stefania seemed like the kind of person who woke up annoyingly early and in an acid-bright mood, purely for the sake of wielding that superiority over others. Who needed to have breakfast at six A.M., really?).

Now, after their patient waiting, the grounds were quiet again.

Ingrid glanced over her shoulder as they walked.

'Wow, guys. This is the most fun I've had in ages.'

Fun wasn't exactly what Magda would have called it. This was more a carefully plotted experiment, which she fervently hoped would not go wrong. Ahead of her, Ingrid was carrying the scroll of parchment. Alarice held the tall lantern, and Catrin was in charge of the token.

There was the possibility that their scheme wouldn't work at all. Like the others had already warned her, it was risky. But more perilous yet was acting too late: and Magda had lost too much already to risk losing her closest friend in the world.

'It'll be okay, you know,' Catrin caught her eye. 'Just this one last step, and then we might get some answers. Right?'

'Right,' Magda mumbled, not wanting to draw further attention. This wasn't just about her, not even close: because these girls were Muriel's friends just as much as she was. Sometimes, she suspected, better friends than she had been.

They reached the Ceremonial Grounds in bitter twilight. Taking care not to twist an ankle, Magda wove between the bluestone monoliths towards the centre: they were sleeping giants, and this was their domain. But despite the fact that no stone was out of place, there was a tangible difference to the aura of the grounds. It emanated from the earth like the stink of a rotting body. It cloyed in the back of the throat.

'Something's changed,' she came to a halt, as if the earth might suddenly turn to swampy marshland beneath her feet. 'Someone's been here.'

Gone was the conspiracy and glamour of the secret trapdoor; the chalk carving beneath the pyre now seemed nothing more than a dull mark in the lawn. It might have felt homely, if this were a place where anything could feel comfortable in its own skin.

'Do you mean the portal?' Alarice peered down to inspect it. 'It should still be working. There's no harm in trying it, anyway.'

'I don't know if it's a good idea.'

'Well, too bad.' Catrin knelt down and extended a palmful of fire. 'We didn't come all this way for nothing.'

They watched as she tried to coax the flame into various points of the earthwork. Each time it was rejected, Magda grew more certain of her assertion: something *had* changed. The Grounds were somehow altered, and would no longer bear them access to the creviced library beneath the earth. That house of cards, red and gold and folded away in secret, was distinctly cut off.

'I'm sorry,' Magda stuttered, at a loss for what to do. 'I should have realised. I should have seen it —'

'Shut up, Corrales. You don't have to blame yourself for everything.'

The flame flickered, pale as chalk.

And then.

A vast billow of light; no heat. A frigid ignition, like molten glass or starlight.

'Is that ...'

'It's perfect, that's what it is.'

The charm of fire was mesmerising. For several minutes they marvelled at the shiftless glow that now riddled the chalk carvings, before cooling to solid grey rock.

'Looks like we have our door,' Catrin stepped back, grinning. 'You just had to ask it nicely.'

*

Over time, some journeys improved with practice. It was the carefully-timed commute, the work trip that crossed the ferry channel, the school run that negotiated the worst potholes, until the routine was elegantly choreographed: each repetition a smoother variant of the dance.

Travelling to the Vespertine Library was nothing like that.

Where Magda had envisioned effortless poise and an imposing entrance, there was a clatter of knees and elbows against its warped gates.

'You said the door was wider than this!'

'It was, I swear!'

The three of them stumbled into the hollow building, gasping for breath. With a splutter, and a rustle of splintered wood, they landed in a sprawl on the floor.

'By the alder,' Ingrid breathed heavily, 'I could kill somebody.'

There was a clanking sound as the desk chair creaked on its hinges. You could feel it before you heard it: the sound of something not minding its own business.

'Half past midnight,' mused the voice of the library, withering and winding from the corners of the ceiling. 'You're nothing if not punctual.'

Magda peeled a piece of paper away from one arm, wrinkling her nose at the damp smell in the air. It was out of character for the voice to appear so suddenly. It would be further out of character for it to help them without some degree of bargaining. 'What made you think we'd come at all?'

'You need something. Visitors of that category tend to be very, very obvious.'

'Well, we already told you what we needed,' she sat up. 'It's not like some big mystery. And you also agreed to help us.'

'Whatever you say.'

Around her, the others were still brushing dust from their clothes. A spill of molten wax lay dripping over the edge of one table. In spite of everything, the place seemed even messier than before.

'Did you always live here?' Magda asked, before she could reconsider the question.

'I'm sorry?'

'Here, in this library. Was it where you grew up? I mean ... What are you?'

There was no reply. Either Magda had touched a nerve, or the voice had somehow found other matters to attend.

'It must have been sort of cool,' she went on, 'being surrounded by all these books. And the forest. And the magical portals.'

'What are you doing?' Alarice hissed. 'Stick to the plan.'

'But it must have been lonely, too.' Magda waited. 'Is that why you're still hiding?'

One of the lanterns fluttered: a punctured lung, dripping with light.

'This is a business transaction,' came the voice's terse reply. 'You came here in search of a book, is that correct?'

'But why did *you* come here?'

'Enough of this nonsense,' it coughed. 'The token. Do you have it?'

'Yes,' said Catrin, to everybody's relief. 'Exactly as requested.'

Heart in her throat, Magda watched as their resident pyromancer moved forwards to the front desk. One thing was for sure: the voice was rattled. And though it seemed cruel, she knew that people were more likely to comply when put under pressure.

'What did you bring, then?'

'Something golden, and very shiny.' Catrin set down a small, locked box on the table, with a certain gentleness that conveyed the value of its contents. Alarice, Ingrid, and Magda all knew the box to be empty. But Catrin was such a convincing liar, that even they wanted to believe.

'Jewellery, or precious metal? You haven't unlocked it.'

'We haven't received our payment yet,' Catrin levelled. 'Do you have the book that can help our friend?'

'The token first.'

Had it not been for the smudges of soot across her trousers, anybody might have thought she had just stepped out of a spring meadow. She made the words sound easy as a summer morning. 'Just remember,' the key twisted in the lock, 'you asked for this.'

Swift as the striking of a match, the flare of golden flame sprang into life: curling upwards from Catrin's palm.

Bright, volatile, hungry.

'You dare to bring fire into *my* house of books?' hissed the voice. 'You were trusted here. You were welcomed here. And this is your repayment of that generosity?'

Magda couldn't answer. This was the threat; the only leverage that they could possibly hope to wield over such a place. It sang with wrongness, and she did not like to think of all those poor books, burning.

But they were desperate.

In all the moments that Muriel could have abandoned her, she had not.

And if this was the price of returning that favour, then Magda would gladly pay it.

'I'm sorry to do this,' she steadied herself. 'The thing is, we need more than what you're offering right now.'

'And you decided an ambush was the way to get it?'

'That's not the point.' She paused. 'So far, everything has been on your conditions. If you want this place to remain unscathed, if you want to help us, then you treat us as equals. Got it?'

'But we are not equals.'

Ingrid took a step towards the desk, menacing. 'Talk to my friends that way again, and you're smoke.'

'You haven't got a clue who you're talking to.'

'What, you think it'd make a difference?' she glared. 'Go ahead. Tell us who you are.'

'It's none of your business.'

The fire was still crackling in Catrin's palm. Magda wondered how long she could keep it going for before it burned out; at present it showed no signs of dwindling. The red in her eyes was more intense than ever, buckling with crimson tears.

'Those are pretty carpets,' Catrin studied the plush velvet flooring, and the intricately-woven jacquard rugs that adorned it. 'Nice curtains, too. It'd be a shame for anything to happen to them.'

Silence.

‘To be honest, I’m not such a fan of that upholstery,’ Alarice prodded at an admittedly distasteful chair in the corner. ‘This has got to be, what, pre-Rift?’

The voice made a desperate noise.

‘You can’t be seriously considering this.’

‘Getting sentimental, are we?’

‘But ... think of the books! Of the priceless antiques!’

Magda pulled the cloak a little tighter over her shoulders. An unseasonable chill was seeping in. It would be better, by far, when the whole place was warm. ‘All our lives, they warned us away from the fire,’ she spoke softly, as if recounting a lullaby. ‘From the libraries. From the wayward woods.’

‘Those are just stories. Old villagers make them up to scare you!’

‘Well, we’ve gotten tired of stories that never come true.’

The princess locked in the castle, withering to bones. The dragon in the keep, forever silenced by a knight’s sword.

Maybe their happy endings would only ever exist in fairytales.

‘If you burn this place, you’ll regret it. Believe me, there are bad things coming, and they won’t spare a thought for your safety.’

Alarice made an almost imperceptible motion towards the door. There was a holloway in her eyes: a sunken tunnel of light that was rapidly thickening to brambles, blotting out the sun. ‘Then we’ll find a way to handle them.’

‘Wait!’

The voice was tripping over its words now, faster and faster.

‘Though this is the Vespertine Library, people do not come here to read. You hail from Fallow ground, but none of you lie dormant,’ it paused for breath. ‘And Cunning Wood is not what it might seem.’

Magda shook her head, exhausted. She'd had enough of this place's cryptic answers; of all its empty mythology. Who was this incorporeal voice to tell them what was dormant? Who was it to tell them anything?

'Enough of this,' Catrin turned away. Then her fingers touched the bookcase, and the first ripple of a flame stroked the corners: smouldering paper, a curl of ash, before extinguishing itself again. 'Any last words?'

'You're making a terrible mistake!'

'Those aren't very good last words.'

'Well, what do you want me to say?'

Catrin hovered. 'That you plead for mercy and you'll agree to help us?'

'Fine,' replied the voice, wretchedly. Except the voice was suddenly a shade louder than before. 'Give me a moment. Let's talk this through, since you've been so irritatingly insistent.'

Magda frowned. Then there was a tap — an unmistakable *tap* — on her shoulder.

She turned around and froze.

Standing in front of them was a boy with a shock of dark hair and the most ridiculous outfit she'd ever seen. It was like looking at a piece of patchwork: his brown waistcoat jarred horribly with the moss-green trousers, and there was some sort of cape swung over his shoulders. What made it truly terrible, however, was the shoes. One was mustard, one was maroon; the only thing matching was the laces. Magda could hardly believe they'd been cornered by a stranger in a library in the woods, much less that he was a walking fashion disaster.

The boy glanced down, then back up again. 'Is something the matter?'

'You,' Alarice took a step back, disbelieving. 'You're not ...'

But she didn't finish the sentence, because there was no mistaking that voice. The *library's* voice.

It was his.

'You're a person,' Magda glared. 'You're the librarian. Where did you – how did you *do* that?'

'I'll tell you, if you stop looking at me like I'm a poisonous snake.'

She stopped looking at the horrible shoes and forced herself to meet his gaze. Freckled brown skin and amber eyes.

'You're the boy, aren't you.'

Somehow, wordlessly, they all knew it. The truth of it was so loud it echoed.

'I prefer to go by Carrick.' He shifted uncomfortably. 'But the prophecy, et cetera, et cetera. It, er, pertains to me.'

Magda had never even seen the Brenin, never seen a picture of him, and yet somehow she should have known that he would look like this. That his *son* would look like this. The perfect prince; the golden boy. Smoke in his voice and fire in his eyes.

She despised him.

The boy raised a hand defensively. 'Magda, I'm not going to –'

'You don't get to call her that,' Ingrid stepped forwards. 'And you owe us an explanation.'

'I'll give you one, if you would only let me gather my bearings.'

Magda tried to see what she had missed before. Those questions in the dark; that voice like burnt sienna. She knew those sounds. Only now, it felt like she'd been cheated of them.

'How glad we are that you finally came around,' Alarice crossed her arms. 'Now that we're on an equal footing, would you care to introduce yourself?'

There was a pause.

Then, looking thoroughly pissed off, the boy stuck out a hand. 'Carrick Madreth. Son of the Brenin, enemy and heir to the house of Madreth. Delighted to make your acquaintance.'

Chapter 54

Dreams

Rhos's visits were becoming more and more infrequent. On the days when she didn't come, Muriel began to miss her company.

'They brought cheese and pickle sandwiches earlier, the ones with the seeded loaf. You would've liked them.'

'Don't worry about me,' was all Rhos would say, smoothing her skirts and uncomfortably clean yellow gloves. 'My appetite's not what it used to be.'

Muriel took a deep breath, wondering if she was allowed to voice the question that was burning her lips. 'Can I ask you something?'

'You can ask me anything.'

'What happened to you, at the edge of the woods that night?'

'At the orchard?' Those green eyes were bullets, an invitation as deadly as they were irresistible. 'I thought you'd never mention it.'

Muriel shook her head, glancing briefly at the bandages that covered the toadstools trailing her arm. She'd hoped they might also be among the effects of Willowdown, but the stern looks from the Ethers told her otherwise. She only wished she could warn the other girls what was about to happen.

What was happening already, if she was honest.

It was ticking through the woodwork; burrowing beneath her skin. There was only a matter of time before it became undeniable.

'That night started with the bird,' said Rhos, gazing peacefully out the window. 'A jay, I think. It was fluttering its wings, alive as anything, but I saw it through the foliage of the woods. That was what caught my attention.'

Those blue feathers, scattered on the ground where she had fallen. Muriel had seen the remnants, too, on the night she'd strayed too close to the Forest. She hadn't even considered their significance.

'I didn't mean to chase it. But you know how they are, jeering at you like little fools. So I took a step, just a small one, to try and get closer.' Rhos paused, her green eyes quivering. 'Then I slipped.'

'You slipped?'

'Or something pushed me,' she picked at a hangnail, the flesh ripping away with it. 'I'm not sure any more. The memories get ... crumpled.'

'What happened after that?'

'I don't know,' the other girl hesitated. 'But something was calling to me, from within there. I had to follow it, Muriel; it was like a siren song. For just a minute I stepped inside the Forest, and it was beautiful.'

Muriel nodded, blinking back the deep grey ache of her heart. 'So you don't remember how you got there.'

'I remember that I was right.' A malevolent gleam came into the creature's eye. 'There was something in the woods. And it was alive.'

*

That afternoon, it was Ether Lorna who came in to check on Muriel. She carried herself with her usual sprightly gait, albeit her sporadic fits of coughing suggested a recently-acquired cold.

'My apologies, Miss Silvana,' she moved around the ward, replacing flasks of water, trays of food, and adjusting dosages with skilful ease. 'I'll be out of your way in just a moment.'

'No need to apologise.'

If anything, Muriel was grateful for the lack of Ether Stefania. While she wasn't exactly fond of any of their guardians, there was a certain warmth to Lorna that made her more congenial. On the cabinet beside her, there was a sheet of daily checks for the medical ward: each signed with one of three names, depending on who had completed the task.

Stefania MacFarleigh.

Rhiannon Mourne.

Lorna Daven.

Muriel couldn't remember the first time she had noticed it, but it brought her no end of curiosity to discover that the Ethers had two names. They were people. Real people! And that lack of mononymous glamour somehow broke the spell of their being tougher or more invincible than the Fallow's lower occupants.

'How's your temperature, Miss Silvana?' Lorna called over her shoulder. 'And do your bandages need changing?'

'They're fine. Don't worry about it.'

She watched as the wiry-framed woman moved down the sick bay, replacing each table's empty jar with new flowers. Some of them were proper vases; others were repurposed metal containers or old mugs. It occurred to her that Lorna Daven could've been a talented wedding florist, someone who took pride in arranging bouquets, in another life.

'Ether Lorna?'

'Yes?'

'How long will it be before I can go back to the North Quadrant?' Muriel asked cautiously. 'I want to get better. It's just ... they'll be worried about me.'

When she looked back, she was astonished to find their guardian looking at a loss for words. It was an expression she had never seen on Lorna's face before. Were those tears in her eyes?

'Sorry,' she apologised quickly. 'I didn't mean to upset you.'

'No, not at all,' Lorna shook her head. 'Of course you're concerned. Of course you must be anxious to see your friends again. And they ... I'll do what I can, okay? I can't promise anything, but I'll try.'

'Thank you.'

She watched as the Ether slipped out the door to the main corridor. A sound like harsh, sad coughing chased her down the hallway.

*

The scent of sugared fruit filled the air, and Rhos was picking at the corners of dinner with relish. Her appetite had gone from non-existent to ravenous in the span of a few hours, which Muriel found disconcerting and amusing in equal measures.

'This is incredible,' she kept muttering between mouthfuls. 'Since when did they make better desserts for the medical bay than they do for the dining hall?'

'What can I say, it's just my magical capabilities. It's a little known fact that veridians can alter the contents of potted strudel as well as forging wild briars and bracken.'

They both laughed.

'Did you always know you had magic?'

'Not that I'd be a veridian, specifically, although I suppose it makes sense. Then again, I think I might've been anything before they told me.' Muriel paused. 'I know what they say, about how the land chooses. But I think people choose, too.'

Rhos set down the empty pot of strudel with a grimace. 'I never chose.'

'Why, what was your gift?'

'I was a shade.'

'A shade?' Muriel spluttered. 'But ... but that's one of the Deathlies.'

Shades were among the most dangerous Folk in the archipelago. Death by a single touch, if the legends were to be believed. Rumour had it they could stop someone's heartbeat with the mere brush of their hand.

By way of answer, Rhos flashed her a rotted smile. 'Turns out I'm not really sugar and spice, and all things nice.'

'Wow,' Muriel repeated. 'Wow, sorry, I'm just trying to get my head round it. That's kind of like finding out your town florist has a side gig as an assassin.'

'Hey, just because I *could* kill people doesn't mean that I did!'

'Is that why you always wore those gloves?'

'Pretty much.'

Muriel looked down to the other girl's hands, sparrow-thin and flayed down to the bone. It was true: she'd never seen Rhos without her gloves. Kid leather when they'd first met. Opal-coloured velvet at Catrin's party. And bloodless yellow suede over her grave-cloth. 'Ingrid said you wore them because they kept you safe.'

'My dad made them specially,' Rhos wiggled her fingers. 'Lined them with slow-worm scales himself. They're impervious to magic.'

The image bolted through Muriel's mind like a lost horse. Rhos, lying like a ragdoll at the edge of the orchard. Rhos, with her mustard-yellow gloves lying discarded in the green. Rhos, almost unrecognisable in her swollen and flaking skin, like an overcooked strudel.

'You took the gloves off that night,' said Muriel, feeling sick to the stomach. 'They were lying halfway across the glade when we found you.'

Rhos didn't speak.

'Something scared you enough to make you take them off. Something was so frightening, that you were prepared to defend yourself, even if you had to kill your assailant. Weren't you?'

'I don't remember what I did,' Rhos folded two stubborn skeletal arms. 'I just remember it didn't work.'

Muriel tried to pinpoint the moment they'd been told the awful news. The chemical stillness of the verdict that Rhos was never coming back, the stony expression that congealed on Ether Stefania's face.

'You said you went into Cunning Wood.' A long, low silence whistled as Muriel put the pieces together. 'But it wasn't the Forest that killed you, was it?'

There were no tears for the hollow dead, for the desiccated. To die was to sink beneath that; to ferment into the gullies of the land itself. Yet there was no mistaking the dry river that ran the course of Rhos's face.

'She said it would be quick.'

'Who?' Muriel sat forward. 'Who said that?'

'She ...' Rhos frowned, concentrating hard. 'She said she could make it painless. But that if I tried to go back, or tell the rest of you, she would make it hurt.'

Muriel shook her head, hurting more than she had ever thought she could hurt. There was only one woman callous enough to promise such a thing. And the next time Muriel saw her, Stefania MacFarleigh was going to pay for what she'd done.

'Rhos, I'm so sorry. I'm so ...'

'Don't,' the other girl flinched away. 'I did what I could to stop it. But it didn't matter, in the end.'

'What?'

'She lied,' said Rhos. This time her voice was different, harder, like cold iron. 'She made it hurt anyway.'

Chapter 55

The House of Madreth

'You know, when they said the prince of the archipelago had gone missing,' Magda cocked an eyebrow. 'I didn't think you'd literally have been hiding in a library for five years.'

'What makes you think I've been in here the entire time?'

She gave the boy a withering look. The pocket of his waistcoat was embroidered with something that had once been silver, and the hem of his trousers was fraying, badly. 'Just a gut feeling.'

'The four of you aren't what I was expecting either, if you must know.'

'Expecting?'

'Grimoire always said that new acquaintances came at unlikely times. You're not the first ones to find this library, you know.'

'Grimoire.' Magda's eyes narrowed. The name was too familiar to be a coincidence. 'You don't know somebody named Grimoire Malgarty, do you?'

Carrick tilted his head to one side. 'How many Grimoires do you think we get in this part of the archipelago?'

'But ... But I know her,' said Magda. 'She's a physician from Wildbriar. And she knows *you*?'

'She's my aunt,' said Carrick, looking a little offended. 'One of the more favourable relatives, although I'm sure the rest of my family would beg to differ.'

'So she knows you're here?'

'I didn't say that.'

'Right. But she knew you before you went missing, which means ...'

'A physician,' mused Carrick, not paying attention. '*That's* what she told you?'

'That's what we were led to believe.'

'Well, I'm sorry to break the news to you the hard way. She's a witch, and a mighty powerful one at that.'

Ingrid, who was loitering at the back of the room, looked decidedly uncomfortable. 'So what if she's a witch? What's it to us?'

'I only meant, you're best to steer clear of folk like that.'

'Carrick Madreth. I don't know how much you know about current affairs these days,' said Alarice, through barely contained rage. 'But since you're the prince, you must be familiar with the Mandate. The one that has made life so incredibly difficult for "folk like that". Your father's work, correct?'

'Of course I know about the Mandate,' Carrick repeated. 'A rather pointed way of making his nearest and dearest suffer, don't you think?'

'This isn't all about you!' Ingrid glared at him. 'You are a missing person, wanted by the Palace, let alone a royal. Don't you think about your responsibilities to your people?'

'Not to mention you've *been hiding in a library.*'

'I was perfectly happy in my library until four strangers came in and threatened arson!'

'Oh, the poor boy,' said Catrin, remorseless. 'You know about the prophecy. Which means you *also* knew that the Forests have been sickening since you left.'

'I didn't choose to leave,' Carrick lowered his gaze. 'They made me go. My father told me that if I ever came back, I'd be dead as soon as I set foot over the doorway. And now, I suppose, he'll get his wish.'

'Consider me moved, Mister We-Are-Not-Equals,' Magda huffed. 'You're making assumptions about our goal here. Why would we want you dead, for goodness' sake?'

'You did seem prepared to burn down my house just now.'

'It's a library.'

'It's a building of many talents.'

'Hang on,' Ingrid frowned. 'I thought the Brenin *wanted* his son back. You're his only heir. Who'd continue the royal bloodline if you didn't return?'

'Him, I imagine. I expect he'd be thrilled if I died out here in the wilderness,' Carrick folded his arms. 'That was probably part of his plan: kill off the weakling, tie up loose ends, and reign until the end of his days. Luckily, I have no intention of complying with his wishes,' he paused for effect. 'Hence, my occupation here.'

'You're saying that you survived, out of spite?'

'I suppose so.'

The group of them exchanged glances, too surprised to speak. Had it not been for the boy's genuine discomfort, Magda would have spurned the story. This boy – this *prince* – had told a tale so unlikely it would've made a fortune teller think twice, and they were expected to just stand there and believe it.

'What about the winter broadcast?' asked Magda. It went out at Invernal, with the same message each time. 'They show it every year. A father, asking his only son to come home. Is that a lie, too?'

'Not entirely. But it's not because of his fuzzy paternal emotions, by any stretch of the imagination.'

He was serious. Magda felt bad for having joked about it, now, but it was too late to rescind her earlier comment. 'If you don't mind me asking, what could he possibly have against his own son?'

Almost bored, the prince flicked her a catlike glance. 'He wants me gone because of a little secret, Magdalena, which you might have heard of it. It's called magic.'

With a snap of his fingers, the air shimmered and blurred. Where Carrick Madreth had stood only moments ago, there was now empty space.

'I don't believe this,' muttered Ingrid. 'We finally find the prince, and now he vanishes?'

'He'll be back,' said Alarice. 'I have to say, that was quite an impressive vanishing spell for a beginner. Clunky, but fast.'

'You do realise I can still hear you?'

Complete with worsted waistcoat, silver buttons and an insufferable attitude, the boy had reappeared. He looked a little less cocky than last time, but it wasn't enough to make Magda pity him.

'Why did you help us with the books before?'

'Because I was curious,' the boy shrugged. 'It's always interesting to have new visitors. Especially when they're trying to use the library for its intended purpose.'

'Do other people not?'

'Some just come to use the portals, and travel through to other libraries. And then there's the occasional search party. Of course, I don't get involved with those.'

Magda's eyes flicked back to the crumpled papers that surrounded them. 'I'm sorry we didn't come to read this time.'

'So I gathered,' he held up his hands. 'You've come to strike a bargain. Care to name your terms?'

For a moment nobody spoke: they were too busy experiencing the surreality of their situation. Standing before them was the prince of the archipelago, a wanted person, and the cornerstone of the prophecy. Was this the standard order of events when dealing with royalty? Magda doubted it. But since when did royalty appear in such an odd fashion as this? He wore mismatching shoes, for goodness' sake. Not even the Vespertine Library could offer a suitable excuse for that.

'If you help us,' said Ingrid, eager to clear the air, 'then we can help you in return. For our part, we'd benefit from access to the collection here at the Vespertine, but we also need someone with a thorough knowledge of the archipelago's wider libraries. That's you. You're the person who could help us navigate our way out of here.'

'Out of here?'

'Out of the Fallow,' Magda explained. 'We're students there by obligation, in training to work at the Palace.'

'The Fallow. So it really did get built,' Carrick muttered, seemingly to himself. 'I never thought that they would go ahead, not after ...'

'I'm sorry?'

'Nothing. Nothing, except I'm sorry to hear it,' he paused, turning towards the window. 'I hope, for your sakes, that you'll not be there much longer.'

'Can you help us, then?'

Through the window, a drowsy cluster of corncockles caught in the havering dusk. They watched them for a long moment, before the boy finally turned back.

'It's a deal. So long as you can help me in return.'

'What's the ask?'

The breeze shuddered once more, like crows in a corn field. The pale blank of the moon, arched rows of wheat, and black silhouettes lifted and rearranged themselves.

'I need someone who can help me break the curse,' said the prince, so evenly that Magda wondered if he had rehearsed the lines. 'Destroy the prophecy for once and for all.'

'Can prophecies *be* destroyed?'

'Not all of it, just the part that says I have to return,' Carrick explained. 'There's got to be a way of recovering the Forests, without my going back to the Palace.'

Afraid, Magda realised. *For all its wealth and glamour, he was afraid of going back there.*

'I'm sorry,' said Alarice, 'but I really don't know how much we can do about a prophecy. Isn't it a bit ... nebulous? I mean, how do you even go about creating one in the first place?'

If Carrick was deterred, he didn't show it.

'Your magic's stronger than mine. There must be some way around it; some loose end that the original maker forgot to tie up. Look at the Forest, for scrim's sake. Everything has its undoing.'

'Why do you care whether the archipelago prospers or suffers, if you're perfectly content in this library?'

'I may well be alive, but make no mistake in my contentment here.'

Inside the library there were shadows, and Carrick stood as far from the light as was possible. He inhabited the darkness like a soft armchair: he was too comfortable, or else hesitant to leave. It had him pinned to the spot, whether he liked it or not.

'I want to travel the land. To see the sights, explore the continent. I want my freedom.' He hovered over the words. 'And here I am, risking all my secrets for a bunch of would-be arsonists in the woods. Some life.'

Catrin cast him a disinterested glance. 'Seems like this is the part of royal heirhood that they don't tell you about.'

'The way I see it, I can help you escape your confinement and you can help me escape mine.' The prince's hands were shoved awkwardly into his pockets, blushing courage as he talked. 'Do we have a deal?'

'I think so,' Magda glanced sideways, to where a red flare of dawn was trickling through the window. 'This library. Are you going to be here three nights from now?'

'Considering my packed social calendar, I'll have to check.'

'I'll take that as a yes.'

'Magda?' Ingrid nudged her. 'We need to go soon. Or it'll be light.'

'Until we meet again,' Carrick drew back, reaching to open the door for them. This time the guile had vanished from his voice. 'Here's your book, by the way. I hope your friend makes a speedy recovery.'

***

People said grief couldn't change you, but that wasn't true. Some mountains were so large they could create weather. And some losses were so great they wrought storms across the land.

Grimoire felt it everywhere she walked: because before the Mandate was passed, there was uproar. Afterwards, there was silence. It turned out the only thing scarier than noise was the total absence of it. And not even she had been able to save her own sister, not when it came down to the last blow.

What did that make her now?

Before the Mandate, she had been the invisible sister. Out of the public eye, by mercy, and largely forgotten by those outside the royal family itself. Why would they look at her, anyway, when Aurelia was so bright she burned?

It was ironic, with all things considered. The Brenin had taken Aurelia Madreth's name in holy matrimony, and tarred her memory. Things had changed so much and yet so little over the centuries: yes, women would inherit first and foremost. Yes, theirs would be the name on the certificate, on the marriage vows, on the property. But theirs would be the singular pain of suffering those men who yearned for times gone by.

Theirs would always be the threat of those times returning.

After the Mandate, some people knew where to turn to and run. It was harder for others, who instead learned how to keep their mouths shut. Not a day went past where Grimoire didn't think about what she had done.

Was he still out there, somewhere?

Did he despise her as she knew he must?

Aurelia had fled, but so had she. Now her sister's child was a lost tidal current, one who dipped beneath the surface chop and the profound depths of solitude. Deeper yet, a fighting fear set Grimoire's nerves on end: had he been spared that terrible gift? The one that had left their family shipwrecked, torn apart by the thing that Elisdair Madreth called a misunderstanding.

She looked down again, at the piece of paper in her hand.

The sea was full of monsters.

And she was slowly becoming one.

***

'That prince has to be seen to be believed.'

'Quite,' said Magda, as they walked back across the orchards. 'I'd almost given up on the whole *lost heir* thing, to be honest. I thought he'd have been found rotting at the bottom of a lake.'

'Who's to say we should believe him, anyway?'

'It's a crazy story,' said Alarice, 'but I think he's telling the truth. It's too weird to have made up. And it tallies with a couple of other things.'

'Like what?'

'Like why the Palace hasn't doubled down on efforts to locate him. We live on a relatively small island. They've got all the fattest bank account in the country. And you're telling me that *nobody* in the elite squadron of royal bounty hunters can find the Brenin's son?'

Ingrid gave a short nod. 'Yet the four of us managed it in less than a month.'

She didn't look too happy. Locating the missing prince should have felt like a triumph, but the victory was empty as a cavern. He was no longer a digit in the code of abstract prophecy. He was a real human with secrets and caprices of his own, which made things so much more complicated than they had been before.

'What do we do now?'

'Don't know.'

It felt like some celestial chain of keys had been thrust upon them, and now they had a responsibility that none one was quite prepared for. In absence of a response, Magda turned over the book which Carrick Madreth had thrust upon them with such haste. *Lyric Spellcraft: The Hollow Soul*, read the spine.

'What kind of a medicine manual is this?'

'Let me see it.' The three jewel rings on Alarice's fingers clinked together as she folded the cover back. 'That's weird. It's full of sheet music.'

'Music?'

Magda poked her head over Alarice's shoulder to see for herself. The first page was a popular folk ballad — one of Muriel's sisters had learned to play it on the banjo, she was fairly certain — but from there on out, the songs got more and more obscure. It wasn't even clear what instrument the last page was intended for: the notes spanned not one, not two, but three staves. Either it was some kind of choral arrangement, or somebody had invented a three-handed piano without her realising it.

'No potions,' Alarice flipped another page. 'And no suggestions on a cure.'

Magda's heart sank.

Though she should have known better than to hope, the librarian had given them the promise of a solution, one that could be sealed within the pages of a novel. She scanned the pages again, searching for some kind of a sign.

The only writing which could be found was a small inscription at the back of the book: *Not everything's in a name.*

'This can wait until the evening,' Ingrid muttered, looking as annoyed as Magda felt. 'I'm going to bed. If Ether Rhiannon asks, tell her I've got food poisoning.'

*

With every minute of Weftwork, Magda felt the familiar strain of magic bleeding between the stitches. The hook dipped; the threads caught. It was small wonder that they named muscle spindles for their tenacity: only a body could carry that delicate tension with more convincing impasse than a seamstress.

But had it always been this way? And how far did the Tidal legacy of sewing extend? She could hardly imagine their powers could influence the more mundane creations, tea towels or bath mats, although their pots and pans *had* always shone with a certain splendour after polishing.

'Miss Corrales? Are you alright over there?'

Magda looked up to where Ether Rhiannon was watching her, concern knitting her eyebrows together. Her hands hovered over the implements, crochet hook abandoned like a shepherd's crook amid a field of sheep. The spindle itself lay half-unspooled, trailing woollen guts across the desk.

'I was just contemplating the best position for the embellishments, Ether Rhiannon.'

'Very well. Keep up the even tension, so that those rows stay smart.'

She picked up the hook again and thought of Muriel. A bad feeling loomed in her heart, but the door to the medical bay remained resolutely locked. For now all they had was the prince, and his library of misplaced secrets.

She intended to wring it for all it was worth.

*

'So do you think we can help him?'

'I think we should try.'

They were sitting in the common room, where the bioelectrics fluttered in and out of time with the clock on the wall. Afternoon had rippled away to another night, whose shadows seemed to stretch to different lengths each day. It created the bewildering sense of living in a hollow — no, a gulf. That was the proper word. Time lapped around them while they sat motionless on the sand, unable to see beyond the rocks.

'If we can somehow alter the prophecy,' said Catrin, 'the Brenin loses all stakes in controlling the health of the archipelago. He won't be the one people depend on any more. Not for their safety, and not for their livelihood.'

Ingrid nodded. 'The Forests will recover. And when word gets out that the prince is alive... Well, as clueless as he seems, you've got to hope he'd do a better job of governing than his father.'

Alarice threw them a reproachful look. 'What if he's no different from his father? What if he makes another law — a *worse* law?'

Magda couldn't think of many things that would be worse than the Mandate, but didn't dare to say it out loud. There were always new and terrible things that a tyrant could think up, and to challenge that seemed like the worst kind of dare.

'How did he get into that library in the first place? He'd have needed to use the doors.'

'With the same magic we used, from what I gathered. That's why he had to leave the Palace, wasn't it?'

'He was forced to leave,' said Magda, remembering the bitterness in his eyes. *My father told me that if I ever came back, I'd be dead as soon as I set foot over the doorway.* 'It wasn't his choice.'

When they had first heard those words, she'd been reluctant to believe the Brenin would turn against his own son. But this was a man who spared no mercy. There were the bodies to prove it, and the fear that shadowed the kingdom like a spider's web: shadow-thin and sticky as molten steel. In spite of his position, the prince had no reason to lie to them.

'A boy who has magic,' said Ingrid. 'How is that possible?'

'It doesn't matter *how* it's possible; it just is.'

Since the Scarp Mandate had carved its terrible path through the landscape, a steep slope fell between those without magic, those who were safe, and the Folk who'd been left to scramble through the lower valleys. It was as poisonous as it was reprehensible. And it appeared that the Brenin would let heads roll sooner than relinquish the higher ground.

'If it's possible for one boy, then it's possible for others,' Catrin reasoned. 'I'll wager there are plenty more people out there, fearing for their lives.'

'People we could help.'

'Only if he helps us first,' Alarice reminded her. There was a distrustful look in her eye: one that warned there was too much hanging on the precipice. Whichever way they turned, some vital element risked toppling out of balance. 'I know what we promised. But we have to keep ourselves safe, too.'

'So we stick together. If something goes wrong, it's us first.'

Behind the tired ache of her heart, Magda knew the others were right. She missed her family more than she could say. And there were promises she'd made back home, duties she owed, before she could go promising things to a runaway prince.

'The group of us,' she repeated. 'That's what comes first.'

*

In its essence, the escape plan was simple. The four of them would pick a dark night and head to the gardening shed, where they could filch a pair of loppers to batter the lock off the door to the medical bay. They'd get Muriel out of there. Then it was time to head underground, through the portal in the Ceremonial Grounds. And finally, once they were through the doors to the Vespertine Library, they would require the help of a certain missing prince to navigate a route beyond Cunning Wood.

It should have been easy to tidy the plan away: out of sight, and out of mind. Most things stayed quiet if you squashed them down hard enough, anguish winnowing away to mottled violet sadness. But that night, no matter how Magda tried to squash them, Carrick Madreth's words tricked their way through the dark.

Though this is the Vespertine Library, people do not come here to read.

You hail from Fallow ground, but none of you lie dormant.

And Cunning Wood is not what it may seem.

The word 'cunning' derived from an old Norse term that meant 'to know', but the Forest presented precisely the opposite problem. Everything they should have known about it was a blank. An impenetrable wilderness, whose faceless venom was its invincibility.

The Vespertine Library. The Fallow. Not everything's in a name.

That was what the prince had told them. That was the part of him that eluded their understanding: the capricious half-truths that made him difficult to take at his word. Yet that subtle warning refused to die away, and danced a fever through Magda's brain. What if there *was* more to those places than met the eye? What if it was another trick in the legend, one they hadn't even thought to question?

'The Selvedge,' she muttered, still wide awake in bed. An idea had caught her and held fast: a fishing hook lodged beyond the barb. 'The places closest to the woods, where people go missing. Rhos, with the forest. And the prophecy...'

She sat up.

She looked out of the window, and wondered if she should tell the others what had suddenly occurred to her. But no: it was better not to drag them into this. Since the dorm room was already half empty, Magda didn't suppose it would miss its second occupant, and so she crept out without a sound. Down the hallway. Down the corridor.

The idea itched in her mind again, wild and terrifying. If she was right in her theory, it would change everything. But if she was wrong, there was no going back.

For silk and the sacred oak, she thought guiltily. *Let me be forgiven.*

Chapter 56
Cunning Folk

Plover hadn't always been a dog.

Most days he stayed in one shape; other times he transformed to a subtle degree. And then there was the occasional century where he chose an especially majestic form, just because he could. A dragon, or an auroch — even a snow fox, once — but for the time being he was perfectly content with the mundane. Being a dog meant having a heightened sense of smell, and pretty much any canine form seemed to reap the same benefits.

It came in most useful at moments like this. From behind the canopy of trees that crowded the Forest's edge, he could already smell who was walking across the North Orchard of the Fallow. It was the same girl he'd led into these woods before, except this time she looked decidedly distraught. He wondered if he should announce himself with a bark. Then again, she would find him soon enough.

'The woods aren't what they seem,' she was muttering, her chestnut hair blowing like rushes. 'Something about ... *names*. Stupid prince. Stupid...'

Plover could feel the way she itched to be gone from this place. But perhaps the most foolish assumption anyone made was that you could leave places behind you. Even if the Fallow was a twisted institution, it ran deeper than these girls knew: from the earth, shot through with silken threads, to its fluted hillsides and warped, winding valleys. From its braided channels to its seams of coal, this land breathed and moved as fabric in the wind – and now the girl herself was following a long, winding trail of yarn.

She was so close to bringing the whole thing unravelling.

'Can you hear me?' A pause. The girl looked nervous, like a rabbit who'd seen the fox and forgotten how to run. 'Tell them ... Tell them I'm sorry. Tell my parents that I miss them. And tell the others where I've gone, if I don't come back.'

Plover watched as she stood up again, breathing steadier than a moment ago. Her eyes were fixed on the Forest. She either knew, suspected, or was incredibly deluded in what she was about to do.

Because that was when she stepped over the threshold and into the depths of Cunning Wood.

Ferns crumpled beneath her feet.

A firefly skimmed her collarbone.

The foliage rippled around her, glittering like waterweeds in summertime.

'What in the –' she was gasping, her face bright with horror. With the simple terror of being alive, and unharmed. 'By the Weaver. It's real. This can't be –'

She broke off.

Plover waited for her to understand. These woods had not killed her on the spot, because Cunning Wood did not grow in such ways. To the girl herself, however, it was probably a shock. The mosses and ferns had not torn her skin; the air hadn't choked off her lungs. Perhaps she thought she'd been mistaken. Her fingers clasped for one of the toadstools sticking out of a tree: hazel gloves fungus, thick and rimy. Slowly her expression shifted to one of wonder, as she realised that touch had left no charred flesh; no trace of scorched skin.

It was time. In the heavy grey form of the gwyllgi, Plover poked his nose out from the bushes and stepped forwards into the glade. *This way*, he urged her, *this way through the trees.*

The girl didn't move.

'It's you, isn't it?' Her voice was strange and faraway. 'Plover. You're here, aren't you.'

Come on, was all he said, waiting for her to join him. Just like he had the first night she'd dreamed of the library. Just like he had been waiting for her to do all along.

And so she did.

At first her steps were clumsy, uncertain. Then she took another. And another. And then she was running, too, skipping through the undergrowth like a young fox, all the way until they reached the clearing where the Vespertine Library lay.

Theirs were the woods, and the woods smelt like home.

*

'You look like you're contemplating murder,' said Carrick, observing the angry silhouette that was darkening his door. Instead of the usual back portal, the grand front gates to the library had swung open, revealing a single hooded figure.

'If you're not careful, I'll do more than contemplate.' Magda stalked into the building. 'Cunning Wood didn't do me any damage, unluckily for you. You owe me some answers.'

Her hair was tangled and the bottom of her skirts were covered with strands of decaying plant matter, but they had completely slipped her attention. She'd just run through the Forest. A Forest that was supposed to be so poisonous its toxins would kill her where she stood.

'How was it possible for me to get here?'

'Well, you opened the door and turned the key, and ...'

'Enough of this bullshit.' She pulled off the ragged cloak and discarded it on the front desk, which was no tidier than it had ever been. 'I should have been dead about seventeen minutes ago. What's going on?'

To her surprise, the prince only lifted an eyebrow.

'So it is true.'

'Excuse me?' Magda glared. 'You're the one who put me on to this!'

'I did no such thing.'

'Then what did you mean with all that talk about Cunning Wood? And that book, with the inscription on names being misleading? I know you think you're very clever, Carrick Madreth, but some of us have got better things to be doing than risking their lives wading into the woods!'

It had taken her the best part of an hour to pluck up the courage, and even then she'd been terrified of being mistaken. But those words, and everything that depended on them... It was too perfect a theory to leave untested. Now she realised she had been an idiot to hang on the words of a perfect stranger, somebody she'd only known had a face for two days.

'I told you as much as I could,' Carrick took a step back, hastily. 'I apologise if my words offended you. I should have been more ... prudent.'

'You can take your prudence and shove it up your arse, Carrick Madreth! I couldn't care less about being *offended*. I care about not winding up dead in a ditch.' She ran a hand over her forehead, hating and hating this wretched place. It was hot, and uncomfortable, and full of lies. 'You said that the Forest wasn't what it seemed. And now you're saying you *weren't sure*?'

'I was fairly certain,' he raised a hand in defence. 'And I suspected that —'

'I don't care,' Magda interrupted. 'Why didn't you just tell me what you knew? Why all the theatrics?'

'You wouldn't have believed me if I told you the woods were safe,' Carrick folded his arms. The low starlight had struck the room with long shadows. 'And if I'd mentioned there was even the smallest chance I might be mistaken, you'd never have dared.'

'To do what you couldn't?'

'Go on, then. Tell me I was wrong.' Carrick caught her eye and didn't look away. 'Isn't that why you came alone?'

For once in her life, Magda wished that looks *could* kill. 'Why don't you do us both a favour, and stop making assumptions about me.'

'It's no crime to care about your friends.'

'I came alone because it wouldn't have been fair to put anyone else in this situation. If I get hurt, it's on my head.' She paused. 'Speaking of which, what stopped you from testing this theory for yourself? Or was this nice little library too comfortable for a royal subject to leave?'

'I'm flattered.' Carrick shot her a venomous look. 'But in spite of what you've seen, these woods aren't safe for everyone. You might be immune to the toxins in Cunning Wood. I, however, am not.'

'And why's that?'

'Because you're one of the Folk,' he replied. 'And I'm just a boy with a half-dose of magic that should never have been mine.'

She looked at him then, and saw what she hadn't before. An outcast from both low and high society. A misfit in the world of magic, and outside it. A harbinger of everything bad that was about to befall the country.

'Who created that prophecy, Carrick?'

'It doesn't matter who left it. The fact is, it's there.'

Magda puzzled over it. Whoever had set the prince's return as a condition for the country's prosperity must have seen great things in the young boy. But why send him away in the first place, if they valued him that much? It was a careful balance of love and hatred; a dance with peril.

'Your powers. What did you mean, when you said they're a half-dose?'

'My mother had a strong bloodline of magic,' said the prince. 'But whatever gifts I inherited from her are weak. It's why I could hide my body, and not my voice. Even a simple illusion like that was tiring to keep up.' An angry blush was spreading across his neck. 'It's certainly not strong enough to keep me protected from a poisoned woodland.'

'You mean...' Magda turned the pieces over in her mind. Slowly, quietly, they were settling into place, quiet as starlight. 'The Forest is a death sentence, except for those with magic?'

'As far as evidence would suggest.'

The words rattled like dice across a table.

'You can't be serious.'

If that was true, then the bodies at the edge of the woods had been real. The whispered rumours had been real: just not quite as she'd imagined. It was a wildfire lie, one that had caught and held an entire village ablaze.

Half-concentratingly, Carrick poked at a wobbling stack of books with his foot. The novel which had been in danger of capsizing slotted neatly back into place. 'I'd never have made such a claim unless the proof was standing in the room with us.' He looked up again. 'But here you are.'

She resisted the urge to wipe the smug look off his face. All she needed to do was breathe: in, and out.

Ten seconds.

Nine.

'Magdalena, is everything alright?'

Five seconds.

Four.

'Are you —'

'I'm sorry.' She shook her head, trying not to cry. There was a difference between angry tears and sad tears, and she was certain he wouldn't be able to discern between the two. 'It's just so bloody infuriating, the way we find out everything a second too late. For Gwern's sake, we could've been out of here months ago. Before any of this happened. Before Muriel...'

'You believed what you saw.'

'It's a mistake I won't make again,' she replied. 'There's no excuse for dishonesty.'

'Everyone in your village probably thought it was just as true as you did.' Carrick picked at a stray thread that was coming unwoven from his shirt cuff. 'Not even I could be sure until today.'

'I'm aware of that.'

'Don't worry, our bargain still stands.' The prince's golden eyes were still lingering on her own, as if he was offering a challenge. The more Magda learned of him, the more he seemed to fit this library: shielding a vault of secrets. 'I'll help you get out of the woods. And you help me with the curse.'

'If you thought we could help you, why didn't you tell us who you were sooner?'

Carrick gave her a thin-lipped smile. 'You've got no idea about the people who've come here, over the years. Bounty hunters. Royal guards. It would cost me my life if I appeared before every stranger who set foot here.'

'What, and you thought I was a safer bet?'

'It didn't seem like it the other night,' he cast her a reproachful look. 'Your friend with the fire was charming.'

'She's a real scorcher.'

'She could have killed me!'

'But she didn't,' Magda shrugged. 'You were lucky. Was that the only reason, then?'

In response, the prince only tilted his head. There was a curiosity — a kind of innocence — in Carrick's movements that reminded her of a young deer she'd once watched on a frozen lake. Skittering its way across the ice, as it learned how the world and its fragile limbs were to coexist.

'The whole lot of you were braver than anyone else who's come here before,' he said at last. 'That, and the threat to burn down the entire library with me inside it. That was also very effective.'

Magda refused to feel sorry for a prince who had been born with every privilege under the sun. But she tried to imagine what that life might have been, growing up among marble halls and rolling rose gardens. Afternoons of cultivated sun, and now the solitude of an abandoned library.

Carrick turned to face her. 'So, no hard feelings? We've still got a deal, right?'

Magda considered for a moment, then pulled the cloak tighter over her shoulders.

'Don't make me regret this.'

'You won't.'

'I can only hope,' she moved towards the door. 'Tell me, Carrick Madreth, what's it like to be a friend of the prince?'

'Oh, I couldn't say.' A worn smile. 'You'd be the first.'

Chapter 57

White Clover

What most people assumed about the House of Madreth was that its royal heirs flourished on the battlefield. Among cavalry and infantry, between friend and foe, under thunder or lightning: that was where the battles took place. It had served his father well, Carrick supposed. And in the fair fields of war, who didn't look good swinging a sword?

Unfortunately, that kind of martial instinct did not come naturally to him. Before he'd learned to fight, Carrick Madreth had learned to cook, and it was a skill which had served him far better than any battle-axe. By the age of seven he'd learned the best recipe for apple crumble, and how to stop chocolate from scalding. It was the perfect interdisciplinary craft: combining precision, speed, and art, all in one. He'd also inherited his father's sweet tooth, which led to no end of disapproving glances from his aunt. *You'll rot his teeth, Elis! Are you teaching him to be a prince or a pâtissier?* But nobody could complain about the crisp smell of cooking apples, and each the time a dessert was served up, the plate came back clean.

All that had changed after his mother left. The Brenin had put a swift end to his culinary education, and Auntie Grim had never come back to visit. He couldn't particularly blame them. He wouldn't have fancied visiting a miserable, spoilt ten-year-old either — and that wasn't to mention the new law. Over time, his mother and her relatives slowly became more like storybook characters than real people. They faded into the backdrop of his childhood.

Days like those were a good excuse to use the doors to other libraries, and pilfer whatever sweet treats he could find from a nearby market. His father never had ascertained his whereabouts on those missing afternoons. But a slice of *teisen y cynhaeaf* could usually be found somewhere, which inevitably helped. And his mother had left him enough magic to work the portals: even if it was the only relic he had left of her.

That was the awkward thing. The singularity of his possessing magic at all, because there was no such thing as a boy among the Folk. He tried not to dwell on it. The girl, Magda, hadn't voiced her surprise, but she was surely thinking it. And there might come a day where she, too, would turn away from him.

He knew it was naïve to think she could be different from the others.

They always left, in the end. First his mother, who had fled with the grace of a willow. Then his father: a closed book, who wound himself tighter and more obscure ever since that fateful day. Not even his aunt trusted him, not really. The grey witch only ever told half-truths. Just in case, Carrick supposed, it ended up being used as a weapon against them.

Just in case he turned out to be exactly like his father.

Rumours travelled fast in the capital, and everyone had found out exactly what kind of a man Elisdair Madreth was after his mother's sudden disappearance. Did he feel some pang of remorse for what he had done, even now? Did he think of the countless families who'd suffered at his hands?

Thought the Vespertine Library was small, it was warmer than the castle had ever felt. Here, the shadows didn't splinter to enemies in the dark. There was always a taper burning at the window, and nobody had to watch their step for fear of landing in a prism of haunted voices.

So Carrick had stayed.

Through the window of the library you could see long swathes of meadow-grass, rich with flowers. One day, perhaps, he would finally be able to go out and pick them. Bird's foot trefoil. Shimmering buttercups. Tall white clover. A flower's growth was a careful miracle of timing, for the sun had to shine at just the right moment; just as the rain sweetened the earth. Then a pollinator set off the chords of change, no sooner and no later than was ideal.

Carrick had no idea who would take the throne after his father.

He didn't care, as long as it was better than this.

Chapter 58

The Witching Hour

The dawn was cold, and unforgiving. Even less forgiving were the expressions of the other girls, who sat wrapped in blankets around the lantern that they'd lit.

'I'm sorry for waking you up so early,' said Magda. 'It's sort of urgent.'

Alarice took one long, scathing look at her. 'You'd better have a good excuse, Corrales. I don't intend to make a habit of getting up at four in the morning.'

'I went back out to the woods,' Magda folded her hands in her lap, surprised by how mundane the truth sounded in cold light. 'I'd been thinking about Muriel, and Rhos, and the weird things that the library told us before, and something just didn't add up. But when I got there, it all made sense. The legends about the poisons; none of it...'

She was interrupted by the sound of Ingrid boiling a kettle.

'Sorry. None of it what?'

'None of it's true.'

There was an exasperated *huff* from the counter of the kitchenette. Beside the main hob, Catrin had picked up a bowl of something and began to crunch. 'I don't know what you think you saw out there, Magda, but I think we could all use some sleep.'

'Are you eating dry noodles?'

'You woke me up at four o'clock in the morning!'

'You're eating dry noodles.'

'And you're trying to tell us that the legend about the Forest's a farce! Which of the two seems more ridiculous to you?'

Magda put her head in her hands. She hadn't even thought about this part; about how impossible it sounded. How in the Weaver's name was she going to convince them of what she'd seen?

'I know it sounds unbelievable, but the woods can't hurt you. That's the truth. That's why I came to wake you. That's why I —'

'Magda.' Ingrid placed a hand over her shoulder, her eyes full of concern. 'We've all seen the bodies. We all know the stories. Right?'

Strange things happen in the cut-between places.

'The bodies we've seen, they were always men. The stories we were told, always concerned ordinary folk.' She waited for them to understand. 'Not women. And never, ever anybody with magic.'

When you said the words *Cunning Wood*, the first thing most people thought of was death. A mess of bones and animal carcasses lounging at the edges, and the legend of those who'd paid the price for their trespasses. To now believe the opposite was more bewildering than the myth itself.

'If you don't believe me, I can prove it to you,' Magda got to her feet, looking for the parting in the undergrowth where she'd clawed her way into the woods. 'Out there, just beneath the spindly ash tree.'

'What about it?'

'That's where I went in.'

'Into the wood?'

'I walked through, all the way to the library. It didn't hurt me.' She was met with incredulous stares. They either didn't believe her, or couldn't bring themselves to know it. 'Everybody knows what plants grow across these grounds, right?'

'I've probably scavenged foliage from most of them, to use as cyanotype stencils,' said Alarice. Her sketchbook was well-stocked and she went foraging every couple of weeks for more flowers. 'What about it?'

'Have you ever seen one of these?'

She held out the branch of sallow, a thin wand whose twisted leaves had clung to the bottom of her skirt on the way back through the woods.

'A willow,' Alarice's eyes narrowed. It was a tree with an inextricable love for water, one which grew on riverbanks and near lakes. Within the orchard, there was nowhere even close to suitable grounds for such a plant. 'You really did go in there.'

Grey velvet encased each of the buds, a silver promise of spring. Hands folded over the slender branch with the aura of a talisman. It yearned to grow, that much was clear, but they stood on fallow ground.

Theirs was not to stretch towards the sunlight.

'We would have known,' Catrin hovered over the willow bough, transfixed. 'Surely somebody would have sensed it.'

'They did.'

'What?'

'Rhos already did.' This time it was Ingrid who had spoken, her hands trembling. 'She didn't die because she stepped into Cunning Wood. She died because they killed her.'

The accusation skated thin ice across the room. Pieces of the glacier broke off as it went, flying loose like shrapnel. An ugly shiver lodged itself in Magda's throat, mangling the arteries beneath her jaw.

'You think that the Ethers ...?'

'You were right. We don't know what they're capable of, Magda.'

The blood dripped. She felt it seep, darkly staining, into the floorboards.

'That can't be what happened.'

Because then Rhos's death would have been for nothing. Not a tragic accident, and not a price by which they learned the cost of trespass. A deliberate act; a toss of coin which always landed featherside up.

There was no iteration of events where Rhos came out of the woods unscathed, and the Fallow could let her live with that knowledge.

'I kept thinking, *if only she'd taken one step less. If only she'd survived.*' Ingrid looked more wounded than any of them had ever seen her. 'Except, as you've proven, there's nothing to survive.'

Magda couldn't answer. Her fingers were scratched with fine lines from the briars and brambles at the undergrowth, but nothing more.

'She must've crossed over just into the border from the orchard, and found out the truth,' said Alarice. She, too, was realising with quickening terror what those events spelled out. Rhos had found out what none of them were supposed to witness.

Ingrid held her head in her hands. 'I should have been there for her.'

'You can't blame yourself for this, Ingrid. You'd have been the first person she told.'

'Which is exactly why the Ethers couldn't let her come back to us.'

They sat there in the frigid dawn air, which turned the colour of pale sheets. The cruel taunt danced before them.

'So this is it?' said Catrin, at last. 'The woods are fine, and we could've walked out of here months ago?'

True, and not true. That speculation came edged in the yearning of a cerulean sunset, because it existed on a plane that didn't quite exist. They had been different girls, back then. Nobody could say for sure that the Forest would have welcomed them as a friend, or if it would have taken them at all.

All Magda knew was that it would take them now.

'It's our last safe place.' Her fingers found the necklace that she'd put on earlier in the morning. It was an opal, milky turquoise, cut in the shape of a feather. 'A refuge where none of the Brenin's forces can get to us.'

'So what do we do when the woods get even sicklier? That's what the prophecy said, isn't it?' Ingrid shot them a desperate look. 'The Five Forests will be condemned to slowly perish, unless the prince returns to Helygen. And he's got no intention of doing that.'

'Maybe it's not what we think,' said Magda. Something didn't quite ring true, even in the midst of their new discovery. 'It gave the prince safety, too. And if we can manage to undo that part of the prophecy, maybe the Forests will get better on their own.'

Safety was not the same thing as satisfaction. But it had been better than the blood-drunk lustre of the Palace halls, as far as a young prince was concerned. Only now did Carrick Madreth understand the confines of his security, and the price at which it came.

'We should check the door to the sick bay,' Ingrid got to her feet abruptly. 'It's almost new moon. They might have let their guard down while they get ready for the Ceremony.'

'Are you sure?'

'If there's even the slightest chance for us to get out, we have to take it. This place is a festering wound.'

They watched as she made her way out and down the corridor. Catrin cast an eye towards the fallen willow branch. 'The Ceremony. They'll have to let Muriel out then, won't they?'

'We could work with that,' Alarice picked at the fraying edges of one pocket. 'The ceremonial cloaks. If we can find some kind of glyph for concealment, we could stitch it in place. Then the robes might be able to hide us altogether: like an invisibility charm. Magda, have you still got that book?'

Shadows stole across the room, lingering on the corner table which held the Everything Teapot. Nobody had used it in months. In Magda's mind, the tiny border of porcelain strawberries turned to hooded figures, cutting a path across the north orchard. The ceramic cups turned to standing stones. And the saucers became a stack of cold white torchwood, bright and menacing.

'We could take some of the torches, and I can craft some lanterns when we get into the woods,' Catrin lowered her voice. 'With that amount of kindling ... Well. Nothing burns better than a couple of old bridges.'

A small flame of hope leapt in Magda's chest.

'Thank you.'

It was immediately extinguished when the door burst open to reveal Ingrid, panting for breath. She was back far too soon, for the distance she should have walked. But it sounded like she had run instead.

'What's wrong?'

'The door was clear,' Ingrid's face was a mask of fright. 'When I got to the medical bay, it was wide open.'

'So where is she?'

The other girl was shaking her head. The words were too bleak to say out loud, and for a moment no sound came.

'She's gone.'

Chapter 59

Opalescence

The first time Muriel had been dragged from her home, she remembered cold white fingers pulling at her cloak. Broken syllables tangling with the wind. The view of her old road, growing smaller and more cluttered into the distance.

Often she recalled the soft croak of pigeons sounding in the mornings; the thump of Plover's tail against the back door. She could picture the way her older sisters dressed at the weekends: eclectic necklaces and dark green eyeshadow that she wasn't allowed to wear yet, although the promise was there. Glistening. Opalescent. Just out of reach.

If she could bear to admit it, Muriel missed Wildbriar the way you missed a photograph. You thought you'd be back any minute to catch it, but by the time you returned it had changed altogether. Although the Fallow had come to mean something to her over the months, it was because of the friendships that had grown here. She would never miss its crooked hallways and odd architecture. And she would certainly not miss being surrounded by a poisoned woodland.

When the Ethers arrived that morning, a part of her knew exactly what they intended.

'Good morning, Miss Silvana.' Ether Stefania's voice was chipped metal against the harsh sun, and in her hands was a silver platter with a cloth placed over it. 'The Brenin sends his regards. We were wondering if you might oblige us in a diagnostic test this morning.'

Muriel shook her head. She didn't like the look of the tray one bit.

'Oh, dear. There's no need for that.' Stefania placed the platter on the side table with unnerving calm. 'How about we have a little chat, you and I?'

'Maybe after breakfast?' Muriel tried to put her off. A jolt of alarm shot through her as she realised that the bed beside hers was empty. Rhos was gone. 'Where is she?'

Stefania gave her a smile that should have been sympathetic. 'It's important that we discuss this as a matter of urgency.'

'But I'm better,' Muriel raised her arm enthusiastically. 'Look. My arm's completely back to normal. I think it would be good for me if to get back into my usual routine, don't you?'

'The Palace has deemed it in their interests to interview you personally, Miss Silvana.' This time it was Ether Rhiannon who had spoken, arriving at the bedside table along with Ether Lorna. 'The decision is yours, of course.'

'For your sake,' Stefania added, 'I hope you won't be objectionable to the royal request.'

Muriel could feel the panic rising in her throat. 'What's going on?'

'You are being given an opportunity. I would advise you to take it.'

'Well, I don't want to go. I want to see my friends. Why won't you let me see them?'

'I'm afraid we can't do that.'

Muriel didn't know which happened first. The thorned tendrils leaping up from the floor around her, or the glass lanterns shattering as dark purple flowers began to blossom. In slow motion, her magic might have looked magnificent: a hundred violet petals tumbling from the ceiling and into the shadow-filled air, thorns springing into a defensive barricade. But there was a deeper sense of terror, of threat, that she knew was behind the sudden outburst of her powers. It was as if every impulse to control it had been broken down.

The storm gates were flooded, and all her body knew was how to protect her.

*

When she woke up, the floor was moving. A carriage. They were back in the carriage, all over again. Except this time, her mother's quilt was gone. Her luggage case was gone. The only things she took with her were the clothes on her back.

'Please don't be alarmed, Miss Silvana,' came a voice beside her. 'This is for the best.'

'You.' She strained to see clearly, her head swimming. 'You traitor.'

'I'm sorry.' There was real pain in Ether Rhiannon's eyes, although Muriel struggled to understand why. 'I truly am.'

'Enough of that,' came another, harsher voice in the front of the carriage. 'You're spoiling her.'

Until the day she died, Muriel would not forgive that voice. She wanted to smash a window, but all the energy had sapped itself from her limbs. It cost her to even keep her eyes open.

'What did I do?' she fought to sit up. 'What did I ever do to hurt you? What did any of us do?'

In place of an answer, Rhiannon only passed a soft parcel of fabric into her lap. 'Here. You'll be needing this when you arrive.'

With a sick feeling in the pit of her stomach, Muriel unfolded the garment to find the same glittering cloak that the Ethers wore. Apart from the slightly shorter hem, they were identical: right down to the name that had been embroidered behind the collar.

Ether Muriel.

'Don't look so horrified,' said Stefania, cloaked by shadows, as the wagon rolled on through the woods. 'You'll grow into it.'

Chapter 60

Nightfall

'She's gone,' whispered Magda. The air sang with the wrongness of it, too shallow to fold itself around the space that her best friend had left.

'I'm sorry, Magda,' Alarice kept saying. 'They must have taken her before we could even stop them. The cart's gone, and the stables are empty.'

'Where did they go?'

'To the Palace. That's what Ether Lorna said.'

The silence burned like silver. And melted away like gold.

'So we follow her,' said Magda. 'Where one of us goes, we all go.'

*

It was a horrible, hot, humid evening as the Ceremony inched closer. The dusk had soured to a thick, moody affair, and clouds like unlanced boils hovered in the lower atmosphere.

In two hours' time they would change into their ceremonial robes. The final preparations were being made to the cloaks, and Magda could feel the calluses that had formed at her fingertips after months of hand embroidery. A leather thimble might have kept them soft, but soft skin yielded no resistance to the spineless world around them.

'Does everybody know the plan?'

Magda nodded, wondering if there was something wrong with her. Her eyes weren't crying. Instead the grief had turned her numb, like a puppet whose name crumpled at the centre of an acting script. She knew the plan like the back of her hand, because the plan was the only thing she dared to think about right now. She couldn't think about Muriel, not if she didn't want to go insane before the pyre was lit. Couldn't. Wouldn't.

'Let's go, then.'

Stay low; wait for the blaze. Then run for the woods.

Ingrid was at the head of the line as they filed out to the Ceremonial Grounds. It felt unreal watching her walk. Even as they stepped barefoot onto the grass, Magda pulled the cloak a little tighter over her shoulders, underneath which she'd secured half of her worldly possessions.

Soon they would be leaving, or at least that was the plan. She tried to focus on Alarice's pearl necklace, which was nearly invisible under the moonless sky. She tried to focus on her own cloak, carefully embroidered for the occasion with a concealment glyph. When the fire was lit, that glyph would come into play, and they would sweep like ghosts into the woods.

The harmless woods.

The woods that were their friends, where everybody else had fallen short.

Magda took one last breath, like a diver about to plunge, and wished she could hold onto the moment for a little longer. Soon they would be running, and the world they knew would slip sideways like water.

*

The Ceremony was a carefully choreographed dance. Magda knew her lines; they all did. And the first player on stage was Ether Lorna, as she always was, with her dark hair swept back neatly.

'Who will be our Keeper of the Flame?' came the smooth, ocean-cragged voice. *Who? Who?* it echoed from the sea. *Who will offer up herself to spare her sisters?*

'We will.'

Next came the Gothic interlude, the ring of standing stones. Magda wondered if they had intended for the Ceremony to be this theatrical: for wasn't there beauty in the casual waltz of bluestone and sunken constellations? This moon she watched with wide eyes, seeing it all in a different light. She saw the hesitation in Lorna's steps, the flinches between her role as Ether and her position as a human being. There was a shiver of reluctance as she chose her target, but Magda couldn't pity her – not after the things she had done. Call it discipline or call it cruelty, the blame landed always in the same place.

Directly over the Fallow girls' heads.

'Catrin Scurlock, you will be our Keeper of the Flame tonight,' said Ether Lorna. 'Please step forward.'

Magda knew she wasn't imagining the smirk on the other girl's face. Her white cheeks were hollow, carved thin with the weight of their long months here. By this point Catrin was more a part of the daylight, of the painted chiaroscuro, than a person with weight and height and real dimensions. And finally she commanded the role that she had been born to play: the leading lady.

'Everybody, light your torches.'

No one moved. Catrin's skirts fell heavy and the deftly stitched glyphs held fast, floating as she moved towards the pyre.

'I said light your torches,' Lorna repeated, looking round in confusion. 'Did you hear me?'

There was no reply. Because this time, they had nothing to lose. The veil had slipped, and for every month that this rite had cost them grief, the wounded truth now ran bloodily across the lawn: a hart sprung free of its snare.

'What are you ... What's going on?'

Still nobody moved. And this time, Ether Lorna looked frightened.

'Don't worry,' the ghost girl on the pyre smiled back. 'I'm your Keeper of the Flame.'

'Come down this instant. You're not supposed to ...'

'Burn?'

An unearthly glow was kindling at the base of the pyre: too warm for metal, too cold for natural fire. The others moved towards her, pulled like paddleboats towards a stormwreck. How did it look, Magda wondered, from above?

Were they still the perfect circle this was meant to be?

Would they burn like the eye of a needle?

'This is out of order,' Ether Lorna took a shaky step backwards. 'I'm warning you, girls. You're to come down on the count of three.'

One.

Magda linked hands with Ingrid and Alarice.

Two.

'This is your last chance!' screamed Ether Lorna.

Three.

She closed her eyes.

The torrid heat of the flames gathered at her ankles, ready and grinning.

'Now.'

*

In the middle place there was no time, no name, no light. Just indistinct grey and a muddle of limbs, each clinging to the other.

'Did it work?' someone groaned. 'Are we ...?'

'Dead?' A hacked-out, spluttering cough. 'I don't think so.'

Magda clutched her ears, which were mysteriously ringing. A scramble of something sharp and thorny had scragged its way over her ankle. It bled a curious, sorrowful colour, but it was not the red she remembered.

Where are we?

'Allie, are you okay? Ingrid? Magda?'

At that point Magda realised that the three other girls were already on their feet, while she lay disgruntled in the earth. 'We're on the other side,' was all she could say, blankly. 'We were on the outside, and now we're on …'

'The inside.'

Through the tightly interlaced tapestry of Cunning Wood, Magda could just make out the silhouette of seven tall standing stones. Stitches she knew, now reworked in twisting green flax: because they were looking at it from a new perspective. There, in the little gully of satin forest canopy, was a perfect sampler of a scene from a storybook.

This time they were watching from inside the Forest.

There in the far clearing, still kneeling beside a smouldering pyre, was the cloaked form of Ether Lorna. The flame itself was burned dead; its prisoners, fled. But they were far away. The woods held them close, no more harmful than the ebb of a summer breeze.

'It worked,' said Catrin, numb with shock. 'The glyphs worked. We really made it.'

'So … now what?'

'We keep moving,' Ingrid staggered to her feet, then lurched to one side. 'We have to go before she sees us. We need to get to that library.'

Magda didn't stir. She was too tired to even reply.

'Magda, get up. We have to stick to the plan,' Alarice urged. 'You remember, right?'

'Right,' said Magda. She was still observing the gash in Ingrid's cloak, where a thin flap was sliced clean from one ankle. 'Um. I think you're …'

'Never mind that. Come on, you have to get up.'

'Not yet,' Magda shook her head. All the energy had drained away from her, despite the fact that she really did want to go with them. She only needed to close her eyes for a few minutes, and then everything would be okay. Muriel would be okay. She would be forgiven. Her mum and dad would give her a gold star for her performance in the school play, everybody would clap, and the curtain would fall down like a guillotine.

'Magda? Are you alright?'

'I'm fine,' she tried to move, and couldn't. 'You know what. Maybe I should stay here, and you can come back for me afterwards. After I've got some rest.'

'Absolutely not,' Catrin winced, hooking an arm under her shoulder. 'How far is that library of yours, Corrales? The prince had better have some training in first aid.'

Ingrid's eyes darkened. 'I'll bloody well kill him if he doesn't.'

Between them they hauled Magda to her feet. Like a many-footed monster, the Fallow girls began to make their way into the forest. With limbs intertwined, they moved onwards: on, towards the Vespertine Library, to the heart of the woods, and to Muriel beyond that.

Muriel, thought Magda, strangely lightheaded, *stay alive, please stay alive.*

Maybe it was the ringing in her ears. Maybe it was the trickle of blood down her neck, because something had not quite gone to plan in that transition, and she wasn't certain she wanted to know what. Besides that, there was so much to fear that she couldn't possibly keep hold of it all. But it was okay: little by little, her friends were holding up the edges of that great weighted canvas for her. It would not smother them.

Just a little longer.

The earth echoed beneath her feet.

Stay where you are.

Heavy, it was so heavy. Other voices seemed to scatter in the clanging silence.

I'm so sorry.

Sorry gets you nowhere, said somebody. Feet get you somewhere. One foot in front of the other. Yes, that's it. One more step.

We're coming with you, Muriel, all of us.

Faster steps now, surer of themselves. She gritted her teeth and felt sharp air.

You won't be alone. The words blurred together. Arms linked together; someone hooked an elbow beneath hers. *Hold on. Just hold on.*

*

The clouds fell all around them. If anybody else had looked, they might have run in terror from the twelve-legged monster that was making its way through Cunning Wood. But Plover, who knew better, watched on.

There was no question of remaining at the Fallow. Its vaulted ceilings were gored with smoke, and its lacy orchards would perish. What would become of the girls, on the other hand, remained to be seen. Should he follow them? Would they even make it past the northern borders?

He waited for a moment, then got to his feet and stretched out the cramped-up vertebrae in his tail. It had grown unaccustomed to wagging after so many months of disuse, but new company and new adventures would see to that.

He took a step.

Then a leap.

Then a bound towards the hurrying crowd. At the heart of things he was no more than a dog, and even a dog needed something to believe in.

END OF BOOK ONE

Acknowledgements

When I first began writing this book, I had recently started work as a sloth technician in Costa Rica. Many days would dawn with golden sun, a beautiful view of the lush forest canopy and, if I was lucky, a couple of howler monkeys making their way through the big mango tree on the corner. However, the wet season would often bring torrential downpours; the dry season, days of scorching heat and no rain whatsoever. Over the last few years I have discovered several similarities between the tropical climate and the process of writing a novel: you never know which days will be easygoing and which ones will throw you an unexpected challenge.

That year in Latin America has had a profound impact on my life. Not only was it an education in the Spanish language, but one in creativity, resilience, friendship, and finding my feet over 5,000 miles from home. Since I came back to England, I was inspired to pay much closer attention to the beauty in the landscapes of the British Isles — which, as I learned, has temperate rainforests of its own! I feel incredibly lucky to have grown up in a country with such an abundance of plant life and deep-rooted mythology. It is one of my ongoing goals to learn more about the lore of the land, and to learn more Welsh.

There are several people who I would like to thank for their support and kindness while I was working on the manuscript for *Gossamer*: without them, sharing this story would simply not have been possible.

I extend my heartfelt thanks to Daria for reading through the first drafts of this novel. Friends like you are hard to come by, and your words of encouragement kept me going whenever the motivation was running dry! Thank you for your insightful comments, endless patience, and for believing in my story.

I'm incredibly grateful to my godmother, Arlene. Your boundless sewing wisdom, sparky attitude, and great sense of humour has been an inspiration to me in every stage of my life. I can't express how lucky I feel to have a godmother like you, and I will always be in awe of your dressmaking prowess! Diolch yn fawr iawn.

Thank you to everybody who has been involved in my education, especially regarding languages. It has been a total privilege to learn Spanish from school to university: thank you to Mirian, Isabel, Clemencia, Leticia, Erik, Jorge, Rich, Elizabeth, Tom, and Kirsty, for teaching me not only what it is to speak another language but what it is to appreciate someone else's culture. Thank you to Eduardo, Perrine, and Nayade for making my term of turtle monitoring in Costa Rica utterly unforgettable, and for inspiring me with your passion for wildlife conservation. Thank you to Sam, Pedro, Sara, Rodolfo, Ana, Karina, and Karen for imparting your knowledge of sloths to me; I have such admiration for your work and it was incredibly special to be a part of it. Gracias a todos por enseñarme tanto y por compartir su hermoso país conmigo.

Thank you to my friends, who have enriched my life in every way. You have seen me through the ups and downs of my time at university, offered kindness and compassion in abundance, and have brightened many a day with your laughter. I cherish the adventures we have shared together.

Thank you to the people who have stood firmly behind the motto *follow your dreams* and helped me to kick some of my aspirations into reality: following dreams is much easier said than done! Special thanks go to Chris, to Patricia, and to Kathy, for supporting me in all my academic and professional pursuits over the years.

Thank you to my fellow artists, writers, musicians, and creators. Amid the grief, upheaval, and atrocities which our world is experiencing, it is sometimes very difficult to make art. You inspire me to keep going, to stay hopeful, and to remember the vast beauty that this world also harbours.

Last but not least, thank you to Pickle and Rafael for your companionship throughout this endeavour. Your wisdom has been invaluable, as well as your helpfully sitting on top of the router, sitting on top of my laptop, and generally squashing any plan that might have allowed for productivity. You are the best boys I could possibly ask for. Thank you to Ziggy, my own stardust dog, for making the world a sunnier place. Taffy, Cocoa, Daisy, Serafina, and Teasel, you are greatly missed.

Finally, I would like to thank my parents for always encouraging me to do what I loved. Mum, your passion for wildlife has made its indelible mark on me. Thank you for all of the bedtime stories, the books, and for showing me that hard work and determination will go a long way. Dad, your bravery and kindness never ceases to inspire me. Thank you for the adventures and for your wisdom whenever I get lost.

Recommended Reading

This novel is a work of fiction. For anyone interested in learning about Welsh mythology, culture, or ecology, I would highly recommend the following texts, which offer fascinating insight on Wales past and present:

The Mabinogion translated by Sioned Davies
Welsh Witchcraft by Mhara Starling
The Lost Rainforests of Britain by Guy Shrubsole
Tir: The Story of the Welsh Landscape by Carwyn Graves

For Spanish speakers interested in Costa Rican culture and folklore:

Plantas comestibles de Centroamérica by Carla Chizmar Fernández, et al.
Cuentos de mi tía Panchita by Carmen Lyra

Other recommended resources:

The Darkness Manifesto by Johan Eklöf
National Botanic Garden of Wales / Gardd Fotaneg Genedlaethol Cymru
Manuel Antonio National Park / Parque Nacional de Manuel Antonio
Santa Elena Cloud Forest Reserve / Reserva Bosque Nuboso Santa Elena

About the Author

Anna Bailey is a Welsh and English author who adores ecological fiction and fantasy. Her passion for languages led her to studying English and Spanish at university, during which time she spent ten months working in wildlife conservation in Costa Rica. As a multimedia artist and avid seamstress, she finds inspiration in handcrafted narratives in all their forms. Her poetry has been previously published in the Rising Phoenix Review. *Gossamer* is her first novel.

Printed in Great Britain
by Amazon

59735488R00283